"What a delight to be immersed in Avery Cunningham's debut. A riveting, dynamic page-turner that transported me through time. I didn't want it to end! At a moment when so much of our history is being willfully obscured yet again, this impeccably researched, sweeping novel is an absolute gift."

—BRITTANY K. BARNETT, author
of *A Knock at Midnight*

"Avery Cunningham expertly evokes 1920s Chicago with shimmering, incisive prose and a bone-deep understanding of her characters. *The Mayor of Maxwell Street* is bold, gorgeous, and deeply moving. This novel is a triumph."

—JESSICA CHIARELLA, author
of *The Lost Girls* and *And Again*

"Avery's writing is lyrical, with sparkling dialogue, gripping intensity, and exquisite scenery that puts you right in the room with the heroine. . . . *The Mayor of Maxwell Street* is a stunning debut and a riveting read. . . . Historical fiction at its finest."

—KIANNA ALEXANDER,
author of *Carolina Built*

"Avery Cunningham's *The Mayor of Maxwell Street* is a page-turner, with an incredible cast of characters you'll want to follow from one surprising, suspenseful turn to the next. Her fresh, unflinching vision of history and the undeniable richness of this story will make this not only a book you'll love, but also one you'll return to again and again."

—V. V. GANESHANANTHAN,
author of *Brotherless Night*

"Cunningham's *The Mayor of Maxwell Street* is wonderfully written and a don't-miss ride of a read."

—DENNY S. BRYCE, author of
Wild Women and the Blues

"Riveting, cinematic, and gorgeously written, Avery Cunningham's debut novel is a true force filled with unforgettable characters who are bound to resonate with readers long beyond its last pages. . . . What a spellbinding, tragic, and powerful read!"

—DR. NONI D. CARTER, author of *Good Fortune*

"I can't remember the last time I read a novel that impressed me so much at every level. . . . *The Mayor of Maxwell Street* will bowl you over from beginning to end."

—REBECCA JOHNS, author of *Icebergs*

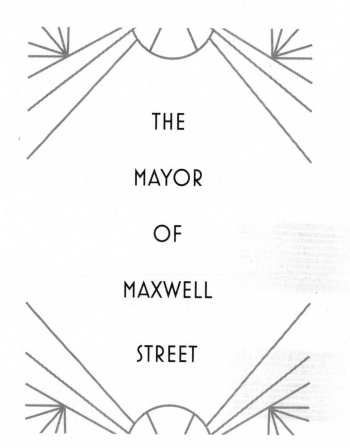

THE

MAYOR

OF

MAXWELL

STREET

THE MAYOR OF MAXWELL STREET

AVERY CUNNINGHAM

HYPERION AVENUE
LOS ANGELES NEW YORK

Text copyright © 2024 Disney Enterprises, Inc.

All rights reserved. Published by MDLC Studio, an imprint of
Buena Vista Books, Inc. No part of this book may be reproduced or transmitted
in any form or by any means, electronic or mechanical, including photocopying,
recording, or by any information storage and retrieval system, without written
permission from the publisher. For information address
Hyperion Avenue, 77 West 66th Street, New York, New York 10023.

First Edition, January 2024
10 9 8 7 6 5 4 3 2 1
FAC-004510-23327
Printed in the United States of America

This book is set in New Baskerville ITC, Mostra Nuova, and Noah
Designed by Stephanie Sumulong
Border art by © Shutterstock

Library of Congress Cataloging-in-Publication Control Number: 2023016393
ISBN 978-1-368-09300-2
Reinforced binding

In a sincere effort to ensure *The Mayor of Maxwell Street* adheres to historical accuracy, terms that many find rightfully offensive are used in this work, including "Negro" and "Colored." This choice was not made lightly, but in the interest of narrative honesty and acknowledgment of our history in all of its degradation and depravity. Please be forewarned that these and other acts of racial, ethnic, gender, and sexual bias/oppression will be featured in this novel. I thank you for joining this exploration into a complex and exciting era in our history with me.

For Liam: my love, my laughter, my inspiration

PROLOGUE

THE BALLAD OF JIMMY BLUE-EYES

What do you see?"

Jimmy saw decay. Mold, and termites, and the final days of a once-living thing. But he also saw a place of meditation. A place for stormy evenings in front of a dwindling fire, surrounded by those who love you. He saw the original architect's grand vision, and he saw his absolute grief.

Like so many great plantation homes littering the South in 1915, White Pine was designed and built by a slave. The architect was told to create the most beautiful house in Alabama, and that he certainly did. But never once had he been invited inside. Now, all had fallen to ruin and desolation. As forgotten as the architect himself, who couldn't even claim his own name.

"I see mahogany," Jimmy said of the coffered ceiling above them. "Amber varnish. Twelve inches at its thickest point. We may be able to save a quarter of it."

Uncle groaned, a sound that preluded long hours and grueling labor. Behind his blind, unseeing eyes, he carried calculations and a log of the region's best lumberyards. Information inherent in a woodworker of his skill.

"A week to bring down," he said. "Over a month for the mahogany. Long job. He won't pay."

"He always pays," Jimmy assured him. "Or face the wrath of Old Man Levi."

"You overestimate the influence of that old man."

"He always pays," Jimmy repeated. And he always protested. And he always delayed. But their work was worth payment, in the end.

Jimmy heard the sound of loose coins jangling in a pocket and turned to see White Pine's heir apparent himself standing in the doorway. Young Junior was twice Jimmy's age but shorter by a head. The privilege that skulked in his shadow made him tall.

"How long is this one gonna take?" he asked.

Jimmy looked to his uncle, who nodded, head down, then said, "A month, at least."

Young Junior rolled his glassy, cowlike eyes.

"Christ, Jimmy," he said. "The way you two swindle my granddaddy, I should call in the sheriff."

Young Junior's laugh was infused with an ever-present threat of the most serious kind.

Jimmy felt Uncle clasp a firm hand around his wrist; cold like steel, and just as rigid. The hand said, *Don't speak. Be invisible.*

Jimmy knew what it meant to be invisible. All his life, people made a sincere effort not to see him. If they came upon him playing in the road, they would cross to the other side. If he said hello to them at the market, they would turn their heads. If there were no open pews in church other than the one next to him, they would stand in the back. Even now, as a fifteen-year-old boy—tall, and lanky, and much harder to miss—neighbors would avert their gazes. The idea of instigating that invisibility, using it as a shield instead of bearing it as a burden, felt incomprehensible to him.

"Oh, Junior, why can't you just leave them two be? I swear, you are the worst kind of bully."

The voice of Cecilia came barreling through the room, much as she often did. She was the last daughter of White Pine, and, like her brother, she woke every day expecting the party to stop at her front door. Barely out of finishing school, she dressed in gaudy colors intentionally out of place in their muted world of greens and browns. Her eyes drifted slowly from person to person, from distraction to distraction, waiting to be entertained.

"What's all this for?" she asked. An unlit cigarette was poised between the fingers of her right hand. Her newest bizarre affectation.

"More of Granddaddy's foolishness," said Young Junior. "No damn good reason for it other than wasting this family's money."

"We only need to replace the coffers in the ceiling," Jimmy said. "It won't be a great cost to your grandfather. As I remember it, it is still his money. Not yours."

Cecilia hid a laugh behind her lace-gloved hand while her brother's face turned the bright red of an heirloom tomato. His top lip—blond hair like peach fuzz growing in spurts—began to curl.

"You best keep a tight leash on this buck," Young Junior said to Uncle, all while keeping his eyes fixed on Jimmy. "His back talk is liable to get you both in trouble."

Jimmy's muscles seized with the desire to give Young Junior just as much as he gave, but he felt his uncle's presence behind him still, tethering his impulses.

"And where you going, all dressed up?" Young Junior asked of Cecilia. "Is it a full moon tonight?"

Without so much as a warning, Cecilia pinched the skin of her brother's forearm and twisted until the grown man squeaked like an ornery hog.

"Dammit, girl!" he screamed. He rubbed at the wound, causing a pink blush to fan out across his arm. "You have the disposition of a cottonmouth."

Cecilia grinned, and in that instant, Jimmy did see the snake in her. He could practically hear the hiss and feel the cold venom pumping through his veins as she bit down. And Young Junior's initial question was valid: Cecilia was dressed to the nines and tens in an ensemble of pink gauze and toile. She preened under their inspection, stretching her neck and lifting her chin.

"Do you like my dress, Jimmy?" she asked. She tilted her head and smiled at him, expectant and assured that whatever answer he gave would be something she wanted to hear.

"It's very pretty, Miss Cecilia," he said. "It suits you."

Inappropriate, obnoxious, and somehow incredibly dull. Yes. It suited her perfectly.

"Brother dear, I need to go into town," she said while setting her hand on Young Junior's shoulder.

"Don't look at me," he said, shrugging it off. "I ain't got time to drive you round like the queen of the damn Mardi Gras parade. Get Russ to take you in the mule cart."

Cecilia's voice rose several octaves when she said, "You would have me ride into town in a *mule cart?*"

By *town*, she meant a wide spot in the road: a post office, a general store, and a Presbyterian church.

"Cecilia," Young Junior said, voice immovable, "you go in the mule cart, or you ain't going at all."

"Jimmy can take me."

"Jimmy?" Spittle flew. Young Junior took a step back and looked at his little sister with critical, appraising eyes. "What game are you about, Cecilia?"

Jimmy could ask himself the same thing.

"The only game, you big lummox," Cecilia said, "is that I have a package of new ribbon straight from Charleston. If I don't go and fetch it today, they're sending it back. Now, Jimmy can take me, or I can walk. No matter what you say, I'm going, and Papi wouldn't take too kindly to hearing of his only granddaughter getting waylaid in the woods 'cause you wouldn't let the local boy run her into town."

While Jimmy internally wished, prayed even, that Young Junior's cantankerous nature would prevent this farce from playing out, he could see in the man's pinched expression that he was considering this and all of its possible consequences.

"All right," Young Junior said. He stabbed his finger into Jimmy's chest, hard enough to make him lose his balance. "You take her directly into town and directly back, you hear me? No stops. No tarrying. And if there is so much as a scuff mark on my Buick, I'll have your hide."

There was so much Jimmy wanted to say to Young Junior. On that and every other day, for years now. But all he could manage was "Yes, sir."

The forests of Wood Acre, Alabama, were awash in the sights and sounds of spring. Everything smelled of wet earth and tilled soil. The treetops swayed high above them, bursts of green amidst the lingering remnants of winter brown. For Jimmy, the only proper way to enjoy all this was behind the wheel of a car. No longer constrained by the distance his own two feet could carry him, the speed of the Buick was *his* speed. Its power was *his* power. Its control was *his* control. And yet, one wrong turn or sudden loss in traction would send them all tumbling into oblivion. Driving—as with everything in this place—was a high-stakes game of chance.

"You can go faster, if you want," Cecilia said from the wide leather seat behind him.

Jimmy glanced at her in the rearview mirror. She sat with her legs crossed, head back, while the gossamer kerchief she wore about her neck trailed behind them like a streamer on a float. There was a self-satisfied smirk on her face, as though she was laughing at her own private amusement. Jimmy wanted to go faster. The idea of pushing the Buick to its breaking point came naturally to him. He glanced in the mirror again. Instead of going faster, he slowed down.

They continued to wind their way down the hill toward town. Houses began to appear. Pine cabins and thin columns of wood-smoke. White men sat on their porches, or chopped firewood, or fixed axles on their wagons. Each one stopped to give Jimmy severe, pitiless glances. There was nothing particularly odd about a Colored man driving his boss's daughter around. But Jimmy, he was an abomination in their eyes. The product of a love union between a Negro man and a white woman—could there ever be anything more unworldly, more unholy? More threatening?

Jimmy allowed himself to breathe easy when he passed the four-mile marker on the boundaries of town. Ribbon from the corner store was an easy stop. Five minutes, in and out. Soon, they would be back up the hill with this ridiculous experiment behind him.

Then he felt a warm gust of air on the back of his neck and the scent of Cecilia's heady floral perfume.

"We two are friends, ain't we, Jimmy?"

Jimmy's exhale came out dry and ragged.

"Friends, Miss Cecilia?" he asked.

"No need to stand on formalities with me," she said. Jimmy flinched at the heat of her finger as she lightly touched his neck. "Please, call me Cilla. All my friends do, and I consider us to be friends."

"I'm not like your friends in town, Miss Cecilia," Jimmy said, more to himself than to her.

She laughed.

"No, you most certainly ain't. You're different from anyone I've met. Always have been, ever since we grew up together."

Now it was Jimmy's turn to laugh.

"We grew up *adjacent* to each other," he said. "I'd be hard-pressed to say we grew up *together*."

"My, that's a fine trick."

Jimmy looked again in the rearview and asked, "Trick, miss?"

"Sounding like a white man. Why, you talk better English than half of Junior's college buddies."

The leather of the driving gloves Jimmy was required to wear groaned as he clenched the wheel.

This is how my father taught me to speak.

"It's so bumpy back here," she said, and Jimmy could hear her bouncing in her seat until the springs squeaked. "Let me ride up front with you."

Jimmy started so suddenly that the wheel jerked, sending dirt from the road shooting up into the air.

"There, see!" she exclaimed. "It's life-and-death. I could have been killed!"

"We're just outside of town—"

"And I won't rattle around like rocks in a can all the way there. Pull over in this ditch here."

Gone were the breezy undertones of Cecilia's voice. It now left no room for debate.

He waited until he passed half a mile, maybe more, without seeing a dirt road or a shotgun house. Then he slowly eased the Buick into a rocky embankment, struggling to keep as quiet as possible. The sounds of an automobile were still foreign in these hills. No doubt, someone heard them pull over. And someone would come to investigate.

Jimmy killed the motor, and within a blink of a bird's eye, Cecilia was tucked in close to his side. Jimmy considered shearing a hole in the back seat just so he could claim that the torn fabric cut her legs. Anything to explain why she was forced to sit up front, alone, with him.

"Why, Jimmy Blue-Eyes. Your hands are shaking."

Jimmy looked down at his hands and saw that, yes, they were shaking. It took him only a brief moment to realize that this debilitating feeling was fear.

"Have you ever been with a girl?" Cecilia asked.

Jimmy looked at her, to gauge her seriousness—or her sanity—for himself. Her expression was deceptively unbothered.

"We should get on," he said. "It's getting close to sundown."

That wasn't too far from the truth. If they hurried, the Buick would beat the darkness. But when Jimmy went to start up the ignition, Cecilia's hand came to rest on his. Jimmy snatched it away as though he'd been burned.

"I would've never taken you to be the shy type," she said. "I've seen your eyes on me, Jimmy. No need to be bashful. I know it's your nature."

"Miss Cecilia—"

"I told you to call me Cilla."

The edge was back. Sharper now, with deadly intent.

"Cilla." The name felt heavy and unfamiliar in Jimmy's mouth. "Your brother would not approve of me addressing you as such."

"Junior can take a goddamn leap, for all I care. Ain't like he's my daddy. Bossing me around and telling me how to behave. If I want you to call me Cilla, you'll damn well call me Cilla."

The ease with which Cecilia cursed her brother took Jimmy aback. She must have seen the wariness in his eyes, the slow withdrawal of a cornered animal. Instantly, that mask of the demure Southern belle was back with its coquettish glances and literal chiming laughter.

"I want to talk about you and me," she said. "*Us*, really. I've fancied you for some time, Jimmy, and I think you've fancied me, too."

"Fancy *me?*"

"Yes! Goodness gracious, boy, don't look so horrified. You ain't no blushing maid. I hear the way the Negro girls talk about you. I didn't take much stock before, but now we're both near grown. And there's no harm in it."

It was like deciphering another language. Jimmy understood the essence of what she was saying, but the details all came together in a frantic heap.

"Are you propositioning me, Miss Cecilia?" Jimmy asked at last.

Cecilia sniffed, as though the sentiment came with a foul odor.

"*Propositioning?* What a word to use. This here ain't nothing untoward, just a talk. Between friends—"

"You keep saying that," he said, "but we have never been friends, you and I. I think this may be our longest conversation."

"Well, what would you expect?" she asked. "An invitation to dinner? Drinking whiskey and smoking cigars with my grandfather? Some of us can't be as careless as your momma obviously was."

That struck Jimmy exactly where and how it was meant to. With harsh, shuddering movements, he shifted the gears.

"Stop it!" Cecilia was suddenly clinging to his arm. There was no illusion of space between them now. "Stop it," she said again, cajoling. "I'm sorry, that was cruel. You must understand how difficult this is for me."

"Of course I understand," Jimmy said. It took considerable effort to maintain that calm, pliable tone that white folks always expected from him. "That's why I'm going to start up this car, take you to town, then drive you back to White Pine."

"You will do no such thing! Why are you making this so difficult? Here, just—"

And they were as close as two people could be. Her lips were on his, and she tasted like something artificial. Store-bought and made to last. As he flung himself back, flush against the door of the Buick, he licked the residue her cherry-red lip rouge left behind. Stained was how he felt. Soiled from skin to bone.

"There," Cecilia said in a slow drawl that she probably thought sultry. "That's better. Isn't that better? Now you can relax, and we can properly enjoy ourselves."

She came at him again, eyes heavy-lidded, and Jimmy dodged away. Cecilia blinked at him, brazen enough to look confused. Then put out.

"Jimmy. If your aim is to play hard to get, you're doing a mighty fine job of it."

"That's not my aim at all," Jimmy said. "This *cannot* happen, Miss Cecilia."

"Don't tell me you're not attracted to me."

"Is that truly what you need to hear?"

"I don't *need* to hear anything. You talk too much as it is. Ugh!" Cecilia folded her arms and pouted with the petulance of a toddler. "I tell you what, I bet Bernie Kidd didn't put up with this, and she has a face like the backside of a cow. Is there someone else you're carrying on with?"

"There is no one else," Jimmy said with all sincerity.

"Then what *is* the problem? Look, we only have to do this once. Unless, of course, you like it. And I like it. Then maybe more than once."

Cecilia's hand traveled up his thigh. With the quickness that one might use to swat at a spider, Jimmy grabbed her wrist and regretted it immediately.

"I beg your pardon," he said, releasing her. "I shouldn't have touched you."

"But I want you to touch me!" Cecilia insisted. "And you should want to touch me. Everyone said you would."

"Everyone?"

"Everyone!" she yelled. "Bernie, Mary Jo. Even Jessica, that witch. Bernie carried on with the tall one who cuts down trees by the lake. All she had to do was flash some leg, and he was all over her. An uneducated girl will be taken for a fool; everyone knows that. These days Rudolph Valentino himself could ask Bernie for a Tennessee waltz and she wouldn't swoon all over the drawing-room floor. Suitors will be calling soon, and I *cannot* be the only one who doesn't . . . well, doesn't know what to do."

Jimmy understood it all now. The trap snapped shut around him.

"I'm no mark in anyone's ledger, Cilla," he said. It was the first true thing he'd ever said to her. Said to any white person, really. No *yes, ma'ams,* or *no, sirs,* or presumptions about who and where they were. Cecilia smiled. Feral and hungry.

"That's more like it," she said. "You should be flattered. I chose you because I really do fancy you. Now, it'll be dark soon. We should hurry. Lord knows Papi will send the battalion out for me if I'm not tucked in by dinnertime."

Cecilia leaned in again. Jimmy held up his hand.

He knew "the tall one." His name was Bartholomew, and ever since they found his father in a shallow grave on the side of the road, he'd taken on every odd job he could to feed his mother and six siblings. Jimmy suspected that Bernie Kidd flashed him a little bit more than some leg, and he suspected that Bartholomew rued every moment of it.

"I'm taking you home," Jimmy said. The Buick came raucously back to life.

"Is that a no?" Cecilia asked.

Jimmy did not look at her when he said, "That is a *never,* Miss Cecilia."

A chill wind passed over him. The final pained, gasping breath of a dying winter.

When Cecilia spoke again, she sounded like a different person altogether. As brutal and assaulting as breaking glass.

"Get out."

"What?"

"I said, get out!"

The choice was not Jimmy's. Cecilia pushed him with unexpected force, and he stumbled out of the Buick and into wet gravel.

"You're as thick as my brother," she said from the driver's seat. "I'm the only white girl in ten counties who'd give your yellow ass a passing glance, and you dare turn me down?"

With practiced familiarity, Cecilia put the car in gear and whipped it so fiercely that it left trenches in the dirt road.

"God damn you for a fool, Jimmy Blue-Eyes," she said.

And then she was gone.

It was well and truly dark by the time Jimmy made it back to Wood Acre. As he walked down the single road that stitched their community together, golden beams spilled out of doors onto the ground before him. The smell of fading cook fires lingered outside every threshold. Their home looked no different than any of the others: built of thin, splintering clapboard once painted white, now turned to a dull gray. Inside, Uncle sat in his rocking chair, smoking and staring into nothing with his milk-white eyes. He hummed an old song. One that had no name and no lyrics. Only a rhythm.

"Jimmy." His voice was muffled by a gnarled tobacco pipe. "Nigh on evening time."

"I know." Jimmy closed the door behind him. "I'm sorry. Got lost on the road in the dark."

"Hm. Not the kind of road you need to be getting lost on."

"I know," Jimmy said again, and recognized the impudence in his tone just as Uncle did.

"Don't snap at me, now. Half the neighborhood's been out looking for you."

Jimmy dropped his body into the matching rocking chair as he would drop a sack of animal feed. Everything in him felt heavy and worn to nubs.

"I know," he said one final time.

"Heard the Buick head back to White Pine round dusk," Uncle said. "They say Miss Cecilia was driving. Didn't know that twig of a girl could drive."

On the roughly hewn edge of a sigh, Jimmy said, "Miss Cecilia is familiar with many surprising and disconcerting things."

He could feel his uncle's eyes on him. Even though they saw no more, the heat of that stare rivaled the heat of an open fire.

"Something you need to tell me?" Uncle asked.

Jimmy wanted to reveal everything in its stark and unflinching truth. His plan had been to do just that. On the long, dark walk back to Wood Acre, he'd talked himself through the conversation, through a thousand such conversations. And yet, something held him back. Call it pride. Call it a new type of terror.

"No, sir."

The silence they dwelt in was dense and layered with things said and unsaid. After all, there was no *true* silence in these parts. The horned owl and the coyote and the bobcat prowled, and their hungry growls made the air rumble like a far-off storm.

Someone was hitting him.

Punching him, slapping him all about his head. A voice drifted above, beyond the submergence of strange dreams.

"—and don't you lie to me!"

Jimmy rubbed the sleep from his eyes and saw Uncle standing over him. One hand held fast to the neck of his nightshirt, and the other was drawn back, ready to land another blow.

"Lie to you?" Jimmy asked, half-dead to the world. He was aware enough to notice the change in the light. A thin blue like dewdrops. Not quite night, but not quite morning either. His eyes drifted closed, sleep pulling him down. His uncle shook him, and his head jostled back until it bounced against the floor.

"Clean out your ears, boy!" Uncle's voice sounded as far away and omnipresent as the voice of God. "I said, did you get fresh with Miss Cecilia?"

"No," Jimmy said, drowsy, and then insistent. "No! I would never be so . . ."

Then he remembered. He closed his eyes tight until stars burst behind his lids.

"Uncle—"

"You best measure your next words to me," Uncle said. "I asked you straight if you had something to tell me, didn't I?"

"But nothing happened! I drove her into town."

"And she drove herself back. You come sneaking home in the midnight hour, her speeding through here like the first bat out of hell. If you don't tell me the truth, I can't protect you, boy. Now, did you touch Miss Cecilia?"

Jimmy pulled the man close and looked into his face, selfishly wishing his uncle could look back and see the desperation in his eyes.

"I did not touch Cecilia," he said. "But . . . she touched me."

Jimmy wasn't prepared to explain further and, judging by the way Uncle's brows lifted and then resolutely settled again, no further explanation was needed.

After a moment, the old man said, "And you refused her?"

A cruel instinct caused Jimmy to laugh and say, "Was I not meant to?"

Uncle's hand came up and landed squarely on Jimmy's jaw. The force made him spin and fall flat on the bare wood floor.

"Too smart for your own good, that's what I always said!" Uncle was up and pacing, ignoring Jimmy's writhing body sprawled out below him. "Just like your daddy. Can name every star in the sky but can't hear the devil knocking on your own front door."

When Jimmy at last had strength enough to speak, he passed over the obvious and went directly to "Who told you?"

"Martha Claxton's girl, Rose," Uncle said. He was sitting again, but his spirit vibrated with perpetual motion. "She cleans rooms up at White Pine. Said she saw Miss Cecilia crying to her brother. Your name was mentioned."

And that, Jimmy supposed, was that.

The frogs in the creek out back had gone quiet. The night was still with tense expectation. Then Uncle stood.

"You need to leave," he said. "Now. You're a damn fool for not running at the start."

The old man moved with swift confidence, easily maneuvering through his home with nothing but memory to guide him. He took the canvas satchel that held a lifetime's worth of woodworking tools and dumped them onto the kitchen table before throwing it with perfect accuracy at Jimmy's head.

"Put your things in. Hurry!"

Jimmy reached out, and everything his hand landed on, he stuffed into the bag. It was deep. Designed to carry a workshop on one's back, and the trappings of his life vanished into it effortlessly. His two sets of clothes, his shoes. His father's battered copy of *Great Expectations*. A thin quilt. It was over in seconds.

Outside, the early morning was warm. A fox barked, and it sounded like the cry of a frightened, lonely child.

"Head upriver," Uncle said as he walked, dragging Jimmy behind him. "You'll land in a place on the border called Red Sulphur Springs. Walk in anywhere and ask for Sam. He'll get you the rest of the way."

"Rest of the way where?" Jimmy asked. "Where am I going?"

"To a better place, Lord willing."

Jimmy still wasn't entirely sure what was happening to him. Only minutes ago, the world turned on an expected, predictable tilt that ordered his days. Now the last of his family was urging him to run from the only home he'd ever known.

A noise grew. Something outside of the clamor of the forest, something offensively human. A glow began to bloom on the eastern horizon, and a mass of angry voices, so solid that they formed a living beast, slunk toward Uncle's home. The man did not turn his head to the noise, but his ears were piqued to it. He did not look afraid. Only very tired.

"Come with me, Uncle," Jimmy said. He held on to his shirt, his arms, anything he could reach. "I won't leave you here. If they can't find me, what'll they do to you?"

Uncle took Jimmy's face in his hands. After all this time, they still felt so large and imposing. The hands of a giant. The same hands that dragged him out of a burning house while his parents screamed somewhere inside. The hands that reared him. The hands that were pushing him away.

"I'm an old, blind man, son," Uncle said. "Ain't much left for them to do to me. Besides, I should've done this a long time ago. Your daddy all but begged me to. Maybe he'll forgive me now. Listen, you just leave here, Jimmy. And you don't look back. Not once, no matter what you hear, no matter what they say. Don't make your father's mistake. There ain't no honor in suffering, not even for the ones you love."

Uncle shoved Jimmy hard, and he stumbled down into the stream that ran behind their home. The older man looked to be standing far above him. The light of the myriad fires shone bright at his back. The mass of voices roared, and someone called Jimmy's name with the vehemence of a madman. It sounded like Young Junior. Then a calmer, older, more exhausted voice spoke. Possibly Old Man Levi himself, come to witness his grandson's folly.

Uncle walked away, right into the mouth of the beast, and Jimmy did not see him again.

The heavy sand of half-dry creek beds clung to Jimmy Blue-Eyes's pants as he ran. Cypress branches snagged at his clothes and tore at his flesh. He fell ten, maybe twenty times, fumbling in the coal-black dark. But he didn't stop. And he didn't look back. Not even when he heard the rifle shot ringing through the night. One long, lone, crystalline note. A wail with no beginning and no foreseeable end.

CHAPTER ONE

CHICAGO | JUNE 1921

A sharp snap of brilliant color caught Nelly Sawyer's eye.

It was a man, or rather, a boy on the cusp of manhood. No older than twenty-four surely, but he wore that youth like an imperial cape, heavy with authority. He stood toward the back: close enough to the door to make a quick exit but immersed enough in the throng to look as though he belonged. It being the repast after a funeral, everyone wore their finest black ensembles, making for a somber, if fashionable, scene. But he was wearing blue. Not even a deep, royal, respectable blue. Rather, his was the blue of an endless September sky. A blue that ushered in thoughts of freshly churned ice cream and tall grass beneath your feet. The color of a Kentucky summer.

It took Nelly's breath away, the audaciousness of it. On anyone else, the outfit would be an instant failure, but on him, the look was uniquely appropriate. As though the rest of the world were the ones out of style, while he was the epitome of it.

Nelly leaned in close to her cousin and whispered, "Sam, who is that?"

Samuel Green politely disentangled himself from a conversation with a fellow Howard man and followed the line of Nelly's sight.

"Not the faintest," he said after a moment's observation. "But then again, more than half of the guests here are strangers to me. This is your *brother's* funeral, for Christ's sake. Where are our cousins? Where are *my* parents, *our* grandmother? Everyone loved Elder. Wild horses wouldn't keep any of our family away unless they were explicitly told to stay away."

Nelly nodded along, but her eyes remained on the boy in blue. His skin reminded her of fresh buttermilk: pale, creamy, and unmarred. In that, he was no different from a majority of the guests. Nelly had never seen so many fair-skinned Colored folk gathered together in one place, all glowing with the warmth of a gilded sun. It made the deep russet shade she, her parents, and Sam all shared feel somehow pedestrian in comparison.

Sam's words drifted in and out of her periphery until she distinctly heard him say, ". . . I was shocked myself to receive an invitation."

"Invitation? To a funeral?"

"Yes!" he said. "Delivered not by a postman, but by a private courier, mind you. Now, it *did* arrive at my DC address, not my parents' home in Louisville, so read into that what you will. Came on embossed paper, too. British card stock."

Nelly exhaled and felt the air grow hot and agitated around her.

This whole affair was morphing into a horrendous spectacle.

All of Chicago society turned out not to honor her brother's short and frivolous life, but to gawk at it. The horde of parishioners at Quinn Chapel AME that very morning had been more interested in gossiping about the premier guests than listening to the bishop's boilerplate eulogy. Throughout the ceremony, the chapel was filled with their cicada-like whispers. Exclamations over everything from the ornate black-orchid arrangements, to the ushers in full regalia, to the mass choir summoned directly and with all haste from a basilica in Italy. Nelly's brother was just a prop, even to their own parents. Another piece of priceless art to analyze and judge for value.

Now the dense, undulating crowd had migrated to their house in Hyde Park. It was one of the largest and newest in the area, designed by Frank Lloyd Wright himself, as Nelly's father insisted on telling every person who shuffled through their front door— even the caterers.

"What other Colored man could book a builder like that?" She heard his voice resound throughout the house, looming over them like a swarm. "And in cash!"

Nelly closed her eyes to contain the ache growing in the very bones of her skull. For years, she'd managed to remain properly invisible behind the monolith of her family's wealth. Her brother had been the star attraction and soaked up that limelight gratefully. Now, without his shadow, the glare of it all left her blinded.

"Howard registration is still open," Samuel said, only speaking where she could hear. "We could leave right now, drive all night, and be in the capital by sunrise."

"We can't leave," Nelly said as she shook her head. Her wig, an itchy pompadour that she had a constant urge to scratch, shifted.

He said, "Of course we can! Besides, look at this lot. No one will notice."

"Please, *everyone* would notice. Don't you feel their eyes?"

Nelly allowed her own to travel over and around them. She and Sam sat at the very end of a dining table the length of a ballroom. It had been imported from a Portuguese villa that once belonged to some princess, and it sat at least thirty comfortably. The glances of the guests who ate and drank at that table were fleeting, but there all the same. Waiting for the scene that would justify their presence, justify the time it took to air out their mourning veils.

And there, again—flickering away like a goldfish in murky water— was the young man. He stood straight-backed, talking amiably with Dr. Daniel Hale Williams. He was closer now than he was before, and Nelly could see him in his fullness. He carried an ivory-pommeled walking cane, and when he spoke, he tapped it against the ground for emphasis. He laughed with his whole face in a way so artfully arranged that Nelly was reminded of an aristocratic portrait. The kind of beautiful visages that were planned over months, down to the final paint stroke.

For a brief, insane instant, Nelly thought that perhaps he was a vision. Or a spirit. He dressed in a way that demanded attention, but only Nelly seemed to notice him. She considered her surroundings. An angel come to escort Elder to heaven, maybe? Or a demon bound for the other place. Knowing her brother, it could go either way.

Then he looked at her.

Polite society dictated that if you catch someone staring, you glance away and give them a chance to correct themselves. This man did not glance away. He stared directly back at Nelly with just as much fascination and intense interest. And not only did he look at her, he looked *through* her. Everything practiced and presumed fell away, leaving her bare. It was like standing in sunlight after a winter's worth of darkness. He was certainly no spirit. In fact, he might have been the only real person in the room.

A rustling sound like raven wings caused Nelly to blink and refocus. Next to her stood a woman a few years her senior, as tall as the day was long. Made even taller by her pinstriped suit. She wore her glossy black hair slicked back in a masculine style that complemented her buttery, red-tinted skin. Nelly took her in all in one gulp.

"You *must* be her," the woman said, jutting her broad shoulders forward on each syllable, as though conducting a symphony with nothing but handless, armless gesticulations.

"That depends on who you're looking for," Nelly replied with a small smile. One of the hundreds she'd given so far that day.

"Why, *the* Penelope Sawyer, of course! I have inquired all over this fabulous house in search of you, but not a soul was aware that you even existed. When I mentioned 'Elder's sister,' I swear half of the people here took me for a liar."

"Elder himself would've taken you for a liar," said Sam, who seamlessly plugged himself into the conversation. "Family obligations spoiled the fun, apparently."

"Well, our beloved certainly did enjoy his fun." She spoke of Elder like one who'd known him for years, known the family for years. She suddenly clutched the long strand of baroque pearls about her swanlike neck with all of the drama and insincerity of a silent-picture actress.

"But where are my manners? Here I am, laying siege to your peace on your darkest day. You must think me awful rude, but when has that ever stopped anybody?"

Somewhere within that jumble of pitched and enunciated words, she stretched out her hand with the force of a bayonet pointed directly at Nelly's neck.

"I'm Sequoia McArthur," she said, "and I am sure the pleasure is entirely mine."

Nelly glanced at Sam, who appeared faintly amused, then took Sequoia's hand in turn.

"A pleasure, as you said." Nelly squinted and saw something in Sequoia's confidence and excess of personality that she recognized. "Should I take you to be Bishop McArthur's daughter?"

With a flourish, Sequoia said, "The one and only. Well, not *only* only. There must be a dozen or so others ambling about all over the South Side. Never could keep track of them all myself."

And with that, Sequoia shooed an older man out of his seat across the table from Nelly and folded her lean body into the chair like a paper fan.

"Your father gave a beautiful eulogy," Nelly said. "Right, Sam?"

"Oh yes, very . . . poignant." Sam rolled the word around in his mouth along with the expensive wine that flowed that day like the fabled milk and honey.

"He exclusively does eulogies these days," Sequoia said. "Much better pay than the Sunday-to-Sunday fare. He had three other gigs lined up but turned them all down when the 'wealthiest Negro in America' offered him everything but the crown jewels."

"That article was not entirely accurate," Nelly said. "My father isn't the wealthiest—"

"Perhaps not." Sequoia easily eclipsed Nelly's attempt at small talk. "But when a fighter is offered a prize title on a technicality, they don't turn it down, now do they? Speaking of titles, your mother certainly does curate a marvelous party. So many kinds of people, so many layers. Like a chocolate Dutch cake. Or caramel, rather."

From anyone else, Nelly would have taken that remark as a sharp cut. However, to Sequoia, it was nothing more than the way she saw the world. No insult. Just her own particular brand of truth.

"Did you know my brother?" Nelly asked.

Sequoia's eyes—gold-flecked and smoky like Theda Bara's— softened.

"I'm sorry to say I did not. At least, not in any meaningful way. Everyone knew *of* Elder Sawyer. His reputation, the staggering fortune he was to inherit. His uncanny ability to turn everything from a lecture to a public execution into a good time. But the man kept to himself more often than not. Honestly, I wish more of his type had that level of commitment to mystique."

Something in that broke Nelly's heart. As a child, her brother wanted nothing more than to be everyone's best friend. Now he was laid to rest surrounded by people as removed as visitors at a museum, observing everything through thick and tinted glass.

"But we've all talked enough about poor Elder," Sequoia said,

27

once again as jaunty as cocktails and Charlestons. "I keep a detailed mental catalog of all the people worth knowing in this city—in this *country*, I'm justly proud to say—and your absence from that list is giving me all manner of vapors. It will not be abided. Seriously, I cannot believe in good Christian faith that we have not met before. Perhaps in Oak Bluffs, last summer?"

Nelly gave another tight-lipped smile and shook her head. "I've never visited the coast. Although on full-moon nights, the bluegrass does remind me of a type of sea."

"That is a charming sentiment," Sequoia said without a pinch of sarcasm. "Lake Michigan is no Atlantic Ocean, but we'll go yachting anyway. Where *do* you vacation? I am envisioning somewhere old-world and expensive. The colors of Morocco must make your complexion glow."

Sam had the audacity to chuckle, and Nelly cut him off with a sharp elbow to the side.

"My family doesn't vacation," she said.

"You mean at all?" Sequoia asked. "Is that not a terrible waste?"

"Daddy believes in spending money on things that earn, not things that depreciate."

"Your father has clearly never passed a winter in the Maldives. Come on now, I'm starting to grow frustrated. Where have you been, exactly?"

Nelly could see that frustration in the impatient bounce of Sequoia's knee.

"Derbies, mostly," Nelly said. "The summers are busy with the races, and then we breed studs in the fall—"

"You're kidding." Sequoia's expression was one of abject disgust. "The derbies I can understand. Wonderful chance to socialize. But *breeding?*"

"Wealth doesn't always come with pomp, Ms. McArthur," Sam said in that low, academic voice he used whenever he launched into some debate.

"Of course not," Sequoia said, "but even you must acknowledge that it's a tad odd. Hiding the only Negro woman with an inheritance worthy of Midas in the middle of nowhere is not only peculiar, it's insufferable. Otherwise, honestly, what's the point of having so much money?"

"Maybe the money isn't the point," Nelly said, and immediately knew it was the wrong thing to say. Sequoia practically licked her lips at the exposed combativeness. Like a practiced hunter, she honed in on the wound and resolved to make Nelly bleed.

"Oh, but *it is*. The money's the only reason folk will remember us come Judgment Day. Ask anyone here about Elder, and they'll cry over his clothes and his parties, his excellent taste. That's what they'll mourn. The experience of his existence. But friends? Relationships? Those seemed to be the one thing his money couldn't buy. In comparison, fast cars that are prone to slipping on wet roads are a dime a dozen."

Nelly only realized she was standing when she heard the loud scrape of chair legs against polished maple floors. Conversation hushed as if on cue, and all eyes turned with ready eagerness. Nelly could see the questions in them, the judgments, the jealousies. These, who were meant to be the pillars of her community.

She began to walk through them, rudely forcing her way at times. No one made a path. Instead, they purposefully gathered about her, closed her in. A chic young woman with feathers in her hair bent close to her companion. Nelly could not hear all of what she whispered in a vicious tone, but she caught the truth of it. ". . . not our kind of people."

The change in temperature came as a jolt to Nelly's system. That prophesied cataclysmic summer was well into rearing its head, and they were barely past the solstice. There was no hiding from the heat in the city. The many windows stared like lidless eyes, bright with a cold fire. Her dress—made especially for the occasion under great duress by a French designer—stuck to her like a second, heavier skin. She had a fierce desire to take off her clothes and run naked through time and space to a world that felt like home.

"May I be of assistance, Ms. Sawyer?"

Nelly turned as though she'd been struck, and there he was.

He stood at a deferential distance, but close enough for her to see his eyes. They were the same sky blue as his suit, and embers danced behind them. They spoke of a curious, calculating mind that took in the whole world with a sober criticism. But there was kindness there, too, from what Nelly could see. It called out to her with all the understanding and acceptance of a long-lost friend.

"No, thank you," she said. "I'm fine. The air is just close in there."

"I can fetch you some ice water," he said with one cautious step forward.

"I wouldn't waste the ice. Lord knows it was purchased at some expense."

The young man reached into his pocket and produced a silken white handkerchief embroidered with the face of a blue jay in profile. He walked through her insistence and presented it to her.

"Take my handkerchief, then," he said. "I keep them in an icebox overnight, and they're cool all day."

Nelly accepted the linen and was genuinely surprised to find it cold to the touch. She held it against her fevered brow, and a calm like cool river water rushed through her.

"That's a nifty trick," she said.

"I grew up in a place that thrives in the summer heat. Staying cool is always imperative."

And he certainly was "cool." As unbothered and undisturbed as permafrost.

"Would you be quite scandalized if I asked for a cigarette?" she asked.

The young man's surprise was there, then gone just as quickly.

"Not at all."

His cigarette case was made of solid, thick sterling, engraved with the initials *J.S.* It looked brand-new and rarely used. When he leaned in close to press the small flame of a match against the cigarette butt, Nelly caught the smell of his cologne. It reminded her of an herb garden: tarragon and sage, rosemary and thyme. Clean, and as ancient as the earth.

Nelly exhaled and allowed the smoke to waft about her head. The haze caused the man's shape to shift and change like an image viewed through death's veil.

"You smoke like a professional," he said. The corner of his mouth was turned up in a smirk that bordered on the improper. Nelly was well accustomed to being teased and knew a jab when she felt one.

Merging her words with an arrogant cloud of tobacco smoke, she asked, "Were you expecting something more sophisticated?"

"I have no expectations, Ms. Sawyer. I try to see every second of this life exactly as it is."

Nelly couldn't quite tell if that was poetic or cryptic. Possibly both.

"Whose son are you, then?" she asked as she motioned back toward the repast.

"I beg your pardon?"

"Everyone our age in there is someone's child, or cousin, or distant relative. You strike me as a lawyer's son. Or perhaps a politician's, with that smile."

The young man flashed that same-such smile, and Nelly felt instantly warmed by it. It was a smile that transformed her into the most important person in the world. At first, she found it endearing, but then she saw the inherent lie in it. Such a smile was a cruel simulation of sincerity. She could just visualize him now: standing before a mirror, monitoring the slightest twitch in the complex muscles of his face until he mastered a grin so charming that it disarmed even himself.

"I see," he said. "No, I'm afraid my family wouldn't be welcome here. Too unrefined."

"In that, you and I are alike." She inhaled again, and asked on the exhale, "Were you an acquaintance of Elder's?"

"Not even that." The young man shifted his weight onto the walking cane. "He loaned me a comb once outside a popular club. He made a recommendation regarding a pomade especially for Colored men. I remember him distinctly mentioning the name: Aida, like the opera. That launched us into a conversation about Verdi and the old masters before his party arrived and we were separated. It was a short, somewhat pointless encounter, but it left an impression on me. His joy left an impression on me. Instead of pretending to make the most out of life, he just *did*. No matter how inane it all turned out to be. When I read that he was killed in an automobile accident, I was genuinely upset. I would've liked a chance to know him better."

At any other homegoing, that story would have meant next to nothing to a family member in bereavement. But for Nelly, it was the most touching thing anyone had yet to say about Elder, and somehow—by association—about her.

"That's very kind of you to say."

The young man bowed his head as though such kindness was a requirement in her presence. His attention quickly shifted and focused somewhere behind them—a white man standing on the veranda of the opposite home. Nelly couldn't quite make out his expression over the expanse of their equally large lawns, but she recognized his posture. Stiff and hard, shoulders hunched with aggravation. He was twirling a pocket watch on a long chain. It caught the sun's light and reflected it back at them. Other white men had come before, to stare and boil like kettles on stoves. And there would be more to follow after.

With eyes on the white man's oscillating pocket watch, Nelly said, "There was another funeral today. Her name was Vivian Jones, a twelve-year-old girl who liked strawberry cake and dime novels. Someone found her strangled behind a church in Louisville with a note pinned to her blouse that read 'No Blacks in Shawnee Park.' My brother was no scholar, or philanthropist, or great figure. Just another party boy. Couldn't even be bothered to tithe at church. Shouldn't all of these upstanding members of our community be paying their respects there, at Vivian's grave, instead of here, at the feast?"

She turned back to face the young man, and a pall had fallen over him. He was still handsome, still the picture of composure, but now infinitely older.

"A grand showing of statesmen and lawyers wouldn't bring Vivian Jones back," he said, "or bring comfort to her family."

"What's the point of it all, otherwise?" She thought of Sequoia and her vacation homes. "Why have all of this wealth and prestige if we can't even protect ourselves from their hate?"

The young man took another step toward her, and Nelly did not stop him.

He said, "I have found in my limited experience that the best defense against hate is complete, unmitigated, iridescent happiness."

He smiled again. She saw a boy peeking through that smile, whose sole purpose was to make her laugh and chase the demons from her heart with sunshine.

Much against her better judgment, Nelly asked, "Would you like to dance?"

His stare made seconds stretch into hours.

"Here? Now?"

"Yes," she said in answer more to her own question than to his. "Elder told me a long time ago that when he died, he wanted dancing at his funeral. The perfect homage to a life lived in happiness."

He was astonished, but not astonished enough to say no. He peeked behind them at the French doors separating their own private exchange from a world waiting to skewer them on golden spears.

"Someone will see," he said.

"Doubtlessly."

"The music isn't right for dancing."

"Don't tell me that a capable young man such as yourself can't dance to Rachmaninoff."

He threw his head back and laughed in a starburst of emotion. A single hair fell out of place.

"Is this how girls from good horse families behave?" he asked. There was a tremor to his voice, an unidentifiable accent. "Accepting cigarettes from strange men, dancing at funerals?"

In answer, Nelly removed the long pin that held her wig in place and felt the sun on her head of thick, tightly coiled curls. So far, life without Elder was a life simply for show. Being present when she wanted to disappear, standing still when she wanted to fly, smiling when she wanted to cry. She hungered for connection, even with this nameless boy who betrayed nothing as she gave him everything. Maybe he was a spirit after all. The kind that drove people to the most fulfilling and delicious kind of madness.

He tossed the walking cane into a corner, along with his suit jacket. His arms were not the spindly things common in the pontificates and celebrities her family had taken to hosting. A working man's muscles shifted under his white cotton shirt.

So, she thought. *We see each other plain.*

He bowed at the waist, and she dipped into a loose curtsy. Their hands reached for each other in unison and met across the distance between them.

"We haven't even been introduced," he said, drawing her close. "Not properly."

"That can be easily corrected. My name is Penelope Ginevra Sawyer of Richmond, Kentucky. Folk call me Nelly. Pleased to make your acquaintance."

On a whispered breath reserved for secrets, schemers, and lovers, he said, "Pleased to make your acquaintance, Nelly Sawyer. Call me Jay."

CHAPTER TWO

A grandfather clock chimed the seven o'clock hour as the Sawyers sat like islands within a great sea, isolated and independent. Even with all the excess food from the repast, Florence Sawyer demanded a proper dinner served with all due ceremony in one of the cleared dining rooms. The only sounds came from the anonymous staff that scurried about them like mice.

Nelly's father was conveniently hidden behind a daily paper, and her mother counted up names in the guest book like a bookie counting up bets. Neither noticed the fourth place setting directly across from them, next to Nelly. It was as though they all expected him to stroll through the front door at any moment; late, as usual. It was senseless enough to be funny.

"I cannot believe you," Nelly said. *"Either of you."*

Her parents looked at her as they would a mute who had suddenly developed the ability to speak.

"Well, you've finally decided to join us," her mother said. Florence didn't give Nelly's declaration enough respect to bother removing her reading glasses. "You were silent as a stone all day.

'Cept, of course, for that outburst at the repast. The whispers you inspired, girl."

"Momma, we buried my brother today. Aren't I deserving of an 'outburst,' no matter the whispers?"

"Not around the people who already look at us like we're damn butchers. Proper ladies maintain their decorum, no matter what. We've had this conversation, Nelly."

Feeling brave and righteously insubordinate, Nelly said, "You never minded my decorum before."

"Yes." Florence's eyes were small behind her glasses and sharpened to a fine point. "A failure on my part. One I mean to remedy. I only wish we had more time. . . ."

She shook her head, hummed ruefully, and returned to ledgering the day's guests.

"Daddy," Nelly said to her father, entreating. The dining table was unreasonably long for such a small group, and she had to raise her voice to reach him. "I mean, honestly. The house? The choir? The fucking invitations?"

Florence slapped the meat of her palm against the tabletop.

"You watch your mouth, Penelope!"

"Flora Mae—"

"No, Ambrose! I lay this calamity at your door." Florence took off her glasses and jabbed them at Ambrose like a dagger. "I told you she was spending too much time at the stables and the races with riffraff, and not enough with suitable people. Now we have a daughter who tears off her wig and throws around foul language like some country imbecile."

Nelly's father grinned in the face of Florence's distress.

"The girl does have a point, honey," he said. "The black orchids were a fine bit of extravagance. And expense."

"For all his foolishness—Lord bless his soul—my Elder understood these things," Florence said in a ragged voice. Nelly was not ashamed to say that she found the sincerity of her mother's grief offensive.

"Don't act like this was all for Elder," Nelly said. She speared a Brussels sprout, and the clang of silver on Chinese porcelain made her flinch.

"Of course it wasn't all for Elder," Florence said. "It was for *you*."

Nelly looked up, and her eyes crossed between her parents. Her father had returned to his shelter behind newspaper pages while her mother stared, undaunted as an oncoming train.

"Me? What do you mean?"

"Did you think all of these fine, upstanding Colored folk traveled from hither and yon just to pay their respects?" Florence asked. "There's some manner of gathering, a 'grand season,' happening this summer. Politicians, doctors, academics, men of business like your father. There'll be people milling about here that we'd never see in Richmond. Good people, with good families."

The epiphany that came upon Nelly came slowly. She'd hoped that the earlier profligacy was purely for silly show, but now she understood that the show was far more intentional than that.

"This was all some kind of social event? A way to put out and put on? For these people, Momma, you can't be serious!"

"Oh, I'm perfectly serious," Florence said, "and you should be, too, now that your brother's gone."

Nelly laughed, loudly, and for the first time that evening, her father looked at her directly.

"You don't think to find me a husband, do you?" she asked him specifically. The high walls suddenly felt very high indeed. Her laugh reverberated up and into the illuminated ceiling.

"Mary and Joseph, Nelly, don't look so horrified," he said. He chuckled, but that mirth didn't reach the wrinkles in the corner of his eyes. "It's about time, anyway. You're nearly twenty—"

"Oh, *God.*"

"—and that was considered pretty old in our day, right, Flora Mae?"

"Daddy, please. *Do not* tell me that we used Elder's funeral as a way to prop me up and parade me around like some thoroughbred."

Nelly didn't consider herself one for melodramatics, but just then, she had a violent urge to stand and shout, or possibly stand and faint.

"And quite a parade you put on," said Florence. "All of these dazzling young women around, and you sit in a corner, hiding behind your cousin. You harp about joining Sam at Howard, but you hardly seem to have the maturity for it."

Nelly swallowed down her hurt like bitter medicine. It was a common conversation, and now she knew definitively how it would end. She did not know her parents to be unkind. Brutal and prone to stinging honesty, perhaps, but this felt like unkindness.

"There'll be a cotillion the last week in August," Florence went on. "Many young ladies from all over the country will be presenting. Your father's club is practically bankrolling the whole thing, so it would be inappropriate for you *not* to participate. You're a great deal more grown than most of them, and this will be your first debut, but I don't see that as a problem—"

"I will not be a part of this," Nelly said. "You certainly can't force me. I'm packing my things and going home, tomorrow."

Her words were confident, direct, but full of false bravado. As useless as an animal beating against its own cage.

"You don't understand what's happening here, do you?" Florence asked. She spoke slowly, as though speaking to an excitable invalid. "Hundreds of some of the most prominent Colored families and peoples from New Orleans to Boston are here, in Chicago, for the next two months at least. Folk who—before Elder died—would've sooner turned you from their stoop than introduce you to their sons. All of their sneering means next to nothing when compared to the fortune you stand to inherit, you mark me. Now they'll be asking after *our* parties, begging membership at *our* clubs. Who knows how high you could rise if you put your mind to it? You have a responsibility to me and your father to do your best in this." She fixed her reading glasses back on the bridge of her nose and returned to the marked spot in her guest book. "No, we can't force you. But I'd hoped forcing you wouldn't be necessary."

Nelly bit her tongue like a humbled child. She glanced again at her brother's empty seat at the table and heard his laugh. He came to Chicago because he craved the excitement, the people, the bright lights. She didn't want to take his place in this world. Couldn't, even if she tried.

"May I be excused?" she asked.

Florence examined Nelly again over the rim of her glasses. She used that same hypercritical, unfaltering gaze when judging whether a horse was ready to race.

"Yes," she said slowly. "Yes, I think that would be best. You need to look well-rested."

Nelly did not bother saying good night and rose from the table. The fabric of her fine black dress swished against the floor, reminding her of the wind shifting through tall, wild grass.

CHAPTER THREE

Nelly sat in her room and wondered at the design's inspiration, for she clearly wasn't consulted. Frank Lloyd Wright's brilliance was beyond doubt or reproach; the angles, curves, and efficient lines all spoke of an intentionality that charmed her. But the individual choices were the choices of a department-store clerk mimicking what they saw in catalogs. Nelly's room was an anthropologist's assessment of what a young lady's "chamber" should be. A *Harper's Bazar* facsimile of her personality. She sat on the large bed's unused mattress like a figure in a diorama.

The knock at her door was abrupt enough to make her jump. It was such a quiet house. The slightest noise sounded off like buckshot.

"Nelly." Her father's voice was beseeching. There was another knock, and another, then the silence left by retreating footsteps.

Serves you right, Nelly thought. *We have nothing to say to each other.*

Suddenly, the sound of keys clanging together on a brass ring and one fitting snuggly into the keyhole of her locked door.

"No!" she yelled, but too late. Ambrose Sawyer was soon standing in her open doorway.

"Dang it, Daddy! Can I have no privacy?"

"Like hell," he said, closing the door behind him. "This is my house, and I won't be locked out of any room I own. I have half a mind to take the lock off this door. What if something were to happen?"

Nelly avoided his attempt at disarmament through fatherly concern and said, "I want to go home."

She sounded like a toddler, even to her own ears. But childlike was how she felt. Other women had families and households to manage at her age, but here she sat, watching her parents move her around like a shiny piece on a new game board.

As Ambrose sighed, his chest expanded, and his dark eyes shone with regret.

"Yes, well."

He stuffed his broad body into one of the room's many decorative chairs. He leaned forward on his knees, wringing hands that tamed wild stallions. He looked as though at any moment he might begin to beg. Even the white men who shifted their bulk around like rutting elephants didn't reduce him to this kind of meekness. It made the palms of Nelly's hands itch, but she was determined to remain stoic.

"Your mother thinks you can be successful here," he said softly, at last. "It's a damn fine opportunity, you see. Not just to find you a husband—I'm sure you could handle that perfectly well on your own—but these young men, they're the sons of politicians, doctors. The presidents of universities. You ending up with one of them could do great things for this family."

"What else could possibly be done for the good of this family?" Nelly asked. "Since that article in the *Times*, we've had more business and admirers than we know what to do with. This shameless house is evidence enough of that."

Ambrose looked about Nelly's immaculately decorated room, and she could see the restrained smile tugging at his lips. There was so much of a little boy still in him. At times, Nelly wondered if all the money and show was some kind of private joke for her father, laughing to himself at everyone else's expense.

"A bit much, ain't it?" he asked with a wink.

"Only a bit," Nelly said reluctantly. "Thank God for the Tiffany light switches, otherwise they'd have proof that we're the outcasts they all take us to be."

"Ah," Ambrose said. "You're damn straight on that point. Outcasts we are." His eyes—hazel and bright with mischief, same as Nelly's—rose to meet her. They hardened with the resolve of an argument won and a point proven.

"You can change that, Nelly. If your family name were no longer Sawyer, but Herndon, or Gibson, or Terrell, we wouldn't be outcasts anymore. Money is all well and good, but if the name isn't right, might as well all be leaves fallen from a tree."

"That's an awfully old-fashioned way to think," she said.

"This is an old-fashioned kind of place, old-fashioned kind of people." Ambrose tossed up his hands, as though to throw away a bad memory. "You know how little I care about all this. Marriages, alliances, that's how your momma views the world. But she hasn't strayed us wrong yet. My father was a no-account, half-drunk farrier who couldn't spell his own name. Now here I am, the richest Negro in the land, and Pops isn't even cold in his grave. Nary a generation has passed between the two of us. Do you understand me, child?"

Nelly did understand. She remembered the early years, when the great stables of One Oak could claim no more than three thoroughbreds and a used-up mare. All of this could blink away with a broken femur or a failed pairing. Still, the little girl in her longed for seamless days stretching on and on into forever, unchanged and unladen by the responsibilities now bearing down upon her.

"They won't take to me," she said to her father. "They'll think me bookish and indifferent. 'Not suitable for family life.' That's how that damnable matchmaker Momma recruited the other year described me, ain't it? Said the only man I'll attract is a desperate one."

"You know I'd forgotten all about that?" he said, laughing. "Elder called her Madame Doodlebug 'cause of her shiny black hairpiece."

Nelly smiled as she remembered avoiding looking in Elder's direction as he made faces to mimic the matchmaker's forever-dour expression and Victorian updo. Her smile fell when she realized that was the last time she saw her brother alive. The same memory must have struck Ambrose, for his usually cavernous laugh seemed very far away, as though buried in a well.

"Don't mistake all of the pomp for forgetfulness, Nelly," Ambrose said. "Your mother and I loved Elder, and we miss him dearly. We miss the boy he was and the man he could've been. But he made his mistakes, plenty of them, and he suffered for them."

"Am I to suffer for *my* mistakes now?"

Ambrose brushed off Nelly's intractability as he would brush a fly from his lapel.

"Child, you haven't lived long enough to make a mistake. Hell, my one hope in this life is that you'll never have the chance."

Ambrose removed a small diary from his inside chest pocket and presented it to her. She flipped through it and realized that every day was accounted for. Dinners, tea parties, society club meetings, luncheons, dress fittings. The fateful day of the cotillion was noted in aggressive red ink.

"Shopping?" she asked. "Do we really need a day set aside for shopping?"

"Several days, as I understand it."

Ambrose produced a wrinkled pack of Chesterfields. Soon, the room was filled with dense Virginia tobacco smoke, careless of the velvet drapes that would hoard the smell for months.

"This nonsense stretches on into October, Daddy," she said. "We'll miss the Travers Stakes."

"*You'll* miss the Travers Stakes, most likely. That's not your concern anymore. Never was, really. I admit, I had thoughts of you taking over the running of this enterprise while your brother married some red-boned girl from DC. You were always such a precocious, helpful child."

Ambrose smiled at her warmly, but it was a dim smile, as though he struggled to see the little girl who had to be lifted onto his shoulders in order to see the tracks, not the young, desperate woman too confused to grieve.

"Don't fret about it much," he said with a shake of his head. "I expect this whole 'grand season' will be just as fun as the races. I might even place a wager, see if I can't make some money off of you yet."

He groaned as he stood. This was his signal that the conversation about the summer was over, along with any hope that Nelly was getting out of it.

"Your tour of duty starts next week." He stamped out his cigarette in the soil of a houseplant. "A polo game outside the city at a man's private home, if you can believe that. A group of the young people are making a day of it. The bishop's charming daughter invited you specifically during your, uh, *absence*. She seemed plum overjoyed to spend time with you."

Nelly pictured Sequoia's silver-screen smile and the disapproving curl under her button nose. She could already feel the vultures picking at her until they struck bleached bone.

Ambrose pinched Nelly's cheek, just as he had when she was a child too afraid to walk down a dark hallway alone at night.

"They'll adore you," he said, and believed it.

The door was open, and Ambrose stood with his wide back filling the frame, but then he stopped. Nelly could see the tension coiled like bands of rope in his shoulders.

"Daddy?" she asked.

He returned to his chest pocket and a crisp square mailing envelope.

"I meant to keep this from you," he said, looking guilty, "but I couldn't quite manage it. How long was your brother playing go-between with you and this pen pal?"

Nelly's eyes passed quickly between the envelope and her father's face.

"A few months," she said. She figured starting with a truth would smooth out the path for a lie. When she had reached out to Elder almost a whole year ago, she'd expected him to ignore her entirely, never mind agree to accepting clandestine messages on her behalf. He had been thrilled, actually. She remembered the pitch of his voice through the scratchy receiver: *Finally, something exciting.*

Ambrose nodded and turned the envelope over in his hands. The seal had not been broken.

"Who is it, then? Some boy?"

Nelly lowered her eyes demurely, feigning shame.

"Yes," she said. Again, not a complete lie.

Her father's grin was lewd and teasing.

"Your momma thinks you're too dowdy for such things, but I always knew better. You're *my* daughter, ain't ya?"

Nelly couldn't say what was more embarrassing: her father's eagerness to believe she'd been fraternizing, or the reality that such a thing was an impossibility.

"Does Momma know about the letter?" Nelly asked.

Ambrose shook his head, but said, "You know this can't go on. Whoever this young man is, it's best to end things now. If your momma did find out, we'd all be in a shit ton of trouble."

Nelly nodded rapidly and reached out for the envelope. Before her fingers could touch it, Ambrose pulled back and left it dangling out of reach.

"I'm serious now, Penelope. I stumbled upon this letter by accident, but I'll be watching now. I *will* tell your mother if I see this like again."

Nelly knew that in all practicality, she was too old to feel threatened by her parents' anger. Yet, her stomach churned the same way it had when she searched among the spice bushes for the switch Ambrose would use to discipline them as children.

"It won't happen again," she said, but this time, it was a full-on lie.

Her father let the letter slip into her grasp. She snatched her hands back quickly and held the envelope to her chest, every inch the besotted girl.

"Smart using your grandma's name," Ambrose said. "Reminds me of something your brother would think of."

Only when the door latched fully shut did Nelly allow herself to exhale. She felt clammy and feverish and relieved. She looked at the envelope, and sure enough, it was addressed to an Ira Brown, her maternal grandmother's maiden name. The mailing address was a Loop postal box; *that* had been Elder's idea. There was no return address, and for that, Nelly was grateful. Her father was sharp enough to figure out some of it, but not all of it.

The typed note read as follows:

Mr. Brown,

Greetings and kind regards.

Thank you for your most recent submission. The tragedy of Vivian Jones's death is allayed, even minimally, by the small joys and pleasures of her life that you were able to share with the world.

I again ask if it would be appropriate for us to meet. You have a strong voice, and while we at the Defender *are accustomed to publishing without bylines, those such as you should not remain in anonymity for long. I believe you are in town for the Chicago Four Hundred's festivities. I admit that this is an assumption; yet, something in our correspondence implies a level of well-to-do associated with this city's Negro aristocracy.*

In either case, there may yet be a place for you amongst this publication's ranks. Your unique journalistic adroitness is youthful and desperately needed in our line of work. If meeting is out of the question, then we shall continue as we have since last May. However, if there is any hope of an opportunity, you may reach me directly at our building on S. Indiana Avenue. It is our new headquarters, and we're all quite proud of it.

Yours in anticipation,

Richard B. Norris
Editor-in-Chief, The Chicago Defender

Nelly read the letter over twice, then folded it into a tight square. She considered sitting down and writing a response at once. *Yes,* she would say. *Let's meet immediately. This is the fulfillment of a dream.* But then her eyes glanced at her bedroom door and its inconsequential lock. She could faintly hear the voices of her parents drifting up like smoke. She expected that they were plotting, she being the cornerstone of those plots.

She took the letter and slid it between the folds of the embossed program handed out by the pound at Elder's funeral. In the photo they used of him, he looked content but unimpressed, as though knowingly posing for his own epitaph. Nelly hated him for leaving her behind in Kentucky while he went off on some grand adventure. She hated him for never calling, for donning their family's eccentricities so effortlessly, for still being the one everyone liked and admired. Hated him for not being there to see what she'd become.

Nelly took the program, and the letter, and her brother's rose-tinted memory, and stuffed them in a vanity drawer. She couldn't very well erase the past. But she could smother it.

CHAPTER FOUR

If not for Sequoia's hat, Nelly would have been completely lost. It towered like the lighthouse of Alexandria.

She in fact saw the hat well before she saw Sequoia herself, and the band of well-dressed, lounging young people who gathered about her. The risers erected for the match's spectators were tall and crowded, and Nelly was just a face among hundreds. She could leave, if she really wanted to. She could turn around and walk back to the city and no one would be the wiser. Then Sequoia turned, and Nelly was caught in her crosshairs. So she smiled and lifted her hand to wave.

As Sequoia stood, Nelly could see the full scope of her outfit. It was impudent, impractical, and fabulous. The bodice was sheer enough to be shameful, blending with full yellow skirts of toile folded one on top of the other like the petals of a blooming rose. It made a striking impression that dulled everyone around her, as intended.

"I thought we were all traveling together, but you show up a whole hour late," Sequoia said once Nelly was close.

"Would you believe me if I said I couldn't decide what to wear?" Sequoia's eyes squinted with suspicious affront and a bit of appreciation.

"Do I detect a smidge of judgment in your tone, Ms. Sawyer?"

"Of course not," Nelly said. "You look absolutely stunning. And I mean that."

That suspicion was diluted by the shine of Sequoia's smile.

"I do, don't I?" she said. "You know, I won this little number off of Joanna Dickerson last summer at Idlewild. Fifteen-love, my best score since. And honestly, if you knew Joanna, you'd know that such a dress is wasted on her. Enough money to finance an entire Jeanne Lanvin collection, but she'd rather go around in wool blouses and plaid skirts like some governess in a tragic novel."

Nelly cringed and stopped herself from self-consciously preening her sensible navy skirt and broadcloth blouse.

Sequoia suddenly grabbed Nelly about the shoulders and pulled her in close. Speaking with theatrical softness, she said, "I told a white lie when we met at the funeral. I've known about you for months, you see. I'm a bit of an admirer."

Nelly guffawed. Clearly, this was some kind of trap.

"No, no, I'm serious!" Sequoia said. "I admire how subtle you are. Give any of these other peacocks just a taste of what you have, and they'd be impossible. Sun Kings and Marie Antoinettes eating cake for breakfast because they can. Elder called you the Rock of Gibraltar, and I think he was right. There's no changing you."

"Is that meant to be a good thing?" Nelly asked.

"It's silver and gold to chameleons like us. Real wealth means feeling secure enough to be yourself. I'm hoping some of that will rub off on me this summer."

Nelly hadn't known Sequoia very long at all, but she had a sense that an olive branch from her was a rare thing. Once offered, it was in one's best interest to accept it.

"Maybe your sense of style will rub off on me, too," Nelly said. "The last thing I'd ever want to be is a governess in a tragic novel."

Sequoia nodded her approval. A truce, then, for now.

Speaking over the din of horses stampeding across a field of paspalum grass, Sequoia called their little outing to order.

"Everyone! Come on now, hush up, listen to me. I am thrilled to introduce the final member of our party: dear Nelly Sawyer."

Nelly stood straight as she faced the collection of Colored young people seated before her. There were about four of them, close in age and all looking at her as one might look at a curious new oddity. Indifferent, but silently hoping for some amusement.

"Now, I'm sure introductions aren't necessary," Sequoia said, "but I'll do the honors for posterity." She started on the right and rolled through them all like a chorus line. "This darling girl is Eveline Syphax with that scandalous Washington history that I of course won't bring up here, Effy, wouldn't dream of it. Mabel Ford from Memphis, but we won't hold that against her. Her cousin Nathaniel Terrell of the DC Terrells—*distant* cousin, as his mother will be quick to say if you bring up their brief engagement. And that light 'n bright Negro over there is Lloyd Younger of Atlanta, or can't you tell by his shoes?"

The yellow wing-tipped man in question removed a porcelain

pipe from between his lips and said, "You're just upset because I wear the color better than you, CeCe."

He doffed his old-fashioned top hat at Nelly, pitched at an avant garde angle.

"Charmé, mademoiselle," he said with as overwrought a French accent as Nelly was likely to hear outside of Europe.

Nathaniel leaned forward to say, "Ignore him, Nelly. He spent a summer in Paris and now fancies himself the goddamn Prince of Wales."

"Please," Lloyd said. "I'm a much better dresser than the Prince of Wales."

The Ford girl—Mabel—extended a delicate lace-gloved hand out to her.

"You must be sweltering, standing there while we interrogate you." Her Southern accent was the slow, old-timey kind that Nelly thought only existed in stage musicals. In Chicago, everyone spoke so quickly, leaving no room for the music. "Come, sit by me so we can interrogate you comfortably."

She settled in next to Mabel and "Nathaniel Terrell of the DC Terrells." Some distance below them, horses that shone as radiant as destriers ran at full tilt while riders in mud-and-grass-speckled uniforms shouted to each other. Nelly shielded her eyes against the sun and saw another set of risers on the opposite end of the field. But instead of sitting in the open, unshaded heat—as Nelly was—several well-appointed pavilions kept groups enviably cool and comfortable.

"My *deepest* condolences, Nelly," Effy Syphax said. She had a full cherub face touched with dark-brown freckles. The parasol she carried cast a spiderwebbed shadow over her chestnut head of hair. "To you and your family. Elder is such a great loss."

Nelly donned that familiar, thankful grin that barely reached her eyes.

"Thank you," she said. "Everyone's been so kind—"

"What happened to the car?"

Nelly's head turned on a sharp swivel to face Lloyd Younger and his obnoxious pipe.

"Excuse me?" she said.

"The car," he repeated. "Never got to see it myself, but I've heard about it. A blue Roamer Roadster with white leather upholstery, right?" He whistled low and slow. "One hell of a birthday present."

Nelly stared at him for a moment. When nothing in Lloyd's curious eyes changed, she snapped on a tight smile and said, "Totaled. They had to fish it out of the Chicago River."

Lloyd sighed, and smoke seeped out between his lips.

"That's an honest shame."

"Clearly, a semester in Paris didn't teach you how to read a room," Sequoia said, gathering the attention back around herself. "Your manners are as crude as ever, Lloyd, and I have resolved to banish you to the hinterlands of this conversation. Nelly! What are your plans while you're in town?"

Even though she'd happily spar with Lloyd, Nelly knew Sequoia's abrupt change of subject was an order.

"I've been drafted into this cotillion nonsense." The group

echoed a begrudging groan all at once, like a congregation.

"Half of us already went through one cotillion or debutant ball or another," Mabel said. "I see no use in making us do the cakewalk all over again."

"It has something to do with all the bumpkins coming in from the South," said Sequoia. She had a lit cigarette poised at the long end of an ebony holder. Matched with the dress and the fearsome hat, she looked like the cover of a Parisian publication. "Some folk hope Chicago will be the next DC."

Nathaniel chuckled dismissively at that. Nelly noted the egg-shaped flask of glass and leather in his hand. He held it out toward her, and when she threw it back, she immediately began to cough.

"Christ," she rasped.

Nathaniel grinned and said, "I thought Kentucky was known for its whiskey."

"Whiskey, yes. Not paint thinner."

"Volstead has made beggars of us all. It's not that bad, once you get used to not having a functioning larynx."

Nelly shook her head and passed the flask on to the next person.

"I rather like the idea of a Grand 'Colored' Season," said Effy. Her pale silk fan moved rapidly as it pushed around the humid air. "Seems terribly romantic, doesn't it?"

"You only feel that way 'cause you're a desirable little deb, Effy," Sequoia said. "Every mother of a Boulé has had their heart set on you for a daughter-in-law since your sweet sixteen last spring." She smiled at Nelly and used the cigarette to draw a wispy heart around her face. "But that was before Ms. Penelope Sawyer here, wasn't it? Now all the matrimonial whispers are of that Biblical Sawyer fortune. Us unwanted old maids must be content with the crumbs that fall from her table."

Lloyd wielded his pipe like a scepter as he said, "Speak for yourself, CeCe. I intend to make a sparkling match this year. Finally get my parents off my ass about a 'career.' As if I could stand a life prescribing oils for bunions like my daddy."

"Will marriage be your career?" Nelly asked, still sniffing after a confrontation.

"Yes," he said. "And why not? That's what they teach the girls, right? To treat marriage like a job? Why can't young men act the same? In exchange for a regular, healthy stipend, I swear to be the most doting and faithful of husbands."

"Is that a proposal?" Nelly asked in a half challenge.

"That depends," Lloyd said. "I plan to be very expensive."

He was a consummate asshole, but a bearable one. Trading blows with him was a welcome distraction for Nelly in the midst of such a brave new world.

Below them, proud polo ponies were black and brown streaks across a field so green it made Nelly's eyes weep. Everything was to regulation from what she could tell. As well-equipped as any competitive arena in the depths of horse country.

"Who is behind all of this?" she asked Sequoia. "This is a private home, right?"

With a lukewarm shrug, Sequoia said, "Some white man with too much money and not enough sense. His son can't play polo worth a shit, apparently, and no professional team will take him. So this 'match' is all for his benefit. Pretend field. Pretend umpires. Pretend spectators. But these seats aren't pretend, let me tell you. I had to cash in a hundred favors to get us this kind of access."

"What about the players?" Nelly asked. They didn't move like actors or amateurs. One young man in particular rode like he was born to it. The sound of his mallet hitting the ball was solid, and Nelly felt it in her chest.

"Oh, they're real enough," Sequoia said. "Those fine young men in blue are with this intercontinental leisure league. Lords, Dukes, obscure millionaires. Some of us came to hunt, you see."

A sound like a cannon shot, then a roar from the field. The natural again. Nelly couldn't see much of his face beneath the protective helmet, but his triumphant smile was luminous. Even his pony had a prideful rhythm to its trot.

After years of making herself small at derbies, races, and horse shows, Nelly had developed an eye for breeds. The natural rode what old heads called a Kentucky Saddler. A slim and jet-black mare with a white star on her head. Not too different from the Kentucky Saddlers her family's ranch bred. But the allure dissolved when she noticed the way the rider's spurred heels dug into the mare's side. The animal started and flinched away, forcing the rider to jerk the lead. For all of their tandem flamboyance, there was a clear lack of communication.

"I imagine you know this scene pretty well," Sequoia said. "Equestrian sports, if that's the word."

Nelly said, "I'm sure we've sold to our fair share of polo teams and players, but most won't tolerate Negroes at their clubs. Not even to work. It wasn't until last year that my father purchased his own box at Churchill Downs."

"Dastardly. And to think of all the money your family makes them. Things aren't roses and buttercups up here in Chicago, but how any self-respecting Negro could live in the South is beyond me." A visible shudder ran up and through Sequoia. "I visited a great-aunt in Georgia once, and once was all it took."

"To tell it true," Nelly said, "I always preferred watching from the lawn, not the boxes. Momma calls it rabble, but that's where you hear the best stories. I was happy to lose myself in the excitement rather than sit prim for white people to comment on how eloquent and well-behaved I was. I even got to see James Lee's clean sweep from the best seat in the house."

Nelly never intended to share so much, but it had been a long time since someone listened to her with such deep intention. No, that wasn't entirely true. She thought of Jay and his seemingly all-knowing stare and desensitized smile.

Another roar went up from the field and leaked into the gathered crowds. The players sporting blue and gold were celebrating with mallets spearing the air, but the people in the pavilions celebrated the loudest. They drew one's attention like rare orchids and Nelly could not look away.

In that first instant, she did not know him as anyone other than a well-dressed white boy of vague means passing an hour of leisure. Like an illustrated ad in a travel catalog. Tailored suit the color of strawberry wine. Slicked-back hair, champagne glass held absently aloft. Eyes like gemstones. And that smile . . .

When the recognition did finally settle, it took Nelly's breath away. The transformation was something without seams, threads, edges, or creases. It was not so much that Jay looked white, or even acted it. Nothing in the way he bent to whisper in the ear of the brunette at his elbow was any different from the way he had whispered to Nelly. Still, there was an essence that radiated from him that couldn't be mistaken for anything else other than white. She tried to read his lips, but it was impossible from so far. What could he say to make them see what she saw so clearly?

The sense of betrayal Nelly felt was deep and unearned. Nearly a week had passed since the funeral, and when her thoughts dared to drift from Elder and her situation, they drifted back to Jay. That comfort she felt in his presence and his strange acceptance. Whatever complicated role he was playing, it had done a number on her.

When their eyes met, his smile did not falter. If anything, it spread and filled his face until his teeth shone like fangs. Any of the oblivious white faces around him would have claimed that smile for themselves, but Nelly knew that it was for her, and her alone.

Jay lifted his glass only just and nodded. Whether in acknowledgment, playfulness, or a malicious type of victory, Nelly would never know.

CHAPTER FIVE

A horn blew, and the game was ended. Some clapped, but most lingered, treating the match like the idle entertainment that it ultimately was.

They all joined a slow progression of guests snaking through the estate's re-created Venetian gardens up to the main house for refreshments; a mix of the pavilion crowd and the more standard attendees like Nelly, but not *wholly* like Nelly. Looking around, she realized that she and the others in Sequoia's entourage were the only Negroes there who weren't grooms, valets, drivers, or caterers.

Nelly spotted Jay's head bobbing easily above the rest. Having seen him once, there was no chance of mistaking him again. The hat he wore was the same pale cream as his skin, and the brim cast a wide shadow. He was still laughing. The sound that fascinated her at the funeral now pulled at something inside her like a loose thread.

Soon, Nelly wasn't being carried by the crowd, but actively maneuvering through it. She didn't know what she'd do once she reached Jay, but her hand flexed from the anticipation. Touching his shoulder and seeing his face as he accepted that, yes, he'd been discovered. She rehearsed in her mind what she would say, what she would ask. Or perhaps she wouldn't say anything at all and just stare at him as he'd so blatantly stared at her.

The queue suddenly split like a river breaking against rocks. One group continued up the hill along a tiled boulevard into some kind of ballroom. Another spread into the lush gardens in intimate parties of three or four. And there went Jay, away from them all.

"Pardon me," she said to those who'd been rudely shoved aside, and then she, too, was away from the crowd and on her own.

Nelly didn't know how exactly she managed to lose him.

One second, Jay was there—trudging ahead in his pink herringbone suit—then he was gone. Swallowed by the unkempt edges of the property. She was still on the formal grounds. She decided in the end to head toward the music. Momma once told her that if you're ever lost in the woods, the sound of running water will lead you home. Nelly figured a pitchy rendition of "Till We Meet Again" was close enough.

After a half hour of walking, she was back among redbrick buildings and wrought iron gates. She heard the familiar sounds of hooves on pea gravel; the sparse, gruff talk of grooms; and the trampling of some stud desperate to reach a mare in heat. Nelly rushed and turned a corner into a stable larger than most houses. Hands exercised massive thoroughbreds, who slowly walked the stable courtyard's perimeter like a living carousel. This setup was smaller than what the Sawyers had at One Oak, but for someone's private residence, it was extravagantly grand.

Unencumbered, Nelly stepped into the courtyard and breathed in the smells of animals, and people, and work. Whatever mania had seized her when she decided to follow Jay began to dim. Someone could easily call her out as a trespasser, and she'd be hard-pressed to dispute them.

One of the horses poked its head out from within its stable to see the stranger more clearly. It was the black Kentucky Saddler with a white star on its brow.

"Hello, champion," Nelly said as she approached it. The horse did not shy away as some do with new people, but rather took a confident step forward. When Nelly caressed its head, she felt it lean into her touch. That white star sparked something in her memory: a colt who came too early and traded a mother's life for its own. Strong in spirit, but fragile in body, fated to die within a week without constant attention. Nelly tried not to grow attached to the horses her family raised, but this one had been different. This one, she'd claimed as her own.

"Can I help you?"

Nelly jumped near out of her skin.

"Jesus Lord!" she said at the crossroads between a gasp and a scream. Her heart beat like an infantry drum. "You scared me near to death. How'd you manage to sneak up on me, walking on gravel?"

Behind her stood one of the polo players in a blue-on-gold jersey. The polo player's eyes narrowed as he said, "You are the encroacher here, but I stand accused?"

"You could have announced yourself," Nelly said. "No use scaring me to prove a point."

The man smiled—stiff and forcefully polite—but still Nelly was struck by its charm.

"Let me start again: Who are you, and what are you doing here?"

His accent reminded Nelly of the breeders of Mexican thoroughbreds who annually came to see One Oak's stock, but more refined. Rich and musical. A song sung in staccato. He looked more exhausted than angry, perhaps even amused, but that didn't dampen Nelly's indignation. She did relish moments like these, quiet as it was kept.

"I am the owner of this horse," she said. The man adjusted his stance from one hip to the other, and his breath came in heavy pants.

"Miss, I fear you are mistaken," he said. "I have owned and ridden this horse for over two years."

"Well then, I am the *original* owner of this horse. I raised her from a colt, and I can tell clearly from the display on the field that you may ride her, but you do not understand her."

The polo player's mouth was now a long thin line. He wasn't much taller than Nelly, so she could look him directly in the eye. They were gentle eyes for the most part. A shade of brown so decadent that they were almost black. When he smiled again, the long angles of his face relaxed.

"Did you . . . wander away from the party?"

"I'm not drunk, if that's you're thinking," Nelly said in answer to his patronizing squint. "My name is Penelope Sawyer. This mare was bought from One Oak Ranch in Richmond, Kentucky, right?"

"I'm not sure. Estrella was a gift."

"Estrella?"

"It is a Spanish name, meaning star."

Nelly smiled as she ran her fingers along the five-pointed white mark.

"Fitting," she said. "I called her Blue Sonata. One Oak is *my* family's ranch, you see."

A fire lit behind the polo player's eyes. His smile was no longer forced but downright joyful, like a little boy meeting a local hero.

"Of course!" he said. "I am *quite* familiar! Even abroad, there's talk of Ambrose Sawyer and his empire. If Estrella is representative of his breeding stock, the praise is well worth it."

Nelly tried not to swell with pride. The praise was directed at her father, what *he'd* accomplished, after all. Whatever success her family knew now had nothing to do with her.

"Even the best-bred horse will fall short with bad handling," she said. "If you keep fighting her, you'll have more than a losing streak to deal with."

"I have been an equestrian since the age of ten, miss. I assure you, I'm perfectly capable of handling a domesticated mare. Today's loss was due to the heat."

"Ah. Heat, terrain, and humidity. The favorite excuses of every mediocre horseman."

"Medi—?"

He stopped himself with a bite to his bottom lip and shook his head with what Nelly assumed was genuine disbelief. She didn't even know his name, and yet, here she stood, calling his expertise into question. The dirt on her hem and the sticks in her hat probably made the dressing-down all the more ridiculous.

"What would you recommend, Ms. Sawyer?"

Now, Nelly was not expecting that.

"You truly want to know?" she asked, wary. He bowed at the waist with a bravado that danced so close to sardonic that it made Nelly square her jaw.

"You can ease up on the spurs for a start," she said. "As I remember it, she's spirited, but not disobedient. If you do the work to teach her where to go and what to do, she'll do it. Blue Sonata—excuse me, *Estrella*—is not some ignorant pony who can't walk the path before her without a guide. With a little effort on your part, your partnership could be more natural."

The polo player nodded along with her lecture, like an attentive student.

"Yes. Anything else?"

He wasn't white, not exactly. His skin was too evenly tanned to be the product of sun alone, and there was a pillowy fullness to his mouth. But the unwitting person couldn't, wouldn't, spot that unless they knew what to look for.

"Do you run her?" Nelly asked.

"You mean exercise?"

"Not exercise as you see it, not *that*," Nelly said, gesturing to the grooms still guiding the horses through the carousel stroll. "I mean running. Letting her set off at her own pace. Like I said, she's smart. She needs more than a casual jaunt to be at her best. Now mind you, I'm no trainer. I'm sure you pay half a dozen people to tell you how to ride a horse. This is just my opinion."

"Of course," he said. "That is, after all, what I asked for. And for all the trainers I pay, not one will admit that I could do better."

He reached out to stroke the horse's muzzle. His touch was affectionate and kind. Nelly could see that his abuse wasn't due to some disregard, just ignorance. If anything, the dent in his brow told her that he'd rather let the horse go free than misuse her.

"You raised this horse, you said?" he asked.

"Yes," Nelly said. "She didn't have a mother, so someone had to feed her and stay with her at night. My father didn't think she'd grow strong. Turns out she just needed time."

Nelly smiled up at a horse that now emitted strength like heat from a hearth. Speaking more to Blue Sonata than the man, she said, "It's good to see her again."

She heard the polo player inhale next to her. He smelled of cigar smoke and licorice.

"You may visit her, if you'd like," he said. "My team will be in Chicago until the fall with little to do between matches. Don't look so grateful, Ms. Sawyer," he said in teasing answer to the spark of appreciation that passed over her face. "This invitation is purely selfish. Any instruction you're willing to offer while visiting Estrella would be ardently accepted."

Nelly found herself laughing with her whole chest, something her mother would pinch her for in the presence of strangers.

"There may be some room in my schedule for a worthy cause,"

she said, teasing back. "Lord knows I have enough to fill up my diary."

The polo player tilted his head in question.

With a regretful sigh, Nelly explained, "This is my coming-out season, apparently. I'm to 'debut' with all of the spectacle of a fresh house fire."

The young man grinned, but there was a curl to the corner of his mouth that Nelly had often seen in her brother before he hatched a scheme.

"My cousin debuted in France last year," he said. "It was a masterfully composed disaster. Then again, my cousin is a prima donna who turns every inconvenience into a crisis. You, however, Ms. Sawyer . . ." His eyes moved quickly, but Nelly did not miss the way he took her in, muddy hem and all. "I am sure you will dazzle."

For once, she could not think of a single thing to say.

"Nelly!"

The moment dissolved, and Nelly turned to see Sequoia standing at the end of the drive that led into the stable courtyard. Her fabulous hat was askew, and everything from the sheer brocade of her bodice to the bottom of her black-and-white pumps was covered in a thick layer of dirt.

"Where the *hell* have you been?" Sequoia yelled. "I've been searching for hours!"

"It couldn't have been more than thirty minutes," Nelly said.

"I have blisters, Penelope!" Her voice was piercing. "These shoes are rented. *Fucking rented.* I trust I don't need to explain the implications to you."

Just over her shoulder, Nelly heard the polo player chuckle softly. Immediately, everything about Sequoia changed. The agitation sloughed away, and her sparkling affect shone through the dust.

"I do beg your pardon," she said to the polo player, for Nelly knew that sugary-sweet tone wasn't for *her* benefit.

The man magnanimously raised his hand like a priest offering absolution.

"Think nothing of it," he said. "Those *are* marvelous shoes."

The simpering sound that Sequoia made was absurd. He was handsome, sure, but not half enough to swoon over.

"What is wrong with you?" Nelly asked.

Sequoia cut her a glance hot enough to light a match.

"I've been running around in my best outfit for the better part of an hour. *That's* what's wrong with me. Just come on. The party's a bust. Lloyd found your driver and is threatening to leave without you."

Where before Nelly was chomping at the bit to be away from this place, now she found it difficult to take those first steps.

"I have to go," she said to the polo player.

"Of course," he answered. The husky drop in his tone betrayed that same regret. "I will call on you to schedule a proper reunion with Estrella, yes?"

"You can try," said Nelly, "but my momma has me booked from here to next Easter. She won't make the room unless she feels it's worth our time."

"I will plead my case, then."

Smiling until her cheeks ached, she said, "I hope you are successful."

Then he was taking hold of her hand and bending low to kiss it. She snatched it back as though she'd been shocked through with electricity and felt the fool for it. The hand that was once holding hers tensed and then closed into a fist before vanishing behind his back.

"Au revoir, Mademoiselle Sawyer," he said. "It has been a pleasure."

She wanted to say more—knew that manners and plain common sense demanded she say more—but words continued to fail her.

On closer inspection, Nelly could see that Sequoia's shoes really were ruined.

"I'm sorry," she said. "For everything. Including the shoes."

Sequoia threaded Nelly's arm with her own, leashing them together.

"It's all applesauce," she said as they began the walk back to the main house. "The only thing you missed was some half-drunk producer mistaking the Venus ice sculpture for his mistress. And they served cucumber sandwiches, can you believe that? These people upset an entire industry to secure the Palmer House head chef, then had him toil over finger food like a housewife."

Only partially listening, Nelly looked back and saw that the polo player hadn't moved an inch.

"You either have the luck of the devil or the devil's luck, Penelope Sawyer," Sequoia said, shaking her head and clucking like some old church mother.

"Aren't those things one and the same?"

"Lord in heaven!" she cried. "Do you even know who that is?"

"Some foreign rich boy?"

"You're really serious. Every white girl from here to St. Louis would trip their grandma for five minutes alone with that particular foreign rich boy."

"What? Is he meant to be good?"

"To hell with being good! That's Tomás Escalante y Roche. His aunt is a fucking marquess, and his father owns half of Mexico. He's practically royalty, Nelly."

Nelly thought back and considered his manners, his stature, his turn of phrase. And the fact that one of the most expensive horses her family ever bred was given to him as a *gift*.

"Is that all true?" Nelly asked.

"Do you think I'd show up to this thing unprepared? I told you, some of us came to hunt. And look at you, bagging the best prize without even trying." Sequoia shook her head again and quickened their pace. "Like I said. Luck of the devil or the devil's luck."

Nelly spared one more glance at the polo player. Tomás, Sequoia said his name was. A strong beam of sun broke through and basked him in a golden light. Even in a soiled, nondescript polo uniform with grass stains on his cheeks, he looked as fresh as newly minted money.

CHAPTER SIX

Nothing?"

"Nothing at all."

"Not a word? You are *quite* sure?"

"Yes! Christ, it's only been a couple of days. Do you think I'd lie?"

"Not sure. Maybe. Wouldn't put it past you."

Nelly had to look away from Sequoia. People were everywhere, and she was doing her best to maintain the barest composure.

"You're a terrible influence," Nelly said. "Aren't you meant to be introducing me to some of these people?"

The Arts Club of Chicago had a sizable exhibit hall, but still, rooms in adjoining office spaces had to be rented for overflow. *Everyone* showed up for the Henry O. Tanner exhibit. All the Negro fraternities and women's clubs were represented, along with their children. Business owners, academics, politicians. The who's who of Colored society, from as far away as California. Nelly had initially taken this "grand season" to be one of her parents' joint delusions. But now, seeing this turnout, she felt the business of it perching on top of her. She felt more the exile here—surrounded by those who thought like her, looked like her—than she ever was in Richmond, and she tried not to hate herself for it.

"Well, you've already met the Mintons," Sequoia said, "and they're the most important people here. Next to Mr. Tanner himself, of course."

"They're the hosts," Nelly countered. "I had to meet them to get into the building."

"I don't know why you're so eager to hobnob, anyway. I doubt even the best of this lot could compete with a prince."

"He's not a prince," Nelly corrected, "and I'm sure he has better things to do. He's as good as white by most standards, better than white by others. What would he look like, calling on some Colored girl? Probably never will, once he comes to his senses. It's not even worth telling my folks about."

"He'd look like a grown man who knows his own business," Sequoia said definitively. The air in the exhibit hall was close, and her lace fan fluttered like hummingbird wings. "Besides, you're not just 'some Colored girl,' whatever that means. You're a stunning young woman who'll inherit enough money, and land, and assets to fill the Great Lakes. If he has any sense at all, he'll show you the proper attention you deserve."

An acquaintance of Sequoia's father passed by, and they engaged in the proper small talk before the lawyer or commissioner was drawn into a conversation with old college friends.

"Stunning?" Nelly asked. "Really?"

"I said what I said, didn't I?"

Sincere compassion was not a color Sequoia McArthur wore often, but it was a flattering shade.

Nelly soon discovered that the only ones there to actually view the art were the white people. It was an open exhibit, after all, and the museum had very dedicated patrons. Seeing them wander about in groups of two or three—looking for all the world like children who lost their parents at a county fair—was as comic as it was tragic.

Everyone else was there to socialize in their silk-lined waistcoats, embroidered gowns, and jewels twinkling on every finger. They shone like stars amidst the firmament. Nelly thought of that morning's sparring match with her mother over what she should wear, and despite herself, she felt underdressed in a simple white frock.

"You know Lloyd Younger, of course," Sequoia said as they wound through the exhibit. She waved at Lloyd, who nodded before ignoring Nelly completely.

"Yes," Nelly said with a sneer. "I think his charm is lost on me."

Sequoia hummed and swiveled her head, eyes touching everything and everyone like the Angel of Death searching for firstborns to slaughter.

"Daniel Stevenson is nothing but charming," she said, pointing at a young man across the way. "His father is quite prominent in New York. Something to do with stocks or investments. Liquid wealth, essentially. He was engaged a couple years ago, but the thing fell through."

He was green-eyed and very fit. Laughing lightly with a young lady who wore velvet peonies in her hair.

"Why did the engagement fall through?" Nelly asked.

"Turns out his charm is a bit of a trap," Sequoia whispered. "I spent a week with him in Oak Bluffs the summer before last. Took me all of five minutes to realize that he's deadly boring. Talking to him is like talking to a taxidermic spaniel. But, like I said, liquid wealth. For some, that's more than enough."

Whoever the peony-bedecked woman was, she didn't seem to find Daniel boring. Her neck stretched as she laughed, accenting the amethyst choker about her pale throat.

They moved slowly among the drifting pockets of people. Eyes would land quickly on Nelly, then dash away at the last moment. A few daring souls held her stare and nodded, or smiled, or raised a wineglass filled with nonalcoholic cider. Nelly intended to smile back at them all, but instead, she felt her face morph into a suspicious smirk.

"I'm not sure what my mother said when she recruited you," she said, "but I'm not looking for a husband." Marquis, prince, investment banker, or candlestick maker. "I'd rather not be here at all."

"Stop all that," Sequoia said. "You're here now, so make the most of it. And your mother didn't recruit me for anything. I volunteered."

"Sequoia! Is that you, dear?" called out a voice within the multitude.

Sequoia steered them in the direction of a fair-complexioned trio. An older couple and a lean-faced gentleman who resembled a panting coyote when he smiled. Sequoia bent down to kiss the woman's cheek, and the sequins in her fitted cap cast a nimbus about her head.

"You're looking radiant as always, darling. A wonder we haven't seen you since Doretha's wedding," the woman said. "Sophia *must* tell you all about our trip to Spain when you have a moment. She was invited to several balls, and even met the king's nephew. He gave her a lovely compliment on her dancing. We did reach out to your father about you joining us, dear, but we never heard back. I hope it wasn't too much of a disappointment."

Nelly did not overlook the stiffness in Sequoia's shoulders, even as she gave one of her bluesy, careless shrugs.

"The bishop can't keep track of his own calendar," she said. "God forbid he spare a second for mine. I suppose Spain is rather pedestrian, anyway. Wonderful for tourists, but not nearly cosmopolitan enough to be a true destination. Now that I think on it, Sophia might be tailor-made for Madrid."

The woman's mouth snapped shut and her self-satisfied smile faltered. Sequoia gave herself a minute to bask in her own conquest before acknowledging Nelly.

"Allow me to introduce my newest, dearest friend, Penelope Sawyer. Penelope, Mr. and Mrs. Pelham of Detroit and their cousin Jason Trahan. I'm serving as her humble guide during her stay, like Virgil through the rings of hell."

"Wonderful to meet you, Penelope," Mrs. Pelham said. "And don't look so shocked. Sequoia here is the master of unconventional introductions."

"You're Ambrose's youngest, right?" asked the older man, Mr. Pelham. He had a thick gray mustache that he fiddled with compulsively.

"I am," Nelly said. "My brother was five years older."

Mrs. Pelham's hand felt heavy—weighed down by a banded gold bracelet—when it touched Nelly's shoulder.

"A terrible, terrible loss," she said.

Nelly didn't feel like faking gratitude for their manufactured sympathy, so she chose not to.

"Elder and I were in the same class at Morehouse. Always one for a good time, as I remember him. Not terribly academic, though," said Jason Trahan. His cravat pin was studded with a night-blue sapphire, coordinated to match the blue in his waistcoat.

"He was only the first in my family to attend college," Nelly said. "I'm sure he did his best."

Even as she defended Elder, she knew it was a fiction. Their parents sent him to Morehouse because that was what upstanding Colored folk did with their sons. The city was always more engaging than the classroom for him. But he graduated, and that was more than any Sawyer going back to the beginning could say.

"How are you enjoying Chicago, Penelope?" Mrs. Pelham asked. "Even with the terrible circumstances, I hope you've begun to take in the sights."

Nelly had to remind herself that this was a vacation for most of them. Under normal circumstances, they'd spend these days at beaches, or camps, or resorts, or exotic destinations. She was expected to fill her time with leisure, not tick by the hours on her bedroom wall like Edmond Dantès in the Château d'If.

"Not as much as I would like," Nelly said. "After the dinners, and luncheons, and club ceremonies, there aren't too many hours left in the day. But *I am* thrilled to see Mr. Tanner's work. I've read about him, and I always wanted to experience his paintings in person."

Mrs. Pelham touched her husband's arm and said, "We were thankful to get a commission from him. Our collection is modest, and his piece gives it such an air of devoutness."

Mr. Pelham snorted before taking a long sip of cider.

"It should've been free. Especially considering how much press our write-up got him, even before he fled overseas."

Nelly thought of the first time she'd ever heard of Henry O. Tanner, and suddenly, things began to connect.

"You're *Robert* Pelham," she said. Sequoia snatched down Nelly's brazenly pointing hand.

"Goodness, Rob," Jason said. "Your reputation precedes you."

"It's only that I am a great admirer of the *Detroit Plaindealer*," Nelly said, speaking quickly to cover her awe.

Mr. Pelham gave Nelly his full, curious attention.

He said, "Child, the *Plaindealer* shut down before you were born. How on earth can you be an admirer of something that's been out of print since the nineties?"

"My father had issues shipped in from Michigan. I passed the time reading what he kept. Your *Woman's Work Ways* column played as much a role in rearing me as my own mother."

Mr. Pelham's expressive eyes crinkled at the corners with a smile. Nelly felt herself blossom and glow. Now, *finally*, something she could sink her teeth into.

"May I ask," she began, "what inspired you to—"

"Is there really so little to do in Kentucky that you read old newspapers to *pass the time*?" Sequoia asked. Cutting her off was no accident, but rather a tactical attempt at redirection.

"I admire a young woman who takes her literacy seriously," Mrs. Pelham said in Nelly's weak defense. "I do wish more Colored youths showed your level of dedication, Penelope. Hardly any of our young men would choose a newspaper over women, or drinking, or gambling these days. After all the work our generation did to rise above those demeaning stereotypes, it breaks my soul to see some of us proving the rule instead of the exception."

"Are you referring to our brethren from the South?" When Sequoia smiled, her teeth looked sharp.

"As a Virginian, I take offense at that," Mr. Pelham said.

"Please, Robert," said Mrs. Pelham. "You haven't lived in Virginia since you were a child."

"Still, it's in my blood. In my children's blood. It's something to respect, dammit. Wouldn't you agree, Ms. Sawyer?"

Quite unexpectedly, all eyes were back on Nelly. Some kind, some frothing with judgment.

"Opportunity is everything," she said. "Especially in the South."

"Says the girl with every opportunity."

Nelly was not surprised to hear this barely veiled barb from Jason.

"Only because my parents had *one*," she said. "Folk coming up from the South have enough to worry about, never mind the so-called stereotypes they may or may not perpetuate. Stereotypes that we give credence by acknowledging."

"No use closing your eyes against the sun," said Jason. "The other day as I arrived from New Orleans, I saw someone stepping off the train from Arkansas with a butchered hog. In a sack. That they carried with them *from Arkansas.* When the sheriffs policing Northern ghettos and the politicians writing Northern laws describe Negroes as unhygienic and ignorant, all they have to do is wait on the train platform for proof."

Nelly felt the steel pour down her spine.

"If you were to board a train for the first time, traveling to someplace you've never seen, what exactly would *you* bring if not food enough to feed your family?"

Sequoia's nose turned up as she said, "Certainly not a hog. Can you imagine the stench?"

"This is precisely why the vote for Colored men is more important now than ever before," Jason said. As he spoke, his chest expanded, and his eyes shone with a staged charisma. "If we can mobilize the population, bully through damned grandfather clauses, we can advance our race so any Negro can overcome these backward shenanigans that pull us down."

Jason paused as if for applause. Nelly didn't doubt she'd hear this speech again in a few years, from a raised dais before thousands of potential voters.

"What about women?" she asked. "You talk about the rights of Colored men, but what of Colored women? We have a harder time than you just getting registered."

"Voting is a man's right." Jason was an excellent orator. His conviction came through in every word. "Just as a household is a right, voting is a right. And yes, a right for our women, too. But—"

"But?"

"*But.* Negro women can be emotional. Prone to all manner of hysterics. What would happen if election day fell on a laundry day? Or a menstrual day? We could end up with a popular vote in favor of a fool because the fish at the market was spoiled. Educated women, now, I can place my trust in them. A university degree is proof of some sense and dedication to loftier pursuits."

Nelly looked around the small circle and saw distracted glances, faces hidden behind fans. Her tongue tickled at the thought of cursing this man down to a nub, but she held back and tried a different approach.

"I don't have a university degree, Mr. Trahan," she said, "and I don't plan to ever earn one. Not by my own will, but by circumstance, just like millions of others in this country. Is *my* vote too hysterical to matter?"

"Circumstance?" Jason asked with a laugh from his gut. "Girlie, 'circumstance' does not exist for you. What's the use earning a degree when your father could simply buy you one? Same as he did for Elder."

Jason's words formed a fist that took hold of her chest and squeezed. She waited for someone to speak for her, to support her, but they all stayed silent as though their lips had been sewn shut. Even Mr. Pelham, who'd shown her such approval and validation, chose to study the stem of his glass instead. Sequoia's face was severe, and her eyes—whether consciously or not—were begging Nelly to disappear.

"Excuse me," Nelly said. She hated that shallowness in her voice. As though they'd succeeded in putting her in her place. "I'm suddenly very warm, I think I need . . . It was wonderful to meet you all."

She heard Mrs. Pelham's intake of breath but didn't stay long enough to hear her niceties.

"I am so sorry," Sequoia said behind her. "Her brother did just pass away."

"Of course, of course, poor girl," said Mr. Pelham.

The last voice Nelly heard from that circle before the crowd drowned them out was Jason's.

"Like I said, hysterical. You can't just storm out of life when the questions become too uncomfortable for you to answer."

CHAPTER SEVEN

There were hardly any paintings on display in the chilled, isolated alcove—five or six at most. But at least Nelly was finally alone with Mr. Tanner's work.

His were ephemeral landscapes snatched from a dream. The river Seine under the light of a pastel sunrise. A lone oak tree on a starless night, gray and sinister. Images that calmed the soul and stilled the mind. Then Nelly came to a piece titled *Salome*. It was no landscape, and it did everything but still her mind.

The figure of Salome was nearly nude apart from a gossamer robe. Her face was in shadow, and a light as if from an open door fell upon her hips and legs. At her side lay the bloody arm of a headless John the Baptist. Nelly didn't know if she was meant to be shamed by Salome's nakedness, or riveted by it. She held herself tight to fight off a different kind of chill.

"Does it offend you?" a voice asked. Nelly turned her head slowly, and there Jay stood, smiling up at the painting in rapt wonder. Nelly was tempted to pinch his arm and confirm he wasn't made of smoke.

"You," she whispered.

"Me," he whispered back. "And you, Nelly Sawyer."

His creamy vanilla suit was cut to stark perfection, and he carried a skimmer hat behind him in clasped hands. Their dance on her home's veranda was the better part of two weeks ago, but it could have been yesterday judging by the ease in his shoulders. The taunt in his tone. As though they'd only just spoken mere moments ago.

"Do you follow me around?" she asked.

The smallest of creases appeared between Jay's eyes.

"Beg your pardon?"

"You stick closer to me than my own reflection. Best mind yourself, Jay. At this rate, you'll get us locked in a scandal."

"If anyone inspires a scandal here, it'll be you," he said. "I've been sitting right over there, minding my business, for over half an hour."

Jay pointed to the opposite corner, and a bench placed to allow for a panoramic view of the alcove. Nelly looked from him, to the bench, then back at him again.

"That's impossible. I would've seen you when I walked in. You're unavoidable, especially in that outfit."

Jay's head slanted like a bird's as he chewed on that observation.

"Is that a compliment or an insult?" he asked.

"Do you have a preference?"

"Insult, I think."

"Insult it is, then."

Nelly turned back to the painting, and whatever comfort and confidence she felt bantering with Jay began to skulk away. She never thought of herself as prudish, but something in this instant—studying this painting with him—felt too crude, too invasive.

"You didn't answer my initial question," Jay said. "Does it offend you?"

Staring at *Salome* with unwavering eyes, Nelly allowed herself to push past the contrition and take in all the artist had to offer. Piano music began to play in the main hall. It sounded muted to Nelly's ears. Filtered through the screen that always buffered her and Jay from the outside world.

"No," she said after a time. "It makes me proud. Proud to be a woman. Is that vulgar?"

"Pride is never vulgar," Jay said with certainty. Nelly had to laugh.

"There're a few preachers and pastors back there who'd disagree."

"I don't have the trouble distinguishing pride from vanity that they do."

"But I contradict myself. I say this painting makes me proud, but Mr. Tanner keeps Salome's face in darkness. To draw such attention to her body like that could be nothing other than vulgarity."

Jay took a step closer and said, "Maybe he's maintaining her modesty."

"By covering her face?" Nelly asked. "Is that less modest than, well." She gestured to the rest of Salome.

"Shame doesn't come from how others feel about you, but from how you feel about yourself," Jay said. "By hiding her face, we'll never know how she feels either way. She maintains her modesty and her control."

His own face had gone pensive. Nelly studied it, just as she studied

Mr. Tanner's artwork. She searched for some hint of what those white people saw. What made them smile so warmly, laugh so companionably?

"I saw you," she said. "At the polo match."

Nelly didn't blink. She didn't want to miss a moment of the shock and panic blooming across Jay's face—and yes, the shame, too—but it never came.

"I know," he said.

She inhaled, and the air whistled through her teeth.

"How could you?"

"Why are you upset?"

"*Why?* Lord, Jay, don't you have any respect for yourself? For your people, for where you come from?"

"You don't know where I come from, Nelly."

"Those white folks would hate you if they knew, you know," she said. They were standing very close now, whispering even though they were utterly alone. "They'd kill you."

Jay had the gall to smile, but it was a fanged, brazen smile.

"What exactly do you think you saw?"

Nelly had to brace herself. Saying the words, even thinking them, felt like one of those two-pronged curses that struck both ways.

"You were passing for white."

Jay didn't jump to defend himself. He tapped his hat against his thigh and swore under his breath.

"I could, if I wanted to," he said. "I won't say I haven't done it before. But what you saw at the polo match was not me passing."

"Oh, that's bullshit!"

Jay jolted back, looking momentarily afraid, then thrilled.

"You never fail to surprise, Ms. Sawyer."

"How are you not ashamed?" she asked, astounded. "I was raised to stand firm in my heritage. I can't imagine pretending to be anything other than what I am, never mind one of *them*."

Far off, the music had stopped.

"Where do you think you are, Nelly?" Jay asked. Pointing behind her, he said, "Some of these families hold skin color in higher regard than education and money. Ask one of them how they feel about passing, and they'll tell you it's an art form."

"Is that why you do it, then? For artistic expression?"

He laughed a trickster's laugh that dissolved the tension as easily as melting ice.

"There are two candy jars, right?" he said. "One marked for Negroes, and one for white folk. The Negro—under threat of *death*—can only take from one jar. The white man, though, he can take from one or the other. He can take from both. Never mind that the jars have the exact same candy; the white man still gets to choose. That is all I want, Nelly. The freedom to choose. I don't want to look like them, or act like them, or be them. But I want their options."

Goose bumps ran up Nelly's arms even though the novel and industrial air-conditioning had ceased blowing. She looked up at Salome, bare and colorless with only her eyes showing through the shadow.

"What do you think they see," she asked, "when they see you?"

Jay followed her eyes to the painting. His smile was closed-mouthed, tight-lipped, and fuming.

"They see what they want to see," he said. "Someone safe, someone harmless, someone confident. This skin, these eyes, it all means nothing if they don't believe in it. If *I* don't believe in it."

"Interesting," she said, and none too convincingly.

"What is it?"

"Nothing. It's just, that isn't what I see when I look at you at all."

Jay had a fine, high brow that pleated when he smirked down at her.

"Truly? What do you see, then?"

"A liar."

Once again, where Nelly had expected to see embarrassment, she saw only amusement. And, infuriatingly, pride.

A disturbance rose in the main hall. A clamor of frustrated voices that made her break away from Jay. She walked out of the coolness of the alcove and was immediately hit by a wall of humid anger. People moved all together toward the exit like the tide of the damned.

Nelly spotted Mabel Ford from Memphis walking swiftly to keep up with her parents.

"Mabel!" Nelly called out. "What's going on? Is the exhibit over?"

Affixing her hat in place with a long, pearl-capped pin, Mabel said, "Over for us. Good ole James Crow has had his way."

"You mean they're booting us out?"

"They're claiming maximum capacity," said Mabel. "Fire codes. The proprietors of the museum told us to clear out 'for our own safety,' or the police will be called."

"I don't see the white people going anywhere."

And it was true. The ten or so white patrons stayed put while the most esteemed of their people squeezed through a skinny door like chattel.

"Christ," Nelly said. "Mr. Tanner's wife is white, for goodness' sake."

"And did you see her here today?"

Nelly had never gotten a good look at Mr. Tanner, but when she *had* seen him, he'd been standing alone.

"Is anyone staying?"

Mabel shook her head as she said, "No. I don't think so. We can't even enjoy our own art unless it's on their terms. Oh, well. Will I see you at the Urban League auction day after tomorrow?"

"If it's in my diary," Nelly said, "then you'll see me there."

"Oh, don't look so glum, Nelly Sawyer. You're doing well! Much better than any of us anticipated."

Already, the hall was emptied enough to appear abandoned, populated with nothing but the ghosts of dead artists. Jay stood alone and oblivious.

"Aren't you coming?" Nelly asked.

"I've been waiting months for this exhibit," he said. "I'm not leaving now."

"But they've told us to . . ."

Then, as clear as the hand in front of her face, Nelly saw exactly what the white people saw. The rules that dictated her life and lives of so many, white or Colored, simply did not apply to him.

CHAPTER EIGHT

The sun was setting against Ethel Waters's stirring vibrato, and Nelly thought of home.

Ms. Waters had a voice that brought childhood smells to Nelly's nose and tastes like honeysuckle to her tongue. The Black Swan Records founder, Harry Price, had given the album to Ambrose directly as a thank-you for a handsome donation. She did not feel such a stranger in a strange land when serenaded with tales of broken hearts and friends gone astray.

Stripped down to her underclothes to combat the wet heat, Nelly sat at her vanity and looked at herself the way she thought Jay might look at her. She saw a liar in him, plain as the sunrise, but did he see the same in her?

Nelly was not surprised when her mother entered without knocking. What did surprise her was the look of absolute glee on Florence's face. Nelly had to turn and observe her straight on, doubting the reflection she saw in the mirror.

Being the daughter of a second-generation sharecropper, no one had ever expected much of Florence Brown. She was big-of-bone and prone to idling by the creek, daydreaming when there was work to be done. But she was bright. Bright enough to believe that those dreams would thrive if only she gave them the energy to grow. So, when greatness in the form of loud-talking, swaggering Ambrose Sawyer came for her, she was waiting a half mile down the road, ready to meet it.

"What's wrong?" Nelly asked on reflex.

"Wrong?" Florence said. "Not a thing."

In quick, long strides, Florence crossed the room to Nelly and turned her head to face the mirror. She watched her mother as warily as a copperhead.

"I can't believe you went out today with your hair like this," Florence said, "and with all of those people about."

Nelly kept her hair wound in two thick braids on either side of her head. It was an old-fashioned style, but it was sensible, easy, and didn't require the labors that kept so many other Colored women "in fashion." She combed it out at the end of each day, hydrated it with one of Madam Walker's solutions, and that was that. Everything else felt like a waste of time.

Reaching up to protect the last braid, Nelly said, "It's fine."

Florence batted her hand down hard enough to sting.

"We talked about this." Her fingers moved deftly as they unwound the strands that bound Nelly's hair until it fanned out around her face in a perfect halo. "If you're determined not to wear a wig, then this all needs to be pulled together in proper company. You're not on a farm anymore, girl."

Nelly stayed quiet while her mother coated her hair in a glossy refiner cream and asked, "How'd the exhibit go?"

There was a trip wire somewhere, and all Nelly could do was wait for the bomb to go off.

"It was fine, I guess," she said. "Apart from being forced out halfway through. I thought having too many people was a good thing for an art gallery."

Nelly tensed as she watched her mother pick up the hot comb that was left warming on the radiator at the end of the day. Tears welled when she felt it close against her scalp, and she struggled to not cry out.

"Oh, stop that," Florence said while the air filled with a pungent chemical smoke. "See there? Much better." Nelly could barely *see* anything at all, but she could sense her mother's satisfaction, and it left a bitter taste. "We'll curl and wrap this tonight. You'll look as snappy as a new pair of shoes for tomorrow."

"Tomorrow?"

Nelly tried to swerve around, but her head was fixed facing forward once again, and none too gently.

"I didn't believe your father when he said you could handle yourself. That man's always had a soft spot for you. He managed to prove me wrong, though, praise God."

"Momma, what are you talking about?"

Florence slapped an envelope down on the vanity top like it was a winning hand of playing cards. The first thing that caught Nelly's eye was the crest: a shield embossed in dark blue ink, flanked by gryphons, dragons, and great birds. A symbol of ancient authority that she didn't have to comprehend to respect. If Nelly had been a betting woman, she'd owe Sequoia a pretty penny.

"I didn't hardly believe it when the courier came," Florence said. "I thought it was some kind of trick. You know how folk've been coming out of the woodwork since that article, sending all kinds of forgeries to the house. But I had your father look into it, and it's all as true as the gospel."

"How long have you had this?" Nelly asked.

"Only a few days, and don't take that tone. You said nothing happened at that polo game!"

"Because nothing did. I didn't even know who Tomás was then. Some enthusiast, no different than any of the other dandies who visit the ranch every year."

Nelly picked up the envelope. The stationery was textured and weighty in her hand.

"The man's not just rich," Florence said. "He's *old money*. His father and uncles played polo, too. He knows his business, according to your daddy. If that wasn't enough, he stands to inherit some kind of title."

"Marquis," Nelly whispered, thinking of his storybook poise. "What else did Daddy have to say?"

"Well, he's a confirmed *bach-e-lor*." Florence broke the word down, syllable by syllable. So elated that her cup runneth over. "He's renting a home in Glencoe that'd put the White House to shame."

Florence wasn't typically prone to hyperbole.

"That's doubtable, Momma," Nelly said.

"All I'm saying is that it's a lot for one person and a couple of horses."

Nelly turned the envelope over and saw that the wax seal was broken. She was doubly grateful that Ambrose had discovered the missive from Richard Norris, and not Florence.

The letter itself was written in impeccable, florid handwriting that turned every word into an intricate work of art. Tomás went on at length about how wonderful it was to meet her. Flattering, beautiful words that reached Nelly through all her skepticism. When he eventually got around to Blue Sonata, Nelly understood why her mother was in such a hurried, primping state.

"Don't you worry," Florence said. "You've already accepted his invitation."

Nelly wanted to crumple the letter in her fist, but it seemed a shame to ruin the finery. It galled her endlessly to be shuttled from place to place without knowing how, or why. She winced when Florence began rolling hot curlers into her newly straightened hair. They were impossible to function in, but she somehow was expected to wear them all night.

Florence began to giggle.

"I'd like to see Mrs. Bousfield turn up her greater-than-thou nose at this family when *my* daughter is the lady of a grand European house. Putting on airs as if she ain't some county schoolteacher no better than any of us."

"It's just a riding lesson," Nelly said.

"It's an opportunity," Florence corrected. She took a silk scarf out of the wardrobe and wrapped it about Nelly's head, closing it in a tight knot until the pressure behind her eyes throbbed.

"I can tell you think well of him."

Scoffing, Nelly said, "Please, Momma, I don't even know him."

"So, get to know him. And let him get to know you! You can be downright delightful when you care to try."

Nelly knew that wasn't a compliment, but she couldn't help feeling warmed by her mother's positive attention.

It hadn't always been so contentious between them. Once upon a time, they were rather close. Florence was the one who taught Nelly how to ride, before Nelly grew from a child into a commodity. However, those memories were buried somewhere deep where Nelly only saw them in dreams. She rarely had those kinds of dreams anymore.

Pleased with her work, Florence smoothed one last hand over Nelly's prepped marcel waves and said, "I think this will do. Get on to bed, now. We're starting early tomorrow."

Florence turned to leave Nelly where she'd found her, but Nelly spoke before she could reach the door.

"Momma, did you know about the cotillion before Elder died?"

Florence stopped in the middle of the room, and Nelly was stunned by the strength in her silhouette. Nelly always thought her mother beautiful in her own eternal, empowered way, unconventional as it was. Ambrose used to even tease Florence about how she "blended in with the cowboys" with her wide-brimmed hat and scuffed leather boots. She worked just as hard as Ambrose; harder, most days. Was more respected in the stables than him, too.

It'll be worth it, children, she'd say after twelve hours taming near-wild horses, feet too swollen to stand on. *Your daddy and I have big dreams. It'll all be worth it in the end.*

When the money came, Florence was prepared to craft herself into a rich man's wife. Something slimmer, more muted, more generally acceptable. Nelly always resented that transformation as a sacrifice, but for her mother, it was more of an ascension.

Florence said, "I'd heard rumors about the cotillion, but I didn't know for certain till we were in the city."

"So, you always planned my role in all this?"

"Nelly, I've planned your role in all this since you were thirteen. Money is well and good, but it's the shield on that envelope that'll protect us when it comes crashing down."

"*When*, Momma?"

"Yes, *when*. For everything does. You're a grown woman now. You can handle the truth. Bed now, Nelly. No one becomes smitten with a burned-out girl."

The door closed, and the room was locked in darkness.

Across the street in neighboring mansions, lights blinked on over portraits by Eakins and busts of lions killed in Ethiopia. Nelly's thoughts turned bitter, and she wondered if her neighbors—with their one hundred years of wealth and security and assuredness that the day would dawn in their favor—rested quite so much hope on so small a moment. If daughters and sons, mothers and fathers, dragged the weight of generations gone and to come behind every step. But she knew the answer to that question, and it made her own house feel even colder, and the scratch of Ms. Waters's album even lonelier.

CHAPTER NINE

The place was excessive. Even by *her* family's exacting standards. Nelly didn't know that such acreage could exist in the middle of a major city. Not only was it an hour's drive to Tomás's home, but once they were waved through the main gate, they had to drive up a winding glade of poplars for over half a mile. The house itself stood like a great gray rhinoceros squatting in the grass.

"My, my, Miss Nelly," said her driver, Murphy—a white veteran from Missouri that her father hired for the sole purpose of making himself feel better. "We're moving on up, ain't we?"

"Yeah," she said. "I suppose we are."

Folk liked to talk about Nelly's family, their prestige and their prosperity, but *this* was something else completely. Something older and secure in its decadence, not walking a constant tightrope like her parents did. Its wealth was measured in centuries, and people like her died hauling its stones.

"Mrs. Sawyer said to come back after two hours," Murphy said from the driver's seat. "Does that sound about right?"

"Yes, sir, two hours," Nelly said.

Murphy tipped his navy chauffeur cap then was gone, kicking up dust as he went. As she watched him leave, Nelly adjusted her stiff jodhpurs and reminded herself of her mission. She was here to help Tomás be a better horseman. The estate, the grounds, the medieval fortress he lived in, and what he thought about her all didn't really matter. And yet, she was so nervous that she incessantly fussed with the stock tie and pin that the "complete ensemble" demanded. The knee-high boots and heavy cotton shirt she was bullied into wearing were made for someone who hunted, trotted, and frequented horse shows, but needed two men to climb into a saddle.

She hoped Tomás wouldn't mock her for such an amateurish display. Or worse yet, take it at face value.

Nelly walked up the wide flagstone steps to the front door and knocked with the heavy brass knocker. The sound reverberated deep within the home like a prehistoric creature's growl.

The door opened immediately. A young white woman in a housemaid's uniform stood in the threshold, annoyed.

"What is this now?" she asked with a nasally accent that turned every syllable into a squawk.

Nelly was oddly comforted by this development. Minor European nobles were a cosmic wonder, but rude and unsuspecting white people were as familiar as her own scars. The devil you know is always more welcome than the devil you don't.

"Good afternoon," Nelly said in polite response to the woman's disregard. "My name is Penelope Sawyer, and I'm here to see Mr. Escalante y Roche. I have an appointment." She'd been practicing the pronunciation of his name, determined to get it right on the first try.

The woman's mouth turned down in an imitation of deference.

"Well, aren't you the uppity one?" she said. "The service did say they were sending one of their best girls."

"Service? No, I'm not with any service—"

"I don't care for you being an hour early. Any other day, I'd send you on and tell you to come back at a sensible time. But it's right you're here now. Mr. Thomas has some fancy lady coming by, and I fear he's never seen the inside of a kitchen. Is this getup a uniform or something?"

Nelly could only imagine the look on the woman's face when she found out that this uppity girl was in fact the "fancy lady" she'd been told to expect. There would be disbelief at first, then anger, then horror. The type of horror Nelly had seen on the faces of many a Negro man or woman when staring down the potential displeasure of someone white and entitled.

"Yes, ma'am," Nelly said. She exaggerated her accent and dived headfirst into all of this woman's assumptions. "A shiny new uniform."

The woman whistled, no better than what she'd use to summon a dog.

"It's awfully queer," she said. Nelly endeavored not to slap her hand away when she reached out and pulled at the wide lapel of the corduroy vest. "If your cooking's worth a damn, you could walk around here in a burlap sack for all I care. Mr. Thomas ain't never home, but when he is, it's nothing but jerky, coffee, and some crumbly foreign cookies. If I wanted to make my own breakfast at the crack of dawn, I woulda stayed home. And you can bet on that!"

The woman laughed companionably, and Nelly laughed with her. Then the woman nudged Nelly with her foot until she stumbled down the front steps.

"Get on, now," the woman said. "Can't have you tramping all through the main house after I just cleaned these floors. You'll find the kitchen door through the herb garden. Probably can smell the burning from here, bless the poor man. God knows you'll be a sight for his pretty eyes."

Still laughing, the maid closed the door, and Nelly could hear the great metal gears turning as the lock slid into place.

Nelly was accustomed to being unrecognized. She knew for a fact that she could walk down any street from Richmond to Biloxi and be treated just the same as any other Colored girl. But Chicago had lulled her into a false sense of superiority. In the midst of so much bowing and scraping, she'd forgotten where she was and who she was. The outfit didn't feel quite so ridiculous now. She ran her hand over the gold-plated buttons and fine hand stitching. The shell cordovan leather boots hugged her calves and whispered as she walked. On her back alone, she carried more than that maid probably saw in a year.

Nelly was thus resolved: she might be entering through the back door, but she'd be good God damned if she left through it. The look on that maid's face alone would be worth it.

The farther Nelly traveled into the overgrown kitchen garden, the stronger the smell of smoke became. And not harmless cooking smoke, but a dark, angry smoke that clogged the senses and threatened lives. It brought back memories of a fierce night at One Oak when a silo was struck by lightning and filled the sky with shadows shaped like dragons.

The smoke billowed out of the kitchen door into daylight, along with a string of muffled Spanish curses. There was a loud bang, then a scream, then the whooshing of a happily fed flame.

"Hello?" Nelly called out. The kitchen was overrun with the smell of burning meat, and while she was sure she could hear Tomás, she could not see him.

She looked about the kitchen and realized that all the windows were closed. With the little ventilation he had, Nelly was impressed Tomás hadn't successfully managed to suffocate himself. She threw open the closest distinguishable window, and as a rush of warm air flooded in, the smoke flooded out. In the newly unpolluted light, Nelly got a proper read of the place.

It was a grand old kitchen with copper pots hanging over a low wooden table fit to prep a feast. The cast-iron stoves and ovens were built into a far wall, and bent over them like a character out of Robertson's *Jekyll and Hyde* was Tomás. He'd started off splendidly dressed, but all that refinement was now coated in a thick layer of soot and food debris. He looked like a blown-out match, smoking hair and all.

"Mr. Escalante y Roche?" she said.

He started and nearly leapt out of his boots.

"Ms. Sawyer!" he said on an exhale. "I thought you were—I don't know who I thought you were. I told the staff to tell me when you arrived."

He glanced at his clothes and the general disarray with the baffled face of a man crawling out of a hole.

"Not so fun being snuck up on, is it?" Nelly asked.

Tomás grinned and said, "Touché, Ms. Sawyer. First, let me apologize. I invited you to luncheon but never went through the trouble of hiring a cook. I naively assumed they more or less came with the house. The gentleman I'm leasing from implied that the regular staff were included in the fee. He conveniently neglected to tell me that 'regular staff' consisted of the girl Sarah and a gardener I still have yet to lay eyes on."

He was rambling, and the faster he spoke, the more his words ran together into this fascinating singsong version of English. As embarrassed as he was, Nelly found some part of it enjoyable.

"All of that to say," he concluded, out of breath, "I came in here two hours ago to prepare a meal. Mind you, the only meal I've ever prepared was canned beans over a campfire. So, as you can tell by that smoking husk, a braised chicken is clearly far beyond my capabilities."

The chicken in question was as charred as a log, practically beyond recognition.

"Canned beans to braised chicken is a bit of a stretch," Nelly said.

Tomás ran his hands along the front of his waistcoat and left blotchy black streaks behind.

"This leaves our luncheon in a limbo, Ms. Sawyer. There is cold coffee and little else."

"I know some kitchen basics that might save us," she said, "but not nearly enough for 'the service's best girl.'"

"The service?"

Nelly sniffed at the poor unfortunate chicken and stifled a gag.

"Your maid took me to be the house's new cook. That's probably why no one told you I was here. She sent me through the back, presumably to rescue you from this catastrophe."

Tomás's mouth dropped open in a look so affronted that Nelly felt guilty that she herself wasn't more upset by the misunderstanding.

"What?" His accent was forward and aggressive, sharpened on the tip of his tongue.

"It was funny, actually," Nelly said. Why she was rushing to comfort his response to her violation, she could not say. Something in his outrage frightened her. "She was so convinced, nothing I said could have changed her mind."

"This won't be abided," he said. "I swear to you. I'll dismiss her immediately."

Nelly caught the sleeve of Tomás's shirt and paused to feel its softness. It was a simple design, but woven from cotton so fine that it slipped through her fingers like water. His wealth shone through in the most minor or most extreme of details. It was as though the frame of his life had been built by someone else and he was resigned to simply hang in it.

"Don't trouble yourself," Nelly said. "It's not worth dismissing anyone over."

"You are a guest in my home. It's an insult to me as much as to you."

"She was only leaning on logic. I can bet that in the one hundred years since this house was built, the only Negroes who walked up that ten-mile drive of yours were coming here to work. Or to *be* worked."

That seemed to take some of the wind out of Tomás. He exhaled, and the fury in his chest deflated like a punctured airship.

His voice sounded chastised as he said, "I'm sorry. I hadn't considered that."

And he *was* sorry, she could see it. Many who said such things when they knew they were in the wrong rarely were. Nelly took it upon herself to lighten the mood and clear the black haze from Tomás's eyes.

"We still have the constitutional crisis of lunch to contend with, Mr. Escalante y Roche."

In time, he gave in to her teasing with a smile and said, "You have a lovely accent, but as I've learned while traveling in America, my name can be a mouthful for some. Mr. Thomas will serve. A good Yankee-sounding name, don't you think?"

As much as she delighted in how the word *Yankee* sounded from his sophisticated mouth, Nelly refused.

"I do thank you for being so accommodating, but no. I was raised to have a very high respect for names," she said. "See, I had a great-grandmother called Momma Phil. She was a white man's child, born during slavery times. At the moment of her birth, her mother named her Ophelia, in honor of the play they weren't permitted to read. When Momma Phil's father came to see her, he looked down at his little daughter and said that the name Ophelia wasn't fit for a

Negress's child. He called her Bert. After his second-favorite hound dog. I will call you by your name, your true name, or nothing at all."

Tomás's raptness made the words of a story rarely told outside of her closest family flow easily with a stranger. He understood its moral in the most crucial of ways.

"Just Tomás, then," he said. "For efficiency's sake if nothing else."

Nelly nodded.

"Very good. As far as lunch goes, Tomás, cold coffee will suffice just fine. After all, this ain't no social call. I mean to work you like a cowboy."

CHAPTER TEN

Blue Sonata was just as lithe as Nelly remembered. The horse trotted up on her toes, constantly prepped to break into a full sprint. Indeed, that's what she seemed to want more than anything. Outside of the constrained bounds of the corral, the land stretched on unhindered. Nelly knew there were other estates—she'd seen them on the drive up—but this property was uniquely isolated. For a horse with the athleticism and drive of Blue Sonata, the temptation to chase horizons must have been devastating.

"Try loosening your hands," she called out to Tomás on his thirtieth turn around the corral with the mare, fighting her the whole way. "You know she can feel your anxiety through the reins. You hold on to them like a lifeline."

"How do I correct her if she keeps veering off course?"

He yanked at Blue Sonata again when she strayed toward the descending sun instead of following the curve of the tall fence that confined her.

"Who said anything about correcting her?" Nelly asked. "Let her move at her own pace, explore the world around her. The horse obviously has enough sense to walk in a circle. You can't assume that every independent decision she makes is a belligerent one."

Throughout the lesson, Nelly strove not to lose any of the respect Tomás had for her or her guidance. She refused to tease, or to joke, or even sigh when he smiled at her and she was reminded of how striking he was.

"The horse is wild, miss. No amount of hand-holding is going to make her a champion polo pony."

Tomás traveled with only one member of his own household: a trainer named Enzo whose face was as sunbaked as Alabama clay. He'd observed Nelly from a darkened corner when she first entered the stable, like an ornery cat. But now they stood close together, leaning against the corral while they shared a store-bought cigarette.

"She's not wild," Nelly said. "She just knows her own mind."

She hoisted herself up and climbed over the high fence. The sky was overcast, but the heat was still pervasive. She could feel the edges of her sculpted hairdo starting to curl with sweat. Soon, all her mother's efforts to force that flat, polished *Vanity Fair* look upon Nelly's head would be a ruin of uneven coils sticking out in every direction.

She approached Blue Sonata with a hand outstretched. All the mare's bluster eased, and her panting became steady and calm.

"Estrella melts under your touch," Tomás said.

Nelly scratched Blue Sonata's snout. "She just recognizes a friend. Listen, I'm obviously not explaining myself well. It might be better for me to show you."

"Are you certain? She could buck and—"

"If she hasn't bucked you, she won't buck me."

Tomás looked doubtful, but he was courteous enough not to hesitate as he threw his leg over Blue Sonata's back and elegantly fell to the ground. He offered his hand, but Nelly laughed it off.

"Oh, no," she said. "No one's helped me onto a horse since I was five."

With a heave, she anchored her weight and pulled herself up. The horse was tall, and it took her a moment to adjust.

"Hello again, old girl," she said with a solid pat to the mare's neck. To Tomás, she said, "I'm gonna take her around a few times. Watch me, not the horse."

Something flared like a dying fire behind Tomás's stare.

"That will not be too difficult, Ms. Sawyer."

To keep herself from simpering, Nelly clicked her tongue and started Blue Sonata in a brisk trot. She kept her hold on the reins loose, used her legs and thighs to steer, but it was hardly necessary. The horse moved as surely as a fish through deep waters. Nelly glanced toward Tomás, and just as she'd instructed, he watched her. Enzo said something close to his ear, and when his mouth turned up in a blessing of a smile, Nelly made herself look away.

She snapped the reins and gave Blue Sonata more to work with. Their trot turned into a cantor, and soon, a full gallop.

"Open the gate!" Nelly yelled, though she was foolhardy enough to jump it.

The gate was flung wide, and Nelly felt Blue Sonata's relief as a great exhalation. She stood up in the stirrups, bent her back, and let the horse run. In seconds, they were out of the corral. In minutes, the stables and horse yard were at their backs and they flew over a man-made meadow. The sound of Blue Sonata's hoofs on virgin, untrodden soil was a timeless rhythm that carried Nelly up and over the world. She looked back and saw a chestnut stallion gaining on them. She should have stopped and waited, but where would the fun be in that?

They ran until the meadow merged with a forest, and the close quarters slowed them down. As Nelly guided Blue Sonata into a lazy trot, she heard the chestnut sidle up beside them, along with Tomás's heavy breathing.

"Tired, are you?" Nelly asked.

Tomás attempted to inhale but ended up gagging.

"Not remotely," he said. "Just woefully out of shape."

Non-native trees trimmed into idyllic shapes and dappled canopies grew in perfect order around them. It was as faultless as a child's memory of when every wild place was a wonderland.

"This is beautiful property," she said, enthralled. "I didn't know there could be so much open space in a city."

Tomás observed the grounds with just as much disbelief, as though it wasn't all part of his sole dominion.

"My one request was enough space for the horses. I have five with me here and fully intend to acquire more as we travel. I admit, I wasn't expecting the equivalent of a country château. Such extravagance has always seemed like an excess to me."

"If this is an inappropriate question, please tell me," Nelly said. Out here, away from all implications of society and decorum, surely, they could speak freely. "But what exactly is your position, or is *status* a better word? Folk say that you're a prince, but I know that can't be true. Can it?" Nelly hated that unsure, gawking lift at the end of her question.

Tomás laughed and said, "Even with all that you Americans did to break from nobility, you have the most fervent obsession with it."

"I'm not obsessed," Nelly was quick to say. "I just want to give you your due respect. If I need to call you 'Your Majesty,' or 'Your Highness,' or 'my lord'—"

"Don't, please, my God." He reached out and touched Nelly's hand to stop her talking. It was large and unexpectedly coarse considering his privileged beginning.

"My family is a bit of a tapestry," he said. "There's some royal lineage—a cousin twice removed who's a duke—but my father would hate to be described as anything other than a landowner. My grandfather was governor in Sonora for a time, and he has some eighty thousand acres in Mexico. My uncle is a very minor Spanish lord, and I spent much of my childhood with my great-aunt in France, who is a marquess. She has no children of her own, so I might inherit the title in her will as a marquis. But for now, I am simply Tomás, the mediocre polo player."

Listening to him talk of dukes, lords, governors, and eighty thousand acres of land stunned Nelly's egalitarian sensibilities. So often, she was reminded of just how close she was to the days when a Negro woman would sell at market for the same price as a lame mule. Tomás's tapestry of a family did not just have a head start. It *was* the head start.

"What does that mean, exactly?" she asked. "To be a marquis?"

"A landed noble too far from a crown to be royal, but high enough for some influence. Little more than a ceremonial position these days. No, polo is our family's passion and legacy now. My father and uncles made sure of that."

Tomás described his family with a clipped, legislative cadence. What Nelly found endlessly fascinating, he seemed to carry like a ball and chain.

"It sounds like you didn't have a choice," she said.

His smile was not sweet, but rather dark and dusted with spite.

"Oh, but I did choose, Ms. Sawyer," he said. "Choose or disappear, those were my options. I had what they called a difficult period about seven years ago. I abandoned my education at Oxford and gave myself over to a rough life in Mexico. I'm Mexican by birth and hated being left out of the fighting when the revolution came. My father eventually tracked me down and signed me up for this leisure league at gunpoint. Truly, he had a rifle trained on me. He vowed to shoot me like the rebeldes who raided his villa if I resisted."

Nelly chuckled and said, "Sounds like a charming man."

"If charm is abrasive, conservative, and self-indulgent, then yes. That is precisely who he is."

"If you could do anything else with your time right now," Nelly said, "would it be still polo?"

Tomás stayed quiet as he looked ahead. The forest began to crowd in around them. The chaos of the natural order overran the formal and orchestrated. Nelly knew he was older than her. Maybe six or seven years her senior, but here, under the cover of twisted trees, she saw that his eyes were the eyes of someone who'd seen a lifetime's worth of horror.

"I would be back in Mexico to help those displaced by the regime change," he said. "It's a terrible thing, to fight for a people and a place but not stay to see if the fighting was worth it."

Nelly knew that hollowing sensation. She felt it every time she submitted an anonymous article to Richard Norris without ever knowing if the changes she advocated for came to fruition.

"They didn't use a gun, but my parents threatened everything else to get me to stay in Chicago," Nelly said. "Now that my brother's gone and they have no other children to bear the load, I must be mindful of my 'duty.' If they even bothered to ask what I want now, I'd suspect they were possessed."

Tomás's voice dropped when he spoke next. It carried the reverence of a prayer spoken aloud in an empty church.

"Then *I* will ask. What is it that you want, Ms. Sawyer?"

Nelly didn't know what made her tell the truth. Perhaps it was the close air and steady clop of horses' hooves, or the sincerity with which he said her name.

"You'll laugh at me," she said.

"I would not dare."

And she believed he wouldn't.

"For a little over a year," she said, "I've been submitting anonymous articles to the *Chicago Defender*. I don't use my name, or even my own address. My brother was the go-between until he passed. Mostly opinion pieces, but some investigative, too. A Colored school in Henderson, Kentucky, had more graduates bound for college than the local white school. I wrote up a piece on it, sent it in. I expected to be rejected—or worse, ignored—but they published it and asked for more."

Nelly had yet to tell the full story to anyone. Not even Elder. She said it all in a torrent that left her feeling breathless. Even just one person knowing made it real and infinitely possible.

"That is a wonderful accomplishment," Tomás said in admiration. "We have not been acquainted long, Ms. Sawyer, but I hope you won't feel patronized when I say how proud I am of you."

"Ah, well. You should really be proud of Ira Brown. 'His' name is the one signed to the letters. Nelly Sawyer is still an inconsequential farm girl with more money than self-respect."

She meant that as a joke, but instead, it came out sounding like the deprecation that she knew it to be.

"There is no shame in anonymity," Tomás said. "It's often the safest choice, especially for a young lady in your public position."

"What public position? No one really knows who I am. At the start, I wrote under a fake name not out of protection, but fear of rejection. Ira could withstand the failure. Nelly could not. But I don't want to be afraid anymore. The editor of the paper asked to meet, and I'm tempted. I enjoy the work. I'm good at it. I might even be notable one day. But my parents wouldn't stand for it if they knew. Not when there are alliances to make." She looked at him. "Marriages to arrange."

Tomás nodded his head, but he didn't speak. His face turned contemplative as the silence lingered and stretched. Nelly could have slapped herself; talking of alliances and marriages as though she hadn't been marched off to his home to secure exactly that. She wouldn't blame him for feeling like a rabbit caught with a snare about its neck.

Afternoon slipped idly into early evening. The air was the warm honey shade of dusk, and the moon shared its sky with the sun. Nelly hadn't checked her watch once since she'd arrived, but she knew the two-hour mark had come and gone.

"It's getting late," she said. "Should we head back?"

Tomás blinked and took in the changing light.

"Forgive me. I've kept you far too long."

"Not at all." She paused, then added, "I've enjoyed it."

Tomás inclined his head.

"As have I, Ms. Sawyer."

They switched mounts for the ride back to the main house, and Nelly observed new confidence in Tomás. He still had a ways to go, but he didn't fight Blue Sonata so assertively, and the mare didn't buck against him. Nelly figured a man of his education and experience could master an ungelded bronco with little trouble, never mind a domesticated mare. Then again, no one managed much when they felt unwanted.

Their conversation was sparse all the way from stabling the horses to walking through the house's antiquated halls toward the main door.

"Do you feel you've improved?" Nelly asked, just to cut the bizarre and sudden tension.

"With Estrella, you mean? Yes, but I have some work to do. My father would follow through on his threat to shoot me if he knew I was out of breath at a full gallop. Next time we meet, I'll be ready for you."

Nelly stopped short, and the leather soles of her boots squeaked against the marble tiled floors.

"Next time?" she asked.

Tomás stopped as well, hands folded behind him in a soldier's stance.

"Unless I am such a poor student, and you refuse to teach me again."

"You've spoken barely a word to me since we came back," Nelly said, more than a little offended. "I assumed I didn't meet with your approval."

His hand was on hers again, clenching it tight. "I apologize. When I dwell on things, my character grows morose. It's a terrible habit that my aunt swears will make me a forever bachelor. It's only, when you mentioned giving up your passions because of what your parents expect, I felt ashamed and angry that you have entertained a moment's hesitation when pursuing what you love."

He took a step into her space, keeping her hand close against his chest. The steady strength of his heartbeat was not too dissimilar from the pace of a running horse. His eyes were wide, entreating, and moved to testify.

"I feared my father's disappointment more than a federal-army bullet, and I let that fear control me. I will regret that weakness and the freedom it cost me for the rest of my life. Meet with this editor, Ms. Sawyer, as soon as you can, and tell him the truth. If you are as talented as I know you to be, he won't hesitate to print your work under any name. Most especially your own."

The pressure at last ruptured within Nelly, and she exhaled. She told herself that the burn she felt gathering behind her eyes wasn't tears. His support could never stir her, because he was a stranger who dwelled in a world so far from her own that she had to squint to see it. Yet, when he spoke, her heart listened.

"Mr. Thomas?" the maid, Sarah, said. Nelly broke away from Tomás with the speed and shame of young people caught necking in the sanctuary.

"Ah, Sarah!" Tomás said, thrilled to see her standing slack-jawed in the hallway. "I was just bidding Ms. Sawyer good evening. Escort her out, will you?"

"Escort *her*?" the woman repeated back dumbly. "Through the front door?"

"Of course," he said. "Or would you recommend I push such an honored guest out the *kitchen* door?"

You could have knocked Sarah over with a ball of lint.

"Until next time, Ms. Sawyer."

Tomás bent to kiss Nelly's hand, and this time, she was prepared. It turned out she was right. The look on Sarah's face was entirely worth it.

CHAPTER ELEVEN

Richard Norris sat alone as the restaurant bustled around him. Loud-talking patrons, silverware clanking together. Waitresses shouting orders to the kitchen staff and kitchen staff shouting back. It was chaos to Nelly, but Richard sat as comfortably as he would in the privacy of his own study. Even as heavy rainwater ran down the window glass and turned the restaurant interior into an Impressionist painting, Nelly could sense how at home he was among the noise. These were the lives he respectfully archived, along with the *Defender's* founder, Robert Abbott.

Occasionally, someone would stop to comment on a recent issue, send regards from family members, or share how much their relatives appreciated the advice that got them up from the South. He addressed them all equally, and thanked them in turn for reading the paper that had grown to mean so much to so many.

"You coming in, sister?"

A man stood under the awning of the restaurant's front door; collar popped against the rain. He held it open for Nelly as water pooled on the checkered linoleum.

"No sir, thank you."

He looked her over, shrugged, and went in on his own. Already, the scheme was off its rails.

Nelly had told her parents that she wanted to tour the architecture without Murphy's surveillance, and thus was loosed. She plotted out her course a day in advance. Knew all the trolleys and trains she needed to catch, the blocks she needed to walk. And then, at the appointed time, she would lay it all out and ask—no, *demand*—that he publish her next piece under her byline. No more aliases. No more anonymity. Not even the unexpected rain dampened her spirits.

However, when Nelly arrived at the door of Chief's Cafeteria on Thirty-First Street and saw Richard settled in as though he'd been waiting all morning, all that careful planning vanished to be instantly replaced with cold terror. She walked to the Elevated station and back, mumbling to herself and endorsing her own anxiety. Say "Ira Brown" never showed up; nothing would change. She could plead an emergency. Send in another article, and in a month or two, her failed appearance would be old news. The secret would remain unexposed.

But she carried Tomás's words in her pocket like a mojo bag that gave her strength. If not now, then never, ever again.

The bell sounded and all eyes were on her. Conversation continued, but it was hushed. This was a place for regulars, and Nelly was in every way someone new.

"Morning, sweetie." A smiling woman greeted her at the low table by the door. She had a cash box and was dealing out receipts into various stacks. "You here for the special?"

"No, ma'am." Nelly stared at the square back of Richard's bald head. "I'm meeting someone. May I?" She gestured toward the dining room.

"Sure thing, seat yourself," the woman said. "There's coffee and water on the cart. Just walk up to the counter when you're ready to eat."

Nelly moved on water-clogged oxfords toward Richard's table. She wished now that she'd stepped into the bathroom first, to straighten herself. Yet, she knew if she turned back, she would walk straight out that restaurant and keep walking.

She stopped next to his table and said, "Mr. Norris."

Her voice was hoarse and easily smothered by the restaurant's noise. Nelly cleared her throat and tried again.

"Mr. Richard Norris."

He looked up from his corned beef sandwich and weekend issue of the *Richmond Planet*, then straightened his back to give her wet hair and soiled clothes the attention they deserved. To his inquisitive journalist's eye, she probably looked like a damn good story.

"That's right." He chased his last bite down with coffee and wiped his mouth with a linen napkin. He was a larger man, a man of presence. When he leaned back to take her in, the chair groaned.

"My name is Penelope Sawyer, sir," she said. She kept a litany going in her head, reminding her to speak up and keep her chin raised.

"Yes?" he said, then after a moment of recognition. "Oh, yes! Ambrose Sawyer's daughter. I beg your pardon; I didn't recognize you from the photos."

"Those are older photos," Nelly said. "And granted, I wasn't soaked through in most of them."

Richard laughed through his teeth as he smiled.

"Visitors here always underestimate a Chicago rainstorm. I've seen kinder weather in the Everglades. Are you enjoying all of the festivities ahead of the cotillion?"

"Yes, sir. It's all been very educational."

"Wasteful's more like it," he countered. "But I wasn't invited to most of them, so I ain't got room to complain."

Nelly nodded until droplets fell from her hair and landed in heavy plops on the floor. She couldn't even muster a polite smile. Richard glanced about, as though to identify someone qualified to claim her.

"May I sit?" she asked in an awkward burst.

"Oh!" He looked at the empty chair across from him. "Any other day, of course, I would welcome the company. Regrettably, I'm actually expecting someone. He's a little late. . . ."

He opened a thick brass pocket watch to confirm that the time was indeed ten after. Nelly was cutting it close.

"Ira Brown, right?" she asked. Richard's head snapped up to her, and his watch closed with a metallic *click*.

"Exactly," he said. "Are you acquainted with Mr. Brown?"

Nelly pulled out the chair before she lost her nerve. Richard again looked over his shoulder for her handler.

"I know Ira Brown because I *am* Ira Brown," she said.

His was the laugh of a nervous man waiting for the grenade to land.

"If this is Mr. Brown's way of maintaining his anonymity, it's not necessary," he ventured. "I'm a newspaper man. I know how to confirm my sources. I'm fully aware that 'Ira Brown' is an alias, and I'd sooner talk with him directly. I don't appreciate my time being wasted. When he's ready to meet with me in earnest, have him contact me. Good day."

Richard took his fedora from the table, crumpling it in his fisted hand, and moved to stand.

"Vivian Jones shared a bedroom with three siblings," Nelly said hurriedly. "They shared everything, in fact, but one thing was hers exclusively. The most precious item she owned in the world: a copy of *The Wind in the Willows*, given to her by her grandmother. It's what sparked her love for books. What drove her out that Thursday evening to visit the mobile library. Where those men ambushed her."

Nelly could see the book now, just as Vivian had left it. A blue hair ribbon used to mark her spot on page thirty-five. All details she'd refrained from including in the article.

Richard eased back down into his chair.

"How could you possibly know that?" he asked.

"Because I saw the book. I saw her house, I saw her room. I saw the last thing she touched before she died."

"That's impossible," he said, but with notably less conviction. "Vivian was from Kentucky like you, sure, but some of those articles came from New Orleans, Arkansas, Virginia."

"I travel with my father to the major races," Nelly said. "We're sometimes there for weeks. I have a lot of time to myself, and the freedom to go where I please."

"Okay." He nodded along, bracing himself for the punchline. "Fine. But can you explain the Chicago address I've been using for my correspondence with Mr. Brown?"

"My brother."

Mr. Norris's mouth formed an O, and he let out a long breath.

"And you wrote every article? All on your own?"

"Wrote them and researched them, to the best of my ability," she said. "I admit, some sources were harder to track down than others. Some wouldn't talk to me at all."

"I can imagine. Your father is the richest Negro in America."

"That's actually not the reason most wouldn't talk to me. More often, it was because I'm a woman."

Richard shook his head and spread his hands flat against the table.

"Mr. Brown—*you*—managed to gain some unprecedented access. Especially for an amateur. We still get inquiries about that school in Henderson. Folk talk about sending their children up there like white people who send their kids to boarding school in the Alps."

That pleased Nelly to no end. No one outside of Kentucky, barely anyone outside of Henderson, knew about the school. She remembered the tears in the school matron's eyes when she saw her classroom, her students, described on the front page of a paper that had readers in Paris.

"I cannot express how grateful I am for the opportunity you gave me, Mr. Norris," Nelly said. "The *Defender* enlightened and inspired me. It showed me a whole reality outside of Richmond. I submitted those first articles because I was moved to do so."

"Ms. Sawyer," he said with a sigh that felt as belittling as a pat on the head. "I am flattered that you were so touched by the work we do, and I was not aggrandizing when I said that you have talent. But your background is—and I'll go ahead and say it—*very different* from the usual young ones I bring on staff. Most have nothing in their pockets but a notebook. Not enough for a train ride home, even if they wanted one, but you!"

He laughed, breathy and awed.

"Just because my family has money doesn't mean I don't care," she said.

"So, tell me."

He leaned forward onto the table with shoulders hunched so he could look her in the eye. The sandwich was pushed to the side, and the air around them smelled of pickles and vinegar.

"Tell me why you care. With your endless prospects, you could commit yourself to anything. Certainly, more profitable pursuits than journalism."

Outside, the downpour continued. People ran by screaming with handbags, suit jackets, and newspapers for shelter.

"Are you from the South originally, Mr. Norris?" she asked.

"Georgia," he said. "For most of my life."

"Then you know the way of things there. We grow up thinking that reality stops at the sunrise and all creation can be carried on a bluebird's wing. Even the bad times are honey-scented memories. Like with most country children, my home was my world. I only had one real friend at One Oak: Tessa, the daughter of our cook, but she was more than enough. Jubilant and clever, she had always been the one marked for greatness. Anyone with eyes could see. She spent every day of her life on the ranch, but she just up and disappeared one day. It took a lot of grown folks telling me to mind my own business, but eventually, I found out about the middling landowner that Tessa's father sharecropped for. People said Tessa's father had a debt. Hundreds of dollars, nothing his family could pay in cash. So they used Tessa to settle the balance. This white man took my friend—who was all of twelve years old at the time—and forced her into peonage. She's still there now, as far as I know. Tending his house, cleaning his clothes, bearing his children."

Nelly remembered the last time she saw Tessa. Haggard and dressed in threadbare clothes not fit for pig slop. Standing in the doorway of a tumbledown shack with one blond-headed child on her hip, and another sleeping in her belly. Teeth rotted by tobacco leered in the darkness behind.

"I begged my father for help," Nelly said, "but he refused. No, not refused. It was like he had no choice at all. The 'richest Negro in America' couldn't stand up to a white man who paid his way in hog meat. It shattered everything I thought I knew about the way of the world. To his credit, my father saw my heartbreak and sympathized. He gave me a copy of Ida Barnett's *The Reason Why*. He said that she managed to make a difference with nothing but pen, paper, and a loud mouth, and that maybe I could do the same. Nothing came of Tessa's story other than pity, but soon, I realized that she wasn't an isolated incident. The hammer that fell on her could come down on me and mine at any time, for any reason. Or no reason at all."

Nelly was not nervous anymore. She felt surer of herself now than perhaps ever before in her young life.

"That's why I care, Mr. Norris," she said in challenge. "I hope it's explanation enough for you."

The famed editor laughed again, but this time, respect lurked under all that consternation.

"The truth is no place for vengeance, Ms. Sawyer," he said.

"Is justice ever vengeful?"

"Oh, yes. Almost every time."

Richard seemed to notice the clock hanging over the cafeteria counter where plates of Salisbury steak, potatoes, and roasted carrots rolled by on a noisy conveyor belt.

"I have another appointment," he said quite suddenly. "I assume you called this meeting to end our correspondence, yes? Now that Elder's gone, I see your parents have made quite the"—he chewed on the right word like the splintered end of a toothpick—"*investment* in you. You have more bookings than Weber and Fields, if you'll excuse me saying."

The dismissal irked Nelly, but not enough to make her change her mind.

"I want to keep writing," she said. "Regularly, and under my own name."

"Your name? Penelope Sawyer?"

"Yes. If you're happy with my work, that shouldn't disrupt anything about our arrangement."

She thought of Tomás and his insistence. The heart galloping beneath his chest.

"You've struck a match to a very mundane Thursday, Ms. Sawyer," Richard said. "Ira Brown is one thing. Penelope Sawyer is something else altogether. I know your father; I've spent the better part of a year spearing him and his inflated ego. If he knew that his only child not only talked to the press, but aspired to be a member of our company? Why, he'd string me up by my toenails, and he'd have every right to do so."

Now Nelly was incredulous. The *Defender* was so controversial that it had to be smuggled into the South in imported coffins. White mayors put out hits on Richard Norris and his colleagues. If he stepped an inch over the Mason-Dixon, he wouldn't step out again. Nothing should stir this kind of cowardice in such a man.

"You're afraid of my father?" Nelly asked.

"You are damn straight!" he said with devout assurance. "You don't become that rich selling horseflesh without inspiring some kind of fear. I know about the jockey who threatened to throw a race if he wasn't paid in full. Sources say he'll never ride again."

"That Vivian Jones article sold newspapers," Nelly asserted, intentionally ignoring the rumor. "I know it did. Forget the fact that no other paper even knew that Vivian had been murdered. Will you really turn me away because of stories about my father's temper?"

"And so my obituary will read if I let you do what you're asking to do."

Nelly was Southern in her blood and bones, and Southern doctrine decreed beyond class and religion that one showed respect to one's elders. Still, she could not help herself.

"I'm disappointed in you, Mr. Norris," she said, and she meant it.

Richard shook his head. He kept shaking it as he looked at the clock behind her. As he looked at the newspaper open in front of them, as he read a headline about another lynching, another wicked murder. Another Negro life sacrificed on a demented altar. One of thousands. One of millions.

"You want a byline?" he said. "All right, Ms. Sawyer. Here's how you get your byline. A shadowy figure showed up in conversation a couple years ago and has inspired all kinds of stories ever since. No one knows exactly where he lays his head, but on the beat, he's called the Mayor of Maxwell Street. There's been some recent coordination among the local bosses across race lines, you see. Italians, Irish, Jewish, Bronzeville. The status quo is them killing each other over street corners, but now they're working together. I suspect this 'Mayor' has something to do with that."

Nelly perched on the very edge of her seat. This was the thing that thrilled her about Chicago, about the news in general. Words and names were pulled out of bloody novels and brought to life.

"None of our staff have managed to dig up more than crumbs on this cat," he said. "But the paper that breaks his story will have the pulse of this city. Something I'll admit to coveting ever since I joined the *Defender*. You give me a profile identifying this person, Penelope Sawyer, and I'll print your name in black and white, come what may."

Nelly kept her peace. The whole truth of what he said was not lost on her. Essentially, it was impossible.

Richard's smile was sympathetic, but vindicated. He rubbed his palms together as though wiping his hands of her entirely. He began to gather up his things and make a show of finishing off what remained of his sandwich.

"I understand," he said, mouth half-full. "Not everywhere can be as simple as Kentucky. You're smart to avoid dancing with murderers and gangsters—"

"I'll do it."

Richard stopped mid-chew. Coughing, he said, "Don't be so quick to jump through the fire, Ms. Sawyer."

"You wouldn't have asked me if you didn't think I could do it," she said.

"Talent and capability are not the same thing. This assignment isn't just difficult. It's dangerous."

"Then why did you offer it to me? You test my mettle, Mr. Norris, and I'll test yours."

Richard couldn't answer that, not without incriminating his own morals. Nelly knew this, and while a smarter person would accept the way out he offered, she ran from it.

Nelly stood, and the suctioning of her wet clothes against a metal chair was loud in a restaurant now gone docile as a cleared field.

"We'll only be in Chicago for what's left of the summer," she said. "I'll have it done by then."

Richard blinked up at her. He looked ready to take it all back. It would be better for him if Nelly failed, or at least gave up. But if she succeeded . . .

"You'll keep this to yourself?" he asked.

"If you mean, will I keep it from my parents," she answered, "then yes. As much as I can. Will you keep your word?"

"If you mean, will I publish your byline," he shot back, "then yes. If you get me this exclusive."

Nelly smiled with her whole body and shook his hand until his watch chain jangled.

"Thank you, *thank you*, Mr. Norris!" she said without a hint of irony.

He said, "You think sources won't talk to you now, just wait. Experience and instinct tell me that you won't get far. This city will wear you down before you step onto the sidewalk. But, for your own sake, I hope I'm wrong."

Filled up with fulfillment, excitement, and the hubris of one desperate to prove oneself, Nelly said, "May I ask you something, Mr. Norris?"

He ran his hand over his face, appearing exhausted and done in.

"As long as it's off the record, Ms. Sawyer."

"Why did you assume Ira Brown was a man? Ira was my grandmother's name. You could have easily assumed it was a woman."

It gave her hope to see that Richard was ashamed of himself.

"I can't explain," he said honestly. "I thought only a man would go through the trouble. It was just an assumption."

"Right," Nelly said, "and if you'd assumed correct, would you give 'Mr. Brown' this test? Even if he'd proven himself for almost a year?"

Richard clicked his tongue against the back of his teeth.

"You presume too much, young lady. Tell me who the Mayor of Maxwell Street is first. Then I'll answer that question."

Nelly was hell-bent on holding him to that.

"Have a good rest of your day, Mr. Norris."

"A hint for a hint, Penelope Sawyer," he said, now standing in his buttoned pinstriped suit jacket and old-fashioned necktie. "You tell me which One Oak horse I should bet on for Saturday's race in New York, and I'll tell you where to start."

Nelly knew the horses racing. They were all individually owned by others, but they were bred at One Oak. None of them were hayburners, but none were champions either.

"Convallaria," she said. "To place. Not to win."

"Don't want to be responsible for my loss?"

"My mother says never bet to win. You'll almost always lose."

"You may go further than I thought in this way of life," he said. "Your first stop should be the Maxwell Street Night Bazaar. It's a fair of sorts, held on Saturday nights before the Sunday Market. Some music, good street food. A little bit of booze, too. It's not exactly something they print in your church bulletin, if you understand me. If you can get those grifters and sneak thieves to say more than three words to you, then you'll be on your way."

Nelly committed the name to memory, and in it, saw for the first time destiny spread out before her.

"Good luck," she said.

Richard donned his hat and gave a gap-toothed smile.

"Thanks. You'll need it."

CHAPTER TWELVE

It was already half after nine on a Saturday night, and Sequoia was a full hour late. Nelly and Sam sat in the front parlor room like naughty children waiting on a scolding.

"We should've picked up Sequoia," Nelly said to her cousin, "not the other way round. I just knew she'd be late the moment she offered to drive."

"The best parties always start late," Sam said. "I doubt this bazaar will be any different."

He adjusted the cufflinks on his snappy navy-blue Jazz suit, something post-war that he considered chic and fashionable enough for Sequoia. When Nelly had called Sam, begging him to fulfill her parents' requirement for a proper escort to the bazaar, he was unyielding. "Papers to write" this, "six hours on the train" that. The only thing that moved him was the promise that Sequoia McArthur would be there. For her, he borrowed a car and made the drive up himself.

Nelly's stiff orchid bob was held in place by a thick-banded bandeau. The extravagant embroidery itched like a tick bite, and Nelly couldn't keep from scratching under the edge with her thumbnail. She kept visualizing a thin line of blood running down the side of her face at some point in the night.

"Why are you so nervous?" Sam asked.

"What?" she said, still scratching. "I'm not nervous."

"Oh, yes you are. If you keep itching like that, you'll hit bedrock. Am I to assume that 'the man' will be there?"

Nelly's thumb paused. Instantly, foolishly, she wondered how Sam managed to find out about the assignment from Richard Norris.

"Man?" she asked with the irreverence of a girl accustomed to getting her "men" confused.

"*The* man. The Catholic polo player, the Mexican prince. The whole family is in an uproar about it."

Nelly's hand dropped into her lap and she closed her eyes.

"Momma's told you?"

"No," he said. "She told my momma, who told me. And my sisters, and the cousins, even Great-Aunt Ethel out in Wyoming. Apparently, he is quite the catch. Can I ask to see the ring, or is it too soon?"

Sam reached for Nelly's hand, but she snatched it away.

"Tomás is barely even a friend," she said. "We met at a polo game, then once again when I helped him out with one of our old ponies."

"Sometimes that's all it takes. I know if he saw you in this dress, he would propose immediately, Grand Cotillion be damned."

Nelly knew the dress was beautiful. It was by a designer named Fortuny, lush and sensuous. But the floor-length mass of gold silk and Venetian beads made Nelly feel weighed down. The dress itself clanged every time she moved, reminding her morbidly of a chain gang she once passed on the way into town.

"Thank you," she said. "I despise it, but thank you. And to answer your question, he's not why we're going. Hopefully, we won't recognize anyone, and no one will recognize us."

The last thing Nelly needed was the daughter of some sorority president or the son of a Negro business association chair slinking away to tell Florence that her daughter was talking the ear off Chicago bootleggers.

"So, if we're not going to rendezvous with your dashing suitor," Sam said, "then why are we going?"

Nelly looked him dead in his eyes as she lied.

"Because it sounds like a fun time, and I don't know about you, but I need a fun time. No more tea parties or luncheons, surrounded by people who do nothing but bring up Elder. If he were here, he'd be falling over himself to go, and he *wouldn't ask questions*."

Sam pursed his lips and narrowed his eyes at her. They were clever eyes that cut through her nonsense easily. But blessedly, he didn't push it.

The still air in the house was suddenly shattered by a clamor like a foghorn. Sam actually ducked, as though at any moment a Molotov cocktail would crash through the window. The noise continued, unbroken, before stopping and starting again.

Sam stood up and ran to the street-facing bay window. As he drew back the curtains, a blinding light eclipsed him. Nelly heard a high-pitched yelp that required no introduction.

"My God," Sam said. "I think she's driving a boat."

Parked squarely in the middle of the wide street running through Hyde Park Boulevard was a white Fiat 510. It was a massive and defiant vehicle, borderline impractical. As Sequoia stood with her foot up on the hubcap, Nelly thought of a circus that came through Richmond when she was a child, and a petite girl in yellow feathers riding an elephant.

"I don't even know you, Ms. McArthur," Sam said as he jogged down the front patio steps to the sidewalk, "but I would not have expected anything less."

Sequoia doffed her chauffeur's cap—a clash with her emerald-green party dress and silver bangles—and beamed with pride.

"If we mean to descend upon the hottest party in town, then with God as my witness, we'll do it in style."

Nelly approached the car as though it were a caged wild animal.

"Is this your car?" she asked.

"*God* no," Sequoia said. "Who do I look like? I won it off of Lloyd Younger at a bridge party last week. You know that boy's obsession with cars. If I didn't have to get it back to him by morning, I'd damn sure pawn it."

When Sam reached Sequoia, he leaned in to press a kiss against each cheek.

"Extraordinary, Ms. McArthur," he said.

"Spare me. Ms. McArthur is my father's ex-wife." Sequoia flicked the brim of his homburg hat so hard that it nearly fell backward off of his head. "And look at you, Samuel! Such a smart suit. Not nearly as stuffy and reserved as when last I saw you."

"Granted, that was at my cousin's funeral, Sequoia."

"And did that stop *me* from looking *my* best?"

"I daresay nothing could stop you."

Nelly saw how Sam squeezed Sequoia's hip and pulled her closer. And here he was accusing *her* of ulterior motives.

With a deftness that Nelly admired, Sequoia disentangled herself from Sam.

"Oh, you ain't seen nothing yet." She crossed to the driver's side of the car. "This thing handles like a wheelbarrow, but it's fast."

"Fast?" Nelly asked. The terrifying image of her brother came to her. Not as he was when they buried him, but as he was when they found him. Mangled, with half his body hanging at a sickening angle out of a smashed windshield.

"Reasonably fast," Sequoia corrected. "I'll be on my best behavior. Remember, this isn't even my car."

Nelly slid into the wide, leather-upholstered back seat. Sam went for the front as though it were the natural choice, but Sequoia's hand jutted out to stop him.

"Oh no, dear," she said. "In the back."

Sequoia revved the engine until the car's frame shook with restrained horsepower. Ambrose insisted on Rolls-Royce for all but one of the family's vehicles, so Nelly wasn't accustomed to such a domineering car. A part of her understood her brother's passion for automobiles now. Horses were animals with their own limitations, but some claimed a well-maintained car would run forever. Such power in anyone's hands was a dangerous, intoxicating thing.

Most especially Sequoia's hands.

"You might want to hold on to something," she shouted. "There's a bit of a kick."

The car jolted and Nelly held on to her cousin as they passed red-faced, gawking neighbors in smoking robes and pajamas. Sequoia waved and cackled, as full of herself as a strutting mockingbird possessed of a loud new song.

The top of the Fiat was down, and Nelly saw the city as never before. Even though they were out in deep night, it was noon-day hot. The air smelled sticky and fragrant, like the scent of coming rain. Sequoia kept her promise and managed not to go too fast, but still, the lights and sights flew by Nelly at dizzying speeds. Whenever she managed to latch on to one image—the golden light framing a marquee, a woman bending down to adjust her stocking, an old man shuffling across a busy street—the world would swing and it all started again. She was cursed with her father's shoddy vision, making it all blur together into something out of a drunken dream. This muggy Chicago night submerged her in its electricity, and she was baptized.

"Penelope Sawyer, are you quite all right?"

Nelly opened her eyes to see Sequoia leering at her through the rearview mirror. She wore blue-tinted driving goggles that made her eyes glow green.

"It's a lot to take in," Nelly said, breathless.

"Such a country mouse. Thank God you invited me. I can't believe you considered doing this alone." She spun around in the seat to look at Nelly directly. "Fantastic frock, by the way. I take back almost everything I said before."

An oncoming delivery truck honked, and Nelly screamed, "Eyes on the road!"

Sequoia veered into her proper lane at the last minute, shooting the stunned driver the bird as she did.

"Do you even know where you're going?" Sam asked over the din of passing cars and rushing wind.

"I don't appreciate that tone, Samuel. Of course I know where the damn Maxwell Street Market is. Only place in the city to find a good deal on stockings."

They took a sudden turn so sharp that Nelly and Sam jostled in the back seat.

"Just a quick detour," Sequoia said as she righted them. "You don't mind, do you, Nelly?"

Nelly wasn't sure what to say. She might have been the executor of this adventure, but Sequoia was their guide.

"Of course not," she said. Sam glared at her, and Nelly could only shrug.

Outside the luxurious bounds of the Fiat, the world shifted and changed again. The bright lights faded and were replaced by hand-painted awnings and shuttered storefronts. The streets were sparse at such an hour, apart from lingering couples and packs of boys with marbles. The lights of downtown burned on the horizon like a never-setting sun.

Sequoia slowed the car until it lumbered down the street at a parade float's pace. Even though Nelly couldn't see her face, she could feel Sequoia's uncertainty in each shallow breath. She reached out a hand and called Sequoia's name.

"Hush," she said bitingly, with a jerk of her shoulder. Then, a bit softer: "Please."

Sam sat up from where he was beginning to doze and took in the neighborhood.

"Where are we?" he asked.

"Deltaîbut," Sequoia answered. "The Greek Delta. Maxwell Street isn't far, and this won't take long. Please, just sit back and keep quiet."

They drove on until Sequoia turned into a narrow, dark alley that hugged the car's lacquered exterior. She drew to a stop and switched off the headlights, plunging the street into a darkness only accented by the occasional streetlamp.

"Wait," she said without turning to look at them, and so they did.

The air was cold in the shade of the alley. Nelly crossed her arms and wished for a shawl. Minutes ticked by, and Sequoia said not a word. She only sat chewing the nail of her ring finger until she pierced skin.

Both Nelly and Sam started when Sequoia sat up. Her eyes were on the building across the street—a modest corner grocer with two floors above. A side door opened, and the head of a white woman peeked out. She was young, with thick brown hair in an old-fashioned updo and a heavy gray cardigan covering most of her body. She looked up and down the empty street, then hustled across, straight for the car. When she opened the passenger door, she got inside with barely a glance behind.

"Sorry I'm so late," she said with a deep, gravelly accent. She immediately shimmied out of her cardigan to reveal a delightful day dress in secondhand, pale-blue cotton. "Ya-Ya took forever to fall asleep, and she hears everything."

"You're not late at all," Sequoia said. "I'm just glad you could make it. I know it was all short notice, and I didn't think you'd get my message."

The woman raised her hand and placed the tips of her fingers against Sequoia's mouth.

"I would not miss it for all the world."

Sequoia dissolved right before Nelly's eyes. Her body went lax, and she briefly leaned into the woman's hand as though it had the strength to hold up the sky. Quick as it was, there was a longing in the gesture that pulled at Nelly and called up a sigh from deep in her chest.

The woman jolted, and she looked into the back seat.

"Poioi eínai aftoí?" she asked. Sequoia cleared her throat and returned to her regularly scheduled herself.

"Agathē," Sequoia said. "This is Nelly Sawyer and Samuel Green. They're friends, don't worry."

Agathē calmed some at that, and grinned.

"Very nice to meet you both," she said in English. "I always hear about the Maxwell Street Night Bazaar's festivities, but my parents never let me go. I'm so thankful to be invited on your outing."

Sam scoffed and blurted, "Invited?"

"Yes," Sequoia said through teeth clenched tight. "This is the guest I mentioned, the one I met in Tower Town. Don't you remember, silly things?"

Sequoia looked desperately between Nelly and Sam. Nelly knew her cousin, and judging by the way his top lip curled as though pulled on a string, he was revving up to lay into Sequoia, and poor Agathē, too. Confused as she was, Nelly still felt that tug at her heart from observing the two together. She understood that whatever this was, it held beauty and needed to be protected.

Nelly crawled forward with a hand outstretched as she said, "Welcome, Agathē! We've looked forward to meeting you."

Agathē took the offered hand and with a strong, grateful shake. Sam had enough sense to hold his tongue.

Sequoia exhaled, and as her anxiety faded, so did the strain between them all.

"Swell!" she said. "We're off, then! Now, I did my research, and based on the advice of a highly reputable source, before we do anything, we must eat. You can get Polish sausage for a penny here, and sfenj for a nickel. The dough is soaked in rum—the real shit, too, from Bermuda—"

Sequoia started the car and pulled out into the street, continuing to talk. The excitement she exuded was real and not painted on for show. After spending time with the talented tenth, Nelly had uncovered a cruel joke about Sequoia being an old maid at the inexcusable age of twenty-six. But Nelly could see just how young and vibrant she truly was in this moment. And full of the purest kind of happiness.

"What the hell, Nelly?" Sam fumed close to her ear. "Is she trying to get us killed, babysitting some white girl?"

Nelly said softly, "Don't trouble yourself with that, Sam. This isn't Kentucky."

Nelly's eyes were drawn down from Sequoia's face to her hand. It was entwined with Agathé's: fingers threading together, palms pressed close one to the other. Like the branches of two trees once separate, now joined and reaching up for the sun as one.

CHAPTER THIRTEEN

When Nelly imagined this festival bazaar, it was as a boozy goblin market. Elegant women with dashing men twisting in the street, up to their chins in booze and confetti. And so she'd committed to dressing the part. But once the walking began, she realized that oxfords and cotton jumpers would have gotten the job done with a lot less mess.

"I thought we were going to a party, not Kilimanjaro," said Sam as he carried Nelly on his back through ankle-deep wastewater in an alley off of Twelfth Street. Sequoia led the way some feet ahead of them. Agathē had yet to let go of her hand.

"No one parks *on* Maxwell Street, Samuel. It requires a bit of a hike," Sequoia said without looking back.

They stepped out of the alley and were in the midst of it all. People flowed down the cleared-out street in a mass of caps, fedoras, and picture hats. Off of the boardwalk, the road was unpaved dirt tamped down by dry heat and hundreds of trampling feet. There were hardly any working streetlamps, but every few yards, a line of paper lanterns dangled between buildings like jewels on a necklace. They flickered with every breeze just as the stars did.

There was no parking on Maxwell Street because the street belonged to the vendors. They were two, sometimes three stalls deep. The actual brick-and-mortar establishments were closed for the night, but twice as many knife-sharpeners, dressmakers, tobacconists, and fortune-tellers were just getting started. Some were confined to two-wheeled pushcarts loaded down with merchandise. Others had freestanding one-room shacks sporting windows, doors, and potbelly stoves. And some were booths in and of themselves, bedecked in watch chains, necklaces, bracelets, and strands of fake pearls. Nelly's ear knew enough to catch some Spanish, and maybe Hebrew, along with, of course, the English, but everything else was as chaotic as Babel.

Sequoia and Agathē walked arm in arm, and Sequoia already had a flask in her hand.

"What are you two doing?" she yelled at Nelly and Sam. "Stop rubbernecking like a bunch of tourists. We need to get moving or we'll miss out on the best of everything!"

Every type of person was accounted for: Negro, white, Jewish, Christian, Italian, Irish. All milling about together with no hint of animosity. Nelly understood now why Sequoia and Agathē strolled these streets with such confidence. Here, a Colored girl drinking with a Greek girl was as common a sight as fishermen hawking trout heads for ukha.

On a corner, Nelly stopped to admire a trio of musicians in corduroy work pants and homespun cotton shirts with sleeves patched at the elbows. Colored Southerners like her; out of place among the shiny suits of Chicago.

"Haven't heard that song in years," Sam said at her side. He'd stripped down to his shirt and suspenders to beat the heat and traded his snappy suit jacket for a cup of lukewarm beer.

"You recognize it?" Nelly asked.

"Sure. You don't? You shame Grandma Dee, Nelly. It's 'Ain't Got Time to Die.'"

Of course, Nelly remembered now. A one-room chapel no bigger than their new foyer. When the money came, worship became a type of distraction that Ambrose and Florence simply did not have time for. At least not in the old way. Newer, more prosperous churches recruited them aggressively and pocketed their tithes with benevolence. Sam was right; Nelly did feel ashamed.

"You don't have to do it, you know," he said suddenly.

"It?"

"The cotillion. This whole grand season, bourgeois white-passing bullshit. I can see how much you hate it."

Nelly scoffed at his presumption.

"You think you know what I feel, *Professor Green?*"

"I do. You may be fair at cards, Nelly, but you have no poker face. Your eyes." He pointed his finger, crossing it over the bridge of her nose. "They tell the whole story."

As though to hide whatever truth he thought he saw there, Nelly directed her eyes back at the performers.

"It's not so bad," she said. "I've met Sequoia, along with some others. It's nice to have friends my own age for once."

Sam chuckled and said, "These people aren't the kind of friends you want. Not in the trenches. Sequoia is fun, but I wouldn't count on her to cover anyone's ass but her own."

Maybe a week ago, Nelly would have agreed. But after seeing Sequoia hang on to Agathē with the desperation of a falling woman clinging to a ledge, she couldn't be so sure.

"We are 'these people' now," she said. "You can run back to DC and play the humble intellectual with your academic friends, but I'm here dealing with it every day."

"That is what I'm saying to you. You do not *have* to be here. Go back to One Oak, or hell, anywhere you want. You can afford it now. You owe your parents less than nothing. Certainly not enough to demean yourself."

"You think I'm demeaning myself?" Nelly asked, wheeling on Sam. "Oh, no. I see. You think I can't cut it."

"I didn't say that."

"You didn't have to. You—like everyone else—believe that I'll fail at this fine high-society life. And what, Elder did so well?"

Sam bore the full brunt of Nelly's vexation. He lowered his voice and spoke softly, as he would to a frightened child.

"The attention of a man isn't enough to stick around a bad scene," he said. "I know growing up, fellas didn't come by a lot. I think Uncle Ambrose had more to do with that than anything. Either way, I get why you might feel compelled to, well, put yourself in an uncomfortable situation."

Nelly could have slapped him. Right in the middle of a crowd, loud enough to be heard a street over.

"Damn you, Sam," she said, and turned from him. She watched the musicians, but only saw how he must see her. Lanky and dark and so accustomed to being ignored that one glance from a handsome man could reduce her to mush. Nelly knew that was how her mother saw her some days—and maybe even her father—but not Sam. He always seemed above that kind of shallowness. It made her want to shock him. Expose her true self and watch all his assumptions about his precious little cousin burn away to ash.

Sam began to laugh, and Nelly turned to see Sequoia stylishly stumbling down the street with Agathē's arm wrapped around her waist.

"I will simply die if I don't get out of this humidity!" She still spoke with an actor's diction even though her legs wobbled like a ship on water. "Not to mention my hair. Agathē's been a darling translator and found us someplace to avoid melting."

Agathē was thin beneath her formless, drop-waisted dress, but she stood solid as a brick wall against the surge of Sequoia's giddy intoxication.

"A woman from Milos selling cutlery mentioned a saloon," Agathē said. "She said it serves gin, and there's dancing."

"Yes, dancing!" Sequoia said, perking up. She took Agathē's hand and proceeded to spin her around and try at the Charleston on two left feet.

Sam asked, "You think you could dance right now, Sequoia?"

"Samuel, if you're implying that I'm drunk, I'll let you know that I haven't been properly drunk in years. This is just a delightful buzz. I could tango circles around you with a gallon of whiskey in me."

"Well, if we make it to this juice joint, I may take you up on that. Did this woman from Milos tell you how to find it?"

"A green lantern," Agathē said, "and that's it. Somewhere between O'Brien and Wilson Street."

Nelly snorted. "That doesn't sound suspicious at all."

Sequoia stamped her foot and kicked up a billow of road dust.

"Nelly Sawyer, you're the one who dragged us all out here. Where is your sense of adventure? Trust me, if we were gonna get waylaid, it would've happened by now."

Nelly didn't think that theory had legs to stand on, but she followed Sequoia and Agathē as they laughed and twirled down the street to the sounds of a Hungarian violin played in an apartment far above them.

Maxwell Street was a place of signs and signage. Each vendor had a placard, some painted onto the walls of buildings or written in chalk on the sidewalk. Everyone advertised everything they could offer, or service, or sell. But this saloon of theirs did almost all it could to be unidentifiable.

They passed it half a dozen times until Nelly spotted a green light flickering timidly between two buildings that rose like dark cliffs on either side. It beckoned them down a boulevard more alley than street, passing men playing dice and young couples finding each other in the darkness. The green light was deceptive—neither close nor far away, but constant. When they were close enough to tell, Nelly understood why.

Three floors up, settled on the edge of a fire escape, was a boy. He sat with his legs swinging in open air while a rope dangled between his knee. Affixed to the end of that rope was a small lantern made of green glass, lit from within by a single candle. This was why it looked so ambiguous from the street. If you weren't searching for it, you could easily convince yourself into thinking it a trick of the night.

"Oi!" said the boy. He was small, but he spoke with an intimidating timbre far too authoritative for one so young. "You all police?"

"I'm not," Nelly shouted back. "I can't speak for the rest of them, though."

When he smiled, one gold tooth glinted in the sickly-green light.

"A'ight," he said. "Step down into the basement behind you. Enjoy y'all's selves."

Nelly descended the narrow steps winding down into a wet pit. She had to hug the wall to keep from slipping on bricks slick with vomit and whiskey. She felt Sam's skeptical hand reach out and take her elbow to steady her.

At the bottom of the stairs lurked another troll at the bridge: a man with legs as short as his muscled shoulders were wide. He was dressed in a factory uniform of denim coveralls and a cap tilted low over his eyes. But Nelly saw the ruby-studded ring on his pinky. His red-boned face was clean-shaven, and a small gold hoop pierced his right eyebrow. He was no working man, and he wasn't trying very hard to pretend at being one. The only light in the murky hole came from the embers in his pipe.

"Evening," he said. His hybrid accent was that of a Southern child raised in fast-talking Northern city streets. "Y'all police?"

"No," Sam said, "and I don't appreciate being asked that twice."

"Meant no harm, youngblood. It never hurts to check. There's a Prohibition on, you know? Cover is three fifty a person."

"Three fifty?" That sobered Sequoia up faster than a cold shower and a hot cup of coffee. "Who the hell is paying three fifty to get into a speakeasy?"

"Sweetheart, I don't set the rates. You all want in? I need to see fourteen dollars total."

All eyes settled immediately on Nelly.

"How do you even know I have that kind of cash?" she asked.

"Oh, please," said Sam. "Uncle Ambrose won't let you leave the house without at least forty dollars."

He might have been correct, but Nelly didn't appreciate the assumption.

There was a sudden high-pitched whistle that pierced the night like an arrow. It came in on a beat, interspersed with drawn-out notes.

"Shit," the doorman said. "Tommy, yank it!"

The green lantern was swiftly hauled up and disappeared over the edge of the fire escape, along with the boy. Only then did Nelly hear the sound of steel-toed shoes coming up the alley and something heavy tapping against the brick walls. They all crouched as low as they could. Nelly was on her hands and knees in dirt and rat feces.

A police officer's mustached face peered down into the gloom. Behind him, a younger cop stood with an electric box lantern.

"Who's down there?" the older one called out.

The doorman transformed right before Nelly's eyes. That leaning swagger became rumpled and staggering. An empty bottle slid from beneath his sleeve, and he made a show of putting it to his lips.

"Eh, Mr. Police Officer, sir," he said in a slurred, comically over-played down-home accent. "It only lil' old me. *Carry me back, yeah, to old Virginny . . .*"

"Just some plastered Negro," the officer said to his partner. "That's Maxwell Street for ya, son. If it's not the Jews sleeping twenty to a room, it's layabouts like him. Their lot are thick on the ground around here, just like the rats. Hey!" The officer beat his baton against the wall, and the doorman jolted as though he'd fallen asleep standing up. "Move on from here, you hear me? No loitering."

The doorman attempted to stand up straight, then sloped down like a tree with a heavy canopy. He gave a half-hearted salute and burped.

"Aye, aye, Mr. Police Officer. I'll be a-shuffling 'long."

The policemen muttered and made their way back to the main street. The doorman watched them go, and as he did, he steadily straightened and returned the bottle to its nook up his sleeve.

"Fucking pigs," he said in his normal voice. "Sorry about that. They walk through here every couple of weeks. The boss has us taking certain precautions. So, as I was saying. If you want in—and if you ain't cops—then it's three fifty each." He winked at Nelly. "Exact change, if you please, miss."

CHAPTER FOURTEEN

Nelly couldn't see a thing, but she could hear, and she could smell. She could feel the stamping of a hundred feet, the clapping of a hundred hands, amidst a fog of cigarette smoke and sweat. A slit of light appeared in the gloom and a pair of eyes looked out at them.

"Yeah?" said a gruff, impatient voice.

"Um, constellation." Sam murmered the word given to them by the doorman. The slit vanished, and hinges groaned loudly as a door opened. Framed by a haze of light and noise stood a thin white man dressed impeccably in a full tuxedo. He smiled at them with as much genteel amiability as the maître d' at the city's finest hotel.

"Ma'ams. Sir," he said with a dapper British accent. "Welcome to the Lantern Club."

It was a one-room basement—long and wide—that covered the length of the building above. A place originally used to store old furniture and furnaces had been revived as something enchanted. The ceiling was so low that Nelly could touch it if she jumped, and every inch was strung with brightly mottled oblong lamps of copper and mosaic glass. The glow turned the dance floor into a living kaleidoscope.

The club was packed with people, most of them dancing. Most looked like they'd just come in off a factory floor, a restaurant's kitchen, or scrubbing toilets at a tycoon's mansion. Others dressed in the way of the old country, wherever that might have been. And one woman in particular wore a million tiny glass teardrops draped so that when she danced, she sparkled like the heart of a chandelier.

All this was filtered through the music's constant, thrumming presence. It drove the energy of the place, and that energy was frantic.

A woman on a stage at the far end of the club perspired and screamed. Her voice was raw and untethered as she sang the familiar song "You Better Run" but not in the old way. Instead of Moses and Sampson, these lyrics told of Thirty-Fifth Street, Lincoln Theatre, and the Stroll. The desperately hopeful spiritual now had a static to it that would have been sacrilegious if not for the way folk danced. Together, they threw up their hands and sang "Run, run, run" in all their accented English. They moved with a current that felt like worship, bringing the song out of the South and into this bright new city of refuge.

"We didn't come down here just to stare," said Agathē once they were seated at a low table smack-dab in the middle of the dance floor. "I want to dance!"

"Drinks first," Sequoia said. "I swear 'fore God, I'm not going out there to embarrass myself sober. Samuel, be a dear, and go fetch something stout for the table."

Samuel looked absolutely affronted, as though Sequoia had asked him to drown a kitten.

"I'm not leaving you all alone. As your escort—"

"Escort is not the same as minder, or did you not know that?"

Nelly stood up just as the heat of their banter began to rise.

"I'll go," she said. "Besides, as we have all established, I'm the one with the cash."

Sequoia smiled up at her with a drunken gratitude.

"You're one in a million, Nelly. Gin for me and Agathē, if they have it. Whiskey if they don't."

"And if they don't have whiskey?" Nelly asked.

"If they don't have whiskey," Agathē said, "then we are leaving this shithole."

Like with most saloons, the bar was backed by a great, gilded mirror that reflected the entire club. Spotting her image in that mirror, Nelly had to catch her breath. She looked frazzled, and dirty, and lost. But she also looked every inch the jazzing flapper with the fly-by-night cares of Olive Thomas. She'd read about such women in magazines, and now here she was, one of their number. Drowning in a speakeasy and wearing a six-hundred-dollar party dress.

The empty bar was manned by a lone bartender, a white woman rounding middle age in another stunning tuxedo. There was no alcohol on display from what Nelly could see. No beer taps, not even any tankards. Every inch proclaimed it as a bar, other than, of course, the presence of liquor.

"Welcome to the Lantern, ma'am," the bartender said. Her voice was intentionally nondescript.

"Good evening." Nelly ran her hand over the smooth, maroon-tinged mahogany countertop. "I would like to order a . . . beverage," she said, and winced. She'd never ordered a drink at a bar. Not even before the Volstead Act.

"Yes," the woman said pleasantly. "What can I prepare for you?"

"Gin, if you have it."

"Oh, we don't sell alcohol here, ma'am."

"You don't?"

"No, ma'am. The Lantern Club adheres to all guidelines and parameters established by the Volstead Prohibition Enforcement Act."

"Well." Nelly cocked her head toward the barrier of smoky gaming tables surrounding the bar where a man operated a fully equipped absinthe brouilleur. "What about what they're drinking?"

"We can fulfill any request," the bartender said smoothly. "Especially for the players. Complimentary top-shelf is included in their buy-in."

Nelly nodded her understanding and glanced at the tables again. One or two had a rowdy bazaar tourist or a sweaty businessman, but the rest were all Italian. And—biased as it was—Nelly presumed, gangsters. She remembered Richard's advice and wondered if this elusive Mayor of Maxwell Street sat among them. They played a mix of rummy, poker, and blackjack, all games she recognized. Nelly was no card shark, but she knew enough. Not enough to win, perhaps, but enough to make people feel comfortable. Enough to get them talking.

"What's the buy-in?" Nelly asked.

The bartender coughed to cover a disparaging snicker.

"I'm not at liberty to say, ma'am."

"Not at all? Not even a ballpark?"

"It's very expensive."

"How expensive?"

"Ma'am, if you have to ask—"

"How do I get a seat at one of those tables?"

Nelly was bent over the counter now, nearly crossing a threshold into the woman's space. The bartender inhaled, held it, then let out a loud huff through her nose.

"The boss has to screen you, personally." That touch of Scotch-Irish came on suddenly. "But he doesn't let just anybody play, hon. Players are grandfathered in: brothers, cousins, friends of a friend. You'd have an easier time getting an invite to the governor's mansion than a seat at the Lantern Club's game tables."

Nelly only smiled. No use telling the woman that she'd been to the governor's mansion, back when they started construction on the Hyde Park house. Apparently, Governor Lowden had a dear affinity for racing horses.

"Is he here? Your boss?"

"You sure you wanna do this? The man's plenty nice, but he won't tolerate you wasting his time."

Nelly took a two-dollar bill from her change purse and slid it across the bar top. The bartender stared at the money a moment and sighed again.

"He's ringside," she said. "In the boxing room. Black suit lined in bloodred silk. Most likely'll be the man with money in his hand."

Nelly could only see the back of this "boss"; the front was occupied with accepting a handful of cash from a jumpy blond who yelped at every punch in the ring. There was a line of similar people behind her, all with loose bills ready to exchange for little strips of paper. The boss's back was slim but straight, and the black of his suit absorbed the light like a hole in existence.

When Nelly was close enough, she stretched out a hand to tap him on the shoulder, but a muscle-bound arm with sleeves rolled up to the elbow jutted out to stop her. Silver scars crisscrossed brown skin the same shade as her own.

"Hold up there," said an older gentleman, wide and baby-faced, wearing a Stetson hat unfashionably indoors.

Nelly tried again to reach forward, saying, "I need to speak with that man."

"You wanting to make a bet?" he asked. "Then you gotta get in line."

"I just have a question about the gaming tables."

"Three-hundred-dollar buy-in, doll."

Nelly reeled back to look the man in the eye.

"Three *hundred*?"

"Will need someone to vouch for you if you ain't got it."

"On me, you mean?"

"You mean to play at ten-thousand-dollar tables with the change in your pockets?"

Nelly lifted her chin to the sounds of a man being pummeled within an inch of his life.

"I'm Penelope Sawyer," she said. "I'm good for it."

"Nelly?"

The unyielding man turned to address the "boss" and said, "You know this girl, Jay Bird?"

Jay at once did and did not look like himself. Same face, same eyes, same imperious posture. But his hair was slicked back flush against the curve of his skull and parted down the middle. The wavy pompadour he often wore cast him as youthfully innocent. In this unexpected light, he was a grown man dressed up as sin.

There was one small consolation. Finally, Jay looked undone. As shocked as Nelly was. She was absolutely the last person he expected to see standing before him in such a place. Whatever poise he strived so diligently to maintain, she'd cracked, and that made her smile.

A man cried out and blood flew seconds before a body thudded against a canvas floor with a sound like raw meat. A referee counted up to three, then a bell rang. Those around Nelly celebrated, or cursed, or raged. An orchestra of emotions was on display from every angle, but Nelly couldn't pull her eyes from the dash of blood across Jay's cheek. He did not lift his hand to wipe it away. Didn't blink as it ran a jagged line down his face, as though it belonged there.

CHAPTER FIFTEEN

Nelly stepped into Jay's orbit, and at its center, there was stillness.

"Are you here alone?" he asked. She'd frazzled him, but he was fighting it admirably.

"She's here with three others," said the man in the Stetson hat. "A man and two women. Came in sloshed half to hell."

How long had Nelly and her friends been watched? Since they walked in the front door? Before then, even? How many dancers were really some manner of spy?

Jay said, "John, take over from here. I'll be back."

Nelly didn't want to give Jay a chance to put together some digestible, probable explanation, but soon, she was standing on her own in the boxing room and he was walking away. John took his spot at the head of the line.

"All right, y'all, no need to fuss!" Nelly heard him yell. "You'll all get what's owed you in due time."

Nelly had practically forgotten where her party was seated, but Jay knew. He walked directly to it without once checking on her. All along the way, people stopped in their dancing and drinking to shake his hand. The murder of gangsters posted at the card tables even halted their gambling long enough to rise and slip Jay a crisp new bill as thanks for some small service. Trailing Jay's steps was like walking in the footfalls of a god. Everything she saw, he held in a subtle sway.

Nelly spotted Sam and Sequoia arguing about something while Agathē looked jittery and bored. Sam was the first to notice Nelly, and when he did, he jumped up out of his seat fast enough to topple the chair.

"There you are! What did you think you were doing, disappearing like that? This place is full of thieves and killers and—"

Sam's attention then shifted up to Jay. He stopped, taking a breath.

"I think I know you," he said, pointing. "Have we met?"

Nelly cut in with, "Elder's funeral. The blue suit."

Sam remembered just as Sequoia did.

"Jay Shorey," she said. She kept her seat as though expecting him to bend and kiss her ring.

Jay peered at Sequoia like a hunter trying to decide if the crude shape in the distance was predator or prey.

"Sequoia McArthur. Your reputation precedes you," he said. "Folk say a club isn't a club until you've graced it with your illustrious presence. Has the Lantern Club finally 'arrived'?"

Sequoia's feathers stretched and fanned at the flattery. She was an unmistakable beauty—copper-skinned, tall, and elegant—and when she stood fully in her power, she was a fearsome thing to behold.

She said, "Depends on the company. Sit down with us, Mr. Shorey. Or must we all stare up at you like the Great Sphinx of Giza?"

Sam choked on a laugh, but quickly corrected himself. Nelly caught the answer to Sequoia's unspoken question in Jay's eyes: *If it's a fight she wants* . . . He pulled out a chair for Nelly, then took his own right out from under a man at the neighboring table. Jay moved the pieces of this place about like his own personal checkerboard.

"Are we not drinking?" he asked of the bare table.

"That's why we came to this watering hole," Sequoia said, "but Nelly vanished and didn't deign to come back with even a glass of milk."

Jay glanced about, then held up a long finger.

"Please, pardon the lack of attention from the waitstaff," he said. "It's been a very busy night."

Seconds later, a Colored woman with bottle-blond hair was setting down four empty flutes and an open bottle. The bottle's label was tattered at the edges, and the script was a florid calligraphy so faded that it was difficult to decipher. Sam held it close to his face and gasped.

In breathless awe, he said, "a hundred-year-old bottle of Madeira."

"With such lauded company," Jay said with a trenchant look at Sequoia, "I thought it appropriate. On the house, of course."

"Jay, that's too much," Nelly said, but he waved her off. Sequoia looked between Nelly and Sam, then snatched the bottle directly from Sam's hand.

She poured a full glass for herself, then one for Agathē.

"Do not mind if *I* do."

Where Sequoia was intentionally impossible, Agathē was endearing and soft. She graced Jay with a darling smile and said, "We appreciate your hospitality, Mr. Shorey."

Jay matched her smile, and their charm dashed against each other like light bouncing between mirrors.

"Am I to take this to be *your* club, Jay?" Sequoia asked. She rotated her glass in slow circles that kept the liquid in constant, sensuous motion.

Jay said, "Oh, no. The owner is very busy, so I manage things in his absence."

"Folk treat you like the owner," Sequoia observed just as a man clapped Jay on the shoulder and "thanked him for the chance" to play the Lantern stage. Jay shook the man's hand but did not stall or break his exchange with Sequoia.

"I suppose that's what happens when you keep glasses full," he said.

Jay offered to top off Sequoia's own glass, but she held her fingers over the rim as she would with a waiter. He moved on to refill Agathē's glass, as graceful as a dancer leaping between partners.

"Tell me, then, 'cause I *am* curious," Sequoia said. "Why is Jay Shorey of San Francisco and Oakland 'managing' a speakeasy on Maxwell Street? Your family has some kind of fishing empire, right? What happened? Did the bay dry up?"

The jealousy that fell upon Nelly was icy enough to make her shiver. She didn't even know Jay's last name before this evening, but Sequoia could recall his family history on demand. Nelly always thought of herself as stone. Capable of standing next to pillars like Ida Barnett, unshakable in the face of mobs. Turns out, she couldn't even resist Jay's flimsy defense of smiles and shared cigarettes.

"You've been listening at the right doors, Ms. McArthur," Jay said.

Lifting her glass to her painted lips, Sequoia said, "I always do."

"My family's business was whaling, by the way. Not fishing. You can imagine how profitable that kind is in this day and age. I'm from a minor branch, so all I can claim is my relative William Shorey's semi-famous name and an empty bank account. Ask any of the talented tenth in this city, and they'll tell you my family prospects aren't worth the salt in the Pacific Ocean."

"Came to Chicago to seek your fortune, did you?" Sam asked. He was already on his second glass of the wine.

"She came seeking me," Jay said. "This nightlife caught me like a falling child and gave me a purpose and place that I never had in California."

Nelly looked about at the people awash in vibrant light and said, "It's a beguiling club."

"Thank you, Ms. Sawyer," Jay said, and Nelly did not miss the genuine sigh of appreciation when he said her name. "Folk are so quick to call Maxwell Street dangerous or deranged. A back-alley ghetto. I wanted them to see it like I see it—as a fairyland. I'm lucky the owner gave me such freedom. Lord knows the electric bill alone could end a less adventurous man."

Agathē motioned between Jay and Nelly, swaying under the allure of premium alcohol, and said, "How do you two know each other, hmm?"

Jay held up his hands, giving Nelly leave to answer that question on her own terms.

"We always seem to be in the same room at the same time," she said elusively.

"Alone, I take it?" Sequoia asked.

Nelly cut daggers at her friend, who peered back with those discerning cat eyes that hoarded information with supernatural efficiency.

"Oh, what?" Sequoia set the glass down, and it landed heavy on the tabletop. She was doing her best to rein it in, but the Madeira was working fast on her, too. Nelly looked at her own glass, not remembering when Jay had taken the liberty of filling it.

"All I'm saying is no one talks to you, Mr. Shorey," Sequoia said. "People see you at all the parties and dinners and *funerals* about town, but no one trades more than a hi and a howdy-do with you. You have no living family to speak of, no people to claim you. Even I didn't know you were in this city until just three months ago. And as you said, I listen at all the right doors."

"Everybody isn't a somebody, Sequoia," Nelly said.

"Yeah, folk say that, but it's not quite true, is it? Just because your family doesn't own a house in Oak Bluffs, Nelly, doesn't mean you never could. Your absence isn't dubious. It's a choice. People may not recognize you when they see you, but they know who you are. Everybody *is* somebody in the end. Unless, of course, they're nobody at all."

Sequoia spoke in tipsy swirls that danced with nonsense, but Nelly understood her. More intriguingly, Jay seemed to understand her just as well.

"I value my privacy, Ms. McArthur," he said, "and after you've been turned out of homes three or four times, the experience starts to lose its luster. I tried getting into the club meetings and charity dinners, but I reckon the great mothers and fathers of this city didn't like me leaving mothballs in their parlors. Old family names don't mean much here unless you can back them up, isn't that right?"

"Our community is as open as ever to those who'll be open to us."

"Oh, right. Once I wore the right suits and shelled out the right cash, y'all were as open as the doors of the fucking church."

That untraceable inflection of his was breaking again. His tone had a heat that simmered and boiled like a pot on an open flame. Sequoia's own usual cadence—as flashy as ragtime—slowly morphed into something untailored. It was surreal, observing these two palatial people stripping each other down to the studs. All the rest of those at that table could do was watch.

Sequoia said, "Bitterness is not your color," and chased a wry chuckle down with the rest of her wine.

"You're kin to that gravedigger from the Second Ward, right?" she asked.

Jay's jaw audibly clenched.

"I think you're referring to Daniel Jackson," he said. "He's my god-uncle and partial owner of this club."

"'God-uncle,' well, well. That's a hastily made-up relation. Teaching you the ways of embalming and racketeering, I gather? I look forward to hearing you explain how a mortician from Pennsylvania is friendly enough with a whaling family in California to be god-uncle to one of their own."

"You know that all Negroes worth knowing know each other," Jay said.

"Oh, so you are a Negro, then? Great to finally get some clarification on that point. When I asked around, the responses were mixed."

Nelly winced. She felt that one like a punch. She cut her eyes at Jay, half expecting him to be up and demanding satisfaction, but he only smiled; and it was not a kind smile.

"You of all people should understand the dollar value of controversy in this city," he said. He glanced at Agathē with an intensity that he tried to downplay, but in truth, it was as casual as a brandished pistol. "Your father has written whole diatribes about romancing outside of our race. The Lord alone knows what he'd have to say about romancing within your own sex."

Agathē gasped and reached for Sequoia's hand. The two of them didn't look at each other, but Nelly could see the panic flowing between them like currents of electricity.

Sam sat up straight, making his presence known to the best of his ability, and said, "Steady there, Jay—"

"It's fine, Samuel," Sequoia interrupted. "Mr. Shorey's just being good at his job. I imagine managing a club is all about customer service, and the best way to serve customers like us is to know our secrets. Same thing that makes my housekeeper such a commodity.

I see why he finds himself so often alone in rooms with you, Nelly. You might be his most valuable 'customer' yet."

Nelly had done her best to let the two of them spar in private, and resented being summoned up for some killing blow.

"Jay is a friend," Nelly said.

"Friend, customer." Sequoia sighed with an airy disregard. "The two can be one and the same. Well, whoever this 'Jay Shorey' is, he has done well for himself. I hereby anoint this club *arrived.*"

"I'm glad you're enjoying it," Jay said. "I tried to model the Lantern Club exactly for customers like you."

"The flaunting and fabulous, you mean?" she asked.

Looking at her with a razor-thin glare, he said, "Yes. And the luxuriously lost."

The silence that covered the table was as thick as the moment after the first shot. The one that turns a thing from a disagreement into all-out war.

Suddenly, a singer let out a yelp from the stage, and the shock had everyone jumping. His voice caught hold of the club's attention and zest, then turned it back out at them. Musicians joined him—fiddle and piano and drum—and soon, tables were emptied, and the dance floor swelled.

Agathē was already on her feet and pulling Sequoia into the dance like a referee pulling a fallen fighter from the ring.

"And what a place to get lost in!" Sequoia yelled as the beat picked up pace. "I mean to dance until I can't remember my own name."

Nelly was sure she said more, but a piano riff took her voice and made it its own. Sam stood as well, loosening his necktie.

"You fancy a dance, Nelly?" he asked, but Nelly knew it was just a gesture. There were several young ladies on the floor doing the shimmy alone.

Nelly crossed her legs to make her point and said, "You know I'm hopeless at a quickstep. Dance up a typhoon for me, Sam."

Sam smirked down at his cousin, then noted Jay, who hadn't moved an inch since he and Sequoia reduced each other to the burning core of themselves.

Sam ran the pad of his thumb across the left side of his face and said, "You have something on your cheek just there, Mr. Shorey. Careful. It'll stain your collar."

Jay touched the blood splatter from the boxing room, now gone dry, and it crumbled to dust as he rubbed it between his fingers.

CHAPTER SIXTEEN

There was no telling time in the Lantern Club. It had no windows, one door, and the only noise was the noise it created. From what Nelly could see, plenty of folk came in, but the only ones who left were escorted out. Even if the doors were bolted, she imagined they would gladly go on drinking and dancing into eternity. Jay took in all of these people with the solemn contentment of a shepherd watching over a flock bound for slaughter.

"What are you doing here?" Nelly asked. Jay's pitying gaze did not change when it fell on her. Clearly, he considered Nelly to be part of the flock.

"I could ask you a similar question," he said.

"Same reason as everyone else: to have a good time."

"No," he said. "This isn't your scene. Although that dress does give you a sufficient head start. I bet you glow like liquid gold when you dance."

Nelly smirked and ran a hand over her beaded skirt.

"Is that meant to be flirting?"

"More like a tribute. I've found that women who take the time to come in here—especially when they clean up like you—appreciate the recognition."

She tilted her head as though to see his teasing from a more advantageous angle. This was becoming the night of young men telling her where she did and did not belong.

"Do you have a cigarette?" she asked. Jay's smirk was smug, but he stayed quiet as he fetched that same silver cigarette case from his breast pocket. It looked virtually unchanged from the last time he had offered it to Nelly. Oddly so, especially for so late in the evening. Nelly would watch her father go through two packs by noon on a leisurely day, and that Sawyer compulsion toward addiction was the only thing that kept her from carrying her own stash.

As Jay lit the end of the meticulously rolled paper, Nelly inhaled and closed her eyes at the familiar, indecipherable taste of his tobacco.

"Damn," she said on a cloudy exhale. "You won't believe me, but I've been craving these since the day we met. What brand do you buy?"

"Ah, so my experiment is a success," he said cheerily. "I asked the woman who rolls these to make the best cigarettes you *can't* buy at a newspaper stand. You can only find this particular taste here, with me, on Maxwell Street."

"Why bother?" Nelly asked. "You don't smoke."

Jay's brows drew together over the bridge of his pointed nose.

"How do you know that?"

She shrugged as she took another drag, relishing the flavor.

"Your case is full. Was the last time, too. It's just an assumption, but no smoker I've ever met walks around with a full case of rare Cuban cigarettes."

Now it was Nelly's turn to look smug.

"No, I don't smoke, Ms. Sawyer," Jay said. "I do, however, spend a lot of time in the company of smokers. It's also an efficient way to make new friends. Worked with you, didn't it?"

Nelly's head teeter-tottered from side to side as if to say *That remains to be seen.*

"I do love your club," she said. "And I *am* having a good time. But that's not why I'm here, not why I came to the bazaar."

"Not to buy dope, I hope. The quality is subpar on this side of town," Jay said as indifferently as he would when talking about sugar and salt.

"Lord, no!" Nelly stubbed out her cigarette in one of the glass ashtrays that adorned every table, suddenly ashamed at her predilection. "Do I look like I'm trying to buy dope?"

"You look nervous."

"Well, when you ask questions like that, what do you expect? If you must know, I'm trying to find someone. I don't have a name, though, and I don't know what he looks like."

Nelly then took in Jay with clear and appraising eyes. If the Lantern Club was a galaxy, a universe, then he was the sun around which all of creation turned. As Sequoia'd said, it was his job to collect secrets and use them to his best advantage.

"You may know of him, actually," she said.

"Really? I'm flattered."

"Yeah, possibly. Someone called the Mayor of Maxwell Street?"

Jay's face dropped like a rock into still, black water, and that honeycomb skin drained of color. He looked terrified. Not for his own sake, Nelly realized, but for hers.

"Are you in trouble?" he asked.

"Trouble?"

"Is someone threatening you?" Jay was urgent now. "Some bad business with your father?"

"What? No, of course not—"

"Then why the fuck are you looking for the Mayor of Maxwell Street? Jesus Christ, Nelly!"

Jay reached over the table for Sam's half-full glass of Madeira and threw it back in one go.

"So, you know him?" Nelly asked when Jay slammed down the empty glass.

"No!" He looked around, collecting himself, and lowered his voice. "No, I do *not* know him. No one does. That's the point. You've been in this city all of five minutes, and already you're sticking your hand in the damn hornets' nest. Who put you up to this?"

"Is it hard enough to assume that I'm pursuing this under my own steam?"

"That's not hard at all," he said, "but I can hope you're not nearly that reckless."

Nelly pleaded, "Then help me. If I'm going about this the wrong way, point me in the right direction."

She now regretted putting out what remained of her cigarette. Keeping a lid on this project was Richard's only stipulation. If she let it all leak out now, her first real opportunity at independence would be her last.

"At Elder's wake, we talked about Vivian Jones," she said. "I don't know if you saw the piece in the *Defender* about her death."

"I did. I'm ashamed to say I didn't know about it until I read the article."

Nelly smiled. That was a small, meaningless admission, but it swaddled her heart in pride.

"*I* wrote that article," she said.

Jay squinted, as though peering back through time to see the article clearer.

"And the one about the Colored school in Henderson?"

Nelly nodded. "And others. I've been publishing anonymously for about a year."

"Hmm. That's an odd hobby for a debutante."

Nelly didn't think he said that to be intentionally dismissive, but still, the use of the word *hobby* struck and caught fire in her.

"It's no hobby," she said. "If I write an exposé about this Mayor of Maxwell Street, the chief editor will publish the piece under my own name. Maybe even make me part of their standing staff."

Jay stared at her for a few seconds with an introspective, serious expression. Then he threw his head back and laughed.

"I appreciate your support," Nelly said and took her first sip of the wine. It was good. Very good. Tasted of flowers and honey in a glass that sweated from the iced chill.

Still catching his breath, Jay said, "So, this is you as a journalist? I suppose you figured the Mayor of Maxwell Street would be standing at a stall with a sign strapped to his chest. And that's why you wanted a seat at a gaming table! I bet you a half dollar that Richard Norris told you this person was a gangster, so you—ace beat reporter Nelly Sawyer—thought playing a few hands would get you in good with the mafioso. Am I scratching the surface?"

Nelly wasn't sure if she wanted to hit Jay for unwinding her plan so snidely, or herself for thinking of it in the first place.

"Just give me a seat at the table, Jay," she said. "You know damn well that I'm good for it. I'll cover my losses if I lose, but I don't plan on losing."

"If you sit down with those men, you'll get yourself killed. I won't be an accessory to your murder."

"You have no right to decide that!"

"I have every right. This is my place, Nelly, and no one gets to the gaming tables without my direct say-so."

"Aren't you some kind of businessman?" Nelly asked, aghast. "I'm all but guaranteeing you a profit."

Jay held up a single finger.

"First off," he said, "never ever imply throwing a game in my establishment. People have lost eyes over less. Second, I can't have some junior reporter sitting at one of my tables, asking questions about someone who doesn't even exist and drawing unwanted attention to the Lantern Club."

"Junior reporter?" Nelly tried to ignore the shrill petulance in her voice. "How dare you! All you have to do is open a door for me, and I'll take care of the rest. Or at least let me interview *you*. With all the folk coming in and out of this place, you probably know more than—"

"Listen to me, Penelope Sawyer." Jay leaned close to Nelly, too close. She picked up on that familiar musk of his cologne, but it was muddled by the smell of sweat, booze, and a little bit of blood. When he spoke, he carried the severity of a long winter.

"This isn't another dime-a-dozen story about Negroes looking for justice. These people you want to trade cards with are deadly. Far too pragmatic to kill over a petty thing like race. They kill over rumors, over rumors of rumors. Keep sniffing after this trail, and sooner or later, the Mayor of Maxwell Street will find you way before you find him. Write about something else. *Anything* else. Turn over a rock in this city, and I promise, you'll find some corruption, or murder, or vice that'll curl Richard Norris's toes. But this? Let this sleep, Nelly. If ever you were my friend, you'll do this for me."

The fingers of Jay's hand brushed against hers, and a shock of static sent a lightning bolt up her arm. Even so close, Nelly would be hard-pressed to say he was Colored if she didn't know him. The features of his face were so ambiguous and formless. She wondered if he ever walked by a mirror and surprised himself, or perhaps it became easy to forget, after a time.

She drew her hand close to her side and said, "But we ain't friends. Before tonight, I didn't even know your name. I might as well be no one but a customer to you. Now, are you going to let me buy in or not?"

Jay's lip twitched. He wanted to speak, but a force like a conjurer's curse bound him up in silence. As though whatever he said next would either condemn her with its savagery, or break her with its honesty. But before he could say anything at all, a shadow appeared at Jay's side.

"Begging your pardon, Jay Bird," said John, the man with the Stetson hat. "But you asked to know when the Genna game was winding down."

Jay stood, pushing the chair away with the back of his knees. The flat of his palm made a pass over his hair to smooth the stray ends.

"If you'll excuse me, Ms. Sawyer. But please, stay as long as you'd like," he said. "John, make sure they get another bottle of the '33, please."

"That's too generous," Nelly said.

"Not at all. I'll put it on your tab. As you said, you're good for it."

Jay began to walk away, but stopped when Nelly called out, "I mean to find this Mayor of Maxwell Street, Jay. With or without you."

He turned slowly, and those summertime eyes of his were tundra cold, and hard.

"Say that name in my club again," he said, "and I'll have you banned. Do you understand?"

Nelly would not abide being threatened, and most certainly not by him.

"What the hell are you so afraid of?" she demanded, rising to her feet.

His grin was snide enough to weaken her knees.

"I see," he said. "You've never been properly afraid before, have you? Well. Maybe you *should* find this Mayor of Maxwell Street.

Whoever he is, he owes you a lesson in risk. Good evening, Ms. Sawyer."

And then he was gone for good. The club embraced and covered him until he could be seen no more. Nelly knew that he'd said those things to frighten her into reason, but it was no use. He was right; she wasn't afraid. She stood at the edge of an inferno and was desperate to feel its scorch and blaze.

CHAPTER SEVENTEEN

Nelly was up before the sun, but even that wasn't early enough to beat the crowds.

They came like something out of the Bible in these shambling, eastern-moving herds, weighed down by baskets and carts and totes made of old quilts. Her head was still fogged from Jay's prestige wine the night before, but she refused to be deterred. Nelly didn't have time for self-pity. Jay Shorey could refuse to help her. That didn't mean she would refuse to help herself.

In the light of day, the Maxwell Street Sunday Market lost some of the bacchanal mania of the Saturday Night Bazaar, but none of the speed. People spoke in a rapid, violent tongue born of trade that ascended beyond ethnicities or countries. Yet, even as they haggled over chickens, and fish, and musty oil paintings, they did so while asking after family and wishing each other good health on the Sabbath. Perhaps more so than any other stretch of road in America, on Maxwell Street, commerce was the only game, and anyone who could pay could play.

Or so she'd believed. By the time Nelly made it to her seventh and most uncooperative stall vendor of the morning, she wasn't so sure.

The man was intransigent. The other vendors would smile, at least. Nod, pretend to show an interest in her questions until they managed to excuse themselves. But he wouldn't offer her that common of a courtesy. He was a young caramel-skinned man, sweating under a heavy wool hat, and he addressed each customer with an aggressive hospitality; all but Nelly, of course.

"My questions won't take long, sir," she said for the third time, voice raised above the constant chatter of the market patrons. But not hearing her was not this man's problem.

A small girl with bare feet and hair cut as though with a butter knife bullied her way to the front of the line. This vendor was one of the few with impressive, fully installed booths as sturdy as any store of steel and wood. Fruit and potatoes, onions and herbs, a selection as diverse as any chain grocer.

The vendor peered over the edge of his stall down at the shoeless girl and said, "Not today, bomboncita. Your mother owes me five dollars still. More, with the interest."

"It's been two weeks, Mr. Fernandez," she said in a faded voice. "If we don't have some food soon, Ma said we're likely to starve or steal."

"You were 'likely to starve' three months ago. She didn't have the money then either. I'm not a charity. I have a family of my own to feed. Your mother has always been a good friend to me, but I can't afford to give the best away. Run on now, child, you're blocking the others. Return with what is owed and you can have your pick."

Nelly moved quickly, opening her change purse and laying out five dollars in fat new silver quarters.

"I'll cover the balance," she said. The vendor looked at her, and the light behind his salesman's bright eyes dimmed.

"Not your money," he said. "Not here."

"It's not for me. It's for this baby girl."

The baby girl in question bounced her eyes between the two of them—hopeful, but with enough awareness of the world to be cynical.

The vendor stood impassive: "I cannot serve you, miss."

"I don't expect you to, Mr. Fernandez. It *is* Mr. Fernandez, right? I just have some questions about the market. No more than ten minutes of your time, sir, I promise."

He considered the money in front of him, the girl close to begging him, and the persistent young woman who grinned in his face. Then upward of twenty folded dollars landed next to Nelly's handful of coins, and another stood among their party. This was the first time she noticed Jay's nails. The cuticles were craggy and broken and coated in dry blood.

"¡Buen domingo, Rafael! ¿Cómo está el negocio?"

Jay did not trip or stumble over the Spanish. He spoke like he was born to it. Hearing him, Nelly felt embarrassed for trying to even trade civilities with Tomás in her atrocious accent.

Clubs like the Lantern didn't reach their zenith until somewhere between midnight and three a.m., and yet, Jay appeared as well-rested as a baby. Not a hint of the punch-drunk party life miasma about him. He presented as an actor appearing on the stage as "Man of Leisure" with his ivory-pommeled walking cane and flat-topped hat set at a dashing angle atop his head. The air was thick with road dust, dirt, and the general mess of a busy street, but his pearly suit remained flawlessly bleached.

"Ah, ¿cómo pueden ir mal los negocios cuando brilla el sol?" Mr. Fernandez said. "Pregúntame de nuevo cuando llueva."

Jay pushed the tight square of bills closer to the vendor and spoke again: "Para Sally y las niñas. Eso debería cubrir su deuda y el resto del mes."

The vendor's smile was all gratitude and amiability, but that ease did not reach his eyes. They were hollow, and Nelly could see a skim of fear icing over them.

"Eres demasiado cortés, Jay. No te acostumbres a regalar dinero. Como un perro, se alejará de tu puerta para siempre si se le da la oportunidad."

"Gracias," Jay said. "Pero este dinero no vagó, tiene un propósito. Deja que la niña tenga algunos comestibles, Rafael."

"Cuando el padre regrese, nos arreglaremos—"

"Sabes tan bien como yo que Joe no va a volver. Si no fuera por Sally, tú, tus cebollas y tus zanahorias se estarían pudriendo en Santa Clara. Ella cedió su lugar en este tramo para que pudieras alimentar a tu familia, y no creas que lo he olvidado. Miramos hacia fuera para cada uno aquí. ¿Derecha?"

Nelly didn't understand the words, but she understood the sharp edge in Jay's tone. He hid it behind a sparkling countenance, but every syllable was a thinly masked admonishment waiting to become an intimidation. Mr. Fernandez looked down at the money, then down further at the sandy-haired girl's vacant eyes.

"¿Esto viene de tu empleador?" he asked.

"No," Jay said. "Sólo yo. No le deberás nada."

That seemed to seal it for the vendor. He snatched up the cash and said to the girl in English, "Wait there a moment, child." Then to Jay: "Your usual?"

"Are they fresh?" Jay asked.

Mr. Fernandez clutched his chest and fell back until he jostled a bowl of figs. "¡Dios en el cielo! Asking me if my goods are fresh. I should ring your pretty bell, Jay Bird."

"Only as long as the Lantern Club can handle the action, Rafael."

Mr. Fernandez's answering laugh waned as he ventured deeper into the depths of his booth. Jay looked directly over Nelly's head and down at the little girl, who remained still and expectant.

"Get on home," he said to her. "A boy'll bring groceries by soon. And don't tell your ma about how this came about, okay? Just say Mr. Fernandez was feeling particularly Christian today."

The girl did not speak. She did not even appear particularly grateful, only nodded once and was carried along by the current of the market.

Jay said, "Folk forget that people live on this street, I think. And the living here is hard."

"Do *you* live here?" Nelly asked. She had no earthly idea where Jay lived. He could be manifesting out of dust and air for all she knew.

"Ah, well," he said with a sigh. "Unfortunate wretch that I am, I'm reduced to sleeping on the El, eating in drugstores, and bathing in brothels. They always have hot water."

"I assume that's where you keep your impressive wardrobe?"

"Oh, no, Ms. Sawyer. I store my suits in a crypt under St. Patrick's."

Nelly was taken aback by his banter. The previous night's quarrel might as well have been a feverish mirage, stirred up by the madness of the club. Jay suddenly ducked as an object the size of a baseball flew at his head. He caught it, and avoided two more. They were warped little spheres wrapped in soiled sheets of newspaper.

"Is this girl bothering you, Jay?" the vendor asked, more warning than question.

"If I was bothering him," Nelly said, "trust me, you'd be able to tell."

Mr. Fernandez twisted up his mouth as though to spit at Nelly's feet and curse her name. She was accustomed to such degradation, but not so blatantly, and certainly not from someone who looked like Rafael Fernandez.

"She's an acquaintance, Rafael," he said. "Vale la pena una tonelada de dinero, así que no seas grosero." Jay unwrapped one of the spheres and a smell wafted up, sweet and sun-kissed. A thick yellow juice oozed out as he bit down.

"Delicious, as always. Next Sunday?" he asked.

"Si no estoy muerto para entonces."

Jay chuckled with a mouth half-full, then said, "Was there anything you wanted from Rafael, Ms. Sawyer? I noticed you were in line before I interrupted you."

The color leeched from Mr. Fernandez's face. Nelly didn't know Jay's place in this strange street-market hierarchy, but whatever it was, it was above Mr. Fernandez. The idea of forcing him to answer her questions while Jay's apparent authority towered over them gave her a pleasant buzz, but she resisted.

"Not at all," she said with a sweetness that only a spiteful Southerner could muster. "I can always visit another fruit stall."

Jay led them away from Mr. Fernandez's booth and into the churn of the crowd. Once they were far enough away for Nelly to speak in confidence, she dropped her composure and groaned.

"I know my tact isn't at its best today, but my God. He barely even acknowledged me, a customer with money in my hand!"

Jay hummed, tickled by the image, then said, "Rafael didn't refuse to serve you because you're obtuse. It's because you're a Negro. Folk back on the island with his shade would take being called 'Colored' as an insult. Word is that he even served in a militia that killed some six thousand dark-skinned Cubans. For him to address you at all shows some progress."

Nelly was at once baffled by the irony and incensed by it. Now more than before, she wanted to talk to the man. To understand how he must have felt when he crossed onto United States soil and was told to stand in the Colored queue. She was raised under the assumption that while Negroes might fight among themselves, when it came to preserving the dignity of the whole, they held the line. Even the talented tenth with their paper-bag tests offered her some solidarity, theoretical and begrudging as it was. The biased men who wrote the laws and maintained the bloody status quo didn't see a distinction, after all. Rafael Fernandez would be slotted into the same subhuman file as Nelly when their judgment fell.

She inspected Jay under the shade of his wide-brimmed hat that blocked the summer sun and kept his face evenly pale.

"He doesn't know that *you're* Colored, does he?" she asked, but knew enough about him to answer her own question. "No. Of course not. Does anyone on Maxwell Street know?"

Jay threw the weight of her examination over his shoulder along with the now useless wad of wet newspaper. Always so cavalier; so dismissive of a reality that honestly terrified her.

"Those who know, know," he said. "I let everyone else think what they want. For all of this street's diversity, some folk here would still take issue with giving a Colored man their money. Them not knowing makes the job easier."

"And which job is that?"

Jay adjusted his coat, and Nelly saw the outline of an envelope—thick and padded possibly with cash.

"You do know why they call him the 'Mayor of Maxwell Street,' right?" Jay asked, completely hopscotching over her question. Nelly had an itch to stay in pursuit, not let him veer away so easily. But he offered something more appealing, and like a dog on a track, she followed it.

"I assumed it's because he conducts business here," she said.

"Nothing quite so literal. It's because he's a thoroughfare. Money, goods, services, vice, information. Whatever you're willing to buy, he sells. Those fool enough to go looking always expect to find him at the bottom. Down here in the mud and the hustle, with us. Most never stop to look up. Where the air's clean and the living is easy."

As he spoke, Jay glanced up toward a clear and boundless sky.

"That's my theory, anyway." He finished off the last of the golden fruit in one wet bite. "If the man's as smart as my god-uncle thinks he is, then he's hiding behind a desk job and a cushy Astor Street address. Anonymity is vastly undervalued."

Nelly laughed, and in answer to Jay's insulted expression, she said, "Men who dress like you don't want anonymity. You want a stage, and a spotlight, and a standing ovation."

"Don't deny me life's simplest pleasures."

Jay's face lifted when someone called his name, but faster than Nelly could catch, a grayness colored in the lines about his eyes and mouth. He took her arm and tugged her in tight at his side, close enough for her to smell the citrus staining his hands and clothes.

"You're being followed."

"What?" she hissed. "Where?"

"To your left. Blue hat. Don't make it obvious—"

Nelly abandoned all of Jay's suave covertness. The idea of a cloaked figure trailing her steps was admittedly thrilling. However, the only blue hat she saw was on her driver, who'd lagged behind to browse a stall of handcrafted tobacco pipes.

Crestfallen, Nelly said, "That's only my chauffeur, Murphy."

Jay's concerned frown flipped into a smile, then bled into a bewildered laugh.

"You had your *driver* bring you to the Maxwell Street Market? He didn't leave the car idling, did he? If so, I reckon that pretty Rolls-Royce of yours is gone for good."

"Some unkind letters have been arriving at the house recently," Nelly said, "and as my parents won't hesitate to remind me, Chicago isn't Richmond. Murphy has been ordered to follow me everywhere.

Sam was bad enough last night. Now I feel like I'm tethered to a big, flashy warning sign that says, 'Avoid the outsider.'"

"How'd you manage writing those first articles for the *Defender*?" Jay asked. "Sharecroppers and schoolteachers can't be any more forthcoming than a cobbler from Poland."

"I didn't always go looking for those sources. Most of the time, I'd start up a conversation with someone I found interesting and hear the story in their lives. After a little digging, I could create a portrait of a region or time or a place made up of stories that came to me with all the variety of birdsong."

Jay held up his finger, and like a choir under a prodigy's command, the market's noise rose. Its chaos was not chaos at all, but an infinite canon sung by a thousand voices.

"Then might I recommend stopping to listen?" he said. "These streets have stories, too. I doubt even the elusive Mayor of Maxwell Street can hide from gossip. What is it?" he asked when she smiled.

"Mr. Shorey," she said, drawing out his name. "Are you voluntarily helping me?"

"Voluntarily? No, *Ms. Sawyer*, I'm not that self-destructive. Besides, I'd wager you're perfectly fine on your own."

Nelly was steadily growing accustomed to Jay's tenderness. It stung at first, but in a way that soon turned pleasurable. She then took note of the sky and the sun. It was high and plump, nearly midmorning.

"Damn," Nelly said. She checked her wristwatch, and sure enough, it was after ten. Apparently, the Maxwell Street Market traded time just as easily as any other merchandise.

"We're hosting a prayer luncheon for the Sisters of the Mysterious Ten in an hour," she said to Jay, already looking for Murphy and a quick exit. "I have to get home."

"Don't say that." He reached for her hand and then checked himself. "I was just starting to enjoy your company."

"Missing me already?" Nelly wasn't always one for teasing, but that blush filling Jay's cheeks like big red apples could not be resisted. "But you're the one who banished me from coming back here."

"It's not that I don't want you here," he said. "One of these old mornings, our rendezvous will be scheduled and planned, and we can take our time. But this Mayor of Maxwell Street business. It's not worth the danger you're putting yourself in, Nelly."

Like Rome, Jay had one true road that never strayed, faltered, or failed. He would be unbearable if he wasn't so consistent.

"Am I utterly incapable to you?" she asked. "I told you what this opportunity meant to me. What do you want me to do, ignore it?"

"Yes, if that'll save your fool life. Do what you came here to do, Nelly. Smile and flatter, make your mark on this society like the deb you are."

Nelly's stomach lurched. Jay had a peculiar talent for turning the harmless into the disdainful.

"I came here to bury my brother. I didn't mean to come to Chicago at all, but now that I'm here, I'm going to use every opportunity to my advantage. Just like you did."

He said nothing as Nelly retraced her steps to intercept Murphy and hurry home. What a waste of a morning. Jay couldn't help but be a distraction, and a part of Nelly wondered if he put himself in her path on purpose.

"Ms. Sawyer!" Jay yelled. Nelly raised her hands in time to catch one of the fruits swaddled in newspaper from Mr. Fernandez's cart. It fit snugly in the palm of her hand and had give when she squeezed.

Jay stood on the other side of a distorted, shimmering wall of air. She could not see the fine particulars of his face through the illusion, so when he spoke, his voice came from every direction. Swaying and unmoored.

"Eat. You'll need your strength."

Nelly asked Murphy to take the long way home, by the lake. She'd never seen the ocean, but as she watched the steady ebb and flow of Lake Michigan dappled in morning light, she felt as she thought she might feel standing on the ocean's brink.

The fruit was messy and delicious, but eating it brought on thoughts of Jay and his echoed warning. Nelly could understand his hesitancy to help if it was based in fear. Yet, for him to see her as the simpering, ignorant girl that so many others carelessly took her to be was a humbling realization. She wanted to prove him wrong. Him more than anyone.

"Quite the riffraff you were associating with this morning, Miss Nelly," Murphy said from the driver's seat. Nelly met his eyes in the reflection of the rearview. "Not the type of young man I think your papa would appreciate walking out with his only daughter. Know I wouldn't let me or mine around his like."

Murphy drifted off as he spoke, but he was just loud enough for Nelly to catch the implication.

"Thank you for your concern, Murphy," she said, "but when's the last time my father cared about 'the type' I associated with?"

"I'm only saying, Miss Nelly. Men don't get that popular by handing out candy canes."

Nelly remembered when Murphy first started driving for her family—he had to get blind drunk to stomach accepting regular pay from a Negro, but now he was comfortable enough to tell Nelly what her own father expected from her.

"I can handle Jay Shorey. Actually, Murphy, I'll be working on a project of sorts while we're here. I may be visiting Maxwell Street again, or elsewhere in the city. Either way, it's not something my parents need to know about. Okay?"

Nelly stared the man down through the mirror. She dared him to oppose her, his employer, but he mercifully only popped his chewing gum and scanned the frothing lake. Nelly settled back in her seat, trusting that an understanding now existed between them.

To avoid staining the interior of her father's precious Rolls-Royce, Nelly used the flimsy sheets of newspaper to wipe residue from her fingers. They were pages out of the *Herald-Examiner*, a sensational publication allegedly distributed by gangsters. This particular torn page held a series of cartoons criticizing creatures great and small— state senators all the way down to code inspectors. She didn't know much about Chicago politics, but when she saw the exaggerated tall hair and ever-drooping eyes of Oscar Stanton DePriest, she knew him at once. They'd met at Elder's funeral, where he spoke of future campaigns and all he and Ambrose Sawyer could do for the community. Confident and certainly ambitious, but sincere from what little she could discern.

This comic was not so gracious.

It depicted DePriest as a chemist flanked by beakers. He was pouring something into a massive funnel that narrowed into a point. From that point came tiny strips of paper falling like ripe fruit from the vine into a bag labeled "West Side Votes." Holding the bag was, unmistakably, Mayor William Hale Thompson. The cartoon's caption read MODERN-DAY ALCHEMY.

When Nelly examined the comic closely, she saw that Mayor Thompson's shadow did not match the man. Where Thompson was wide, his shadow was lean. Where Thompson wore a ridiculous ten-gallon hat, his shadow donned a formal stovepipe. And Nelly couldn't be sure, but it looked to her as though the shadow had the smoking barrel of a pistol aimed at Mayor Thompson's back. Underneath this twisted silhouette was the blurred and runny inscription *See Me for a Deal, Sundays Only.*

The artist's signature was tucked into a pinch of white space in the far corner of the image, tiny letters printed as though with the point of a safety pin. Made to be ignored. Made to be missed. *M. Harjo.*

Nelly's face stretched into a smile. Not a waste of a morning at all.

CHAPTER EIGHTEEN

Nelly checked the address again. A piecemeal name torn from a back-issue comic strip wasn't very much to go on, but Chicago city administrators kept exceptional public records.

When the matrons of the "grand season" held a tour of the Central Library—the cotillion's chosen venue—Nelly made valuable use of that time poring over census archives. The rest was putting up with Murphy's grumbling while she traversed the far reaches of Chicago conducting cold calls. It took her the better part of three days to get to this particular address, and as proud as she was of her work, she wondered if the building would be just another dead end.

It was a dour gray brownstone on the back side of Cottage Grove Avenue, but those who lived there did their best to highlight moments of beautiful life. The front lawn was used as a vegetable garden, neat and lovingly cared for. Flower boxes adorned every window, and somewhere inside, a recording of "Dardanella" played. The disrepair and neglect did not erase the loveliness of the building, or the people who dwelled inside.

When Nelly knocked at the front door, a middle-aged woman with skin the dusky shade of a pecan shell answered. Secured about her head was a checkered scarf, and her body appeared stretched in a denim jumpsuit.

"Can I help you?" she asked with a pronounced Florida twang. Her eyes were gray and piercing as a hawk's, and Nelly feared that they could see right through her.

"Hello, ma'am!" Nelly used her most effective churchgoing, child-rearing, well-intentioned lady-of-society voice. "My name is Penelope Sawyer, and I'm here on behalf of the Alpha Suffrage Club of Chicago. Election season will be here soon, and I'm preaching the gospel of the vote, especially for our Negro women. Might I take a moment of your time to discuss your options for getting your voice heard?"

The woman glared at Nelly with deep-set, tired eyes. If such a look could fire bullets, Nelly would be dead.

"Miss," said with the same intonation as *fool*. "Much appreciated and all, but I'm heading out the door. Do you have any pamphlets or whatever that you can leave?"

"Of course!" She didn't. "But there's nothing like connecting with someone person-to-person. I won't hold y'all up for long. Even just a second could mean the difference between a champion governing over our city and our people, or a tyrant. May I ask, Ms. . . . ?"

"It's missus. Mrs. Harjo."

Nelly smiled in earnest. She took her tracker's thrill and channeled it into her performance.

"Yes, thank you. May I ask, Mrs. Harjo, have you registered?"

The woman peered back into the depths of the brownstone, as though looking for someone to relieve her of her post, then faced Nelly again.

"No, miss. Never saw much of a point."

"Begging your pardon, but you couldn't be more mistaken. The points are endless! I can register you right here, while you're free."

Nelly lifted her leather briefcase, which she'd stuffed with old magazines to mimic the weight of official forms and documents. The woman coughed once, then spat into a vase by the door.

"Fine," she said. "Come on in, then, Ms. Sawyer."

And like a Greek through Troy's impenetrable walls, Nelly walked inside.

The apartment was really just a large room with screens partitioning kitchen from salon from bedroom. The brownstone had once housed a single family, but now each room was a dwelling. This space was formerly an interior room with no way out or in other than the front door. Nelly had grown up with an excess of space. She could walk for hours and not see another human soul if she wanted. This lack of windows and the rejuvenating clarity of natural light reminded her of a mass tomb.

The woman poured herself a glass of something brown from a bottle cooling in the icebox, then dropped into one of the kitchen chairs with a groan.

"You said this wouldn't take long, right?" She drank deep from her glass. "What do y'all need from me? I can tell you where I work, but that's pretty much it. I have no family here, and I can't speak for my parents—"

"Allow me to apologize in advance, Mrs. Harjo." Nelly abandoned the pretense and spoke to the woman plainly. "May I call you Marta?"

The glass slid from Marta's fingers and landed right side up on the kitchen table, sloshing the hooch onto her lap and shoes. Her eyes went to the door behind them. She was going to rush Nelly. Make a break for the door and be gone, possibly forever. "I'm not here to cause trouble, Marta," Nelly said. She kept her hands flat and open on the tabletop, a sign of submission. "I'm a fan of yours, actually." Within the briefcase's fake stuffing, Nelly found the old comic strip. She'd ironed it under bricks, then kept it out in the sun to dry. It was faded and cracked, but just as vibrant as the day it was printed. Marta looked down at the picture as though it were a blight.

"Harjo is a unique name," Nelly went on. "There are sixty in Chicago, according to the city census, and only seven *M.* Harjos. The first one I tried was a meatpacker in the West Loop. He was Norwegian by birth, and didn't understand English well enough to read an American newspaper, never mind draw for one. Very nice man, though."

Marta chewed on the inside of her cheek as she cut her eyes at Nelly, the liar who'd deceived her way into a private home. Only those who meant harm would pull such a trick.

"You can't prove I made that," Marta said before Nelly could even ask.

"I don't want to prove anything. To tell you true, I'm not even here about the comic itself. Just what's depicted in it." Nelly stretched the paper out on the table between them. "I know who this is." She pointed at DePriest. "And this." Then at Mayor Thompson. "Now, I have a theory about him." She slid her finger over the debonair shadow. "But I just need to be sure."

Marta had strong, imposing lips that convulsed in a fleeting show of appreciation.

"A funny picture," she said and took a loud sip from her glass.

The walls of Marta's apartment were as thin as a silk slip. The voices of neighbors above and around were so present, they could have been right there in the room with them, watching the stalemate play out. Two women chatted about a new bride's unfortunate condition, possibly while shucking peas into a bowl. The needle skipped on the "Dardanella" record until finally someone gave up and switched to Paul Whiteman. Children ran screaming across a landing while a dog barked several lots away.

"Let me introduce myself properly, ma'am," Nelly said by way of a fresh start. "My name *is* Penelope Sawyer, but as I'm sure you've gathered, I'm not here with the Alpha Suffrage Club. I'm a journalist. This comic could be the key to unlocking a great mystery in this town, and if my theory's right, then the character you cast in Mayor Thompson's shadow is the person I'm looking for."

Marta finished off her drink with a soft belch. Nelly could tell by the healthy shine of her fingernails that she wasn't born to a life where women wore denim coveralls and wrapped their hair to avoid being sucked up into some insidious machinery. Whatever wind she rode to land in Chicago was a strange wind born of necessity.

"Child, didn't anyone ever tell you there's no use in chasing shadows?" Marta asked.

"But this ain't just any shadow, is it?" Nelly scooted her chair closer until her chest bumped against the table's edge. "I know a little about cartoons and the value of empty space on a page. If each mark in this picture didn't have a purpose, it wouldn't be in the picture. I could understand if you're saying that beneath Mayor Thompson's everyman swagger, he's some upper-class fraud, but that's not quite right. He's an honest-to-goodness cowboy. Maybe you're saying he associates with gangsters who'll hold a gun to you while they haggle, but why would Thompson be holding a gun to himself? Call me prideful, but I keep going back to my own theory, and I can't move on from this until I know for sure."

A clock on the wall chimed the hour. It depicted the face of a grinning sun with hands pointing the cardinal directions. It was perhaps the most beautiful thing in the sparse apartment.

"That's a wonderful heirloom," Nelly said. If Marta refused to answer her directly, maybe she would answer indirectly.

Marta sniggered and said, "It's no heirloom, Ms. Sawyer. My husband bought it at a corner store for a dollar. He said I worked long hours and never knew when to come home. The roads turn treacherous at night in Pensacola, and he liked me in the house by sundown."

Nelly fought the impulse to pry. Her fingers twitched for a pencil and paper, but she curled her hand to still them.

"May I ask you something, Marta?"

"Will it get you out of my home any faster?"

Nelly grinned. "Maybe."

"Fine, then. Ask your question."

"What brought you to Chicago? Alone, especially."

Instead of answering, Marta stood and returned to the icebox to refill her glass. The time was drifting away. Nelly had told Murphy she'd be no more than an hour. The man wasn't nearly as domineering as he liked to pretend, but Nelly didn't doubt he'd come looking for her if she lingered too long. For the sake of his job alone if for no other reason.

"My daughter, Becky, is with me," Marta said when she sat back down. "She's a pretty girl, like you, and naturally kind. When this white widower down the road started giving her gifts when she turned fourteen, she thought he was just being neighborly. We all did. He'd always been harmless enough, never spoke an ill word to no one. But one day, Becky was late getting home from school. Four hours late. The widower brought her by as the moon was rising. He said Becky had 'stopped for fresh orange juice and a chat.' The time got away from them. Becky never spoke of what happened that evening; she didn't have to. Coming to Chicago wasn't a choice. It was just the way things had to be."

Marta appeared strained, as though the telling of the tale was just as painful as the living of it. Nelly thought of her own terrible change from girl to what they called "a woman." The hungry smiles and lewd expressions that made her very skin feel like a transgression. Florence had told her not to smile, not to make eye contact, not to ever appear receptive, or worse yet, repulsed. There was no room for courage growing up like that. As a Colored girl, you learned early on to see your own body as a threat and an ever-present danger.

"It's hard here," Marta continued. "Harder than Florida somehow. I'm an educated woman with years of good work experience behind me, but the best this promised land could do was a place on a factory floor making fifteen dollars a week. Good enough pay, but before the cash is in my hand, it's swallowed up by rent, and food, and the twenty cents it takes to go from one end of this city to the other. I tried for an entry-clerk job, but any Negro girl they hired had to, at the very most, be brought up local. At the very least, be light enough to pass."

"Is that what you were in Pensacola? An entry clerk?"

Marta turned the empty glass around until it scratched against the wood of the table. Her assessment of Nelly was harsh and unflinching. She looked down again, at the discarded comic strip, and the muscles of her jaw shifted like a cow chewing on crud.

"I drew comics," she said. "For the *Colored Citizen*."

Nelly knew the *Colored Citizen*, a small but thorough publication that reported on everything from heart disease to economic policy in France. And if Marta worked for one paper, she could very easily work for another.

"You have so much experience," Nelly said in sincere amazement. "I wish I could've been with a paper like the *Colored Citizen*, or any paper. If my parents knew I was doing this interview, they'd lock me up and damn me as a lunatic."

Nelly laughed, but Marta didn't laugh with her.

"One thing they never tell you—persistence is the toughest part. Not the job. Not the work. Staying the course will wear you down faster than anything, especially once the money dries up, or the friends disappear, or the family stops coming round. You start off thinking your passion will sustain you. Then you come home to a place like this. I wish I'd seen the truth of things when I was a young person like you."

Nelly straightened her spine in prideful defiance and said, "I mean to stay the course, Marta. So I can achieve something greater."

The older woman's laugh had a rough-hewn edge.

"And you see where that gets you."

Marta's laugh soon turned into a cough so violent that it made Nelly's own ribs ache. She stood without thinking to pour some water from the tap, but Marta held up her hand, refusing her. Her last hack brought up a mucus more red than yellow. It landed with a significant *plop* in the bottom of her empty glass. Marta looked at the residue with a passive kind of terror.

"Six months was all it took," she said. "We breathe in all kinds of shit at the factory—fibers, dust, little chips of metal—but if you cough too loud, you're sent home without a day's pay. I thought drawing cartoons for the *Herald-Examiner* would remind me of what I had back home, what made me strong. Help me stay the course. Turns out, they just made me heartsick."

"So, this *is* you?" Nelly asked, pointing at the comic.

When Marta sighed, the last of her resistance seemed to leave her.

"Yeah. It's me. It's an old one, though. I've stopped signing with my real name since then. How'd you get ahold of it?"

Nelly didn't want to wade through the particulars, so she only said, "It was thrown out with some garbage. I came upon it completely by chance. You don't much care for Mr. DePriest, do you?

I thought he was Chicago's bright new star for Colored progress and prosperity."

"Oh, they're all bright new stars," Marta said. "They burn out eventually. Pensacola—hell, every inch of the South—may be damned by its history, but Chicago takes a demented delight in its own damnation. Corruption is cash here, and once you're in the arena, there's no getting out of it."

"I'm impressed you still keep your ear to the sidewalk," Nelly said, part compliment and part question.

"Politics is all anyone ever talks about in this city. I housekeep at a gentlemen's club to make ends meet. All manner of aldermen, and commissioners, and secretaries come through there in every kind of state. It would straighten your baby hairs to hear the talk they use so freely around me. I'm just the Colored girl scrubbing their floors. What use could I have for secrets that set the wheels of this whole country turning?"

Marta winked then, and Nelly saw a glimpse of the firebrand who'd arrived in Chicago with a talent and an eye that refused to move blind through the world. For all that to shrivel down to such a sodden, sickened spirit devastated Nelly. To think, this woman might very well have been Nelly's mentor, in another life. Someone she could look up to and learn from. If only they had the time.

"This means a lot to you," Marta said, tapping on the comic strip. "Doesn't it? Enough for you to lie your way through my door. I'd be within my rights to shoot you where you sit, Ms. Sawyer, for such an invasion."

When the fourth M. Harjo had brandished a cleaver at her head seconds after she knocked on his front door, Nelly pondered if this was safe or right. What business did she have, forcing her way into these lives, blind to the consequences? But then a new lead would emerge and she'd be too caught up in discovery's dance to care much about herself. Or anyone else.

She said, "My brother passed not too long ago. He was the type to never turn down an experience or adventure, no matter how farfetched. I used to think he lived that way 'cause he was careless, but no. He cared more than any of us. Cared enough to make the most of his life. If finding the Mayor of Maxwell Street is the only thing I ever do, then I'll do my best. Lest the curtain close before I get the chance again."

Marta smiled at Nelly like a long-gone friend who only comes to mind during sad and lonesome times.

"The curtain's already closing, child," she said. "That's something else they never tell you until it's too late."

The sun-faced clock began to chime.

"Becky will be home soon," Marta said. A purposefulness came to her face. She sniffed, thumbed her nose, and Nelly felt that they were now—*finally*—talking business.

"Hear me, girl. I can tell you what I know about the people depicted in this comic, including the Mayor of Maxwell Street. I even know where you might find him. But there's something I need you to agree to first."

Nelly was never one to haggle; whatever the price, that was what she paid, without question. If Marta asked for something beyond her capabilities, Nelly knew she would compromise herself to get it.

"Anything," she said.

Marta paused, surprised at Nelly's quickness, but she didn't stall for long.

"Becky *cannot* return to Pensacola. No matter what happens to me. I didn't trek across half this country and abandon the man I love for her to go back to that life just 'cause she thinks she has no other choice. I don't know what you can do for her, but whatever it is, it must keep her in Chicago."

Against her better judgment, Nelly thought of options. A college education, maybe. Well-earning work. A community. She herself didn't have many connections in the city, but she knew people who did. Jay's face came to her once more, along with all the hands he shook and the eager smiles cast his way like coins down a lucky well.

"Becky's a good, smart girl," Marta rushed to say. "She's in school now, but she wants to be an accountant one day. Can you believe that? A Colored girl from the back side of Florida moving around the money of millionaires. And she'll do it, too. Whatever you contrive, it needs to give her a fighting chance at that life. A better chance than she could ever have back home."

Nelly could hardly help herself most days; what on earth could she do for some teenager driven out of the South by a white man's vulgar privilege? But she looked at Marta Harjo. Looked at all this woman had sacrificed, and accomplished, and sacrificed again. Even a thousand miles from home in the depths of despair, she'd found a way to express the brilliant essence of who she was. Nelly professed such resolve every day. Fought and deceived the people she loved the most to claim it. Now was her time to manifest it.

"I'll do what I can," Nelly said. "I promise."

CHAPTER NINETEEN

They huddled together under the awning of the Lake Forest train depot.

"Fucking Chicago," Sequoia said. "When they say rain, expect snow. When they say sun, expect rain."

"*Cold* rain."

It was early morning in high summer, and when Sequoia said to dress "for mischief and dancing," Nelly chose a daring beaded gown that left her feeling exposed in every way: bare arms, bare back, and all in black. That was Sequoia's most severe stipulation when Nelly approached her about getting into what Marta had called "the Ebony Masque"; whatever Nelly wore, it had to be black. If Marta's smoking-room intel was correct, this black and tan party would be Nelly's best shot at seeing the Mayor of Maxwell Street face-to-face. It was where the elite, lauded, and notorious of Chicago crossed color lines to mingle without society's oversight. And it was Nelly's most promising lead yet.

"Why didn't we just drive here?" Nelly asked while they stood with a handful of other black-draped men and women, all shivering together like crows on a telephone wire. "We could've figured it out, even without an address."

"Impossible," Sequoia said. "These things are *highly* exclusive. No one knows where they're held, not ever. You can't even get an invitation without a reference."

Sequoia was more comfortable in a tailored tuxedo, complete with top hat and tails. The smoke from her cigarette and its long-handled holder fizzed and faded as it melded with the rain. Sequoia was made for this flapper age. At times, Nelly had to tamp down a wonderstruck jealousy when she saw how her friend dressed and carried herself. Style had never been a priority for Nelly, but in Sequoia McArthur's company, she felt obliged to put her best foot forward.

"Now, look here, Ms. Penelope Sawyer." Sequoia stamped out what remained of her cigarette into the red brick of the train depot, leaving behind a pronounced black mark. "This Ebony Masque is not like the luncheons, or the teas, or anything they've thrown together for the 'grand season.' You'll be bumping noses with real Chicago society here, and I know how difficult banter can be for you in mixed company."

"By real society, do you mean white society?"

Sequoia gave her a condescending clap, congratulating her on an honest attempt at being snide.

"I mean that you will not be the richest person in the room," she said. "The last Ebony Masque was held in the Palmer Mansion, and the one before that had a Romanov for a guest of honor. This one is rumored to be hosted by one of the Lake Forest Big Four, who some of us thought would never stoop so low for social clout. I guess you can only be the most desirable debs in Chicago for so long, especially now that the war is over. Not to mention all the gangsters who show up at these things. Just be careful. Don't make me regret cashing in my biggest favor to get you into this party."

"This is your first time at one of these?" Nelly asked, a bit astonished. Sequoia had such an encyclopedic social knowledge that Nelly assumed that she always spoke from intimately personal experience.

"Not for lack of trying," she said. "Usually, the only Negroes who get invites are performers or artists. *Entertainment*, for lack of a more dignified word. All fascinating people that the white socialites and politicians can use to make themselves feel more cosmopolitan. When I mentioned that the wealthiest Colored heiress from sea to shining sea wanted in—even on such short notice—my contact practically broke out in tongues. I know that I owe you for being such a doll when I brought along Agathe to the Night Bazaar week before last, but this isn't an act of goodwill. I promised these people that you'd make sparkling company. So don't let me down."

Nelly wrinkled her nose at an image that felt uncomfortably similar to the hours she and Elder had spent reciting Paul Laurence Dunbar for her father's early investors.

"Why on earth would you want to be friends with such people?"

"Who said I wanted to be friends? When you haven't been born at the top of the hill"—Sequoia motioned with the butt of her cigarette at Nelly—"then everyone you meet is a rung that lifts you up. Just because circulating isn't taught in schools doesn't make it any less of an essential skill. By the by, your folks won't be looking for you later on, will they? 'Cause this thing can go for days, and if I have to turn around an hour after getting there just to make sure you're tucked into bed, I'll never speak to you again. Except to hex you."

Nelly would have laughed, but the more she thought on it, the more she believed that if anyone could lay a hex, it'd be Sequoia McArthur.

"I told them I was surprising Tomás," Nelly said. "We've spoken on the telephone a few times over the last week, but we haven't seen each other since I visited his home for that riding lesson. I said that his team had an early game somewhere outside of town, and I wanted to cheer him on."

Sequoia looked away, baffled. Her mouth turned down as though she'd walked past a trash bin and caught a bad stench.

"Well," she said. "That's quite adorable."

"Thank you. I think. And you can't mean to stay out here for actual *days*, right? Won't your own people wonder where you are?"

"Oh, my father doesn't give a baptized shit about what I do. I once stayed at a poker table in Cicero for four days straight, and he only cared that I didn't make it back in time for the Affirmation of Faith on Sunday morning. But it wasn't a complete loss. I ended up winning a necklace of real pearls right off the neck of some lily-white coal heiress from Wyoming. I mean, *really*. Someone from Wyoming has no business at a Chicago card table."

Nelly found that all exceptionally sad. Since coming to Chicago, she'd been blindsided by her parents' attention and care, suffocated even, but that was nothing compared to the void of indifference.

"Is that true, Sequoia?"

Sequoia cooed and brushed her hand against Nelly's cheek as an older sister might.

"Dear heart," she said, "don't cry for me. I don't plan on living this half-life forever. When you marry Tomás and move into your château, I will set myself up as governess for your little princelings. I meet all the basic requirements. I play piano, know parts of the *Odyssey* by heart thanks to Agathē, and I've been told that I'm fluent in French when I'm drunk."

Nelly was prepared to shoot Sequoia down, insisting that she and Tomás were just friends, but she stopped herself. If such a dream kept her friend from sinking into the wretchedness that was her "half-life," Nelly wouldn't dare undo it.

"I've been meaning to apologize," she said, "for the way Jay spoke to you at the club. He had no right to be so abrasive."

Sequoia's laugh was as scornful as poison.

"Child, I could count on one hand all the seconds I've wasted bemoaning Jay Shorey's miserable attitude. I've done my best to give that boy a wide berth since he bubbled up out of the quagmire, and you'd be smart to do the same."

Nelly ducked her head and said, "I don't know, Jay seems like a good enough time."

"Oh, sure. That's his job, ain't it? All I'm saying, Nelly, is to proceed with caution. I'm a partial connoisseur of diamonds, and everyone always forgets that diamonds are just rocks. Dull, blunt, boring, and fucking priceless. But people don't want priceless. They want flashy. And the knockoffs are always the flashiest."

A humming rose around them. The heads of the other party guests lifted and turned, stretched out almost into the road. Nelly peeked through the downpour herself and saw an unexceptional black bus lumbering toward them.

"Is this really necessary?" she asked when it came to a stop at the curb.

"I told you, exclusive," Sequoia said. "The anticipation is half the fun. Folk place bets on who the host might be, and one year, an ambassador from Argentina made literal millions when the odds turned in his favor. I don't reckon I'll make a fortune, but a few hundred at least, if I'm right. And I'm rarely wrong."

When the bus turned off of a wide, tree-lined boulevard toward the Lake Michigan shore some fifteen minutes later, people began to gasp and whisper and fill the vehicle with a palpable excitement. Even through the rain, Nelly could see the impeccable detail built into every aspect of the estate. Winding drives, manicured lawns, English gardens plucked out of a countryside pastoral. Like so much of what Nelly had seen of Lake Forest thus far, it strove to convince the guests that they were somewhere else. A grand deceit of brick and stone.

They pulled into a gravel motor court where already a queue of buses, roadsters, limousines, coupes, and even one or two horse-drawn phaetons snaked ahead of them. People filed out, all decked in the most extreme of black attire. A few took this to be a costume party and came dressed as panthers or masked plague doctors. Waiting in line at the main door were a fair share of Colored folk, but the distribution was not equal. Nelly understood now why Sequoia had such difficulty securing an invitation. To this crowd—whose knowledge of Negro society barely extended beyond Bill Robinson—Sequoia must have been as insignificant as trampled earth under their pointy-toed shoes.

~\|/~

Nelly felt a rush of cool air as she stepped through the mansion's foyer and into a marble-floored entrance bedecked in rose petals the color of fresh blood. The hall swam with a hundred conflicting sounds like music and shattering glass. The smell of spilled wine clogged the senses until Nelly had to stop to take it in at once with eyes wide open.

"Treat it like a fancy-dress dinner," Sequoia said with significantly less wonderment. If anything, the gaudy home and overwrought decorations only disappointed her. "Start on the outside of the plate and work your way in. If anyone, and I mean anyone, gets fresh, slap them. No questions asked. Remember to eat, or the very strong liquor they tend to serve at these things will inevitably go to your head. This isn't one of the Urban League's church socials. If you don't want to dance, you do not have to. If you *do* want to dance, somebody's aunt won't collapse from the scandal of you doing the fox trot with a white boy. That's what most of us are here for anyway."

It was not a lot to remember, and technically quite simple, but still, Nelly was overwhelmed. As much as she resented the rigidity of those "church socials," they had rules. The absence of rules was what gave the Ebony Masque such appeal and such peril.

Sequoia pushed against Nelly's shoulders until her back was straight, then pulled at the hem of her dress so it fell in that quintessential *Vogue* profile that turned her body into a geometric shape.

"You look like a million bucks," she said. "If all you do is float around without speaking to a soul, you'll be a screaming success. Now, if you'd tell me exactly what it is you're searching for at this party, I might have more relevant guidance."

Nelly trusted Sequoia, but the woman collected information as others collected rare coins. Nelly didn't savor the thought of rattling around in Sequoia's pocket, waiting to be used.

"Since coming to Chicago, I've realized just how much time I've wasted," Nelly said. "If my parents have their way, I'll be married and settled by Christmas. At the very least, engaged, and all for the sake of the family. Today, I want to do something for myself."

This—all of this—was profoundly selfish. Yet, there was a joy in being selfish. Without the weight of generational expectation, every second became a shot of electricity that lit Nelly from the inside out. Sequoia nodded her acquiescence and stepped away from her, pleased.

"Let's make a circle, then meet in the middle," she said. "I look forward to hearing all about your exploits."

Sequoia went left, into a murky room where people moved languidly, as though through water. Someone handed her a pipe. Nelly went right, toward the sound of music and dancing, and voices crying out for more.

No one had ever described Nelly as subtle, and she hoped they never would. So, when she saw Mayor Thompson himself—red-faced and laughing with Jack Johnson and his new young wife—she took the direct route and walked straight at him.

She'd been at the party for over an hour by this point and had done exactly as Sequoia had suggested: float. There were dozens of rooms, and salons, and libraries, and galleries, and each had a theme. Nelly passed by a gaming room, dark and smoky, where guests played cards or bent over billiard tables. Another room was put together in excessive defiance of Prohibition. Every type of alcohol was available and free for people to sample from a seemingly endless supply. Nelly could pour a stein full of a cognac once owned by Napoleon, if she wanted.

In the end, she found Mayor Thompson in a miniature dance hall. A band fit for the Cotton Club played, and white heiresses danced with Negro boxers, all dressed for state mourning. Nelly thought of her brother. When he said he wanted dancing at his funeral, this was what he'd envisioned.

Mayor Thompson had his back to Nelly, but the ten-gallon hat gave him away. The champagne she drank under the pretense of assimilation was full of bubbles that made her feel weightless and brave.

Lead with the name, she thought as she worked her way through the partygoers that bordered the dance floor. It was painful to admit, but Nelly's greatest asset here was her name. It got her through the door, lifted her high enough to stare these men and women who used Negroes as ornamentation in the eye. In this place at least, she could lean on who she was, or she could be buried under it.

By the time she saw the man, it was already too late. All she could do was brace herself as her shoulder collided with his.

Her champagne glass toppled and spilled in sticky streaks down the front of her dress, and the glass breaking against the floor was like a gunshot splitting the ambience. People screamed, the music stalled, and Nelly was left breathless and terrified by the sudden attention. She saw Mayor Thompson turn away from Jack Johnson, wrinkle his nose at the display, then move on to a different room.

The man who ran into her was apologizing, dabbing at her dress with the hem of his suit jacket. Her vision was full of him and his bumbling. Forgetting herself, she gave him a strong push back just so she could catch her breath.

"Shit," she said at the mess. Any attempt at fading into the tide of the party now seemed impossible.

"This is my fault, miss," the man said.

The most abrupt thing about him was his hair. A red so vibrant that it captured all the shades of autumn leaves. He was older, closer perhaps to Jay's twenty-four, or twenty-five years, but he had a full cherub face. When he smiled, buttons formed in his cheeks. It was a nervous, apologetic smile that dampened the intimidation of his stout body.

"As much as it is mine," Nelly said. "I wasn't looking where I was going."

"You did seem determined. Like you were coming for someone's head."

Nelly glanced again at the exit she just saw Mayor Thompson take, and sighed.

"Something like that."

"Let me get you another drink," he said.

As if summoned, a waiter came to stand at their side with a tray of tall champagne flutes.

"Thank you," she said as she accepted what was offered. "It tasted expensive. I hate to have spilled it."

The man looked at the broken glass, already being cleaned up by an innocuous member of the staff.

"It's not that expensive. Trust me. I've been coming to these things for years."

He didn't look like the moguls and socialites she'd envisioned as Ebony Masque regulars. He kept shifting from one foot to the other, adjusting to new shoes. His suit was refined, but ill-fitting and out of style.

"This is my first Ebony Masque," Nelly said before taking a long sip of the champagne, perhaps longer than needed.

"I thought so," he said. His eyes raked over her slowly, soiled dress and all. "I would've remembered you otherwise."

Nelly wasn't accustomed to flirting, especially not with some overeager white boy. She remembered Marta and her daughter Becky, and didn't know whether to feel flattered or trapped.

With an open hand, he said, "Rowan Byrne, at your service."

Nelly looked at it, skeptical, before accepting.

"Nice to meet you, Rowan. I'm Nelly."

He had a large hand with a firm grip that could have crushed her own with minimal effort.

"Are you a boxer?" she asked, then regretted not keeping that to herself. Nelly had no stamina for alcohol. It always managed to make her think and speak heedlessly.

Rowan also looked down at his hand—wide with freckled fingers.

"I've done some brawling in my time, but I wouldn't call that kinda thing 'boxing.' How about you, Miss Nelly? You one of the cabaret girls?"

Nelly's laugh was indecently loud.

"No," she said. "*Christ*, no. I dance like a cross-eyed chicken. I just came here with a friend. She let me off on my own to see if I'll sink or swim."

"And how are you managing so far?"

Nelly pulled at her wet dress and said, "Sinking. But maybe you're here to rescue me."

Rowan's attractiveness was rugged and unexpected. As she took another sip of champagne, Nelly reckoned that she liked looking at his face. He sported a bashful grin, but his green eyes were confident and assured of what they wanted.

"It's gotten a bit hot in here," he said. "Mind stepping out onto the veranda to cool down?"

The fresh air cleared the popcorn from between Nelly's ears and made her steadier on her feet. Rowan watched with a fascinated expression as she smoothed out her hair and dabbed at the sweat along her neck. Not disrespectful or lewd; just appreciative. More often than not, Nelly faded into the background when young men came to call. The mystique of male attention was lost on her, and even when she felt her most lonely and filled with desire, she didn't seek it out. But since arriving in Chicago, she'd begun to accept that her beauty had a weight and a price. And more importantly, it had a power.

She moved close to Rowan and let her arm brush against his.

"You mentioned that you're a regular here," she said. "I didn't think something as secretive and selective as the Ebony Masque was partial to 'regulars.' I still don't know how my friend got us invitations. I believe a blood sacrifice was involved?"

With his hands in his pockets and shoulders curved in toward his chest, Rowan cast the shadow of a little boy made to stand outside while his parents conducted business.

"The truth is, my *boss* is a regular here. He's got a thing for black and tan parties, and this is the most fashionable black and tan party in the city. I just come to make sure no one tries to start up trouble."

Nelly honed in on that, thinking of his brawler's hands.

"Do a lot of people bring their bodyguards to parties held in millionaires' mansions?"

Rowan smirked and said, "More than you think. Probably half of the men you see around here, out in the open, are bodyguards. The real bosses are hidden away, making deals."

Nelly looked out over the grounds with its gardens, and stables, and barns, and docks. There were countless places for groups of five or six to gather and hold meetings that would never be documented. No one to witness politicians sitting down with the gangsters they'd vowed to eradicate. Marta was right; if the Mayor of Maxwell Street was to make an appearance, it would be here.

Nelly turned her body full on toward Rowan's, practically "flashing her virtue," as her mother would say.

"Do you know a lot of these people? Being a regular and all," she said.

Nelly suspected it wasn't often that someone asked after his opinion. The men who were told to stick to yes and no answers were all secretly philosophers and theologians at heart.

"Oh, sure!" he said. "Once you get 'em talking, these Gold Coast types, they tell the whole story. Who're you trying to meet? I helped Gloria Swanson into a limousine once, if you want her autograph."

Nelly made her face stretch into a smile alive with enthralled wonder.

"Nobody quite so glamorous," she said. "You'll laugh, but I've always been interested in Chicago politics. I come from a small town where nothing exciting ever happens. All of the intrigue, the corruption, it's invigorating. I was hoping to speak with Mayor Thompson himself, actually—"

"Shit, I know Big Bill," Rowan said immediately. "The man's a blowhard, but he'll bend over backward for flattery and a pretty smile. I'd be happy to introduce you."

Nelly felt her mouth begin to salivate. She touched the swell of his pectoral and felt the muscle go taut under her fingers.

"Would you really, Rowan?" she asked with a breathy, exulted sigh. "I would *love* to ask him some questions about his campaign. Lord knows he's always been a friend to Colored folks. I'd be so grateful."

Rowan's smile took on a roguish edge. He closed the space between them and pressed until his barrel chest was flush against hers. His fingers began to play with the small silver beads of her bracelet.

"How about this, Miss Nelly?" he said. "Not only can I get you in front of Mayor Thompson; I'll give you a tour of city hall myself. But first, you have to dance with me."

"You wouldn't mind dancing with a cross-eyed chicken?"

His hand closed around her wrist, holding her to him.

"Not a cross-eyed-chicken as beautiful as you."

If Nelly wanted to be a journalist worth her salt, that meant doing anything and everything for the story, including flirting with unsuspecting white boys. So she pressed her luck.

Rising up on her toes to whisper against his ear, she said, "I'll do you one better. Introduce me to the Mayor of Maxwell Street, and you can take me out."

This close to his face, Nelly could hear the grinding of Rowan's jaw as his teeth slammed together. He pulled away just enough to look her in the eye.

"The Mayor of Maxwell Street?" he asked.

Nelly did her best impression of an innocent, reckless girl who threw around big words without knowing what they meant.

"If you know Mayor Thompson," she said, "then surely you know the Mayor of Maxwell Street. I know he's here somewhere, but I'm too shy to ask after him myself. I can't tell you how much it'd mean if you did this for me."

Rowan's eyes roved carefully over her face. Nelly wasn't a half-bad actor, but under such intense evaluation, she felt her veneer begin to crack.

"Yeah," Rowan said without a smile. "I might know who you're talking about. Why'd you wanna meet him?"

Nelly shrugged and considered biting at her lip the way she'd seen jazzy women at racetracks do when they were looking for a good time. "Like I said, I'm interested in politics."

Rowan made a cynical sound almost like a growl, low in his chest. Tersely, he said, "Dinner. Let me take you to dinner, and I'll get you in a room with the Mayor of Maxwell Street."

Nelly would have said yes if he'd gotten down on one knee.

Rowan's mood shifted as soon as they left the veranda. He guided her through the edges of the mansion in silence, telling her when to stop and when to turn, and only that. Like a man taking his last walk to the gallows.

Soon, they were staring down a long, windowless hallway. There were no doors on either side, but one ahead of them, at the end. Massive shaded red lamps ran in a uniform row down the center of the ceiling, and in the absence of natural light, everything was cast in a misty crimson. Rowan stood with hands in his pockets, his baby face oddly blank. When Rowan wasn't grinning, especially in this bruised light, he appeared quite vicious.

Nelly reached the door and ridiculously wondered if she should knock or just burst onto the scene like the villain in an Italian opera.

"We should hurry." Nelly started when she heard Rowan's voice directly at her ear. For such a thickset man, he could make little to no sound when he wanted to. "He isn't alone often. This may be the only chance you get before we're both missed."

Nelly remembered Richard Norris's condescension. The way he smiled at her with what he took to be respect. She would give him something to respect.

Nelly turned the knob, pushed the door open, and stepped inside. It was a bedroom. A perfectly preserved suite in an abandoned hotel. A single skinny window let in a sliver of gray light. Apart from the ghosts, there wasn't a soul in that room but her own. And Rowan's.

She heard the *click* of the door's lock just as a corded arm strapped around her body, and a hand pressed a kerchief over her mouth and nose. When she inhaled, her head filled with the smell of clean cotton.

Nelly often described herself as observant, aware, impervious to lapses in judgment. But now, here she was with a strange man, in a strange place, and he appeared to have every intention of killing her.

"Be still," she heard him say with disturbing calm. Nelly refused. She bucked and threw her head back again and again until she felt the dull pain of his nose cracking against her skull. Rowan cried out, and his hold loosened enough for her to take a loud, gasping breath. She broke free and went scrambling for the door.

When Rowan grabbed her again, he was done playing at tenderness. His bicep lodged against her throat as he locked his arm about her neck, and she knew there was no fighting out of that. "Brawler" that he was, his choke hold was surgically precise.

She clawed at him, kicked, let out voiceless screams, but he did not let go. Blood from his broken nose leaked down onto her shoulder, still warm.

"Be fucking still," he said again. "It'll be over soon."

The edges of Nelly's consciousness began to break off and float away. Her thoughts came in random, muddled pictures that smudged like ruined makeup. The scruffy old dog who patrolled One Oak. Elder's collection of empty perfume bottles. The ribbon Vivian Jones used to mark her place in her favorite book. Her mother's singing.

Rowan looked down at this wretched sight and dared to shake his head. Nelly reached to gouge out his remorseful eyes, but that took the last of her strength. The world came to her through a veil like frosted glass.

In the seconds before surrender, Nelly thought she heard her grandmother's voice telling her to pray.

CHAPTER TWENTY

She came to in darkness.

Nelly's mouth felt raw and packed as though with dry leaves, and her throat constricted when she swallowed. The tough, scratchy material affixed over her eyes provided full coverage, allowing for only the occasional gap of light. She was tied down to a chair. Something silky dug into her wrists and ankles every time she moved. Good knots, too. The more she struggled, the tighter they became.

Frantically, Nelly ran her mind back through the party. She arrived with Sequoia. Couldn't have been more than an hour ago. Or maybe two? She lost track of time while watching the dancing. And there was champagne. The white boy with fire-truck-red hair and his face in the bloody haze. Unbidden, she heard Jay's voice like a scratchy record in a neighboring room. *You're an amateur. This is dangerous and out of your league.*

No, she thought. *I won't give him the satisfaction.*

Now was no time to panic. She was somehow still alive, thank God. Not debilitatingly injured. She had the awareness of her right mind, and time to figure out what to do next.

There was a muggy smell: old books that needed airing, shelves that needed dusting. She heard the humming of an electric fan. She could even feel the sporadic gusts of hot air against her bare legs and arms. The circulation of the fan reminded her of someone breathing deep in sleep. But, no. There *was* someone breathing. Wherever she was, she wasn't alone.

"Hello?" she said softly. No answer, but the breathing picked up. She coughed and called out again. "I know you're there. I can hear you."

"You won't believe me," said Rowan, "but I am really sorry about all this."

"Rowan? What the hell is going on? Where am I?"

"Just answer their questions," he said, ignoring her. "Be straight and don't give 'em any mouth. If you tell the truth, they'll probably let you go unharmed."

Unharmed? Nelly strained against whatever bound her, hard enough to make the chair wobble.

Rowan went on talking.

"Just don't lie. Everyone always tries to lie right off the bat, and it never works out. My boss, he likes hurting people. He'd especially like hurting you. Don't give him an excuse."

Nelly closed her eyes to keep herself oriented. Strange how the room could still spin even when she couldn't see it.

Rowan's sigh was full of trepidation, as though *he* were the one bound and suspended like a cow waiting to be butchered.

"I didn't mean for any of this—"

"Fuck you!"

Nelly found her voice, and the curse bounced off the walls. Good. She hoped it made his ears ring.

There were footsteps in the distance. Several of them. Furious footfalls that meant business, all walking hard and fast toward her. Nelly dwelled on that word again—*unharmed.* She knew enough about herself to know she had no tolerance for pain. If they meant to torture her, she would tell all. She *had* to stay focused on the present; not possible, terrible futures. Nelly could answer their questions as sweet as any primrose belle. Maybe, if she stood strong in her resolve, they would even answer hers.

A door opened and a gale of sweaty, angry energy came through.

"This is her?" a new voice said. It was gruff and laced with a self-important authority. A king who crowned himself and thought that was the end of it.

"Not much to look at."

The harsh bluntness this next man used reminded Nelly of breeders describing a horse up for sale. That, more than anything, told her she was in some considerable trouble.

"What happened to your nose?" the self-crowned king asked in the blackness.

"She fought me," Rowan said. The room broke out in laughter, and Nelly tried to count the individual voices. More than three. Maybe as many as five.

"You're saying that little darky got the drop on the Wolf of West Englewood?" said someone with a pronounced Italian accent. "You've kept this boy too long out of the ring, Mikey. He's getting soft."

A hand touched her face, and she jerked away. Whoever this was smelled of the same spiced cologne that her father used. His hand grasped her chin and lifted until she was forced to extend her neck. She winced when she felt the burn of swollen skin close to her collarbone.

"You could've killed her, Rowan," a Negro man said.

Negro, Italian, white; this strange cast grew ever larger and more motley.

"Rowan's a grown man and knows his business," said that toneless auction-block voice. "If he wanted the girl dead, she'd be dead."

"Why are we even still talking about this?" This man was notably younger than the rest, younger than Rowan. His voice had an anxious edge that kept it high and trapped in his nose. "I mean, what have we come to? Mayor Thompson, you can't be in the same room as some beat-up, hog-tied Colored girl!"

Nelly stopped breathing. So, one of them was Big Bill himself. All of this could be a halfway blessing.

"Ah," the Italian said. "Seems the girl is paying attention."

"Then let's get on with it."

Footsteps again like infantry boots coming fast, then bright, assaulting light. Nelly squinted and felt a pulsing behind her eyes. Steadily, the room came into focus. It was a library or a study, which explained the smell. She was right about the number of men, too. Including Rowan, there were six of them.

Mayor Thompson sat in a thick leather chair while caressing a stubby glass of liquor. He wheezed as though fresh from a long walk and looked very put out by the whole proceeding. Behind him stood a fidgety young man who paced compulsively. Every time he glanced her way, he shook his head until his ears turned red. The Colored man stood to her right, by Rowan, who had a red rag pressed to his nose. Nelly knew this man. Another Chicago Colored society figure of some note. A lawyer, she thought.

The Italian was to her left. He sat back against a writing desk in one of the sharpest suits Nelly had ever seen. He cut an impressive figure; blond and brown-eyed, with bookish round glasses that peered out through the fog of his cigar smoke. He looked at her like a newly discovered butterfly pinned and dissected under a microscope.

Then there was the man who stood directly before her. Pale in every way. Patches of his skin blotched red by the sun. With him leaning in so close, Nelly could see thin pink scars across his cheek and throat. She did not have to guess that this was Rowan's boss, the one who wouldn't mind hurting her.

"The poor thing looks scared half to death," said Mayor Thompson without much pity.

"Good," the scarred white man said. He had what once might have been an Irish accent, stirred as it was within America's melting pot. "This will go a lot faster if she's scared."

His smile was like broken glass.

"What's your name?" he asked her. Nelly held her tongue. Would have swallowed it if she could. He fetched a chair from the writing desk, letting the legs screech as he dragged it against the floor. He sat down close enough for their knees to touch. She tried to squirm away, but it was no use. There was nowhere to go.

"You don't know who I am," he said, "otherwise, you'd answer me when asked."

The Negro man scoffed and said, "'Cause everyone should tremble in fear of the great Mikey Hannigan, right?"

Nelly's interrogator turned to look at the man and said, "Some people should, yeah."

She knew that name. Not well, but it scratched at a memory. She saw it printed in the pages of a paper once, next to photos of fighting in the streets.

"Maybe the Colts have lost some of their bite," said Mayor Thompson.

With that, she remembered exactly where she'd seen the name "Mikey Hannigan" before. He was listed as one of the white gang members who'd contributed to the madness and violence of the 1919 riots. And if Mayor Thompson's reference to "Colts" meant the infamous Ragen's Colts, then Mikey was in the Chicago equivalent of the Klan.

"Her name is Nelly," said Rowan. Nelly's eyes slid over to him. If Mikey Hannigan was Rowan's boss, that meant Rowan was a Colt just like him. She regretted every smile.

Rowan continued telling it all like a proper little traitor: "I cut her off heading straight for Mayor Thompson. She looked damn serious, like a runaway train. She said she was interested in politics."

The nervous man—some kind of a secretary, Nelly assumed— waved his finger at Rowan.

"At least someone is paying attention!" he said. "That was supposed to be your business, Mikey. You, and Tony!"

Tony, the Italian, held up his hands and said without a hint of remorse, "I was in the middle of a very good hand with three thousand dollars on the line. You could not expect me to abandon that just to make sure Big Bill didn't jeopardize his wedding vows."

Scattered laughter all around, except from Mikey.

"Nelly the Nigger who likes politics," he said, and the room went still. He reached into his pocket and pulled out a straight razor with a mahogany handle. The blade glinted clean and bright as silver.

Holding the straight razor aloft like an empty wineglass waiting to be filled, Mikey said, "Ain't no need to make this difficult. We'd settle with who you are and who you work for. And why you're using names like 'Mayor of Maxwell Street.'"

The blade was no prop. The edge was chipped from frequent use, but still sharp. Rowan coughed, and when Nelly glanced his way, he looked petrified. With his top lip caked in dried blood, she saw him mouth, *Please.* In answer to him, to Mikey, she shook her head. In a flash of metal, the tip of the blade was pressed against her chest. The steel was cold and sent chills rising across her skin.

"You know, growing up," Mikey said conversationally, "me and my friends used to think your lot didn't bleed red blood. We figured it'd be brown, like shit water. I know now that isn't the case, but sometimes I still wonder. Shall we find out together?"

The lawyer stepped forward, but not close enough to put a stop to things.

"What are you playing at, Mikey?" he asked.

"You all said you wanted answers, right? This is how we get answers."

Mikey's hand came up from nowhere and struck Nelly square across the face. The chair jostled from the force, and if not for the ties that bound her, she would have fallen to the floor. The pain flared out from her jaw, up into her hairline, down her neck. Tears came, and she couldn't even lift her hand to wipe them away.

"Feel like talking now?" Mikey asked.

Nelly's arms and shoulders ached as she righted herself. She pondered how she must look to these men. Absurd, and vulnerable. Primed to take this abuse. The lawyer turned his back, while Rowan had the decency not to look away. Mayor Thompson chewed on the ice in his drink, and it sounded to Nelly like her own skull breaking in two.

Before, she had been only afraid. But now she was furious, and that made her reckless.

Nelly snorted hard, then spat directly into Mikey's face.

"Che palle!" Tony said. "These parties get better every year."

Mikey wiped at the phlegm with the back of his hand, leaving a satisfying gray streak. Despite herself and the peril of her situation, Nelly smiled.

"Rowan, she come here alone?" Mikey asked. Nelly's smile collapsed in on itself.

"She came with another Colored girl," Rowan said. "Some pastor's daughter from the South Side. She's been in the opium room for a while."

"Fetch her for me, will you? Maybe she'll be a little bit more chatty."

Immediately, Rowan moved for the door.

"No!" Nelly's voice was hoarse, pleading. "No, please. She has nothing to do with this."

Mikey clapped his hands and said, "Ah, she speaks! Shame, we were starting to have a little fun."

Oh, she could speak, all right. And now that the seal was broken, she meant to say her piece.

"First off, how dare you?" she said to Mikey, to all of them. "And I'm not working for anyone, if that's what all of this is about."

The secretary sneered and said, "Watch that tone. Don't you know your betters, girl?"

"I've been restrained, beaten, and I thought that one with the bloody nose was going to strangle me! Is this meant to be the behavior of my betters?"

Mayor Thompson shrugged as though to say *She does have a point.*

The lawyer spoke with a hand to his chest, a show of deep repentance.

"Necessary precautions, Miss Nelly," he said. "I promise, as long as you cooperate, you will be treated with the utmost respect. You must understand, the Mayor of Maxwell Street is not a name that gets spoken often. Not out loud, anyway."

They suspected her of being some kind of spy, maybe a federal agent. If she came across as a threat, she had no doubt they'd make her disappear.

"I heard the name at a party," she said. "Someone mentioned him. I couldn't tell you who."

Mikey laughed. "Oh, you'll have to do better than that."

Tony put out his cigar in a half-full champagne glass until it hissed. He stood up straight and began to unbutton his suit jacket.

"Shall I give it a try?" he asked, and Nelly felt a desperate desire to run. Mikey Hannigan was violent and hateful, but this Tony was methodical. She could tell that by simply looking at him. Insulting his pride, spitting in his eye, would do nothing but feed his curiosity as he broke her.

She was grateful when Mikey said, "Sit your guinea ass down, Tony. I know how you hate getting your hands dirty. No, she'll lose the attitude and speak plain if she knows what's good for her. We can stay here all night."

As he toyed with the handle of the razor, Nelly had a sudden, gruesome vision of her own blood merging with the red dye of the very expensive rug under her feet. She could just see her mother standing at her back, shaking her head, complaining about how the stains would never come out.

The door opened and Jay Shorey came tumbling into the room. He took deep, full-body breaths, like a man who'd been running very fast for a very long time. Running as though for his very life.

When he looked at her, a warmth bloomed in Nelly's chest. She knew she was not safe, and yet, she felt *saved.* Jay's mouth moved, and she thought he might say her name, but then he took in the rest of the room. Sniffing hard, he wiped away the sweat from his brow and tugged on the hem of his waistcoat until it lay flat against his chest. He stepped in and closed the door behind him.

"Gentlemen," he said. "Apologies for being late. This place is more locked down than an heiress's boudoir."

Tony opened up a globe-bar to pour something clear as river water into a glass and said, "Eh, you'd know a bit about that, wouldn't you, Jay Bird?"

He winked as Jay accepted the glass, and the men began to laugh. Hee-heed and haw-hawed, as though beating and interrogating young women was the natural way to pass a weekend.

Jay brought the glass to his lips, and over the cut-crystal rim, he looked at her.

"Ah," he said casually. "Penelope Sawyer. We meet again."

Mikey wheeled on Jay.

"You know this girl, boy?"

The white men wouldn't have noticed, but Nelly, and possibly even the lawyer, saw the way Jay bristled at the word *boy*. He gathered his composure while taking a stiff drink and was soon himself again.

"I thought everyone at least knew *of* her by now. She's Penelope Sawyer, Ambrose Sawyer's daughter." Blank stares all around. "Oh, honestly, gentlemen, don't you read? Ambrose is the horse breeder from Kentucky," Jay explained. "The papers call him the 'wealthiest Negro in America.'"

The men all started grumbling at once, and Nelly felt the control begin to slip. Mikey was the only who didn't move. And neither did his razor.

"What the hell does that have to do with anything?" he asked.

Jay refilled his glass and said, "Nothing at all. Unless you mean to kill her, of course."

Rowan propped himself up against a bookshelf as though he might be sick.

"You make that sound like a problem," Mikey said.

"Well, her father is excessively rich," Jay said. "Since building his house here, he's given money to almost every union, organization, fraternity, and municipal service in the city. Including the police." Jay let the implication of that hang and swing. "If anything were to happen to his daughter, cops would be on you like flies on shit."

Mikey growled as he stood and stared Jay down. Nelly took her first real breath now that the blade was no longer pointed at her, but she tensed when she saw it pointed at Jay.

"I don't trust this kid, Bill!" Mikey yelled at Mayor Thompson.

"Stop waving that toothpick around, Mikey," the mayor said. "You don't have to trust him. He just represents similar interests, is all."

Jay nodded and said, "Dan would say the same thing."

"And where exactly is the stingy becchino, your god-uncle?" asked Tony.

Jay took a slow appraisal of Nelly's bruises, and his lip turned up in unfeigned disgust.

"This ain't exactly how he'd like to spend a Saturday. There's something perverse about seeing Negro-killers at black and tan parties."

When Mikey laughed, it was with his whole mouth. It reminded Nelly of a baboon's snarl.

"Killing her is not an option," the lawyer said. "But it's clear she knows too much already."

Jay walked through the room seemingly without direction. They all stood rapt as they watched, even Mikey, who looked at the ready to cut him.

"Maybe you're all asking the wrong questions," Jay waxed. "Yes, the young lady knows something. Can't put the genie back in the bottle, right? Doesn't much matter *how* she knows, though, but *why*." Jay finished his oration with a keen stare back at Nelly. He spoke without words. The subtle entreatment of his eyes told her to lie, and to make it damn convincing.

"What do you want with the Mayor of Maxwell Street, Ms. Sawyer?"

Nelly felt the glares of the other men digging into her, groping for whatever answer would satisfy them best, but she stayed focused on Jay and his confidence in her.

"I heard that he dealt in secrets," she said, "and I have secrets to sell."

"Whose secrets?" Tony asked. It was unnerving, bearing the force of his full attention.

"My own. I hoped to find him here, or at least someone who could point me in his direction."

"Someone like Mayor Thompson?"

Rowan hadn't spoken in a while, and not once to her directly since the others came in. Nelly didn't want to address him, to look at him.

"I thought he might have an association," she said to the portrait behind his head.

The secretary cried out for God's mercy.

"Well, this is just perfect. A damn banana split with cherries on top! Is that the going word, that Big Bill Thompson is the middleman for shysters like the Mayor of Maxwell Street?"

Mikey ran his straight razor along the hard line of his jaw. "Wouldn't be too far from the truth, I'd say."

Mayor Thompson stopped chewing his ice. He stared at Mikey, and Nelly saw the source of the man's imposing stature that was so effectual in politics.

"What put this slander in your head, child?" Mayor Thompson asked her.

A deep pit opened in Nelly's chest. She *could* reiterate that this was all just gossip floating around boozy parties that had no origin and no name, but that wouldn't get her home. Not even with all of Jay's stalling and posturing. She'd read once that the best and most believable lies were filled in with shades of truth. And so it had to be the truth—a half-truth even—or nothing at all.

She couldn't look one of them in the eye when she said, "I saw a comic in a newspaper."

Mayor Thompson stomped his foot, and it was like the quaking of an oak tree as it fell.

"That damn Negro cartoonist again!" he said. "I thought we dealt with that libelous woman."

"Apparently not well enough," said the secretary.

Jay held up his hands like a Renaissance jester announcing the end of a scene.

"The girl heard some gossip," he said with his back to her. "Folk hear gossip every day. Ms. Sawyer is harmless. Brazen as all hell, but harmless."

As the men chuckled together, Nelly saw the window closing. Saw herself fading behind Jay. He thought he was saving her, and perhaps he was, by making her seem small and insignificant. But Nelly knew she wouldn't have a chance quite like this again.

"It ain't all gossip," she said with a raised voice that cut through the mirth. They *couldn't* forget about her. Not yet.

Jay spun around and didn't bother guarding his disappointment. If he could, he'd slap a hand over her mouth to shut her up.

"The man exists, or you wouldn't be so quick to prove otherwise," she said. "I still have secrets to sell. I don't need to know who he is, or where to find him. Just pass along my message. In exchange, I'll share whatever price the Mayor of Maxwell Street is willing to pay with whoever sets up the meeting."

Jay spoke to her in a low, warning tone that labored not to betray their intimacy.

"Ms. Sawyer, you don't know what you're saying."

"I know enough, Mr. Shorey," she said. "Please, I don't want trouble with anyone here. I just need help, and it seems the Mayor of Maxwell Street is the only one who's worth talking to."

The men were quiet. The air was as still as the seconds before the horn blew and the race began. Then Mayor Thompson stood. He really was a massive man, almost as wide as he was tall, solid in a medieval way. He made a show of kneeling down until his knees creaked and he could look at her directly. His eyes were small pits within the expanse of his tanned, flat face.

"You listen to me now," he said. "I don't know what game you think this is, or what kind of talk you've been partaking in. But whether or not this Mayor of Maxwell Street fella exists, your search for him ends *today*. If I should personally hear of you sticking that cute nose in things that don't concern you, it won't matter how much money your uppity daddy makes. Old Mikey here will just as easily carve you up like a holiday roast for free. Is that quite clear?"

Nelly smiled. Pleasant and charming, a Georgia peach's smile. She hoped it was bright enough to hide the truth.

"Yes, sir," she said.

Mayor Thompson smiled back. He pinched her bruised cheek.

"There now," he said as he rose. "Let that be the end of it! And no hard feelings, of course, Ms. Sawyer. I bet on your father's horses every month, and every month, I earn a pretty penny without fail. I admire the man and his spunk. Go on, Mikey, turn her loose."

Mikey shook his head and began to look at each of them in turn, as though he were counting, calculating the odds of getting his way.

"The girl is obviously lying, Bill," he said. "Give me ten minutes. Alone. She'll tell us the truth of it."

Mayor Thompson slapped Mikey on the back hard enough to upset his balance.

"I trust Ms. Sawyer's word emphatically," he said. "Besides, if the dear girl is lying, then she'll learn that there are consequences for fibbing in my city. So, if that's finally *all*, I'm getting back to the party. Edith Wilson is scheduled to sing, and I'll be good God damned if I'm missing that."

He nodded again at Nelly, and mimed doffing his hat.

"A pleasure, Ms. Sawyer," he said. Then, to the rest of them: "Let's do this again, boys."

He left with his nervous secretary hustling at his heels. Without him, authority seeped out of the room. Nelly fully expected Mikey to resume his perusal of her person in his own time, in his own way, but instead, he cursed and motioned toward his fellow conspirators.

"Come on," he said, then began undoing the knot binding her left wrist. Jay took her right, and the lawyer and Rowan awkwardly knelt at her feet. Tony kept his seat, only lifting his head to observe them better.

"Apologies for not recognizing you, Ms. Sawyer," the lawyer said. "My name's Harold Sterling. I've been out of town, and I missed the chance to meet you at one of the cotillion events. My condolences on the loss of your brother. I would appreciate your father not hearing about this misunderstanding. I mean to run for alderman the year after next, and he's already committed a handsome sum to my campaign."

Nelly stopped his sniveling short and said, "He won't hear about this from me."

Mikey jerked at his knot with the tenderness of a sailor mending a fishing line.

"Oh, she'll keep this to herself, all right," he said. "Or she'll be seeing me again."

Nelly considered trying her luck at biting him.

"I certainly hope so," she said, sneering.

Mikey sneered right back, accentuating the poorly healed cut that split his bottom lip. He said, "Jay, since you're so familiar with the girl, make sure she leaves here, quickly, and without any fucking fuss."

"I can't just disappear," Nelly asserted. She trusted Jay, but she wouldn't put it past Mikey to ambush them once they were off the property. "I came here with someone. She'll ask after me if I'm gone for too long."

"I know the young lady," said Harold. "My family worships at Olivet. I'll let her know not to worry."

Nelly felt the blood rush back into her fingers and toes, and she flexed to clear away the thousand pinpricks across her skin. When she tried to stand, her legs buckled, and Rowan was the one to catch her. She snatched herself away from him so viciously, she almost fell again.

"Don't you touch me!" she yelled. "Ragen's fucking Colts, Rowan? You aren't satisfied enough tormenting Negroes out in the open, now you have to come poke at them like animals in a zoo? Do you flirt with Colored women just so you can harass their men later? Be quiet!" Nelly held up her hand to stop whatever silly apology he thought sufficient. "For you to turn me over to the likes of Mikey Hannigan makes me ashamed of how quickly I trusted you."

She didn't fight when Jay took her hand and marched them to the door. Tony stood at its seam, and Jay made a show of lifting Nelly's arm, implying the urgency of his mission. Tony smiled, then presented Nelly with a calling card of thick stock. Florid and heavily embossed, it read ANTONIO GENNA and the word *architect* below it, along with an address.

"The Mayor of Maxwell Street is not the only one who trades in secrets," he said. "If your problem persists, my brothers and I could be of assistance."

As bold as the sunrise, he lifted the thin strap of Nelly's dress and nestled his card against the crook of her right shoulder. It remained there like the tags they used to mark colts waiting to be sold.

That seemed satisfaction enough for the mafioso. He moved aside and waved at Nelly as Jay rushed them out the door.

Nelly's glance back was short, but in it, she saw her time in the library frozen in stark relief. The men were gargoyles. Hunched and snarling and churning with malice. All people who shouldn't even know of each other, never mind be acquainted enough to stand in a room and talk conspiracy. It was a moment stolen from a nightmare, and as suddenly as it had begun, with the shutting of a door, it was ended.

CHAPTER TWENTY-ONE

Jay dragged her behind him without pausing. Through halls and corridors and secret rooms. His steps were assured, as though he owned the house and his hands were the ones that placed every brick.

They ended up joining a steady flow of staff passing with ghostly silence through the inner workings of the mansion. Jay's world was a world of spirits, Nelly realized. She thought of the polo game and the mystical ease with which he appeared and disappeared from sight. Grand houses like these had so many unlocked kitchen and garden and cellar doors; Jay had no intention of waiting to come in through the front.

Nelly surfaced out of the mansion somehow back where she'd started in the motor court. The heavy smell of the outdoors and the glare of rain-washed roads made for a striking transition. She had no sense of time. Barely any sense of place. Days might have passed in that library.

The pain came to her in fits and starts. First, her muscles ached, and when she coughed, she immediately choked on the tightness around her throat. She lifted her hand and poked at the hot bruise. If that was Rowan showing restraint, she shuddered to think what actually murdering her might have looked like. She thought suddenly of her parents. They figured she was somewhere elegant, reeling Tomás in with her rod and hook. If something terrible had happened, they wouldn't think to look for her for days. By then, there wouldn't even be a body left to bury.

Nelly jumped when she felt Jay's hand on the indentation of Mikey's ring in her jaw. Right. She'd forgotten about that one, too.

"Excuse me," he said as she shied away. "May I?"

Nelly exhaled and nodded. His fingers came back to stroke the welt rising along her cheekbone. She leaned into his touch and the coolness of his fingers. After being treated so roughly, Jay's gentleness lulled her into a shell-shocked placidness.

"I'm sorry," he said. His eyes shone, wet and outraged. "Fucking Rowan Byrne. We're lucky Mayor Thompson was bored enough to get involved. Tony and Mikey are unpredictable, and Harold's just a coward."

Nelly went over their names again to keep them sharp. She could always place a face, but names came to her with difficulty. A branch of the Chicago mafia, the Irish gangs, politicians, and Colored ones at that. If she came to Richard Norris with this alone, he'd say that not only was she an amateur, but a delusional one.

Her laugh started dry and sullen, but soon turned hardy. Exhilarated. Laughing until tears came to her eyes.

"You're in shock," Jay said.

"Yes. Probably. This couldn't have gone any better."

"What?"

"I came here hoping something like this would happen," she said. "Okay, maybe not *exactly* like this—"

Jay's hand fell limp to his side.

"You're insane. What, did Mikey smack you so hard that it knocked your brain loose?"

Nelly lurched back and said, "That's a low blow, Jay."

"You could have died today, Nelly!" he screamed. "Jesus, Mikey 'the Butcher' Hannigan was seconds away from making you sing like a springtime sparrow, and you're what? *Happy?*"

"Yes! You couldn't find a more random group of men in a variety show, but somehow, they were all willing to kill over what I had to say. That's the very definition of a lead. Besides, I was faring fine before you showed up."

"*That* was fine?"

"They were giving me more than I gave. Your interfering shut me down. I'm not some princess in a tower, Jay, pining for you to rescue me."

Jay breathed hard, gasping between each word.

"What was your plan for getting out of there, princess?" he asked. "After they took their time cutting you open, wringing you dry for every lie you've ever told, what then?"

"You keep trying to scare me, but I'm not scared," Nelly said. "I'm not scared of them, or their threats, or their bogeymen. I told you that I can and will tell this story without you, and that's exactly what I'm doing. I don't need your help!"

"Oh, but you *do* need me. Without me, you'd be fertilizing Barbara

King's rosebushes right now. Should I list all the things each of those men have individually done to snuff out an inquiring mind? They don't just kill the problem. They kill the problem's family, its friends, its lovers, everyone who's ever shown it a passing kindness. Hell, if they find out that I lied for you, I'll be the next on Mikey's list. You're not the only fighter in this ring."

Nelly had never seen Jay so scared, and that was the crux of it. He wasn't even angry with her, not really. But his fear was a wild and menacing thing.

"I'm sorry for the risk you had to take to help me," she said, "but I will never apologize for executing a plan that worked. I came here to do a job, Jay."

"But why?" he begged. "*Why?* You talk about 'a job' like you don't know where your next meal is coming from. Look around, Nelly! Look at where you are, what you've just been through. Surely none of this can be worth it."

"It's worth it for my freedom!" Nelly crossed the space between them until she could stare directly up into his face, breathing in all his rage. "Why is it that you get to make something of yourself, and I don't? You'll say that you had no other choice; well, neither do I. I refuse to live and die in obscurity, Jay. This article is my first, maybe my only, opportunity to be something more than 'Ambrose Sawyer's strange little daughter' or 'so-and-so's strange little wife.'"

"You'd prefer it if I did nothing back there in the library," he said. "If I let it all unfold without saying a word. Even if it meant watching you die?"

Nelly swallowed down her instinct to soothe and to placate. She couldn't comfort him with a lie, so she'd honor him by telling the truth.

"Yes," she said. "If that got me closer to finding the Mayor of Maxwell Street, then yes."

Jay covered his mouth. There was a sopping desperation to him that made Nelly nervous. The little birdsong that remained sounded hesitant and lost in the aftermath of the storm, too afraid to sing.

"These are dangerous people, Nelly," he said. "Back at the Lantern Club, I asked you to let this go not because I didn't believe you could manage. Lord knows you've proven that today. But I could never stand by and watch them hurt you. If you walk into the fire, then damn me for a fool, I'm walking in after you."

The picture Nelly had constructed of Jay over the past weeks was a skewed and self-centered one. Surely a man who shucked off his own race when convenient was innately egocentric. And yet, here he stood, willing to risk it all for a practical stranger.

"I would never ask that of you, Jay."

"Of course not," he said with resignation. "But what else can I do?"

Jay's eyes went to her neck and the fading purple bruise.

"I could kill Rowan Byrne." It wasn't a threat, or a confession, or a wish born of a violent passion. It was a promise. As predestined as Judgment Day.

"I wouldn't recommend it," Nelly said. "I've heard he's a pretty good brawler."

Jay laughed without opening his mouth.

"You would know, wouldn't you, slugger? Damn good hit, by the way." He tapped the bridge of his nose, a bone that Rowan now had to stitch back together.

"Would you believe me if I told you Nat Love taught me how to throw a punch?"

This time, when Jay laughed, he showed his teeth. As much as she might try to downplay his interference, she knew that her danger was real. She might never tell him to his face, but she owed him her life.

Jay wiped the teary scales from his eyes and took in the empty courtyard.

"Since a cagey veteran of the Somme isn't shadowing you," he said, "I assume you came on the buses? Well, they won't be back till midnight. We'll have to walk."

"Walk? All the way back to the train station?"

Jay unbuttoned his black dinner jacket as he said, "All towns like these are the same. One road in, one road out. If we head west, eventually, we'll find civilization. It's either that or stay and wait for Mikey to change his mind."

He handed her his jacket, noting the runs in her stockings and the welts up her arms. She looked like something the cat threw up, then dragged in.

"Oh, come on," he said. "Don't tell me a country girl like you isn't up for a little hike."

The challenge stung, but it fulfilled its purpose. She snatched the jacket from him and set off limping down the manor's drive while his footsteps crunched on the gravel behind her.

"You know, Nelly Sawyer, I never pegged you for the ruthless type. But I think I was mistaken."

They were not long into their walk from the King estate. Most cars passed them by, but a few slowed down to stare at the seemingly white man escorting a Negro woman on foot into town. One man stopped and asked if they were lost. Jay had responded with all his cool dispassion and said, *Just walking my maid to the train. The wife took the Pierce-Arrow out for shopping and that was ten hours ago.* She thought he might apologize later for casting her as the servant in his hastily made-up drama, but he never acknowledged it. He created a role, and she was expected to play it.

"The cartoonist Mayor Thompson mentioned," Jay went on. "It's Marta Harjo, isn't it?"

Nelly stopped in her tracks.

"You know about her?"

"I'm the one who found her. At least the first time. How'd you ferret her out?"

It was not the image of Jay knocking at Marta's door and presenting her with a fatal choice that unnerved Nelly; it was how quickly the image came to her, and how quickly she accepted it.

She shook off this suspicion and carried on toward the western horizon, saying, "I used the census archives."

"No kidding?" Jay laughed at himself. "I never thought of that."

"Damn you, Jay!" Nelly said, harsher than she intended. "What the hell do you mean, that you found Marta the first time? What are you doing here? What are you *always* doing here?"

"Glad to see your thank-you is still so sincere."

"Don't do that. You know I'm grateful for your help, but your reach is long. Who are you to those men?"

The bright sun soaked up what was left of the rain, turning the air into a wet sheet that clung to their skin and mixed with their sweat. When Jay ran his hand over his face, he left it flushed and blotchy.

"When I first came to Chicago, I just wanted to be useful," he said. "My god-uncle, Dan Jackson, always takes care of his useful people. When Mayor Thompson had a problem with a clever cartoonist, Dan was more than willing to charge a fee for my help."

"You sound no better than a servant," Nelly said.

Jay was impeccable at morphing his face like fresh red clay into whatever visage he wanted. But one thing he could not hide was how gray he became in his moments of anger or disappointment. It was the most fascinating thing. Within seconds, he would age years. Another break in his chain that once seen couldn't be unseen.

"That's the wonder of America, Nelly," he said with harsh gusto. "Even servants can rise, if they work hard enough. As to why I'm here, at the Ebony Masque, I came with the talent. A lot found this gig by way of the Lantern Club. Crooners from Alabama aren't always comfortable in mansions with rich white folk. Bad memories, and whatnot. I like to offer my support."

Nelly remembered the way Jay radiated in the club. How every person gravitated toward him, flush with gratitude and a selfish awe. They looked at him like he could give them anything. Like *they* would give him everything.

"They pay you, don't they? To perform at the club?"

"Sure they do," he said. "Don't wince like money burns when you spend it."

"These people come here with nothing, Jay. You take the little they have, and for what? Five minutes on a speakeasy stage?"

"I offer access. Big band leaders look for talent in the Lantern Club. If the talent makes good at the Empire Room, or the Panther Room, or the Paradise, those big band leaders might offer me a cut of the earnings. Out of thanks."

Nelly scoffed and said, "Shouldn't you help poor Negroes up from the South out of the goodness of your heart?"

Jay scoffed in turn: "Who does anything out of the goodness of their heart, Ms. Sawyer?"

They carried on in the silence. There was a noise to it, though. A mosquito's maddening buzz.

"Why did you call me ruthless?" she asked when she could hold it back no more.

For a long while, Jay did not speak. She thought maybe he hadn't heard her, or rather, didn't want her to hear the truth of what he had to say.

"Marta swore not to publish anything else," he answered eventually. "Swore not to tell anyone that she was behind those cartoons. You saw how Big Bill reacted when you said she was still active. And yet, you gave her up. I was watching your face, Nelly, you didn't hesitate."

It struck Nelly like an accusation, but Jay did not look remotely judgmental. As the corner of his mouth turned up with a twitch, she saw that he was delighted.

"I had to," she said feebly. "They needed to hear something easy to believe, or I would've been in more trouble than even you could talk me out of."

"Isn't there some kinda code among you newspaper folk about turning over sources?"

It wouldn't have hurt more if Jay slapped her across the face.

"The comic that led me to Marta was published months ago! I didn't tell them where to find her, and I definitely didn't say that she was still making cartoons."

"Oh, but they'll be looking for her now. The warning was meant to be just that: a warning."

Nelly stared at Jay with her lips pressed hard together. She wanted to properly stand up for herself, but there was nothing to endorse. She had known the risk when she brought up Marta. She was no better than an animal playing with its food, letting it go on believing in the hope of life.

Nelly said, "You found her once before. Could you find her again? Get a message to her? I'd do it myself, but I figure this lot will be watching me now."

"That's a big ask, Nelly."

Nelly reached out and grabbed his waistcoat. He made to back away, but she was stronger than she looked.

"I can't take back exposing Marta," she said, "but I can at the very least give her a head start. I made a promise."

When Jay spoke, the mix of gin and old coffee made his breath pungent.

"I just told you how those men who order up murders like lunch rely on my discretion, and now you're asking me to betray it?"

"Whatever they're paying you—"

"I don't want your money." Her mouth snapped shut. "I'll try to get to Marta, but that won't erase what you did. You're a Negro woman born to more opportunities than our grandparents could fathom, and yet you'd risk life and limb for a fucking lead. You don't have to do any of this."

"Is that all there is to life?" Nelly asked. Her tears smarted as they filled in the cuts on her face. "What's the point of having choices if you can't go after what you want?"

Nelly let him go. She wished she could run from him, but she could only walk, swiping at her face as she went. The last thing she wanted in that instant was to see the pity in his eyes.

"I'll help you."

His voice was a whisper, and she had to stop and turn to hear him clearly.

"What?"

"With the Mayor of Maxwell Street," he said. "I'll help you."

Jay's long legs bridged that distance in seconds. He was still so young. Men twice his age spoke to him as they would an equal. But here—surrounded by ancient trees on an abandoned road—his stylish clothes seemed more like a poorly fitted costume.

"I remember when the cost for my freedom came due," he said. "Christ forgive me, but I paid it. I think sometimes of what my life would be if I made the right choices, the safe ones, and it makes me sick. I'll spare you that reverie, Nelly Sawyer, if I can."

His words came out like a foreign language. She stared without understanding.

"But you said it was dangerous for you. You were terrified the last time I asked for your help."

"Yeah, it is dangerous. But it's more dangerous for you. If I never see you at the mercy of men like Mikey Hannigan again, it will be a day too soon."

Nelly moved fast. Jay was tall, so she had to jump to hug him properly. At first, she simply hung there, clinging to his shoulders and breathing in the old-world texture of his cologne. Soon, his arms closed in around her, and even when she dropped to the ground, he did not let her go.

CHAPTER TWENTY-TWO

The afternoon crowds set the sleepy suburban train station to buzzing. Workmen, businessmen, families dressed for an afternoon's travel. And so many Colored women. Young and old, they filed off of the incoming train with heads bent under their hats, and eyes looking everywhere except at the white folks who brushed by them. It stunned Nelly, how so many could be so blatantly ignored. These women who doubtlessly cleaned their houses, cooked their meals, and rocked their children to sleep at night.

"I wish you'd let me take you to the Lantern Club," Jay said as they waited in line to buy tickets back to the city. They stood behind a battalion of loud-talking young men in identical white suits, which made the process slow going.

"I asked Murphy to wait for me at the station," Nelly said. "He's been there for hours already, and I can't just leave him with no explanation."

"But you also can't go back home without cleaning up. You look like you've gone three rounds with the champ."

"Your charm is as eviscerating as ever, Jay."

Despite her brittleness, Nelly figured that he had a point. She'd only seen her reflection in the windows of the station as they entered it, but that was more than enough. Her cheek was visibly swollen where Mikey had struck her, and the bruise around her neck was inflamed and angry. Jay tied one of his handkerchiefs about her throat to offer some concealment, but the contrast of her shimmering black dress and the white linen ascot made her appearance all the more obvious. She looked very much like someone who'd been in the wrong place at the wrong time.

"I'll be fine by the morning," she said. "As long as I avoid my parents, no one will be the wiser, and that won't be hard to do. So, when do we start?"

The line moved an inch, and Jay whispered a curse.

"At this rate, we'll miss the train," he said, distracted. And then, "I'm sorry, *start?*"

"With looking for the Mayor," Nelly said.

Jay's expression was bewildered, and the dark bags under his eyes were stark in the clear light of day.

"Don't get ahead of yourself, Nelly. I'll be in touch when I have something to share, but in the meantime, *do nothing.*"

"Do nothing? If you think I'm gonna sit still while you play maestro, you have another think coming."

The line moved again, and someone behind gave Nelly a none-too-kind jolt forward, directly into the back of one of the boisterous young men.

He turned around immediately.

"I beg your pardon, miss. Are you quite all right?"

Nelly knew that voice. The excitement she felt came on suddenly, sincerely, and she reached out to grasp his hand. Beneath the brim of his silk-lined checkered cap, Tomás Escalante y Roche smiled.

"Ms. Sawyer," he said on an exhale. His smile grew, and his other hand closed in on top of hers. Again, with an infectious enthusiasm, "Darling Ms. Sawyer!"

Nelly was struck by his attractiveness all over again. His grin stole her breath and made her thoughts and words jumble together until all she could focus on was the color of his eyes.

"I am so sorry," she said before anything else. "My behavior has been inexcusable. I could have at least visited you."

"Think nothing of it. You did warn me that I'd have to fight for your time this summer. I'll endeavor to make a more heroic effort."

Next to her, Jay cleared his throat. The look he gave her was teasing and wicked.

"Pardon my manners," she said to Tomás. "This is Jay Shorey, he's a . . . well?" She didn't exactly know how to introduce Jay. Gangster? Headhunter? Speakeasy proprietor?

"Local entrepreneur," she finally settled on. Jay nodded slowly, impressed. "And Jay, this is—"

"An internationally acclaimed number one needs no introduction," Jay said. He held out his hand to Tomás, who accepted it eagerly.

"C'est toujours un plaisir de vous regarder jouer, monsieur, ou préférez-vous l'espagnol?" Jay said in smooth, impenetrable French. Tomás's hand stilled, and he stared at Jay with a slack jaw.

"English is quite fine," Tomás said once he'd recovered from the shock. "I'll take any opportunity to practice."

"And how do you know our 'darling' Ms. Sawyer?" Jay asked, waggling his eyebrows at Nelly. If Tomás noticed Jay's callow goading, he didn't let it show.

"She did what no one has dared since we landed in the United States," he said. "She told me I was mediocre."

Nelly remembered how cutting she'd been when they first met, and felt a strange embarrassment.

"It was only a suggestion. Tomás owns one of my family's horses, and I thought he might adjust his form to bond with her better."

Tomás rested a hand on Nelly's shoulder with the intimacy of old friends. His thumb—absently, it seemed—brushed against her clavicle. Jay's frozen smile was for Tomás, but his eyes were seething and intent upon her.

Oblivious, Tomás said, "You are too humble. It is thanks to you that we won today's match against the North Shore Club. Estrella runs like a dream, Ms. Sawyer. Your touch seemed to invigorate her."

Nelly simpered. There was no help for it. All the derring-do that had carried her through the day faded when Tomás cast his unconstrained joy upon her. Jay made a trivial, disbelieving noise that became lost in the rush of the train station.

"And you, Mr. Shorey?" Tomás asked. "How are you and Ms. Sawyer acquainted?"

Before Jay could answer with some brash innuendo, Nelly said, "We're part of the same social circle. Jay has quite the standing in the Colored community here in Chicago, don't you?"

Those words soured as Nelly spoke them. For a sobering instant, she saw herself standing in a flock of other Negro women with impressive husbands and sons, discussing the "community" and one's standing within it.

"Are you both returning to the city?" Tomas asked.

"We're just leaving a party. Mr. Shorey was kind enough to escort me home a bit early," Nelly said, and immediately knew she'd said too much. If this got back to her parents, there would be questions, and she'd be slow to offer up any believable answers.

"Then you're free this evening?"

Nelly had no good reason to refuse. In fact, she didn't want to. She warmed at the thought of passing an evening in Tomás's company. Compared to what she'd just experienced back at the Ebony Masque, it would be a relief. Besides, her parents already figured she was off somewhere adorning Tomás's arm. It would fulfill their every expectation if she stepped out with him that evening. Would they even notice her roughed-up appearance? Would they even care?

"Yes," she said. "Yes, I guess I am."

Tomás clapped loud enough to make Nelly jump. "Wonderful! Then please, allow me to stake my claim and treat you to dinner. I owe you a proper meal after that luncheon fiasco. My pride has been slow to mend ever since."

His charisma grew all about Nelly like a coiling vine, making his excitement her own.

"Very well," she said. "As long as you promise not to cook."

"Not tonight. The Marine Dining Room makes a much better braised chicken than me. Of course, Mr. Shorey, you're welcome to join us."

Tomás remembered Jay just as Nelly had forgotten him. He stood silently throughout their banter, watching it with a sniper's focus. He caught every word, every glance, that passed between them and cataloged it away. Nelly had seen this look in him before, when observing others—but never when observing her.

"I would hate to impose," Jay said, but it wasn't a real objection. He gave Tomás all the time he needed to offer a more vigorous invitation.

"It's no imposition at all," Tomás said, right on cue. "I'm curious to hear more about your entrepreneurial pursuits, Mr. Shorey. Business has always been a fascination of mine, especially American business."

Jay held up his hands as though he were helpless to refuse and said, "It's a date, then."

He looked down at Nelly, and the way the light caught like a blaze in his eyes brought up an old memory in her: when she surprised a bobcat feeding in the hills at the edge of One Oak's property. Those piercing, intelligent, savage yellow eyes as it pulled the intestines out of a deer's stomach.

"Jimmy?" A voice spoke among the dozens. Small and insignificant. Then, again, louder: "Jimmy Blue-Eyes?"

Jay's face went white. A real white. The white of a cold, frozen death.

He spun around, and behind him stood a young Negro woman about his age. Dark-skinned with a cleft upper lip and cheeks that turned up when she smiled. And she *was* smiling at Jay. It was a jubilant expression that Nelly might expect to see on the faces of those dead and gone when they meet again in heaven. The woman's hands shook as she clasped her pocketbook.

"Sweet baby Jesus," she said. Her Southern accent was undiluted. "It *is* you. I never thought I'd see you again."

Jay stared the woman down, looking as terrified as a sinner facing the reaper's bloody scythe and all the wrongs that a lifetime could wrought.

The woman ran at Jay and took his limp hands in hers. Closer now, Nelly could see that she was crying. Large, honest tears that smudged her beautiful face.

"Oh, Jimmy. I should've said something. I should've done something. Lord knows Miss Cecilia was a liar to the end. And your poor old uncle."

"Stop," Jay said, but the woman didn't seem to hear. She went on, clinging to Jay all the while.

"We thought you dead all these years. I swear on my momma's grave, I've cried over how we treated you and your people. I pray every day for forgiveness, and now here you are, standing right 'fore me as whole as Sunday morning. Praise God, Jimmy. Praise God!"

"Ma'am, you are mistaken." Jay's voice was mechanical and soulless. "You do not know me."

The woman shook her head, sending tears in every direction.

"Of course I know you. We grew up together, Jimmy. It's me. Rose Claxton, Martha's girl. You *must* remember me."

"Ma'am, I do not!" Jay pulled his hands out of the woman's grasp with such force that she stumbled forward. "I told you once before that you don't know me. How could you? Do I need to repeat myself?"

Nelly didn't recognize the acidic cruelty that came out of Jay. Or, at least, she didn't recognize it *in him*. She'd heard it plenty of times from the white boys who frequented the derbies in the throes of a tantrum when a Negro porter dropped a bag, a Negro waiter spilled a drink, a Negro laundress failed to get out a stain. It was as menacing as a raised first.

The woman stood hyperventilating in the middle of the train station.

"Sir," she said. She shrank right before Nelly's eyes. "I apologize, sir. I took you to be—"

"I don't care!" Jay snapped. "Where you come from, manners must not be part of the basic education. Let me enlighten you. Running up to strangers and accosting them is unacceptable in this city. Or would you rather hear this from the police?"

The woman gasped, turned, and ran out of the train station. As she left, the hubbub picked up again. Everyone—Colored, white, and otherwise—went on about their business without a second thought.

When Jay turned back to face her and Tomás, his features had gone lax and sickly, the clammy pale of a dying man.

"Forgive me." He said this to Tomás. "I just remembered I have some business here in Lake Forest. Mr. Escalante y Roche, would you mind escorting Nelly back to the city?"

Tomás's European, gentrified etiquette had him rallying quickly. He moved toward Jay, partially blocking Nelly's body with his own.

"Of course, Mr. Shorey. It was a pleasure to meet you."

Tomás held out his hand, but Jay was already away from them. The city-bound train screeched as it came barreling into the station. The noise was like the helpless screams of a wounded animal. A deer caught in a bobcat's maw, crying out for mercy as it died.

CHAPTER TWENTY-THREE

It took nearly forty minutes for the train to leave. The ticket collectors, the porters, and even the conductors were all at a baffled loss for what to do.

"I do not see what the issue is," Tomás said. "I purchased two first-class tickets. By law and logic, we should *both* be seated in first class."

Nelly stood beside Tomás, silent, watching him come face-to-face with the bullheaded ideals that ran like lifeblood through every vein of American existence.

"I understand that, Mr. Thomas," the conductor said. He was a burly man who, in Nelly's deduction, would gladly manhandle them off the train if he had to. "And we'll be happy to seat *you* in first class with complimentary service from the dining car. But your companion's just not welcome. It's the policy of the company."

"Are you liars as well as fools? I ride this train almost every day, and I cannot count the number of Negroes I've seen traveling to and from Chicago in peace."

"Yes, sir, in the third-class coach, or even second. Not in first class."

Tomás exhaled like a fuming bull. Nelly would not say so out loud, but some part of her was enjoying this. It was horrifically satisfying to see a stranger beat at Jim Crow and point out all its malicious flaws, but to no avail. His futile frustration was like an exorcism of all Nelly had ever felt at the hands of such people, but could never express.

One of the ticket collectors held out his hands, pleading, and said, "We would be happy to reimburse you."

"I don't want to be reimbursed!" Tomás yelled. "I want to take the seats I paid for and enjoy a pleasant ride home. Me, *and* Ms. Sawyer. Deny us this, and you will deny us our basic rights as passengers. I'm prepared to stand here all day and stall this train indefinitely until you either seat us or force us from it."

Tomás crossed his arms, daring someone to uproot him. The conductor looked over Tomás's shoulder at Nelly and sniffed. As though he could clear his nose of her smell.

An older gentleman with a thick gray beard and a pre-war suit stood in first class.

"I have a very important meeting within the hour," he said. "If this train is not moving by then, I will hold this company personally and fiscally responsible."

Nelly did not know this man, but his words—more so even than Tomás's—inspired some true ire. Passengers began to mention appointments, and litigation, and forfeited jobs. The conductor swore and slapped his hand against his knee.

"Fine," he said. "Fine! But you two are the last off this train when we pull into the city, all right? We can't give others any ideas."

Tomás's smile was triumphant. He looked back at Nelly, as though expecting a full complement of gunfire salute. She offered only a small, appreciative nod.

Instead of wooden benches that gathered everyone together like sardines stuffed into a tin, in first class, passengers sat in plush green armchairs that swiveled away from the aisle. Airy and elegant, it represented the height of rail travel. And the barrier remained open so everyone who could never afford such accommodation would see it and dream. The engine sounded, jolted, and they were moving south to lackluster applause.

"What a horror," Tomás said once they were seated. "Is this what you experience every time you travel, Ms. Sawyer?"

He appeared engorged with his own heroics, having defied evil and defended her honor. It was adorable how easily he assumed all such problems were now solved.

"Actually," Nelly said, "every time I've traveled by train, it's been in a private car. Whether or not the 'company' allows Negroes in first class hasn't really mattered when we're the only ones on the train."

Tomás simply stared. He looked astonished, and even a bit suspicious. Nelly winked to break his trance.

"Well, Ms. Sawyer," he said as he leaned back in lush seating. "Consider me humbled. Of course, how could I assume that one such as yourself would travel with such meager trappings?" He waved around them at the mahogany siding, crystal sconces, and velvet drapery. "I must seem quite the bumbling fool to you."

"Not at all. You took a serious risk standing up for me. They could've booted you off the train, or worse."

Tomás shook his head, dismissing the risk and Nelly's concerns easily. Such a thing, in his mind, was practically unfathomable.

"I travel mainly by train now," he said. "Days at a time, and all across this grand country. Such routine makes it easy to forget that I was refused access on a train once. It's been so long now, sometimes I wonder if I just imagined it all."

Where normally Tomás's features were soft—princely, even—now they were chiseled and hard enough to chip a tooth on. He picked at a loose seam on his sleeve until the pattern unraveled.

"In Europe?" Nelly asked.

"No, even though France and England have their own senseless biases to contend with," he said. "It was at home. In Mexico. I was six or seven then. My mother came from the valley, and her people named themselves Yoeme. What you might call 'Indians.' The government took it upon themselves around that time to either move them or exterminate them. My mother wanted me to know her family, her people, before they were gone forever. She resolved to take me into the valley. We arrived at the train station in the early morning. When my mother tried to purchase tickets, the conductor called her a bruja and me a bastardo maldito, then spat on her cheek. Even knowing that my father could tie him to his saddle and drag him through the desert until his skin came off in ribbons, this man refused my mother. Not so different from the way that surly gentleman refused you, Ms. Sawyer. But she didn't rage and threaten all of my family's wrath. Just took my hand and told me to walk. She had to carry me after a while. I remember resting my head on her back and pretending to sleep as she cried. It was dusk when my father finally caught up to us and brought us back to the villa. I didn't see her leave it again until they dragged her out."

Tomás had remained perfectly still throughout his story. The only thing about him that stirred was his eyes. They twitched across the outside landscape with a frantic quickness. As though they could not settle on any one thing in the blur of an ever-changing world.

"Dragged her out?" Nelly asked. Tomás looked away from the window and down at a gold-banded ring on his pinky finger. It was a cameo depiction of a woman's face carved into coral the color of fresh blood. He turned the ring around until it left a perfect trench in his skin.

"I was not meant to see it," he said. He ran the pad of his thumb over the details of the woman's face. Long curled hair and a solemn mouth set in a hard, resolute line. "It all happened very late at night, but her screams woke me. I saw her pulling at my father's shirt until the fabric tore while men with machetes hauled her away. They packed my mother up like an animal carcass and threw her in the back of a wagon. My father watched them leave. There wasn't even the pretense of a funeral in the days that followed. She was merely gone, and we all were given regimental orders to go on without her."

Nelly felt the resentment in him. She heard it in the serrated edge of his voice, an edge she carried within herself at times. She, too, was expected to move from day to day as though Elder had never existed. As though his death was a bad smell that refused to dissipate, so after a while, you lived in it. Ignored it. Refused to give it a name.

She couldn't watch Tomás wrestle with these feelings—long

buried and raw—alone. She took up his hand, and he held fast.

"May I tell you a terrible secret?" he asked, but he didn't wait for her permission. "I've allowed my society friends to believe I joined the war in Mexico for justice. Or freedom, or purpose, or—Dios me libre—'adventure.' In truth, I went back to find my mother and defend her as a man in a way I never could as a boy."

"What happened to her was not your fault," Nelly said. As clear as that was to her, she suspected no one ever bothered to make sure that was clear to him.

"I know that. And it's not my father's fault. I know he loved my mother once. Marrying her against his family's wishes was tantamount to a sin, and the deception broke him in the end. But that will never excuse his cruelty."

"Did you find her in Mexico?" Nelly asked. Silently, she added, *Alive.*

Tomás gave a her a sad smile and said, "No. What I did find was a love for my homeland. I didn't even speak fluent Spanish when I joined the Revolution in 1915. It was what I needed to do. For myself, and for my mother's memory. Although I still hope that my father will redeem us both and tell me where I might light a candle for her soul."

Nelly was unaccustomed to death, for Elder was the first relative she could remember losing. The concept still baffled her; how someone could be there, and whole, and filled with the very essence of life one moment. And dust the next. She couldn't begin to comprehend all the loss Tomás experienced fighting and killing in a revolution, all to avenge a ghost.

"What's your mother's name?" Nelly asked.

"Mecha is the name she was born with," he said, "but when she was baptized into the Catholic faith, she changed it to Josemaría."

Nelly said, "I'm not a Catholic. I can't light a candle for her soul. But at One Oak, we have a crape myrtle tree that folk sometimes hang a blue bottle on to honor the lost. I'll add a bottle for Josemaría when I return. And one for Mecha, too."

A tension like a taut guitar string thrummed around them. Tomás began to lean forward, and for a charged second, Nelly thought that he might kiss her. But the moment passed with the shudder of the train. He released her to straighten his tie and dab the wet sheen from his eyes, and when he smiled, Nelly was stunned into sitting up straight by how similar he looked to Jay. It happened lightning-strike fast, and she couldn't pinpoint where the similarities ended and the differences began. And yet, the resemblance was there all the same.

"Goodness," Tomás said with a self-deprecating laugh. "I don't think I told the priest quite as much at my First Communion. For your sake, I pray your other suitors aren't nearly as depressing."

Nelly's tongue suddenly felt very heavy. As though a dry river stone had settled on the floor of her mouth.

"Suitors?" she asked. She sounded asinine—she *felt* asinine.

"Forgive me," he said. "I know our time together has been short, but I thought my intentions were clear."

Nelly squeezed her mouth shut until the muscles in her jaw clicked and groaned.

"You're the first to say as much to me. To me directly, not to my mother or my father. Or to assume that nothing needs to be said at all."

"I would never presume. I daresay, I don't think I've even met your parents. How disgraceful of me."

The devious turn to his smile told Nelly that he didn't find that disgraceful at all.

"Don't succumb to your shame so quickly," she said. "You'll meet them tonight. When you pick me up for dinner."

"Yes." The word came from Tomás as a yearning sigh. A fond nostalgia for something yet to occur, and with it, that stench of a child's fear was washed away.

The outside transitioned from suburb to city. Less grass, less green. More smokestacks and the patina of sunlight on the glass facades of downtown buildings. A double rainbow had appeared in the sky. It glowed, solid enough to touch, and Nelly allowed her mind to glide down its vivid spires into the diamond-studded lake in the distance.

"That gentleman you were with in Lake Forest, Mr. Jay Shorey." Tomás pronounced the name slowly, and with all the proper inflection. "What manner of business is he in?"

Nelly was within a hair's breadth of forgetting that unpleasantness with Jay. She had no idea if the way he'd cut that woman was the extent of his capabilities, or just the glassy surface.

"That is the sphinx's question," she said. "The only one with the real answer is Jay himself. I only know that he manages a nightclub on Maxwell Street."

"I see," Tomás said. He began to turn that ring round on his finger again. He flexed his hand when it began to cramp. "I suppose that explains it."

"Explains what?"

"I felt— I'm not sure. I felt like a book that knew it was being read in his presence. I have only ever felt that way with men who want me to be comfortable so I can be better served. More willing to buy whatever they have to sell."

Tomás was only speaking plainly. What he experienced was what everyone sensed when favored with Jay's attention. Still, he'd caught on to a scent, and Nelly felt a defensive responsibility to put him off of it.

"That's why his patrons are so loyal," she said. "He knows what you want before you can even ask for it. You should visit his place; it's called the Lantern Club. Great music, great liquor, a huge space for dancing. My first time was like walking through Alice's looking glass."

Tomás's closed-mouthed smile pushed up his cheeks and slanted his eyes.

"Sounds thrilling."

Nelly heard the period on the end of that. A *fin* to the conversation that she was secretly thankful for. She turned back to the window and the rainbow, but it was a waning memory now. Out of the corner of her eye, she saw Tomás. He was biting down on his lip until the skin turned white, staring right at the bruise still raw across her cheek.

CHAPTER TWENTY-FOUR

So, this is where you hide."

Jay's eyes went to her immediately, and they were panicked. The eyes of a fox pinned down under a clear, open sky. His hand beat out a rhythm on his chest like an old woman trying to restart her own heart.

"Fucking hell, girl," he said with a relief so tangible that it deepend his voice. "I could've killed you."

"With what? You don't carry a pistol."

"You know that for certain?"

"I'm from the South, Jay. I know what a concealed weapon looks like."

Nelly took lazy steps down into the tailor shop below the Weisenfreund Yiddish Theater. The windows were stocky and let in a silver, smoky light like a religious temple. Clothes were everywhere in all variations of completion. Strewn across butcher tables, hung from plumbing pipes, stacked in neat piles on chairs. She fondled the fabric of a dinner jacket in the final evolution of its creation. Velvet the color of wine, so sensuous that it made her flush.

Jay stood atop a platform in the very center of the room. He wore bits and pieces of what might one day be a tuxedo.

"How'd you find me?" he asked. It was odd seeing him so incomplete. A part of Nelly wanted to look away and give him time to compose himself.

"Your man John at the Lantern Club," she said. She picked up a cut of thick tartan cloth. The plaid appeared infinite as it crisscrossed in an ancient pattern. "He remembered me from my first visit and was told to give me whatever I wanted."

She smirked up at Jay when he cursed.

"I didn't mean that literally," he said, as though speaking to John directly. "You could be here to kill me for all he knows."

"Who says I'm not?"

Jay shook his head at her, grave as a schoolteacher wielding a ruler to rap against the knuckles of uncooperative students.

"This place is sacred to me," he said.

Nelly looked about at the clutter and dust, but Jay held up his hand before she could point out the obvious.

"It ain't much to look at, I'll grant you, but it's still sanctuary. I'm not used to sharing it with people."

It was deceptively easy to see Jay as only a specter who appeared and disappeared on his own terms. Not entirely human; a character she could tear out of a novel. But in this strange place, there was no character to hide behind. She reached out and held the wide lapels of the tuxedo jacket between her fingers, then ran her hand over the ivory double-breasted waistcoat and its glossy gold buttons.

"I like the suit," she said.

She was relieved when he accepted the olive branch for what it was. He adjusted his stiff collar and pulled the waistcoat flat over his abdomen.

"My tailor said all white for a formal tuxedo is unheard of, but I insisted."

Nelly grinned and said, "The first time I saw you, you were wearing robin's-egg blue at a funeral."

"Sapphire blue, Ms. Sawyer, please."

"*Sapphire*, of course. What's this one for, then? A firing squad?"

"Tempting, but no. It's for the cotillion. I know the ladies were told explicitly to wear white, but no one said a thing about the men."

"You're going to the cotillion?"

It was already the start of August, meaning the gala slumbered only a few weeks away, but Nelly had allowed herself to become distracted. The excitement of her partnership with Jay—of her budding friendship with Tomás—made the cotillion and all its speculations burn like a dull, flickering light in the far-off tomorrow.

Jay looked down from his elevated height, his face a cross between amazement and a resigned, expected disappointment.

"Where do you think I am when we're not together, Nelly?" he asked. "I have a life outside of our daring exploits, you know. Or do you figure that I sit on a shelf, waiting patiently for the moment you'll need me?"

Nelly swallowed to keep herself from telling the truth. *Yes*, she wanted to say. *That's exactly it.*

"Are you escorting anyone?" she said instead.

"Christ no," said Jay, quick and glib. "I'm not what some well-to-do parents might call 'desirable' right now. Dan is attending, and you're not the only one who needs to make a debut." He peered at her over the faceless head of a mannequin. "Why do you ask?"

The old hinges of a door suddenly groaned open, then closed with a mechanical *clang*.

"You are very lucky, Jay Bird," said a concealed voice moving closer to them. "This is the last yard I'll have in stock for months. A custom tuxedo is quite a task in under three weeks. Despite what you may think, you're not my only— Oh."

A man of middle age appeared around the bend of a high stack of folded neckties. He was island-dark and dressed in a long black suit. The only spot of color about him was the embroidered kippah atop his head. The rimless glasses he wore down on his nose trapped the light, creating a glare across his face. He held a cut of gold silk in one hand, and a lit cigarette in the other.

"So sorry, but I'm closed for a private fitting, miss. Come back in an hour or so?" The man spoke in a melodic accent. He nestled the cigarette in the corner of his mouth, not really smoking it, but rather caressing it with his lips.

"She's with me," Jay said. "Abe, this is Penelope Sawyer, a friend. Nelly, this is Abraham, my tailor and sole source of happiness."

"Welcome to my humble shop, Ms. Sawyer," Abraham said in an exhale of tobacco smoke. From the smell, Nelly could tell it was one of Jay's. "I'm not used to the company of the gentler sex down here in my cave. Not even my wife will make the journey anymore. Please, excuse the mess."

He began moving things into loose stacks and sweeping threads and cuttings onto the floor, so she'd have a place to sit.

"I must say, Abraham," Nelly said, "it's an honor to meet the man responsible for Jay's sense of style."

Both men laughed together as Jay stretched out his arms so Abraham could pin the silk to the lining of his jacket.

"That careless abandon you call a 'sense of style' long predates me," Abraham said while sticking Jay right below his waist. Jay barely flinched, only smiled with a cruel promise of retribution.

Nelly watched Abraham dance around Jay with an enviable assuredness. She was herself no seamstress—she'd wasted half a day trying to reattach a button—but she could appreciate how the man took his charge and transformed him into something impossible. Like Raffaele Monti taking cold, hard marble and turning it into supple flesh, dancing fire, and gossamer cotton.

"Do I even want to know why you sought me out almost two hours early? Is your house on fire?" Jay asked with partial sarcasm.

In truth, Nelly couldn't pass up this opportunity to surprise him. It was an immature but enticing impulse. The chance to see him in an environment he did not dictate was a rare delicacy. But telling him that was out of the question. The last thing she wanted was another reason for him to doubt her conviction.

"Can I . . . ?" She pointed at Abraham, who bent nearly in two while adjusting Jay's inseam. Jay followed her gesture, then swept the concern away.

"Abe is practically my confessor," he said. "You can speak your mind."

Nelly was hesitant, but after watching the way Abraham kept his eyes firmly fixed on his task, she continued.

"Your note was cryptically vague, and I wanted to know what I was walking into. Does this 'friend' you mentioned even have a name, or do you expect me to do the interview blindfolded?"

Jay narrowed his eyes at her and said, "I for one don't plan on catching a hot bullet just because the girl who does your hair thinks she can earn a couple bucks selling what she reads in your mail."

Nelly's parents did have a history of opening her letters. Perhaps she wasn't giving Jay his due for thinking ahead.

"What about the flowers you sent along with it?"

Abraham instructed Jay to turn, so his back was to her. She could not see the expression on his face when he said, "I figured the dashing Mr. Escalante y Roche was the type to send flowers. Disguising my correspondence as his own was less suspicious than some kid from Maxwell Street with dirt on his nose slipping an envelope under your door. Your parents *did* assume they were from him, right?"

They had. *She* had. Tomás sent flowers almost immediately after their first dinner, and when the second arrangement arrived not two days later, Nelly's heart fractured just a bit when she realized it was some kind of hidden code from Jay.

"Clever," she admitted. "But if your aim was to play at being Tomás, five dozen white roses was a tad too ostentatious."

"Ostentatious, you say?" Nelly could feel his mind working like one could feel the vibrations of a great machine churning in the earth. "He sent carnations, didn't he?"

Nelly gaped.

"Yes, actually. How did you—?"

"Pink ones?"

Her mouth stayed open. When Jay turned back to face her, his smile was victorious.

As Abraham helped him out of the tuxedo jacket, Jay said, "Your interviewee's name is Pony Moore. He's a pretty successful gambler. Owns a couple of saloons in the Levee, or what remains of it. He doesn't know who the Mayor of Maxwell Street is, but he knows where he's been. I'm hoping your editorial instincts will weed out the rest."

Abraham's cigarette was down to a stump when he stepped back from Jay and gave him a once-over before letting out a hopeless sigh.

"This is all I can do with you today," he said. "Go ahead and take it off. I'll have something more substantial next week. And please, for the love of God, eat something. If you lose any more weight, no amount of alterations will make this suit hang properly. Laura has already threatened an appearance at that club of yours with a platter of kugel. You know my wife never makes a threat lightly."

"If my memory serves, Laura is a wonderful dancer," Jay said, stepping down from the platform. "I might not mind passing a night with her at the Lantern Club."

Jay ducked when Abraham swiped at his head, then ran to hide behind a thick, tall screen erected for changing. While Abraham made notes in a thin pocket journal, Nelly was drawn back to the velvet suit that stood proudly among the wreckage of lesser ensembles.

"Is this suit for Jay?" she asked.

Abraham came to stand next to Nelly. He smelled of leather and that strange campfire burning of a Singer sewing machine when pushed to its limit.

"He's asked for it, but no," he said. "This I made for myself. It is the suit I am to be buried in."

"Christ. That's awfully morbid."

He laughed at her appalled expression.

"My wife says the same. Our faith decrees that all are to be buried clean in a white shroud, but when I go to meet God, I plan to make a statement. May I tell you something in sincerity, Ms. Sawyer?"

Abraham's intimacy left Nelly at a momentary loss. She'd just met this man. But the frankness of his open eyes, flashing behind his spectacles, made her receptive.

"Yes, sir."

"It warms my heart to see Jay spending time with a friend," he said. "He works too much, and the people he works for use him like a soldier. I've known the boy since he first washed up in Chicago, but only now am I beginning to understand his whys and his hows. I hope he can be himself with you. Or whatever self that makes him most happy."

"My time with Jay isn't social," Nelly said, even though his admission touched her heart. "He's helping me with something."

Nelly dwelled on what Jay had said earlier about Abraham and his trustworthiness. She knew from experience how valuable the knowledge of a seamstress or a tailor could be. Her own was a reliable source for her mother, who planned entire wardrobes based on the fashion tastes of gossiping neighbors.

"I'm writing an article," she said, "for the *Chicago Defender*. We're interested in the origins of a man called the Mayor of Maxwell Street, and his role in the shift I've witnessed personally in vice across this city. I don't want to stop his business. Nothing like it. I just want to know his story." Nelly glanced at the screen that shielded Jay. Fabric rustled as he changed. There was no way he could hear them, not unless they were trying very hard to be heard.

"Is his a name that your customers might whisper?"

Abraham gave her a knowing look.

"Even if they did," he said, "I couldn't tell you. There's no love lost between me and the Catholic church, but Jay's comparison was not far from the truth. I respect the sanctity of something shared in confidence." Nelly was discouraged until he said, "What I do know of the Mayor of Maxwell Street, I know from what I've seen with my own eyes."

"You . . . Do you know him?"

Abraham removed his glasses to clean them with a handkerchief, and the change un-aged him instantaneously. He was still a good deal older than her, but there was a smooth youthfulness to his face. The only hints at his true age, at the density of the life he'd lived, were in the spiderweb of wrinkles around his eyes.

"We share a mutual friend," he said. "A man named Sam Mason. Well, Sam Mason is the name they gave him in school. By the time I met him, he'd forgotten his Ojibwe name. I was born in Barbados, and when I came to New York as a young man, the best work I could find was stitching together socks in the Garment District. My wife's family only agreed to our marriage, even after I converted, because

Sam guaranteed a loan to bolster my business. We've stayed in touch, so it was no surprise when a parcel came through the mail from him. But the package wasn't for me. It was addressed to someone simply called 'the Mayor.'"

"And not Mayor Thompson?" Nelly asked.

Abraham's grin was bittersweet when he said, "*Not* Mayor Thompson. Like a fool, I called up to city hall and told them a package came for Big Bill. They told me that Mayor Thompson wouldn't have his dirty laundry sent to some Colored Jew in a West Side back alley, not to mention his custom suits. I considered forwarding the package all the way back to England where it came from, but a few days later, a boy dropped by to fetch it. The next month was the same, and the month after that. This all started maybe eight months ago."

"I see," Nelly said. She pulled at a curled patch of hair near the base of her neck as she looked back toward Jay. He would be ready soon, and most likely wouldn't appreciate her endangering Abraham by roping him into her enterprise. "What does your friend Mr. Mason do, exactly?"

"It isn't very genteel, miss."

"Neither am I."

Abraham smiled until his cheeks shaped his face like a Valentine's Day heart.

"No, I suppose not if you're cavorting with Jay Bird," he said. "To put it simply, Sam is an actor. He's played a thousand and one roles. That's why he sought out my services at the start. Every performance demanded a new ensemble, and I worked fast."

"Has the package for this month arrived?" she asked.

"Not yet. The days are often random; could be the first of the month, or the last."

The changing screen shifted, and Jay emerged in a notably more subdued navy suit that reminded Nelly of a bank teller. She rushed to open her change purse and handed Abraham a calling card with an address and a phone number for the Hyde Park house.

"I'd appreciate it if you called me when the next package arrives," she said. Then she gave her full, smiling attention to Jay.

"I swear, I don't take this long to dress, and I have three times the choices you do."

Jay straightened his sunflower-yellow necktie and said, "Exactly. When you have fewer options, you can't afford to fuck up a first impression. Abe, I left what I owe on your desk. I'd be mighty grateful if you didn't tell Laura I'm a day late and a dollar short."

"Wouldn't dream of it, Jay," Abraham said. "Your business helps us pay rent. It was a pleasure to meet you, Ms. Sawyer. God willing, we'll see each other again soon."

Jay was too busy lecturing Nelly on how "this would never work if she didn't listen to him" to notice the conspiratorial look pass between her and Abraham. She decided to keep this development to herself. Jay was intent on guiding the ship from now on, but she wasn't delusional. The day could come when her cause would jeopardize his own, and vice versa.

CHAPTER TWENTY-FIVE

The luxurious Marigold Hotel Tearoom was entirely empty apart from the servers who came to ask after them, and a concealed stringed quartet playing Chopin. There was an eerie absence of life and activity. They waited while the sky changed from blue, to pink, to a burnt red. The walls and ceiling were made of glass, and so elevated above the city streets, the tearoom floated like a castle in the clouds.

"I didn't know they rented out this room," Nelly said. "Especially to Negroes."

Jay said from his tufted lavender settee, "They don't under normal circumstances, but the maître d' owed me a favor."

"Do many people owe you favors?"

One of Jay's intricately manicured brows of blond, brown, black, and burgundy rose in a kind of amusement.

"I thought Pony was being interviewed here today, not me," he said. "Anyway, I wanted to choose someplace respectable."

"Not on my account, I hope."

"I would suggest nothing shy of perfection for you, Nelly Sawyer."

Nelly looked at the sharp point of her mechanical pencil and briefly considered stabbing Jay in the knee with it.

"In all seriousness," he said, "Pony lives for this type of thing. He doesn't respond to money, or favors, or stuff. His only weakness is flattery. The man's the Colored boss of Twenty-First Street, after all, and that's nothing to shake a stick at."

She heard Pony Moore long before she saw him. The heels of his shoes on the tiled floor. The jangle of jewelry. There was no hurry in his step, and he stopped several times. When he finally did round a massive crystal vase exploding with violets, he stopped and held up his hands in surprise. His drooping hound dog eyes lit as though this whole rendezvous wasn't in a set location, at a set time, to which they had all agreed.

"Ah!" he exclaimed. "Jay Bird! Don't tell me they let your mulatto ass in here. Did you at least wipe the shit off your shoes first?"

Pony was a small, older man well into his late seventies with a mustache like pencil shavings. When he advanced on Jay to shake his hand, his head barely reached the younger man's chin. But his presence was titanic. He soaked up all the light and sound with his two-tone shoes, Palm Beach suit, Alpine hat, and a diamond the size of an eyeball padlocked to the front of his shirt.

"Thanks for your time, Pony," Jay said while shaking his hand. "I know this is a busy season for you."

"Anything for Dan's boy. I've managed to stay off that bastard's bad list for twenty years, and I don't mean to start now. How's that blind pig of yours, still turning a profit?"

Nelly had the distinct sense of being ignored. She wondered if he mistook her for Jay's secretary, or worse, his date.

She thrust out her hand right between the two of them and said, "A pleasure to meet you, Mr. Moore. Thank you for taking this meeting."

Pony's eyes were a bright amber brown, and they took her in with the care of a connoisseur. He undressed, categorized, and appraised her so thoroughly that the sensible gray suit she chose because of its sobriety felt as revealing as Josephine Baker's feather skirt. He licked his lips before taking her hand and kissing her fingers.

"I do declare, Jay," he said. "When you said journalist, I was expecting some old brick house of a woman. You're pretty enough to be on the stage, Ms. Sawyer."

She pulled until her hand jerked out of his hold. He rubbed his fingers together, as though to work her essence into his skin.

"You know who I am?"

She began to scrutinize every petal in the tearoom, anticipating an ambush.

Pony said, "Of course! Your daddy just joined the Negro Business League. That makes he and me colleagues now. I like to keep good tabs on my colleagues, and their children."

Nelly glared at Jay, her self-styled partner. They'd agreed that going forward, an alias would be in both their best interests. He swore not to use her real name except when speaking in the strictest confidence.

Wary, Nelly said, "I hope your connection with my father won't jeopardize this interview."

For all of Chicago's size and scope, it was no bigger than Richmond when it came to connections. Her family name seeped into all things, like groundwater.

"Not at all, young lady. I can't stand that illiterate fucking farrier. Struts around this city like he invented money and every which way to spend it. No offense meant, of course." Pony patted his flat, practically concave stomach and said, "Do they serve tea in this place, Jay Bird, or am I to sustain myself on flowers and perfumed air?"

Jay motioned Pony ahead of them to a low round table festooned with cold cuts, sandwiches, tarts, cakes, scones, clotted cream, and Lapsang served from a porcelain tea set. When the man was far enough away, Nelly inched close to Jay and sneered.

"The fuck, Jay?"

"I know," he said, "but he's as good a source as you're likely to find in this city. Compromised or not, he's worth your while. Besides, it's not like this is your first time dealing with difficult men."

Surely not. Compared to most, Pony Moore was simply eccentric.

"Can he be trusted?" she asked.

"In matters of business, always. Then again, he did allegedly frame the Everleigh sisters for murder, so you be the judge."

Pony waited for them to sit before pouring for the table. His plate was evenly distributed with savories and sweets, and he intentionally started with the sandwiches, just as Nelly had been taught by a finishing school matron. Curt as he was, it was clear he'd done this before.

"So," he said after wiping lemon juice and mustard from the crinkled corners of his mouth. "You want to know about the Mayor of Maxwell Street. When Jay Bird approached me, I almost shot him for good measure. Bringing that man up never does anyone any good. But what can I say? I have a natural curiosity."

Nelly sat poised with her pencil and pocket journal open to a crisp blank page, unsure of how to begin. Past interviews had taken place in crowds, or behind buildings, or in the alcoves of a church. This was orchestrated and formal; so much so that Nelly felt more an amateur now than ever before. When she glanced at Jay—who sipped from a milk-less, sugar-less tea—she wondered if he'd arranged it in such a way on purpose to prove some kind of a vicious point.

"I'd actually like to start with you, Mr. Moore," she said.

His hand halted as he reached for another finger sandwich. He drew the hand back and folded it over his chest, leaning away as much as he could manage in the high-backed chair.

"I'm nothing to write home about, honey," he said. "Just an old man born in a tobacco field. No different from any other Negro who comes North for money and peace of mind."

"But not quite like any other Negro," she said. "Not every cook, or seamstress, or lineman in the South Side has a jewel pinned to their chest."

Pony reached up to fondle the diamond with a covetous affection. He wore it like a charm that could shield him from the evil eye and coat his steps in fortune.

"You familiar with the ancient Egyptians, Ms. Sawyer? Bit of an obsession of mine. Their thoughts on death have always been a comfort compared to the brimstone I was brought up to expect.

One of these old mornings, my bell will ring and a bullet with my name on it will strike true. *That's* why I wear this diamond. No matter when or where, I'll have enough to bribe that ornery ferryman to row me across the Lake of Flowers and take me on to Paradise. I like to be prepared."

Jay had yet to say a word since they all sat down together, but his rigidness had a noise that made his presence pervasive. Nelly shifted over, away from him, and watched Pony internally debate whether or not to try the ham or start in on the palm-sized cakes crafted to perfectly resemble marigold blossoms.

"Did you always aspire to be a businessman, Mr. Moore?" she asked.

His laugh was all in the throat; a cynical, tropical birdcall.

"No Negro from the Southland 'aspires' to be a businessman," he said. "Just to make a half-decent living, stay alive. Your daddy could tell you all about that. Now, go on and eat something, child. I never trust folk who don't eat when free food is offered."

Pony watched as she bit into a shortbread cookie that tasted of lemon and honey. Watched as she scraped cream onto a scone and ate several cranberry tarts. When he seemed satisfied with her progress, he continued: "I saw a need and I filled it. I'm thankful it's a type of thing that folk will pay money for."

"Considering that," Nelly said, "would you describe the Mayor of Maxwell Street as a businessman?"

"Damn straight!" He slapped the table. "He's the best of us. The goods he trades in have no mass, weight, or mouths to feed, so there's no overhead. Folk barely even know what his business is, and still, they'll pay out the ass for it. He's remained more or less invisible, which is damn difficult these days. Half the people who've worked with him ain't never seen his face, never mind heard his Christian name."

"Yes, I've noticed. Is he just some haint made up to keep gangsters and corrupt politicians honest?"

"If you'd asked me that a year ago, I would've said yes. No one person could ever link up all the neighborhoods, give all the players a reason to trust each other, like he supposedly has. It's mythical. But that was before I went and met the man."

"You *met* him?"

Nelly dropped her pencil mid-stroke. It slid down the curve of her open journal, onto the table, then landed heavy on the floor. Pony went on sampling the delicacies as though he hadn't just thrown a stick of dynamite into a trench. She took time fetching her pencil so as to not appear too unsettled.

"What did he look like?" she asked evenly.

"Haven't a clue." Pony raised his hand to usher over a server, who appeared in seconds with a fresh pot of tea.

"Oh. It's only, when you said that you've met him, I assumed you meant . . . physically?"

"It was hard to make him out, you see. Saunas around here keep it intentionally murky. Not polite to interrupt a man's private time."

As Pony spoke, Nelly felt like a fishing line struggling to unwind itself. She looked to Jay for some kind of support, or validation, or help, but he was thoroughly engrossed with his nail beds.

"Let me understand you, sir," she said. "You met the Mayor of Maxwell Street in a sauna where the steam was so thick that you couldn't see his face? How do you even know that's who you were talking to? It could've been anyone!"

Pony Moore began to laugh.

"Calm yourself, girl. Ain't you got any appreciation for a yarn?" He added a few more cakes and pies to his plate while Nelly gradually strayed into mania. "The Mayor and I had an appointment. Like death, he didn't tell me the day nor the hour, but I knew him when I heard him. Dignified, he was. Spoke clean English with no accent that I could place. A white man; not old, but not exactly wet behind the ears. Frozen somewhere in between. Not a lot of white men speak to me with respect, but he did."

Nelly rushed to piece together an image of the man Pony described. Not young, not old, a voice that you could find in any crowd. A featureless spirit made of smoke that could be blown away with a sturdy gust of wind. She thought the mystery would solve itself with a physical description, but it was too much to hope for.

"What was your business with him?" she asked.

"You want to get my throat slit end to end? I can't tell you that! There's a net made up of powerful, spiteful folk around this man. If they knew I broke ranks, I'd be dead before dinnertime. Such is the deal you make when you seek out his services."

"If he required such secrecy, how'd you get in touch with him in the first place?"

Pony drained his teacup and said, "I mentioned something to someone once. The rest wasn't up to me."

"You're telling me that the Mayor of Maxwell Street's entire network is run on gossip?"

Nelly was coming to find that every society's foundation stood on idle chatter that spread and took like a match to fresh tinder.

"Not gossip, young lady," Pony said. "Fidelity. Something that, for men in our business, is as sweet as the love of a good woman. And just as elusive. If you've ever been close to a person as they die, you'll know that they talk a lot in the end. That's how he spoke. Damn sad, really. So yes, I know the Mayor of Maxwell Street, Ms. Sawyer, and he ain't no story. The man's as real as sin."

A sudden brightness illuminated the space above them. A crystal chandelier reflecting its electric bulbs off the glass ceiling like man-made stars. The string quartet was now gone, replaced by the clatter and mutterings of a shift turning over and new servers coming to relieve the old. Evening was upon them.

Next to her, Jay stretched his long body and yawned.

"I believe that's our signal," Pony said. "I'm afraid we'll need to wrap this up, Ms. Sawyer."

Nelly looked between Jay and Pony while they rose around her.

"No, please," she said to Pony with a hand stretched out across the table. "We're just getting started! Did the Mayor contact you again? What did you pay him? How long has it been since you met?"

Pony looked apologetically at Jay, a show of asking permission.

"There's no time," Jay said. "The theater opens soon, and you have tickets for *Don Quixote*, I believe?"

That was all Pony needed to hear. Already, he'd moved on from this enticement to savor the next. All Nelly could do was stand, shake his hand, and say, "I'd appreciate it if you kept this conversation confidential, sir. At least until the work is done."

"Don't you worry your pretty head," he said. "I'm no snitch. And who'd believe that the daughter of the wealthiest Negro in America sat down for afternoon tea with a soggy old pimp like me, eh?"

As when he'd arrived, Pony left as though he had all the time in the world. The tearoom lost its exclusive and exclusionist gloss when he ran his finger over the marble-topped tables and pocketed a silver butter knife.

"Was that beneficial?" Jay asked once they were alone again.

Nelly flipped through the chicken-scratch of her notes and said, "I don't know. I can't begin to make sense of it yet. But we're getting close. Thank you, Jay, and I mean that."

Jay's response was as flippant and casual as always, but his warming color betrayed him.

"Folk rarely pull knives in upscale tearooms," he said. "At least not during working hours. I'm just sorry I couldn't get you more time."

"I know you did your best."

Staff appeared from behind paneled walls to change out settings and rearrange furniture. In violent contrast to the Chopin, a jazz ensemble warmed up their instruments with inharmonious scales.

"If you're hungry," Jay said, "I can have the chef here treat us to an early dinner. He's a friend and won't mind the work if you don't mind eating in the kitchen. We can share a meal. Talk strategy for your next move."

As appealing and intriguing as that sounded, Nelly looked at the darkening sky and marked the time.

"No, thanks. I need to get going."

"Have somewhere to be, Ms. Sawyer?" It sounded like an incrimination.

"Tomás is taking me to the ballet," she said. "He refuses to believe I'm a terrible dancer, so he's created a kind of experiment to test me."

"You're a fine dancer. Shit, I should know."

This came as a shock. They never spoke of the day they met, not in any depth. That first dance existed somewhere between dream and memory. If Nelly thought of it at all, it was in the dark, at night, when summer heat made her restless.

"I couldn't tell by the way you disappeared after," she said. "I looked for you, but you were as gone as last Christmas."

"Leaving you wasn't what I wanted. Trust me on that."

In the month since Elder's funeral, Jay had learned so much about her. Seen her at her most vulnerable, knew secrets that could ruin her future. She was trusting him with the most delicate facets of herself. And yet, when she looked at him, Nelly still saw an equation impossible to decipher.

※

They left the tearoom in a large service elevator that rattled all the way down. Whatever price the maître d' had to pay, it didn't include a return trip in the mahogany-paneled guest elevator. Otherwise, the esteemed patrons might wonder if the Marigold Hotel had changed its policy on serving Negroes after certain hours.

"When will you have something else for me?" Nelly asked more or less to distract herself. It was a slow, lumbering ride in a hot box that held humidity like a bucket holds water.

"Will you be at the NNBL dinner this Saturday?" Jay asked. When Nelly nodded, he said, "I'll have something for you then."

"Are you sure? Today's Monday. You'll only have a few days."

"I'm sure. As long as you don't bum-rush me before then."

"I apologized for that."

"Did you? I must've missed it. Ah!"

Nelly watched Jay reach into a trouser pocket and pull out a tin box the size of his palm. It depicted a smiling woman in blue with flowers strewn through her dark hair.

He said, "I would advise not sharing these," then motioned for her to take it. Inside, ten identical cigarettes were lined up in tight little rows.

"I shouldn't accept this," Nelly said without meaning a word.

"Nonsense. You'll be the chicest, most popular gal at the ballet."

Nelly wanted to do the considerate thing and wait until they were outside, but it was difficult to resist. She pressed her tongue against one of the cigarettes and tasted the intricacy of the tobacco. Before she could ask, Jay was there with a lit match.

"Dinner, then the ballet?" he said, soft as the flame that danced between them. "Tomás wasn't bluffing when he promised to spend more time with you."

Nelly drew deep and held it there. She knew that this comment hid a question with a right answer and a wrong answer. She let go, and while the elevator filled with smoke, she said, "You don't approve?"

"Don't approve? Quite the opposite. I congratulate you." He shook the match once, and the flame blinked out. "Securing a serious suitor now will make this project of yours easier to pull off. He'll be so dazzled by your charms that he won't notice you fleeing from the ballroom to chase down a source."

At times, Jay's teasing was like being poked with a very small, very sharp stick.

"Tomás is a friend. Same way you're a friend," she said with some vinegar. "I have no serious suitors."

Nelly didn't know why she lied. She felt an instinct toward self-preservation that badgered her to keep Tomás and her relationship with him a secret from Jay and that erstwhile animal hunger in his eyes.

"Is that what you think?" he asked. His tone was as amorphous as the smoke that lingered in the elevator, trapped with nowhere to go. "I remember you at the Henry Tanner exhibit, Nelly. All of those desirous men and their desirous stares. You were like a white stag in a room full of hunters."

The elevator came to a hard stop. They were in the bowels of the hotel, among the hot water furnaces and popping pipes. Naked bulbs flickered every few feet in sporadic bursts down the hallway ahead of them.

"Follow this hall, then take the first door on your right," Jay said. "That should lead you to the alley behind the building. I'll wait here and come after, just in case someone's watching."

Nelly swallowed what she knew to be an irrational fear of the darkness and stepped out of the elevator.

"Have you ever actually been hunting?" she asked Jay. The long hallway before her soaked up her voice, then shot it back at her in a distorted echo.

"Can't say I have."

He stood alone, cloaked in a sickly green shadow. He struck her as not a hunter himself, but a predator. The kind that didn't kill you outright but stalked you until you fell dead from exhaustion and hopelessness.

"I have," she said. "I'm not a half bad shot on a clear morning. Even with all the dogs, and the horses, and the trackers out since dawn, at the end of the day, the hunter who bags the stag isn't the one with the best shot. Just the one who gets there first."

CHAPTER TWENTY-SIX

Richard Norris didn't acknowledge her as she sat down next to him. Nelly didn't neglect to notice that her seat alone had been empty in a room where people pressed against open windows for space.

"Did you have any trouble getting here?" he asked.

"No," she said. "I'm curious, though. Why are we doing this in a church basement at six in the evening, and not at your office at a sensible time? I had to convince my folks that I'm out and about with Sequoia McArthur."

"A mentor of mine always preached the value of a 'teachable moment.' Do you know what this gathering's about?"

"Gathering" was an understatement. The fellowship hall of Galilee Baptist Church was packed to capacity—standing room only—and the collective outrage of the assembled men and women had the moldy smell of fruit gone rotten. All those present were Colored, and most from the Southern low country, the Delta, Appalachia, and the Bayou. Nelly heard all their variations in the demands they hurled at a white man stammering on a stage at the head of the hall.

"Times have changed," he attempted to say loud enough to be heard over the multitude. His good ole boy, South Carolina accent stung like a provocation. "We are willing to increase pay by at least thirty percent; better than anything you all could ever get here in Chicago!"

"How 'bout the food you make us pay to grow?" shouted back a one-armed man with his right suit sleeve pinched off at the elbow. "The air you make us pay to breathe? The women violated, the young men killed? You gonna increase that by thirty percent?"

A roar rose up in his wake. People were on their feet, pointing, yelling, crying out the names of family left behind, living and dead.

Nelly said, "The Southern Metal Trades Association. They're trying to convince Negroes to go back to Dixie, right?"

"They're getting desperate," Richard said. "I've heard from friends and relations back in Georgia that they're closing down whole depots to keep Negroes from leaving. Forcing trains to reroute or just pass their towns completely. I've even heard of white men in masks holding conductors at gunpoint."

Such was the arrogance of the South, resorting to petty acts of violence against companies with enough money and might to summon whole armies. Guns, and masks, and aggravating disruptions would not stop the turning of the wheel.

"And no one's challenged them?" Nelly asked, shocked at their gall.

"What's to challenge? If one town's station is closed, folk will just go to the next one over. And the next one after that. And the next one after that. Illinois Central ain't gonna ignore all the money they make funneling Negroes north, west, and east. These boys can throw around all the threats they like. Eventually, those looking for a way out will find one. He knows that."

Richard pointed at the SMTA man and his placards comparing wages in Chicago to "improved" wages in Montgomery.

"When will they learn that it's not about money?" she asked. "It's about life and death."

"They have to acknowledge that we have lives worth living first. We usually ask associates to write up things like this, but I offered to come down here myself. Greenwood is still on my mind, and nothing can be quite as cathartic as watching some white man eat his own shit."

Richard finally turned to her and whatever he saw seemed to meet with his approval.

"You look well for someone chasing down demons," he said. "I hope I didn't go too easy on you."

Nelly straightened the boat neckline of her dress and made an effort to look professional. His odd compliment lifted her up and sent her crashing down all at the same time.

She said, "If you'd asked for this meeting a week ago, you'd have seen a welt the size of a horse apple on my cheek. This article had me looking like the last fucking ring of hell."

She couldn't tell exactly what put such a terrified expression on Richard's face: her story, or her language.

"What happened?"

"An uncooperative source," she said, and left it at that.

"I see. I assume, then, that you have an update for me."

Nelly opened her pocket journal to the page of notes arranged specifically for this meeting. When she began to read aloud, Richard stopped her.

"No time, Ms. Sawyer," he said. "Just the broad strokes."

She closed the journal slowly and curved her fingers around its spine as though to absorb the points she'd spent hours refining. She feared that if she just opened her mouth and spoke, she would ramble and lose herself in the minutiae.

"You were right about the Mayor working across syndicate and ethnic lines," she said. "I know firsthand that he's connected to the Italians, the Irish, and city hall. Bronzeville, too."

Richard grunted and nodded for her to continue.

"He seems to deal in secrets. Favors, most likely. Someone offers up something important to him, he does something for them in turn. There's a lot of fear surrounding the man, too. Not so much fear *of him*, but fear of those invested in his success. And his name has nothing to do with Maxwell Street in any literal sense. According to one source, they call him that because of the diversity of his commerce."

"Makes sense enough," Richard said, "but there are no real bosses in this city; everyone works for someone. Who does *he* work for?"

Nelly hadn't considered that. This figure was spoken of with such reservation that he seemed to be a force unto himself.

"I don't know," she said frankly. "He doesn't belong to any specific group, ethnic or otherwise. The only physical description I have is that he's a white man of indeterminate age. Maybe British; it's possible he has a delivery of English suits sent to this tailor based out of at a Yiddish theater once a month."

Richard's brows shot up, creating deep creases in the skin of his forehead.

"White?" he said. "Are you certain?"

Nelly hesitated, questioning that certainty, then affirmed, "Yes. My source was very confident. I haven't heard anything to the contrary."

Richard scratched at the short brown-and-gray curls coming in after his last shave. Nelly recalled helping Elder shave when they were young and the first pubescent hairs came in on his face and neck. He was terrified of the changes to his body. Ambrose called it the mark of manhood and insisted that Elder go without shaving for an entire winter. The experience crippled her brother, and Nelly thought with an ache of how he couldn't stomach his own reflection until summer. Such a strange, insidious thing death was. It made the deceased more present as ghosts than they'd ever been in life.

"Who exactly have you been talking to?" Richard asked.

"I beg your pardon, but I can't tell you that," Nelly said. "I've already exposed one source."

"It'll all come out in the article, anyway. You do realize that, right?"

Nelly ran her tongue over her teeth and tamped down the urge to smoke. She knew this would happen. This addictive impulse. That's exactly why she never carried cigarettes with her.

"Do you know the name Marta Harjo?" she asked.

Richard seemed to be measuring his words, figuring up an ideal amount of information to share without giving away too much.

"Yes," he said. "She was a cartoonist with the *Colored Citizen* down in Florida before she came here. I've seen her work. She one of your sources?"

"One of her cartoons was my first real lead. If it wasn't for her, I'd still be picking along Maxwell Street like a sightseer."

"Is she the one who gave you that welt you mentioned?" Richard asked with a peculiar half smile. "I've only had the pleasure of meeting her a few times. I would've brought her on at the *Defender* if our political views weren't so contradictory. She seemed like the type to choose fight over flight."

"She threatened as much," Nelly said. "I wasn't exactly forthcoming when we met, and she had every right to sock me. No, I had the misfortune of meeting Mikey Hannigan."

"Mikey 'the Butcher'?" Richard looked about, lowered his tone, then said, "You had a run-in with Ragen's Colts?"

"Well, not *intentionally*," Nelly said to his fearful outrage. Richard dropped his head and began to rub the pads of his fingers hard across his closed lids.

"Ragen's Colts are not to be trifled with. I don't know what you said or did for them to let you go in peace the first time, but there won't be a second. This has gone on far enough, Ms. Sawyer."

"We haven't even begun," Nelly said. "The Mayor of Maxwell Street isn't just a person, he's an idea. Proof of the changing times in this city. There's so much to discover here, and I'm not afraid of animals like Mikey Hannigan."

"But you should be. As eager as you are to shuffle off anonymity, Ms. Sawyer, you're not just some faceless, nameless beat reporter. They know who you are, and they know you don't mean to stop. Some of my other reporters, they can work stories like this because they fade away. You, as much as you may resent it, stand out, and always will."

Nelly wouldn't tell him that her name saved her from Mikey Hannigan. Her name, and the promise that she was worth more to them alive than dead.

"I know the risks," Nelly said. Her eyes connected with a woman her own age, a child bouncing on her lap. She sat next to a man in overalls with a weathered, tired face. Nelly could see the miles they'd walked in their knotted hands and thin necks.

Richard spoke like a disappointed father who had seen his child make a terrible mistake: "You're not like these people. Your risks are nothing compared to theirs."

The bite in that struck Nelly deep enough to hit bone.

"Why?" she asked. "Is my life not worth living the way I want to live it?"

"It's not about worth, child, but value. You have talent and grit, but that's not always enough. Whatever choice you make, you have to want it more than anything in this world."

This here was a man Nelly respected, idolized to a degree. His clear underestimation of her wounded more than just her pride.

"I'm not some sixth-generation heiress born to excess," she said. "You say you've been writing about my family for a year; then you know where my people come from. My mother picked the same cotton as her great-grandparents, and my father was born in a pup tent. I watched them work until they didn't even have any blood left to bleed, and all because they knew that they were deserving of more. Like them—and even *despite* them—I will give whatever it takes to live the life that is best for me."

The energy of the hall made a dry, furnace-like heat, and Nelly watched a long line of sweat travel down from Richard's hairline to the hinge of his jaw. His dark skin appeared polished, scrubbed to shining.

"It's easy to make such proclamations when you're young," he said. "Before the responsibilities set in, and the real implications of what you stand to lose. Right here, in this fellowship hall, you tell me that you'll do whatever it takes to be a journalist. But what will keep you from changing your mind when the price gets steep?"

Nelly squared her jaw and said, "With all due respect, sir, you don't know me. No price is too steep."

Richard's face was drawn, forlorn, and stoic. Riddled with doubt. It was the look of a man who'd opened a door that could no longer be shut.

"Right," he said with an air of portentous finality that spoke of ill-omened ends, "but you won't be the one to pay it."

The SMTA agent made the bizarre decision to open himself up to questions. A rare few had honest concerns about what life was like back home. Not for themselves, but for the siblings, and parents, and friends. If they had some happiness, some improvement to their lot, it would make the guilt of carrying on without them easier to bear.

Then, quite suddenly, Richard said, "Did you know that Marta Harjo is dead?"

The hall, even with all of its fuming noise, went quiet for Nelly. Only the sound of her breath leaving her lungs in a sharp exhale.

"What?"

He did not meet her eyes. Nelly stretched her neck, straining to see his face.

"It was yesterday—or maybe the day before—that they found her on the West Side. She'd been shot. My office is trying to get in touch with her people down in Pensacola before the city buries her in a pauper's grave."

It was a foolish, selfish question in the grand scheme of things, but at the time, all Nelly could think of was her promise. That one thing Marta required in exchange for the information that likely killed her.

"What about her daughter?" Nelly said. "Becky Harjo. What happened to her, is she okay?"

Richard's eyes were distressingly blank, but honest.

"I don't know."

⎯⎟⎟⎯

For all the rest of the evening, dread hung around Nelly's neck like a noose.

It tightened as Murphy drove her home past a lake so dark that it reflected the light of the night sky. As she sat at dinner with her parents and apathetically answered their questions about her "progress" with Tomás. Which automobile he preferred, what he ordered at dinner, the tone of his letters, the sincerity of his smile. As she unbound her hair and oiled it for bed. As she turned off the light and laid herself down on sheets with the sterile smell of white soap. Then, alone in the dark blue fog of her bedroom while Chicago danced, and fought, and drank, and ate, and tossed in fitful sleep, Nelly cried. Not a mournful cry, but a terrified and repentant one. She knew that she'd traded Marta's life for her own. And the guilt broke her heart. Or rather, the absence of it.

CHAPTER TWENTY-SEVEN

You," Sequoia said straight off, "have some explaining to do." She cornered Nelly at one of the silver punch bowls filled with a thick, honey-colored concoction of strawberry, orange, grapefruit, and spiced cinnamon. She hadn't dressed to impress for once. It was odd to see her in the same old sequined and square frock as everyone else.

The pretense that league business would be done at this National Negro Business League dinner fell away to pieces as soon as guests arrived at the home of Dr. Carter Evans and his family. From there, the true purpose of the dinner took hold: pushing young people together until one of the odd pairs managed to stick.

"Good to see you, too, Sequoia," Nelly said. She took a sip of the punch and wished that it was whiskey.

"You're astounding. First, you beg me to get you into one of the most restricted parties in the city, vanish halfway through, then Harold Sterling shows up out of nowhere to say that you've fucked off out of Lake Forest entirely. I, a perfect friend, fear the worst and call up to the house, only for Miss Florence to tell me that you're busy and will have to call me back. Busy all day. *For eleven days!* And don't get me started on your whirlwind romance. I had to find out you were doing the tango at the Marine Dining Room from *Mabel Ford* of all dull people. And after all we've been through, Nelly Sawyer. Where the hell do you get off keeping this from me?"

Nelly bore it all with a closed mouth, puckered from the sweetness of the punch. The easiest thing would have been to tell Sequoia the truth. Nelly didn't know when she might need more of her unique insight. But telling Sequoia felt like a line that once crossed, could not be crossed again. Her two worlds had managed to maintain a thin barrier thus far, and Sequoia's involvement could bring the whole illusion of separation crashing down.

"I'm sorry," Nelly said. "I can't tell you why I had to leave the Ebony Masque like I did. I can't tell you why I've been out of touch for so long. It's not that I don't trust you, there are just certain things that you don't need to know."

"This has something to do with Jay Shorey."

Sequoia made this declaration with concrete certitude. Nelly's explanation, meandering as it was, didn't put even a dent in her tenacity.

"This has nothing to do with him," Nelly said.

"Oh, yes it does. I know he was at the Ebony Masque; I saw him, Nelly. He disappeared just as suddenly and completely as you did, and you have been in the strangest of moods since the Lantern Club. I told you he wasn't worth the time God gave a fruit fly, but you just can't seem to stay away."

"Jay's ability to be a constant inconvenience is annoying," Nelly said, "but purely coincidental."

"Is he your lover?"

Nelly choked. The cup jostled, and punch sloshed out and onto Mrs. Evans's pink Chinese area rug. Sequoia had no patience for it; she snatched the cup out of Nelly's hand and passed it off to some poor, mystified boy standing nearby.

"If he is," Sequoia said while Nelly gagged, "then I suppose, technically, I can understand it. But, darling, if you're looking for a harmless fling, I can make more appropriate recommendations. More discreet ones, too."

"How could you even ask me that?" Nelly said once she regained her equilibrium. "I'm here with Tomás, for goodness' sake!"

She motioned over to the hapless man in question, who was doing a valiant job dodging questions from the founders of Delta Sigma Theta Sorority. His courteousness didn't waver, even when President Sadie Mossell demanded a no-nonsense explanation for how Tomás fighting on the side of the revolución while his family maintained full economic control of an entire region of Mexico wasn't a conflict of interest. For a man alone in potentially hostile territory, he handled himself admirably.

Nelly had gone radio silent in the days after the SMTA meeting and Richard Norris's damning revelation. For twenty-four hours, not even her father could coax her into the open. She couldn't sleep. She couldn't eat. She could hardly glance in a mirror without seeing Marta Harjo's ashen, lifeless face staring back. However, when they told her through a closed door that Tomás was calling, she answered. The sound of his voice drew out her despair like a lodestone.

He'd learned of the NNBL dinner through enterprising Florence and would not be dissuaded from accompanying Nelly in all his winsome glory. Nelly doubted she would attend the dinner at all, but there was no telling him that. Not when he sounded oh-so-ecstatic.

I want to see who your people are, he'd said over the telephone. *Where you come from.*

She remembered letting a billow of Jay's tobacco smoke out of the window and watching fireflies float through it like birds through clouds. Those cigarettes had been her sole comfort as she attempted to outrun a Marta-shaped ghoul yelling at her from the corner of her room.

Into the receiver, she'd said, *This* is not *where I come from.*

Tomás's laugh was made deep and smoky by the static of the telephone line.

I suppose we'll get to that, too. We have time.

And so, Nelly found herself with her back to Dr. Evans's wall while Sequoia made quick work of her entire operation. Damn her for her intuition, and damn Nelly's blindness to it. Not even her parents were paying full attention to her in Chicago, but Sequoia was.

"I had a life before this summer," Nelly said. "Aspirations that I held close to my heart, and if I choose to pursue those aspirations— even with someone like Jay Shorey—that's my business. I'll tell you everything someday, and you'll realize that it's all far more scandalous than a secret lover, but for now, leave me alone. Please."

Nelly felt on the edge of tears, but Sequoia spared no sympathy. Her eyes became razor blades, slender and sharp, that sliced through Nelly's entreating despair with a butcher's proficiency.

"You are a terrible bullshitter, Nelly Sawyer," she said. "You're a fine liar, but if you're going to pull off this little cloak-and-dagger charade of yours, you're gonna have to learn how to bullshit. Ask Jay, since you're such great pals. He's a damn virtuoso."

Sequoia hiked her hem to a pink and gold-gilded flask tucked into her garter. She smoothed down her skirt, opened the flask, and dumped the entirety of it into the punch. It was a bright, clear liquid, probably gin. It would be several hours most likely before someone noticed that their drinks were spiked.

"This thing is on track to be as entertaining as a trustee board meeting," she said. "You'll thank me later."

A hand reached out and plucked the flask out of Sequoia's hand. Lloyd Younger wrinkled his nose and handed it back to her as one would a soiled diaper.

"Excellent taste, as always, CeCe," he said. "Did you sample that at your local basement apartment bathtub?"

For all the inexplicable aggravation Lloyd caused Nelly when they were required to be in each other's presence, she could not fault his style. Not even Jay could've pulled off white British plus fours at a formal dinner where everyone else was in black tie.

"Ms. Sawyer," he said with a Cheshire-cat smile, "there's a nasty little rumor going around that you're going to be a princess."

His look back to where Tomás continued to withstand brutal interrogation was not subtle.

"You should know, all the mommas and papas are very upset about this. Daddy chewed me out the other night for not locking you down the day we met, even if my interest in you is purely anthropological. Why, this very intrusion is a bit of a last-ditch effort. You've been summoned by our fathers, Nelly, and I was given direct orders to fetch you."

Behind them, Nelly saw the outline of her father's back standing within a group of other men. The NNBL was a mark of arrival for Ambrose Sawyer. It represented the joining of an organization, of an ideal, that had long eluded his vision of himself and his family. He hoped to be chairman one day. Before they had set out for the party that evening, Ambrose told Nelly as gently as he could to do her best that night. Tomás was an intriguing development, but in the end, he was more a proof of that quintessential Sawyer eccentricity than a suppressant of it. Another example of how Nelly's family went above and beyond to show that they were bigger, flashier, and louder than everyone else.

Sequoia was right, as she often was. If Nelly meant to make it through what remained of this "grand season," she would have to extend beyond lying and put on an ovation-worthy performance.

"Ah, here she is!"

Ambrose wrapped his arm around Nelly's shoulders, saying, "I was just telling Mr. Jackson here about your race with Tomás. They were off down Lakeshore Drive like a pair of Pegasi, I tell you. The fastest I've ever seen Nelly go. Now, she may be the better rider, but that race proved that nothing can count out a One Oak horse. Tomás only won by a hair, but a hair was all it took."

In the midst of her father's story, Nelly took in the circle of people around her and felt a chill along her neck. Including Lloyd and his father, there were six men in the circle. Three of them she knew, and they—in one way or another—knew her.

Harold Sterling looked the most sickened by the whole situation. He glanced at Nelly just long enough to nod in greeting, then made a point of studying his shoes, or his punch cup, or the general décor. Pony Moore was not nearly as shamefaced. He went on ad nauseam about how lovely Nelly was, how obedient and compliant a daughter. All the while, he grinned as though they were thieves caught up in a shared heist. Jay was the only one who maintained his dignity. He offered Nelly a warm smile and complimented her dress. The passive comment of a flattering stranger.

"What were the stakes in this legendary race?" asked the tall, older gentleman to Jay's left, an oak among saplings. His eyes did not blink as he looked upon Nelly. They were like black marbles, round and hard enough to pluck out of his head. He made an attempt at a smile, but it was little more than an uneven gash cut across his face. She took this to be Daniel Jackson, Jay's god-uncle that she had heard so much about.

"If I won, we were to visit his home in Mexico," Nelly said. "If he won, he'd have the honor of escorting me to the cotillion. The hair decided it."

"The cotillion?" Jay sounded legitimately surprised, as though

Nelly had announced that Tomás was taking her to the moon. "Does Mr. Escalante y Roche even know what the cotillion is?"

"He's done his research," Nelly said.

Jay seemed smaller standing next to Dan, even though they were just about the same size. That impervious cloud that always floated about him was diminished, and Nelly realized that they were equals here. Both reduced to their basic function as children or charges of their elders.

"That's quite the catch, Ambrose," said Pony Moore. "I wish my daughter was stepping out with a marquis, and not some freeloader who thinks he'll change the world with a harmonica."

Ambrose could not contain his pleasure at their adoration. He puffed out his chest and, like a strutting rooster, made himself big.

"Ah, he's a good boy. Swell with a horse, too. Florence is ready for wedding bells, but I'm not so sure yet."

A chorus of shrill laughter went up from the parlor and a group of wives and mothers, standing in a similar circle. Florence Sawyer stood among them, awash in the pink light that comes from being part of a whole. There was nothing quite as validating or mortifying as when beautiful, wealthy, elevated women stretched out their diamond-encrusted hands and said, *I choose you.*

Lloyd's father sighed like a man crucified and said, "Whose idea exactly was it to choose Chicago for this . . . what are we calling it?"

"Grand season," Harold Sterling said.

"Ah, yes." Dr. Younger's face drooped under the weight of an exhaustion as deeply embedded as cancer. "Negroes up North always go on about standing apart from the white man, but then insist on a half-assed attempt at being just like 'em. Our roots are in New Orleans, Charleston, Atlanta. Not here, where we're all refugees fighting for a square inch of living space."

"I'll be damned if I pick up and move to fucking Atlanta for a summer," Pony said. "At least I can walk down Wabash without some planter's son asking for my freedom papers. And there's no need to fight over an inch of space when you own the block."

"I did suggest Richmond at the last conference. It's noted in the log, and not a one of you voted for it," Ambrose said.

Lloyd snickered and spoke before anyone could think to stop him.

"Are there even any Colored folk of note in Richmond, Kentucky?"

Dr. Younger's hand came up and struck Lloyd across the back of the head hard and fast. Nelly blinked, and Lloyd was standing erect. She blinked again, and he was stumbling to the floor. When he righted himself, the fire was firmly extinguished in him.

"Excuse my son," Dr. Younger said, unmoved by such a sudden act of violence. "His only skill is running his damn mouth. I wish he had your god-nephew's initiative, Dan. Jay has made quite the name for himself."

Where Dr. Younger's touch was destructive, when Dan laid his hand on Jay's shoulder, it was compassionate and proud. Lloyd sniffed hard to draw up wayward tears, then joined the circle of women on the other end of the house. Nelly was the only one to watch him leave.

"Gentlemen," Dan said. "Are we going to pretend that we brought everyone together here to match up our children?" He swept his hand over Nelly as though highlighting a valuable piece of art. With Lloyd gone, she and Jay were the only young people left. All they were missing was an altar.

"Chicago breeds politicians of every ilk and stripe," he said. "Good ones, too. That time has passed on for old heads like us; but children with unfulfilled potential are like unpicked fruit—a waste. I have every hope that Jay could be alderman one day, maybe even state representative. Or Congress; who knows with these changing times."

"You're awful young to be considering politics, son," Dr. Younger said. "That kind of pursuit requires a great deal of capital, of experience. Education, too. Where, by chance did you study? To my recollection, there ain't but a handful of Negro institutions out West."

Jay took a fair while to arrange his words.

"I haven't had the honor of attending college. After my family passed on, Dan was kind enough to take me in. I started working at a young age, never had much time for—"

"Business came first. You all understand," Dan interrupted. His hand went from Jay's shoulder to the back of his neck, pinching. "One year in business is more an education than four in a classroom. I attended Lincoln, and in time, Jay will do the same. In five years at least, he'll be ready for a campaign, don't you worry. Hell, half the money in this room could buy that seat for him. A Dejoie from New Orleans. A Ford from Memphis. A Sawyer from Richmond."

Dan let his deep voice carry that statement around the circle. The men nodded, muttered, whispered muted agreements. Jay's eyes were a thousand miles away.

Ambrose was the first to break the stillness.

"He is an impressive young man," he said. "I wish you the best of luck, Shorey."

Nelly knew her father. Had lingered at his elbow long enough to translate his personal language. Whatever proposition Dan had just made, Ambrose's answer was a resounding *no*.

Dinner was a classic, elegant affair at a long dining table that just managed to accommodate everyone. Silver candelabras cast trembling light over faces bright with conversation.

"Are you having a good time?" Nelly asked Tomás, who was just starting up a dialogue with Marjorie Joyner. His smile was a constant, and he spoke to everyone with such animation about the most banal of topics. That sparkling education and access to the world's most elite social clubs apparently hadn't allowed for opportunities to mingle.

"I'm having an *exceptional* time," he said. "I've met the most captivating people tonight, Ms. Sawyer. Your community is . . . it's not what I expected. What about you?"

Nelly hadn't told Tomás about Marta. He knew she was upset, but he did not know why. Even still, he'd made every considerate effort to lift her spirits with a grin or a kiss to the hand.

"I enjoy watching you have a good time," she said. "And I'm glad you insisted."

Across the river of candlelight, Jay stared at them. He watched Nelly through the soup, and the seafood. The roast, and the quail.

Only when the dessert was finished and the coffee was poured did he give up and glance away.

After the dinner, all the young women and men were instructed to stand and march to the third floor, where a large space had been cleared. Parents and relatives followed them up until all stood in a close circle. Sequoia appeared next to Nelly with a refilled flask and an intoxicated glow.

"Is this the part where they sacrifice us, do you think?" she said.

Mrs. Evans, their hostess, came to stand in the middle of the circle. She rang a small glass bell to demand their attention.

"Well, everyone," she said in a demure whisper of a voice. "Carter and I thank you all for joining us this evening and choosing our home for such an essential gathering. There are many here who I haven't seen in years, and it's a blessing to fellowship all together at last. Now, could the young women who'll be debuting this summer, and the young men present, please step forward?"

Sequoia gave Nelly a strong push, and she lurched to the front of the crowd. They all looked confused and terrified, ideally suited for sacrifice. A tall woman in silks came to stand next to Mrs. Evans. She moved with long, flowing steps that were a dance in and of themselves.

"Congratulations to all of the young women who will enter society this summer," she said in a Creole alto. "And congratulations to the young men who will escort them. I am Madame Blanchett of the Théâtre National de l'Opéra in France, and your parents have summoned me here to make sure the night of your cotillion is a glorious one."

No, Nelly thought. *They're not going to sacrifice us. They're going to make us dance.*

Madame Blanchett looked to be wearing ballet slippers, and she walked through the room as though on the stage.

"On the night of the cotillion," she said, "you will dance the Viennese waltz. A romantic, elegant dance that will highlight your collective grace. My assistant and I will go through the basic steps with a small group; then we will observe the rest of you. I will need ten volunteers: five men, five women."

By "volunteers," Madame Blanchett meant "the chosen." Her assistant—a gorgeous young man with coppery Grecian features—came around and selected people at random. When he approached Nelly, she didn't move.

"No," she whispered. "Please."

He ignored her, took her hand, and pulled her like a dog on a leash directly toward Jay.

The two of them were placed within inches of each other, along with four other couples. Madame Blanchett's sole instructions were to "follow her," as though that would be enough to master an entire waltz. Jay was the only young man who stood with back straight and eyes unaffected by the many eyes that watched them.

"Here we are again," he said.

"It must be fate."

"That, or a timely suggestion."

"God, Jay," Nelly said, smiling. "Did you bribe her to pair us?"

Jay tried his best to look crestfallen.

"What do you take me for, Nelly Sawyer? Of course I didn't bribe

Madame Blanchett," he said with an inflated French accent. "Just asked nicely. This is the safest way for us to speak. "

A needle was moved on the gramophone, and Strauss began to play. Nelly reached for him first. His hand on the middle of her back forced her to stand tall, straining the muscles in her shoulders. Now, knowing Jay as she did, Nelly was suddenly nervous and hyperaware of her own failings.

"I should warn you," she said before the score changed and there was no turning back. "I don't know this dance very well. The lessons my brother and I had were basic, at best."

Nelly could feel the heat of Jay's hand through her silken white glove. His grip was secure, steadying in its confidence.

"Just follow me. You'll pick it up soon enough."

Then, like the races, they were off.

The Viennese waltz was fast, and Jay kept a furious pace. The continuous spinning was deeply disorienting. Nelly tried to find someone or something to focus on, but everything became reduced to formless shapes. They stopped moving long enough for Jay to push her away, then draw her back in, turning her as he did. She ended up with her back pressed against his chest. Throughout it all, their hands stayed locked tight together and her feet lost direction.

"Don't look down," Jay said. "That's the fastest way to fall."

"Why are you so good at this?" Nelly asked.

"I'm not *that* good."

"You're better than you have any business being. This here's supposed to be a lesson, and you're breezing through it like it's the Texas Tommy."

"Oh, I'm impossible at the Texas Tommy," he said. "My mother refused to teach the newer crazes. She glorified the classics: quadrilles, the polka, reels, and tangos. A little bit of ballet. And, of course, the waltz."

This was a rare thing indeed. All Nelly knew of Jay's family was the story he'd told Sequoia that night in the Lantern Club. A part of her had come to think that he had no parents. That he was constructed out of clay, fully formed as he was, and an ingenious god breathed life into him.

"Your mother was a dance teacher?" she asked. The composition was taking a slow, twilight turn, and Jay's pace slowed to match it.

"Before she met my father, yes," he said. "She had a small school in San Francisco. My father though, he was hopeless. He decried dancing as bourgeois because he had no rhythm, so my mother danced with me, her last student. I think it was the only thing keeping her sane some days."

"Was she . . . ?" Nelly swallowed to wet her mouth and wash down the inherent intimacy of her question. "Was she the white parent? Or was that your father?"

Even though Nelly was held by him—nearly flush against his body—there was a vastness like eons between them. The hold he had on her loosened, and she felt him slipping away.

"That was a terrible question," she said. "It's just, you are the first mulatto I've met raised by both a mother *and* a father. There're plenty of children with white daddies who won't claim them, but never anyone like you."

Jay's face took on the complexion of a porcelain bowl made up of a thousand faded gray cracks in the glaze. Nelly knew she was in a hole, and she began to dig herself deeper in earnest.

"Maybe things in California were easier for them—"

"It was terrible for them," he said. His voice was that of a ghost, raspy and waning. "It was terrible for them everywhere."

Then she was in the air. Lifted up by the waist with only her hands on Jay's shoulders to keep her grounded. Nelly thought of her first time on horseback. When a new colt spooked and took off at full tilt. All she could do was hold on.

As soon as she was on the ground again, she felt Jay's breath tickling the skin under her ear.

"Do you still want a seat at the table?"

She turned her head quickly. "What?"

He *tsked* and said, "Eyes forward."

Nelly snapped her head back into place.

"I said," Jay whispered, "do you still want a seat at the table?"

The dance instructor clapped once, and they were spinning again.

Nelly had made this decision only in her mind. Privately, during the unholy bleakness of the night, when the devil skulked in and asked to make a deal. To tell Jay would be like the sealing of a spell. The magic would bind her and going back would require a terrible ransom.

"No," Nelly said. "No, I can't."

He spoke as though he hadn't heard her: "You're not supposed to know about it without an invitation, but I can vouch for you if you can get yourself there. I'll be with you the whole time, so what happened at the Ebony Masque *will not* happen again."

Nelly halted the flow of the dance and stood still. She needed to say this with her head clear and her feet planted.

"You've been a great help to me, Jay. But I'm not doing this anymore."

Jay glanced about at the other couples, still stumbling through the waltz, and said, "You mean dancing?"

She held up her hand.

"No. The article. The Mayor of Maxwell Street. I can't do it."

Jay tried to laugh but stopped himself almost at once. He looked at Nelly as he would at some great master's half-finished painting, forever lost in the ill-defined realm of potential. His eyes flicked over her shoulder, and she knew that they landed on Tomás.

"I didn't think you could be so easily distracted," he said, incensing her like a thrown-down gauntlet.

"Marta Harjo's dead, Jay."

Nelly waited for the outrage, but the very shade of such emotion didn't cross Jay's face. He appeared irritated by the admission. As though Marta's murder was a sudden change of plans that risked upturning an otherwise successful evening.

"Yes." He said it like a fact, as common as the coming dawn.

Nelly scoffed, already close to tears at just speaking the words out loud.

"She's dead because of me," she said. "I used her name, and now she's gone and her daughter's lost, maybe forever. Take comfort in knowing that you were right, Jay Shorey. This story is clearly beyond me."

"You're giving up? After all you've done, that *I've* done?" Jay said. The score was reaching its rapturous climax.

"I'm not giving up. I'll go back to Mr. Norris and ask for another assignment. He's already offered before. But if I continue on this path, I know more people are going to get hurt."

"Of course they are. Did you think this would be easy? Bloodless? I saw you threatened within an inch of your life, and you hailed it as a triumph!"

"I can take what's thrown at me," Nelly said. "Marta didn't know that telling me about the Ebony Masque would put her very life in danger."

"But *you* did."

Jay's voice was flat as the mirror's face. With the dancers spiraling around them, it appeared to Nelly that they were trapped in some crawl space between worlds. Forever watching the dancing, and the merrymaking, and the normalcy of everyday life, but never experiencing it.

"You had to have known," Jay said. "No, I know you did. You didn't need to give them Marta. You made that choice because you knew it would ingratiate you to those men, get you closer to what you needed from them. You said you wanted this, Nelly."

Was he disappointed in her? Ashamed? The one thing she thought he might rejoice to hear, and he spat it back in her face like a viper's venom.

"I do!" she said. "More than anything. But I won't offer up people like tithes before an altar. There has to be another way."

"And if this is the only way?" Jay asked.

"Then there's no way for me."

Nelly's hands shook. Not from the decision to give up on the article, but the failure of it. She'd staked her future on this one experience, this one opportunity. And like Strauss's enchanting composition, it was over and done.

"I thought this would please you," she said.

"Don't act like you're doing this for me, Nelly. Not after all the times I begged for reason."

"What do you want, Jay, hmm? For me to cry? For me to tell you all the ways you were right about me?"

"But I was wrong." Nelly did not know his hand had moved until she felt it on her chin, then her cheek. To touch her in such a way was all but forbidden in mixed company. His blunt nails ran along the curve of her jaw, a threat and a promise. "I was wrong about so many things."

The noises of the guests in the fabricated ballroom filled in the crater left by the music. Jay took Nelly's hand and bent under the pretense of kissing it.

"You're not ruthless," he whispered. "You're just naive."

Nelly snapped her hand away and said, "At least I'm not cruel."

Jay's smile was vacant and insidious like an old, empty house.

"No, you're never cruel, Nelly. But you are a coward."

CHAPTER TWENTY-EIGHT

Nelly felt like a fool. An entitled, sanctimonious, interloping fool. It was early morning on the day before the cotillion, and all the debutantes were assembled in the Black Belt to do the "good work" of scolding hardworking folk about everything from their clothes to their speech. The National Negro Women's League thought this would be the perfect experience for those fortunate enough to enter society with such splendor and spectacle. To teach them humility, to nurture their devotion to service. Nelly felt no humility as she stood with her basket full of pamphlets in front of a tired woman in striped coveralls. Only shame and a soul-deep desire to leave this place and scrub away the mark it left on her.

The woman had the thin eyes of a person accustomed to little or no sleep. A hard wind blew from the east, and Nelly swore that she heard the foundations of the three-story tenement give.

"Good morning, ma'am," Nelly said with an apologetic smile. "My name is Penelope Sawyer, and on behalf of the National Negro Women's League, I welcome you to Chicago."

She read the lines just as she'd been instructed, but with a sheepish lilt.

"Welcome me?" the woman said. Hers was a Bluegrass accent like Nelly's. "I've been here five years. Bit past time for a 'welcome,' don't you think?"

Most of the people Nelly had met in that tenement alone were long overdue for a welcoming committee, but according to the old settlers of Chicago, every Negro who claimed Georgia, or Florida, or Tennessee was "new," no matter how long they'd lived in the city.

Nelly handed the woman an embossed pamphlet prepared by the League. It was several pages and included a long list of places *respectable* Colored folk were expected to go, *respectable* ways they were meant to wear their hair, how to walk, how to eat, how to use public transportation. It was the type of document given out to the foreign-born as soon as they stepped on American soil. A reminder of how *other* they were, and how inhospitable their new home would be. It was a demand for them to help themselves if they wanted any help at all.

"How many did you give out?" asked the doe-eyed Lillian Binga. She was only sixteen, and as the niece of Jesse Binga, she would have been the most desired debutante of the season if not for Nelly. Nelly felt like an old, bitter maid next to this cheery young woman with amber skin and an unquenchable smile.

Nelly checked her basket and said, "Maybe six. One man set it on fire and used it to light his pipe, though, so not sure if that counts."

Lillian laughed as though Nelly had said something funny.

They walked in a slow-moving herd down State Street past drugstores, tailors, barbershops, and grocers, all owned by Negroes. It was a bustling stretch, and Nelly had to press in close to the other girls in order not to be jostled about. Some of the young ladies tried to hand out pamphlets to random men and women, whether they were originally from the South or not.

"Lillian, have you ever been to this neighborhood?"

"Not really. My family tries to keep me pretty strict to school and church."

"But isn't your home a few blocks from here?"

Nelly had visited it only recently, when the debutantes had a dress fitting for their custom white cotillion gowns. She remembered specifically how her father and Jesse Binga talked at length about bomb threats from disgruntled white neighbors. Mr. Binga had personal experience and carried that mantle as a point of pride.

"Oh, you know," Lillian said. "Chicago is such a big city, and I've only been here half a year. You can walk a block from your front door and be in a whole new world."

"Ladies!" called out one of the committee chairs at the front of the procession. She was as militant as John Pershing, shouting out orders every few minutes and demanding they walk in a uniformed, synchronized line. "We'll be riding the Elevated soon, so be sure to have your change ready for tickets. Stick together, please, no dawdling."

The stairs up to the El station were crowded. A rush of people came down out of the most recent train, pushing Nelly flush against the unstable railing. That is when she saw a familiar face passing by. The cleft lip lit the fuse of her memory, and the eyes. Downcast and distracted now, but when Nelly first saw them, they were alight with the joy of finding something that had long been lost.

"Excuse me," Nelly called out. The woman kept on walking. "Excuse me, miss!"

Nelly peeled herself from the railing and chased her onto the sidewalk.

"Miss!" she cried again. "Miss Rose!"

The woman stopped and spun around, scanning the post-train horde with wary, weary eyes that settled on Nelly. She took in Nelly's Sunday school white dress and wide-brimmed hat with certainty. She wasn't one to forget a face either.

"It is Rose, right?"

Rose's stance became defensive. She nodded and closed her hands in front of her.

"It is," she said. "I don't think I ever got your name, miss."

"It's Nelly Sawyer." The wind stirred up and nearly yanked the hat from Nelly's head. The ribbon tied about it loosened and blew away, winding through the sky like a tiny pink dragon.

"Can I treat you to lunch?" Nelly asked over the unnatural howl of the Chicago wind.

Rose scoffed and said, "It ain't even noon yet, Ms. Sawyer."

"Well, how about some coffee? I don't mean you any harm, I just want to talk."

Rose looked over Nelly's outfit again with a bit more derision, lingering on her basket of pamphlets.

"What could you and I ever have to talk about?"

Nelly could tell a lot about a person by how they took their coffee.

Her mother liked it black and with a little bit of grit, as bitter as the ranchers who worked their horses. Her father wanted it sweet. So sweet that it was more dessert than beverage, and with a shot of whiskey to "keep him honest." Her grandmother mixed coffee in with oatmeal and had three bowls for breakfast. Since moving to DC, Samuel drank his coffee in what he called the French style—a messy sludge that went down like petrol. Elder never was one for coffee. On the rare occasion he did partake, he threw it back like a shot. Black as a moonless night with an egg white stirred in.

Rose Claxton requested that her coffee be hot, hotter than she could stand. She added cream, sugar, and honey, then spent over a minute stirring it all together. When she drank it, she cherished it with closed eyes. She set down her mug and noted Nelly's own empty hands.

"You don't drink coffee?" Rose asked.

Nelly shook her head and said, "Not really. It gives me the shakes. But please, have as much as you want. Order some food, too. All on me."

Rose closed her hand around the mug and looked to be bracing herself against it.

"I thank you," she said. "Coffee is as precious as jewels in our home these days. Lord knows, some mornings I need it. The Bible says man can't live on bread alone. Not to be blaspheming, but I just might be able to make it through on a cup a day."

Nelly laughed at the rapport, thankful for it, then peeked at the black-and-white maid's uniform under Rose's sweater.

"Were you coming from a job when I met you by the El?" Nelly asked.

"And another one starts after lunch. It's funny, I thought coming up to Chicago meant I wouldn't have to clean no more houses. Turns out that might be the only thing I'm suited for."

The restaurant they'd chosen was quiet. It lulled in that bizarre hour between a blue-collar breakfast and a white-collar lunch, so the only souls left were those with nowhere to go or nothing to do. Nelly and Rose were practically alone and left to their own devices.

"I'll tell you right now," Rose said. "I don't want any trouble. Not from you, and not from Jimmy neither."

It made Nelly wince; thinking of Jay, but also hearing him called by another name.

"You'll have no trouble from me, Rose. And none from Jay—excuse me, *Jimmy*. He's a friend to me. I just want to understand him better."

Rose had a charming laugh. Tinkling like silver and rain.

"A friend? Really? Jimmy never took to friends back home. He was a sweet boy and liked pretty well by everyone, but he didn't seem to want the company. Would rather be alone with his books."

Nelly knew of Jay's remarkable command of languages, but she had never seen him read before. The image came pleasantly: Jay curled in a comfortable chair, engrossed in a novel or a book of philosophy. Glancing up as she walked into the room. Holding out his hand to pull her close.

"When was the last time you saw him?" Nelly asked to beat back the fantasy. "Before the train station, I mean."

Rose looked into the coffee and, as though she could see her past reflection in the creamy film, began to pull at her hair and press down the bags under her eyes.

"Years and years," she said. "Not since the war. He was James Glass when I knew him, but we all called him Jimmy Blue-Eyes. Most of us ain't never seen a Colored boy with eyes like his before. They scared me when I was younger. I thought they meant a demon walked around in his skin."

That day at the train station had planted a doubt in Nelly that festered like an infection. She never completely believed that he was "Jay Shorey" from California—unknown and unclaimed—but the alternative meant that everything she'd come to resent and even admire about him was a lie.

"Rose," Nelly said, "what Jimmy said to you in Lake Forest was unacceptable."

Rose tried to downplay her hurt, reduce it and make it small, but it came through in the way her rounded fingernails rapped like crashing waves against the table.

"It wasn't the most welcoming place for a boy like him, back home in Wood Acre. The white family that lorded over the place tormented him without fail, and in all manner of ways. Jimmy always knew he had options, you see. He couldn't touch them, he couldn't see them, but he knew they were there. Not much those people could do with a Negro who wanted more for himself. And the rest of us weren't none better. What he needed after his folks died was a community. All we gave him was a cold shoulder."

As Rose spoke, Nelly thought of Sequoia and all her damning suspicions. Jay was everything she had warned Nelly he'd be. Yet, there was pain amidst the deceit. After all, there had to be a reason for him to run so far, and for so long, that even he couldn't remember where he began.

"I'm a bit of a storyteller, Rose," Nelly said, "and I would like to know Jimmy's story."

Rose shook her head and said, "It's not a happy story, Ms. Sawyer."

No. Such a thing wouldn't be appropriate for Jay. Whatever his story, it must be tragic.

CHAPTER TWENTY-NINE

The heat of the night was stifling. Already, two young ladies had clean passed out, and several others gathered at cracked windows, praying for a breeze. Nelly stood with Effy Syphax and fanned her with a folded program to keep her paste-like makeup from smearing. Majestic as the Central Library was as a venue, it was not partial to ventilation. Especially where the young women were stored alongside books and shelves cleared out to accommodate the ceremony in the great hall. The debutantes were told to arrive a full two hours before the gala's planned start, and now they waited, sweating in the wings like players before an impatient audience.

"I can't believe I'm doing this again," Effy said. "It was scorching when I was sixteen, too. My knees buckled during the presentation, and they had to bring me round with vinegar. I was so embarrassed that I wished they'd just left me on the floor. I cried during my first dance. Sobbed so loud they could hear me over the music. Has it started yet?"

Nelly stretched to see over the heads of thirty women and girls assembled backstage, and the world she saw glittered. Candlelight and diamonds, chandeliers and champagne glasses. She heard laughter, chatter, silverware against porcelain, a soft classical score threading delicately amidst it all.

"I don't think so," she said. "It's a full house, though. Everyone should be here by now."

Effy lifted her arms to air out the natural musk of many frenzied bodies pressed close together.

"Oh, thank God! I feel like a pig in a damn stall."

Effy was a small woman, and when she stopped to look up at Nelly, the surprise and mild amazement in her almost pitch-black eyes were evident.

"You are quite the beauty tonight, Miss Nelly," she said.

Nelly's reflex had always been to shuck off such compliments. But she stalled when she remembered how she'd felt staring at her reflection after hours at the mercy of beauticians, and seamstresses, and stylists. Every example she had of the beautiful was notably slighter and more pastel than what she inherently was. Early on, she established that her nose was too wide, her hair too woolly, her bones too big, and her skin far too dark. No one bothered to contradict these assumptions, so she consumed them. Digested them. Eventually, embodied them.

And yet, there she'd stood. Fully aware that what she saw in the tall mirror could only be described as *beautiful.* The white silk of the gown draped in decadent folds that whispered across the floor in a short train. Jeweled straps held up the bodice, weaved through her soft bob, and closed about her neck in a thick chain, turning her skin and hair into galaxies. The features she'd so long counted as a disadvantage became stunning.

A bell rang out in the main ballroom, and Nelly heard the muffled voice of Mrs. Bousfield, the cotillion's Master of Ceremonies. There were the intonations of welcome, acknowledgment of the sponsors, the significance of the event. Scattered laughter after an ineffectual joke; then the ten-piece band struck up "Casta Diva," accompanied by the soprano Estelle Clough.

The debutantes shuffled quickly into an orderly line while their minders adjusted gloves and straightened hems. One after another, they were pushed through a curtain and out onto the stage. The girl in front of Effy—a Hurley from South Carolina—disappeared in a hail of applause. Effy began to shake. An older lady in a bronze turban reached out for her, and as Effy started to wobble, Nelly caught her by the shoulders and whispered, "Don't you dare faint! There's no way I could follow that up."

Effy laughed just as the curtain opened and she stepped into white light.

The turbaned woman grinned at Nelly. "You're next, sweetheart."

When Nelly fisted her hands, she felt an unpleasant clamminess. She'd reminded herself all day that she wouldn't let herself be undone by this cotillion. She was not a debutante, this was not her "season," there were a thousand more important things at stake. However, when they pulled the curtain aside and she saw her father standing in a black tuxedo, Nelly cared more for those seconds in a pretty white dress than she did for anything else in the world.

"Well done, old girl," Ambrose said. "That'll show 'em."

He walked her from the stage down to the parquet dance floor. Tomás stood among a long line of other escorts. He was more a prince than ever in a splendid tailcoat so ornately embroidered that the gold thread rippled in the light.

"You actually wore the uniform."

As he kissed Nelly's gloved fingers, he said, "What else should I wear in the presence of a goddess?"

Their first dance was that damned Viennese waltz, but Tomás took to it like a shot. With his background, he'd probably learned to waltz as soon as he learned to walk, to speak, to shoot, and to hunt. Nelly knew she looked faultless in his elegant embrace. Like a little wooden doll spinning in a music box. She glanced down to count her steps once, and only once, then heard Jay's voice. *Eyes forward.* Lifting her head, she saw him.

He was partially concealed in the back of the ballroom, but recognizing Jay was now second nature to her. His ivory tuxedo was just as stylish and bold as he'd promised. Bold as the eyes watching her now. Unreadable and sad, filled with something too forlorn to be desire.

☀

They had two hours of peaceful propriety. Another waltz, then a banquet where the debuting couples were scrutinized and prayed over. The hope was that one or two of the pairs could bridge the continental distance between the centers of Negro wealth and create a real aristocracy. Such was the real point of the "grand season":

to turn the Negro elite into a class with the economic power and breadth to compete on a national level. It was to be a night of possibilities for their community in defiance of the inevitable corrosion brought on by Jim Crow and its ilk.

Tomás performed his role to perfection. He visited each table, accepted every introduction. Laughed at Ambrose's jokes, paid Florence all manner of flattery, and remembered the names and faces of each guest at the NNBL dinner. The hall was filled with the acclaimed and celebrated of their insular community, but Tomás was the unofficial guest of honor. Everyone wanted to rub shoulders with royalty. Even when he maintained that he was just a polo player, that didn't keep the stars out of their eyes. And like a fish on a line, Nelly allowed herself to be dragged along. His charm gave her poise. His elegance made her stand tall. For once, *she* wore all the glittering finery, and it did not wear her.

When ten o'clock struck like a curse, all that changed. The band gave up on waltzes and turned to the Charleston, and the fox trot, and the black bottom. Skirts were hiked, and young men stripped down to trousers and bibbed shirts. The floor was littered with abandoned kid-leather gloves like October leaves.

When Lloyd Younger asked Nelly to dance, she asked if he was drunk.

"Don't be like that, Nelly! Aren't we pals?" he asked while doing the quickest shimmy-shake she'd ever seen. No, they weren't pals. But they weren't enemies either. He taught her and Effy Syphax how to do the Texas Tommy, then spun her about so fast that she thought she might fly.

Nelly hadn't spent much time among young people before Chicago. She'd grown up surrounded by men and women whose sole purpose was either to teach her, mind her, or ignore her. Adopting a stern façade was the only way to be taken seriously. So, now, to make up for lost time, she laughed like a child.

Since discovering journalism, Nelly had convinced herself that the bubbly joy like what she experienced at the cotillion was undeserved. How could she so effortlessly sport those rose-tinted glasses while people who looked like her starved, and bled, and cried, and died? How could any of them? If the greatest weapon against hate truly was "complete, unmitigated, iridescent happiness," then why did a part of her cringe every time she passed a glass surface and caught the reflection of her own smile?

Nelly collapsed at Sequoia's table after three encores of a Broadway melody. Tomás volunteered to acquire refreshments for them both, then attempted to cross the dance floor like an explorer crossing the River of Doubt. And as lively as the party had become, Sequoia's presence among its bacchic gaiety was unusually subdued.

"Sam sends his love," Nelly said. "He couldn't make the trip, but he asked you to save him a dance for next time. He's been practicing."

Sequoia grinned around the lip of her flask.

"Sweet Samuel. He should be practicing, with that shoddy footwork of his."

"But why aren't *you* dancing? You could out–Lindy Hop every person in this room."

"I am not dancing alone at a cotillion like someone's little sister."

"Then dance with me. Or Tomás! He wants to samba, but no one is brave enough to try."

"You're a dear," Sequoia said, although it didn't sound like a compliment, "but for me, it's either dance with the one I want, or not at all."

Nelly was confused only long enough to notice the way Sequoia's eyes tracked one of the caterers. A long-legged white woman who went from table to table serving small chalices of ice cream. Her smile fell on all with equal, unforgettable adoration. Nelly'd met Agathē only once, but the girl's serene attitude left a mark on all who passed through her midst.

"A Negro cotillion with Greek caterers," Nelly said. "How exactly did you pull that off?"

"There are some benefits to sitting on the Junior Cotillion Planning Committee," Sequoia said. "Not fucking many, but one or two. All I had to do was put Agathē's family at the top of a list. I may not be able to dance with her, but I can watch her, and smile at her, and pretend like I'm having a good time."

She took another drink. A long one with her head thrown back, and the ruby necklace at her throat bobbed as she drained the flask.

"I'm sorry." It was a hollow offering, but it was all Nelly could give. The thick kohl around Sequoia's eyes made them all the more penetrating, especially when narrowed with such precision.

"Don't be sorry, Nelly," she said. "Dance. Laugh. Simper while Tomás fetches your punch. But for the love of God, mean it when you do. You have no reason to pretend, so don't embarrass the rest of us by trying."

The shame Sequoia conjured in Nelly quickly turned into a righteous anger.

"I don't understand you," Nelly said. "You were the one who told me that Tomás was an excellent catch. You and everyone else insisted that this was the best thing that has ever happened to me. Damn near a miracle! But now that I'm actually close with him, I'm being insincere? What exactly do you want from me, Sequoia?"

"The truth." Those twenty-six years reared by a preacher came out of her then. She spoke with all the damning authority of an avenging angel. "The whole fucking truth, Nelly. I know this isn't what you want. Maybe it's what you want right now, love-drunk and stupid, but not in twenty years. Not even in two. The day's coming when no one will give a shit about what you think, only what you can do for them. Stop beating the devil around the pole and show us who you really are while it matters. Ah, we were just talking about you! Your ears must've been itching."

Jay appeared before them as though from moonlight. Up close, Nelly could say definitively that his tuxedo was a raging hit. Instead of washing him out, the white and gold gave him a supple, sensuous glow.

"Good evening, Ms. McArthur. That is a wonder of a dress. Dyed with the blood of your enemies, I'm assuming?"

Sequoia flexed her shoulders like a bird fluffing its wings. "Tell me, are you *always* the bride at every wedding and the corpse at every funeral, or do you pick your opportunities to upstage with some intentionality?"

"So says the woman in red. Besides, I thought we agreed to split the weddings and funerals down the middle."

Sequoia's grin was all poison. She shook her wrist, and Nelly heard what remained of her liquor sloshing around in the bottom of her flask.

"Looks like I'm all out. You working tonight, Mr. Shorey, or should I refill this myself?"

She didn't wait for an answer. She stood and forced her way through the gala, nearly knocking over one of the catering staff. The big-eared boy in white stared after her with shotgun barrels for eyes.

Having successfully dueled Sequoia into submission, Jay finally turned his gaze on Nelly. In the aftermath of their falling-out at the NNBL dinner, a gulf had formed between them. Briefly, they were strangers again. But they knew each other well enough not to waste time.

He held out his hand and said, "Dance with me, Nelly."

There was something new in the way he said her name. A soft warmth like a dying fire. Nelly glanced about for Tomás while Jay kept his hand suspended there. Easy and patient, as though the choice had already been made and all she had to do now was accept it.

"You know," he said, "it's often recommended—nay, *encouraged*— that young ladies dance with more than just one beau. Wouldn't want to give the impression of having favorites, would we?"

"Is that a dare or a threat?" Nelly asked.

"Oh, that's entirely up to you."

A dare, then.

Nelly took Jay's hand, and he pulled her to her feet.

The dancers swayed in tight couples like birch trees in an autumn wood. The band was playing a bluesy take on Abel Baer, and it turned what Nelly always considered to be frivolous melody into an intoxicating waltz. Jay led them into a listless box step, and Nelly allowed herself to be soothed by his cologne's pinewood scent. She rested her head against the swell of his chest, right over the steady *tap, tap, tap* of his heart.

Up above, the hall's famous glass dome gleamed. Nelly didn't know such a thing of beauty could exist in a library, of all places. She doubted many of the Negro citizens of Chicago did either. A child born in the Black Belt may go their entire life without witnessing this fairyland, simply because it had not been created for them. The realization made the music as grating as the clank of chains in Nelly's ears.

"What will they say about all of this?"

Jay's head shifted at her temple.

"They?" he asked.

"The people a hundred years from now. Our grandchildren and great-grandchildren. They'll see pictures from this night and hear stories about all of this excessive glamour in a building that won't even let Negroes through the front door unless they pay for the privilege. Will they laugh at us for our hypocrisy? Damn us?"

"They'll say it was a charmed life," he said. "Hell, that's what I thought when I stepped into this ballroom. It felt like a mistake, or a lie. What else could it be, right? A room full of Colored folks who aren't here to clean or to serve, but to *enjoy* in enough splendor to rival Olympus. I spent so many years breaking my back to survive, and thanking God for the strife. But this night—*you*—it's proof that we can hope for more. That we can be more, and all on our own terms."

His voice harbored an old wonder. The kind that children felt when they believed, even for just an instant, that all the phantasms of their dreams could be real.

"Is that what you want, Jay?" Nelly asked. "A charmed life?"

With his mouth so close to the taut skin of her neck, Nelly felt more than heard him say, "I want it all."

She knew the contentment she felt wouldn't outlive the song, but while she had it, it was everlasting.

"I know I'm not the first to tell you this tonight," Jay said, "and Lord knows I won't be the last. But you are beauty itself, Ms. Sawyer."

Nelly laughed on impulse. She could never tell how much of Jay's flirting was sincere or just another attempt to commandeer a conversation.

She said, "You think so? I'll pass on your compliments to the dress."

"It's not the dress. Look at me, Nelly." Jay went still, and Nelly had to push back to peer into his face. She'd long assumed that she was numb to his ethereal attractiveness, but faced with it now, there was no avoiding how handsome he was. Those eyes—a person couldn't fathom that kind of blue.

"I haven't been honest in a long time," he said. "I lie to everyone, about everything. I lie to myself. But when I tell you I care for you, Nelly, I—"

"I know," she said. "Jay, I know. I know *everything.*"

Confusion morphed Jay's features. Then a brutal understanding. A shadow fell over those luminous eyes like a shroud. His eyes roved down over her nose, her mouth, her chin, to the rope of diamonds that dangled about her neck. A vision came to her. Nelly saw his hands coming up to close around that rope. Twisting and twisting until the diamonds cut into the skin of her neck and made her bleed.

What happened next happened quickly.

Jay's attention shifted over her shoulder. The hammer of a pistol slid back and locked. Someone screamed.

"Mind your place, nigger."

Then fireworks.

Nelly dropped to her knees to stop the ringing in her ears, but in vain. She couldn't hear the first bullet as it struck Jay in the chest. She couldn't hear the second, or the third. She had to watch, deaf to the world, as Jay took one breath, and another, and then crumbled to the floor not to rise again.

The shooter was dressed all in white, and his eyes were fearful and pubescent. He hadn't even grown into his big round ears yet. The smoking gun in his hand looked like a toy Nelly could buy in a corner store. When he lifted it in her direction, she scrambled away and opened her mouth to yell. Something snapped into place at the sound of her voice. The boy shook his head, dropped the gun, and ran.

CHAPTER THIRTY

top the bleeding.

Nelly unbuttoned Jay's waistcoat with trembling fingers. Amidst the running, and the screaming, and the unholy racket of musicians tripping over instruments, she tried to keep her focus on the blood staining her hands. There was a lot of it. More than she'd ever seen, and it was everywhere. When she went to wipe her hands across her dress, she left wide wounds in the silk. The harder she rubbed, the more it spread, until it covered her completely and the smell of death made her want to cry.

"Stop it," she said. "Pull your shit together, Sawyer. Stop the bleeding."

There were two wounds that she could see. One in the upper right quadrant of his chest, another grazing the left side of his abdomen. The third bullet was spent somewhere on the parquet floor. The chest wound gushed like a geyser, and Nelly had to press Jay's suit jacket against the hole with the full force of her knee to stanch it. A warm pool spread out from his insentient body in every direction.

"Jay, I need you to wake up," Nelly said. She bore down until her muscles ached. "Jay! James!"

His eyes opened. He looked at her, blinked, and smiled.

"You know my name?"

Nelly's body stilled when she heard his accent. Strong Alabama hill country, and as native to the Southland as dogwoods.

"I do. Do you know mine?"

"You're . . . Penelope Sawyer." The name came to him with some difficulty. "And I've been fucking shot."

He was alert now. Suffering, and mad as all hell, but awake. Nelly glanced up at the chaos unspooling around them. The dance floor was emptied, banquet tables overturned. People disappeared down the Carrara staircase to the first floor, and soon, they would be alone.

"Help!" she yelled. "Help, we need a doctor!"

Jay's bloody hand came up and closed tight around her wrist.

"No doctors," he said.

"What? What do you mean? The place is half-full of doctors."

"No doctors, Nelly. No hospitals, no police."

"If you don't get some medical attention, you'll die, Jay."

"Then I die."

Nelly hauled off and punched him square in the gut. She wasn't nearly as sorry as she should have been. She had half a mind to keep going and finish the job.

"Ms. Sawyer!" Tomás yelled. He stood at the top of the stairs while people hurried past, hands cupped around his mouth. She waved until he spotted her. When he dropped to his knees beside her, he slid in the fresh blood. He touched her face, her shoulders, her arms, looking for the wound that produced so much carnage. Then he noticed Jay.

"Dios mio," he said with a shivering sigh. "We need to get you a doctor, Mr. Shorey."

Together, Nelly and Jay said, "No doctors."

Jay took a while to find Tomás. He looked around him and above him, winking away disorienting pain, but when he finally settled on his face, he said, "Doctors will have questions. Questions I can't answer without trouble. Trouble for me, and trouble for the people I work for." He tried to sit up, but his head wasn't an inch off the ground before he cried out and fell again. "I just need to get home and out of the open. If the cops get to me, I'll be better off bleeding out in this shitty library."

He took a shallow breath and wheezed on the exhale.

"I'll get you home, Jay," Nelly said.

"You are getting the fuck out of here." Nelly refused, so he appealed to Tomás's naturally heroic sensibilities. "Get her out of here. Please. Throw her over your shoulder if you have to."

Tomás looked across Jay's broken body to Nelly, and she hoped he could see just how impossible such a thing would be. He might try, but she'd fight him, and he'd fail.

"Ave María llena eres de gracia," he said as he took off his gorgeous court uniform. He said it again as he used it to stanch the blood. He looped Jay's limp arm over his shoulder and heaved. Nelly took the other arm and pressed her hand to the savage gash in his side where the blood came out slow like sap from a tree.

They emerged on the Garland side of the library into a bright harvest-moon night. Nelly could hear yelling from the cotillion guests as they spilled out onto Michigan Avenue just a half block over. Tomás and Nelly had dragged Jay screaming from the great hall, but now he'd gone utterly silent. If not for the feel of him breathing in her ear, Nelly would've pegged him for a corpse.

Tomás eased Jay onto a curb, then looked up and down the alley to get his bearings.

"Stay here," he said to Nelly before setting off at a jog south, toward Washington Street.

Nelly held Jay as she would a child. His head was flush against her chest, and she rocked back and forth, more for her own comfort than for his. Blood seeped from the wound at his side, and Abraham's marvelous white creation was red as a sailor's last sunrise. Behind closed lids, Jay's eyes searched through a darkness only he could see.

"I need to tell you something," he whispered. They were the first words he'd spoken since the ballroom.

Nelly swatted at him and said, "Hush up with that. You're not gonna die, so stop trying to make a deathbed speech."

He surprised her by laughing.

"You'd deny a man his dying words?"

Headlights appeared at the bend in the road. Nelly was already lifting Jay and reaching for the door as Tomás's Stutz Bearcat came to a stop so sudden that the wheels lurched. It was a stripped-down roadster made for high speeds and steep curves with barely enough room for a driver, let alone her and Jay's gutted husk.

"This car," Jay slurred. "This is a nice car."

He was pressed against the passenger door, and the whole cockpit filled with a stench like dying animals.

Nelly shook him by the shoulder until his head bounced against the interior canvas top.

"Focus, please!" she said. "You said we needed to get you home. Where's home?"

"I told you, Nelly, I sleep on the El—"

"Dammit, Jay! We cannot stay here."

Jay's breath made imprints of steam like snowflakes on the window's glass.

"Okay," he said. All his concentration went into speaking with a clear, loud voice. "Head west on Randolph. If I live long enough, I'll tell you where to go from there."

Jay dwelled in the shadow of a cathedral. A great beast of a building that crouched over delis and post offices, brick walk-ups and converted townhomes. As Nelly pulled Jay out of Tomás's car, she felt the eye of Holy Innocents Church frowning down at her in pious judgment.

What have you done? it said. *What horror have you brought to this quiet place?*

His apartment's darkness was absolute, but once the light of a streetlamp filled out the gloom, Nelly could see things clearly.

It was a home fit only for the dead or the nearly dead. A cramped attic space with walls that leaned until they met in a pitched roof. Bare brick siding and timber floors that gave with every step. The furniture was possibly abandoned, included with the apartment only because it was there to begin with. A bed, a chest, a steamer wardrobe, a spindly rocking chair. The only thing that made the attic a technical residence was the coal stove. And all of it was covered in a sheet-white layer of dust. It seemed impossible that a person as graceful, and elegant, and effortlessly stylish as Jay could ever live in such a place.

He fell against the bed with an earthen sigh. His body sank into the mattress, crusted over with sweat like a locust shell. Tomás immediately leapt into action.

"Is there water?" he asked as he unwound their hasty tourniquet and helped Jay out of his undershirt. It stuck to his skin and came off with a grisly tear.

"In a pitcher," Jay rasped. "Above the stove."

Nelly moved without being told and found the stoneware pitcher, half-full of stale water and the corpses of wayward flies. She pulled a cotton work shirt from the wardrobe—moth-eaten, but clean—and began to rip it into strips. The deadliest wound turned out to be in Jay's shoulder, not his chest, as Nelly had first assumed. A small, perfect hole that was charred at the edges. While she cleaned it, Tomás lifted Jay into a sitting position to examine his back.

He hummed and said, "The bullet's still in you. I don't see an exit wound."

"Should we try to get it out?" Nelly asked.

"No use. Not here. We'll do more harm than good. It may be with you forever, Mr. Shorey."

"A memento mori," Jay named it. "As if I needed another reminder."

The second wound was an ugly gash near the curve of his hip where a bullet skimmed but didn't penetrate. Tomás said it would need stitching; in Mexico, he saw a man procrastinate closing up a wound like that and took five days to die because of it.

Through teeth clenched tight to keep him conscious, Jay said, "There's a woman a few buildings down. A seamstress called Kasia. She has steady hands, and she owes me a favor. She'll come with enough encouragement."

Nelly didn't need to guess that by encouragement he meant money. Her change purse was somewhere back at the library, but Tomás had a clip full of bills in his chest pocket.

"I'll go," he said. "We'll need more water, and something for the pain, I think."

Jay groaned his thanks.

"You should move your car while you're at it," he said. "Roadsters like that aren't common in this neighborhood. It'll draw attention."

Nelly followed Tomás to the door. They stood close, and in such pitiless light, he was no sporting gentleman with money at a loss on how to spend it. The steadfast cut of his jaw betrayed memories of a hundred such bullet wounds and desperate attempts to save a life, perhaps even his own.

"Pack the bullet hole with cotton to stop the bleeding," he instructed. All the overtones of flattery and flirtation were gone;

they spoke as equals, comrades with backs against the wall. "Use as much as you need. It's a furious wound and will bleed all night, but it's not fatal. Not yet, anyway. That business by his hip needs to be managed until this seamstress arrives. Clean it, bind it. With God's grace, Mr. Shorey will see the morning."

Both their hands were marked with Jay's blood, fresh and old. Less than an hour ago, they were dancing to a brass band under painted glass and chandeliers.

"You must regret winning that race now," Nelly said.

"I never regret a win, Ms. Sawyer. Although, as spoils go, this is . . ." He drifted off to glance at Jay.

"It doesn't matter now," Tomás said. "I'll return as quickly as I can. Lock the door behind me."

Nelly heard the rush of his steps as he descended to the street. Soon after, the purr of his Stutz starting up and pulling out into the night.

"He's a good man."

Jay stared at Nelly with red-rimmed eyes. His body stretched across a bed originally made for a child, every limb extended. The blue light touched his skin and made him as ephemeral as a spirit. Like Saint Sebastian filled with arrows and caught in rapturous agony, Jay was still beautiful. More so now because his crafted prestige was shot full of lead and there was no illusion left. Bloodied, broken, but no less stunning, the feelings he conjured in Nelly were real.

"He is," she said. "Better than either of us deserve."

She shredded more old shirts and wrapped them layer by layer around his chest until the flow of blood was slowed, but not stopped.

Nelly moved on to the bullet hole. Clean and packed, it looked harmless enough, but she could not blot out the image of him draining like a butchered hog on the ballroom floor. She tried to stop her crying before he noticed, but his eyes were ever watchful, even in near-death.

"Don't you dare cry for me," he said as he touched her face.

She swatted his hand away and said, "Fuck off, I'll cry if I want to. You should be dead. Someone just tried very hard to kill you."

"Clearly, not hard enough."

She pushed off the bed and began to pace. Her heels left ruddy shoeprints on the floorboards.

"This isn't a joke, Jay. I'm covered in your blood!"

"I didn't mean for you to be involved in this, Nelly. I told you to leave me—"

"Leaving you wasn't a damn option. You know I would've dragged you out of there on my own if I had to, you *know that*."

"Of course I know that. Shit, with your record, you would've taken a bullet meant for me to make a statement."

"You take that for granted, Jay!"

"I never wanted it in the first place!"

He stood and took a step, but it was a step too far. Nelly rushed to him, and they went down to the raw, splintered floor together. Jay's body shook from the shock of rising and falling so quickly, and Nelly wrapped her arms around him, as though to bind him to this world. To make her strength his own and have him whole.

"I never wanted your friendship, Nelly," he said in a sigh that threatened to break into a sob, "but now that I have it, I don't know where I'd be without it."

She didn't allow that tenderness to pierce her. There was no point telling him how helpless she felt seeing him like this. He didn't need to know that she was grateful for him, too, and he never would.

Nelly helped him onto the edge of the bed. When she pressed a hand to his brow, it was wet and far too cold for such a balmy summer evening. She chewed on the inside of her cheek until it raised a sensitive bump that tasted of blood.

Looking down at the bullet hole maybe for the first time, Jay said, "Christ, that's ugly."

It *was* ugly. The blood had clotted, thankfully, but a yellow reeking pus coated the edges of the cotton packing.

"Tomás said it should be fine for now," Nelly said. "As long you're not bleeding."

"Not to sound ungrateful, but how does an international playboy know about gunshot wounds and blood loss? I didn't think polo was such a violent pastime."

Nelly took what little remained of the water and wet a rag for Jay's face and chest. She knew enough to suspect that the trauma had his blood running hot. At least his teeth had stopped knocking together from the pain, but whether that was a good thing or bad, she feared to ponder.

"He fought in Mexico during the revolution," she said. "I'd bet money that you're not the first bullet-riddled carcass he's come across."

"Of course." She was impressed and a little upset that he managed to sound sardonic in such a state. "It's not enough these days to be titled, rich, educated, *and* handsome. A fella has to be a war hero, too, to get anywhere in life."

Then he gave her a drowsy, crooked smile.

"He's in love with you, you know."

Nelly kept her focus on the rag in her hand and the way the lean muscles of his stomach contracted when she passed over them.

"You don't know that," she said.

"Oh, I do. I suspected before, but now I'm sure. He wouldn't be here tonight unless he was blissfully, madly in love with you."

"If that's true, what the hell does that say about me?"

She looked into his face, expecting to see that trickster's grin that always seemed reserved just for her—the shared, private jest—but he did not smile. Jay's remaining good hand came up to grasp hers, and the wasted water from the rag ran between their fingers. Eyes lidded and lost wandered over her face. Searching, digging. Imploring her to open up some secret door and let him in.

Jay sighed, and she felt his breath against her lips when he said, "I wonder."

Outside, a car door closed. Nelly jumped away from Jay, but he didn't let her go.

"Nelly—"

"There's no time."

She pulled once, hard, and he released her. Climbing onto the bed to reach the apartment's lone window, she peered out to see if Tomás had managed to find this seamstress and stopped short.

Under the light of a single pre-war streetlamp, there indeed was a vehicle parked exactly where Tomás's Stutz Bearcat had been. But this was no little speedster—rather, an old model Ford big enough to fit six. Two men were climbing out the back, while another two stood surveying the streets. One glanced up. Nelly couldn't see his face under the shadow of his top hat, but she felt his eyes.

"Jay," she said. "Is anyone supposed to know about this place?"

"Not anyone alive."

"How about the dead?"

When she looked at him, Jay's sudden, comprehending fear mirrored her own. Nelly ran for the door and bolted the lock, but she knew that would do no good if four men were coming to kill them.

"You have a weapon here?" she asked, already searching blind. "A rifle, a knife, something?"

Jay attempted to rise but didn't get far before falling back, clutching the gash at his side.

"A revolver," he said. Then, pointing: "A carpenter's bag in the chest."

The chest itself was near empty apart from a gaping sack made of worn canvas. When Nelly opened it, she was so startled by the neat stacks of cash that she almost closed it again. Seven bricks of one-hundred-dollar bills bound up in twine. Fifty thousand dollars total, maybe more.

This was the type of cash folk buried in tins, in a field, miles from the house and warded with redbrick dust. Not stored in a dusty, creaky chest, lying about for the mice to eat. More than anything, people with that kind of accessible money didn't bathe in brothels or pay their tailor in monthly increments. Either Jay was hoarding it all for some ominous, unknown reason, or he was hiding it. Was this pathetic little apartment just an elaborate kind of camouflage? She found the Smith & Wesson under the cash.

"Jesus, Jay," she said as she checked the cylinder. "This thing's rusted half to hell. Have you ever even cleaned it?"

Blessedly, every chamber was full, but it was an old gun. Barely maintained. Nelly would have a better chance at shooting herself than anyone else.

"You have to go," Jay said, pulling her to her feet.

"Where? Out the window? This is happening, Jay. Four men, six bullets. I have two chances to miss. So, I won't miss."

She cocked the pistol and realized that her hands were shaking. No, that wouldn't do. She had to be stronger than that.

"I've never shot a person before," she said in the guilty whisper of a last confession. "Rattlesnakes and rabbits. A coyote or two, but not a person."

Jay's forehead came to rest against hers. He breathed in long, steady bellows that filled her like the thrum of a pipe organ. By and by, her hand stopped shaking.

"I can't let you fight for my life, Nelly," he said, and it sounded like goodbye.

There was a knock at the door. Short and precise. A promise that if it wasn't opened from within, it would be kicked down from without.

Elder was the one who taught Nelly how to use a gun. Folk tended to forget how good of a shot he was, when speaking of her brother and the life he'd led. He could out-gunsling Bass Reeves. As kids, they would shoot milk bottles and old horseshoes on the backside of land her father now owned.

Don't paw at the damn thing, he'd say. *Loose, Nettle, loose hands! Now, I know your ass can throw a punch. Stand like you're 'bout to blacken my eye, one foot in front of the other. Okay, so aim. No, no, keep both eyes open. That's right. Just focus, and . . . let go.*

Nelly flung open the door and put her hand on the trigger. She aimed at the face in front of her, then stopped. She knew that face.

"Penelope Sawyer. This is a surprise."

Daniel Jackson's marble eyes looked at her now with a pleased satisfaction. As though she were an unexpected but welcome present. Jay's god-uncle was decked in formal white tie, probably straight from the cotillion. Three Negro men in black suits stood behind him in a wall of bodies and hands reaching for gun holsters. Nelly knew that all her supposed skill with a pistol would do no good. They would have her between the eyes before she could take in the breath needed to shoot.

Dan glanced down at a revolver not fit to shoot squirrels and laughed. It was a grating sound that showed off all his wide white teeth.

"If you mean to use that, girl," he said, "now would be the time."

CHAPTER THIRTY-ONE

With so many bodies in the apartment, Nelly appreciated just how small it really was. The standing men had to tilt like a house on stilts to avoid knocking their heads against the slanted roof.

Nelly sat on the bed with Jay, hands flat on her thighs as instructed, the gun now confiscated. Dan insisted that they couldn't take any risks. Dan claimed the chair—a rickety old rocker that cried like a cat in heat with each sway. Every time she glanced at the man guarding the door, or the one by the stove, or the one standing sentry at Dan's shoulder, she realized that the only way she was leaving that room tonight was if they *let her* leave.

Dan ran a white-gloved finger over the arm of the rocker and rubbed in the dust with the pad of his thumb.

"I haven't been to the Polish Patch since the war," he said. "Smart of you to set up here, Jimmy. Before tonight, I would've sworn up and down that you bunked in the Levee. That's where I went first. Had to knock a few heads to get the truth of it."

Jay alternated between leaning back as far as he could go and curling forward with his head between his legs. Fresh gore drained from the saturated cloth packed into his shoulder and ran down his chest like a red creek. Nelly reached out to steady him, but the man at the door *tsk*ed when he saw her move, so she stayed still. Dan spoke as though he couldn't even see Jay's injuries; couldn't *smell* them.

Nelly said, "Mr. Jackson, I don't know what—"

"Did I say you could speak?"

Dan's voice did not rise above polite conversation, but still, it seized her like a hand about the throat. She was more frightened now than she had been under Mikey Hannigan's knife. At least then she could see and measure the threat. Dan was as much an unknown as the dark side of the moon.

"It pains me to see you like this, Jimmy," he said, looking at Jay's ruined body with revulsion. "Maybe it was naive of me, but I've always thought of you as impervious to material things like bullets. Lord knows everything else has bounced off you. You mentioned once that your momma was German, but with your luck, I swear the bitch must've been Irish."

Jay groaned as he dragged himself upright. That insult seemed to bounce right off of him, too.

"This changes nothing," Jay said. "The Genna brothers only care about Maxwell Street. Move production to the Stroll, and by next year, the investors will recoup twice of what we'll lose without the Lantern Club."

Dan's eyes widened to wrinkle the brown skin of his leathery face.

"You know this message came from the Gennas?"

Jay looked at Nelly briefly, then said, "I had a theory they might try something like this. The boy's accent put the seal to it."

Much of what happened in those moments before Jay fell was a patchwork that Nelly still struggled to see in its entirety. But yes, she *did* remember that the shooter had an accent. He wore a caterer's uniform, so she'd assumed he was Greek. Just as everyone in that ballroom assumed he was Greek. He'd walked right through the back door with a platter of dolmades in one hand, and a weapon in the other.

Dan nodded, then removed his gloves. Acting without the slightest instruction from him, the man at his shoulder packed and lit a tobacco pipe. Dan reached up to accept it and took in three strong pulls like a chimney. When he let it out, the apartment filled with a smoke so thick that it made Nelly's eyes water.

"You had a theory," Dan said, "and you didn't share it with me? With any of us? With the Mayor?"

Nelly's ears burned at the name. Even the allusion to his presence plucked at her curiosity like the string of a fiddle.

"I didn't want to alarm anyone unnecessarily," Jay said.

"Don't talk to me like I'm one of your fucking marks, Jimmy. You didn't tell us about the Gennas to save your own black hide. When you came to me about liquor, I told you what you were up against. The Italians were the first to snatch up the bootlegging income and settled the particulars among themselves. The rest of us fell into line and were happy to do so. But you, Jimmy boy, you with your fresh ideas and that unobstructed mind that's made you such an asset to me. You said there was an easier way."

"And there is, Dan."

Jay sagged back with an arm wrapped tight across his middle. Dan shook his head at the sight, as though Jay were a derby-winning stallion, a champion, now too lame to run. He snapped at the man standing taut by the stove, who produced a sterling flask and offered it to Jay. He drank until it was near empty, then passed it on to Nelly, who finished off the rest.

"Whatever the Genna brothers might think," Jay said with a bit more substance, "I don't want the South Side to control all the bootlegging in Chicago. Just our own. If they had bothered to talk to me first, I would've told them the same."

"Talk to you?" Dan sneered. "You're telling me that for all your languages, you can't understand Chicago's mother tongue? They said everything they needed to say with a bullet. Fucking hell, I'd have less trouble if they had managed to kill you, Jimmy."

"I'm thankful for everything you've done for me, Dan."

"Are you?" The embers in the pipe's bowl flared with each angry inhale. "If that's the whole truth, boy, why didn't you come to me when they popped you? Didn't you know I'd take care of you?"

Jay licked his top lip, and Nelly saw that he was deeply frightened. She'd come to rely on his fearlessness and felt adrift in such a dangerous new world without that confidence.

He said, "I know how you hate mess. I figured I ought to clean this up myself, the best way I know how. Lest you clean it up for me."

Dan's smile was wistful. As though he'd already made up his mind about what he meant to do. When he sighed, it was with a heavy forlornness.

"I'll take care of the Genna brothers," he said. "At the next card game. You're right that the money we've made from liquor is . . . significant. If we can keep that income by moving the stills to the Stroll, I'll be happy for it. Take all of your Maxwell Street action to the Italians. Everything else, we'll make ourselves."

Jay reached out to take Dan's hand and seal this decision with the only authority they both respected.

"You won't regret this, Dan. Thank you."

"Don't thank me, Jimmy." Dan upended the bowl of his pipe and dumped a smoking clump of tobacco onto the floor, so close to Nelly's feet that she had to jump away to avoid being singed. "This shit *was* a fucking mess. If they'd tried to get at you on the Stroll or at the market, that would be one thing. But they shot you at a cotillion in front of this country's most well-to-do Negroes. Your blood might have been a warning, but *that* was the real message. That they can, and will, touch us anywhere. Months of good faith convincing folk that Chicago is a future worth investing in are now as spent and worthless as the bullet that hit you. We'll continue with this bootlegging enterprise because of the work owed and the money promised. But know this: I won't raise up half the South Side just to avenge your honor. I love you, and when I thought you'd died, I mourned you like a son. It'd be a lifetime's loss to lose you, but if you call down more trouble from the Gennas—or any of the Italians—I'll turn you over to them myself. And I won't ask for permission."

Dan's face was a wasteland, void of sympathy or a hope that he spoke in exaggeration. Nelly was horrified by such frankness from someone who claimed to love Jay as a father would. Then he fixed his attention on Nelly.

"Now. What are we to do with you, my girl?"

Nelly hated the sensation of being a point on a list. She knew the feeling well from her own mother. Florence had always been brutally efficient, but ever since their temporary resettlement in Chicago, Nelly had functioned as a task to be completed. She barely tolerated such treatment from her own family; she'd be damned if some stranger dismissed her with such indifference.

She reached into her bodice and pulled out the last of Jay's rolled cigarettes. She'd been saving it for the end of the night, a kind of celebratory smoke, but now was as good a time as any. When she held it out toward the man with the mechanical lighter, he glanced down at his boss for instruction. Receiving none, he set the flame against the paper and ignited it.

Nelly took a long drag and released it directly in Dan's face.

"Oh, I'm sorry," she said with synthetic sweetness. "Am I permitted to speak now?"

Dan grinned at her impudence. He sat far back in the rocker and crossed one leg over the other, as though he'd just captured her queen and was tickled to see how she'd respond.

He said, "Forgive my earlier brusqueness, Ms. Sawyer. In matters of business, my coarser side tends to show. Let me start off by congratulating you on a stunning debut this evening. You made quite the impression."

"It's not a night I'll soon forget," Nelly said.

Dan huffed like a steer, as if to say, *Boy, don't I know it.*

"I'm tired," he said. "It's been a long night, and I'd like to see the cold side of my pillow before morning. I'm going to ask you a few simple questions. All you need to do is give me straight answers, and I swear on the lives of my children, no matter what those answers might be, no harm will come to you."

"Oh, really?" Nelly jutted her chin toward the man at the door. "Then why's that one looking at me like a bull's-eye?"

The man in question moved aside the flap of his gray duster to flash the butt of a Remington as polished and dangerous as his smile.

"These are working men, paid handsomely to look after my best interest," Dan said. "A girl who answers the door with a loaded revolver might be considered a danger to myself, and others."

The men all laughed in a solemn echo like a storm roiling in the night.

Sitting up prim as a red maple, Nelly nodded at Dan and said, "Ask your questions, sir."

"What do you know of the business young Jimmy here is involved in?"

Nelly turned down her mouth, simulating deep thought.

"I know he manages a club off Maxwell Street," she said. "The Lantern, I think it's called. Anything else I just learned tonight. Here. From you. An undertaker who has to pay armed men to intimidate half-dead playboys and debutantes."

"Whoa there. Let's not insult each other, Ms. Sawyer. I think you know well enough by now that I'm not just some undertaker, and the man you call Jay Shorey sure as hell ain't just some playboy. I expect honest answers out of you. Now, did you see the face of the man who shot Jimmy?"

Yes.

"No. My back was to him."

"That's good. How did you manage to get here all on your own?"

Tomás.

"A Yellow Cab."

"That right?"

"The cabbie didn't ask questions."

Dan looked impressed.

"That's something to remember. Does anyone know you're here?"

Tomás. Tomás, out there somewhere, possibly walking up the stairs right now with some grizzled old seamstress.

"No one," she said.

"You're sure?" Dan asked. "Because the very last thing I need is your wrangler of a daddy bursting in with a shotgun and all that cowboy justice."

She repeated herself: "No one."

Dan swept cold eyes over Nelly. Her face, her bloody hands.

"You're about as lucky as Jimmy, Ms. Sawyer," he said with gentle regard. "The Lord must have the same plan for you two."

The rocker let out a godless wail when Dan stood. He was quite tall, and the shadow he cast by the witching hour's light was long.

"You'll need to keep your head down for a few days," he said to Jay. "The assassin they sent had piss-poor aim. I'll float it to the Mayor that I want a meeting, and a truce while the bad blood settles."

His eyes cut over to Nelly, and he motioned with his head for her to follow him. When they got to the door, she walked out first, followed by Dan. Remington stayed behind in the apartment while the other trigger men returned to street level. Nelly folded her arms across her chest, suddenly cold.

"Tell me the truth now," Dan said. "How's our boy faring?"

Nelly took another pull from her cigarette, then sent ash like snow falling over the landing into a makeshift courtyard.

"Better than he was before. He bled a lot at the cotillion, but I think he's out of danger now."

Dan wiped at his mouth and mumbled a thanks to God.

"Does he need a doctor?" he asked.

"I don't think so. Just looking after."

"Well, I don't think our boy's ever had too much of that." He smiled at her with an old man's endearing indulgence. "He speaks of you often. Silly things when he thinks no one's listening, and I'm beginning to understand why. I daresay he'd allow himself to be shot all over again if it meant spending another evening in your company. Nothing quite as healing as a pretty girl's touch."

Nelly's smile was much less beguiling.

"If it's all the same to you, sir, I hope to never be here, doing this, ever again."

"Aye," he said. "Me too."

Dan beat against the door, and it opened at once. Remington peered out at him with his hand on his weapon. His unease in Nelly's presence was more flattering to her than a dozen bright red roses.

"Yeah, boss?" he said.

"We're leaving. Give the girl back her gun. You know what, give her your duster, too, before she catches her death."

Remington handed over both without meeting Nelly's eye. She checked the cylinder and exhaled when she saw each bullet in its corresponding chamber. Having it in her hand made her more solid, somehow. More prepared for whatever came next.

"Get word to me should Jimmy take a turn," Dan said. "He'll tell you how. And, child? Don't be slow to use that old Smith & Wesson. If someone knocks at that door after me, you shoot them."

Nelly gave the revolver a twirl and slipped it smooth into the jacket's pocket.

"Like I should've shot you, Mr. Jackson?"

The old man threw his head back and bellowed. There was a candy smell to his breath like overripe peaches.

"Charming girl," he said. And as he made his easy way down and away: "Charming, charming girl."

CHAPTER THIRTY-TWO

Nelly put her back to the closed door and shook. Tremors ran all up and down her body until her bones knocked. Christ, but she wanted to cry. She had never been so scared of a person, of what they might do. Dan Jackson was just another man with weight to throw around, yet she felt marked by the Devil's own hand.

"What did he say to you?"

Jay sat on the edge of the bed with his hands braced against his knees, as though he might launch himself up at any moment. There were plans conspiring behind his eyes. She knew that wild look, had seen it in young horses, difficult to break, in the seconds before they decided to bolt.

"He asked if you were going to make it," she said, "and if you needed a doctor."

"What'd you tell him?"

"I told him you'd be fine."

Jay sagged back like a puppet with cut strings.

"Good. That's good."

"But why is that good, Jay?" she asked. "Tomás and this woman, wherever they are, may know enough to stitch you back together, but sooner or later, you'll need a real doctor."

"Not from Dan, Nelly. Trust me."

He drew himself out across a pallet that sagged in the middle and lay very still. Nelly checked the door's lock again, then sat in the rocking chair. She thought of her bed at the Hyde Park house, of a bath hot enough to scald, and felt such a yearning that her mouth began to water.

"Dan has been good to me," Jay said. His hand covered his eyes, his nose, and part of his mouth. "But all his talk of sons and fathers is just talk. As long as I'm standing, I'm of use to him. If a doctor tells him otherwise, he'll put me down."

"Is that what he came here to do?" Nelly asked.

"Probably. If you hadn't been here, certainly."

That gave Nelly little reassurance.

"Will he come back?"

"Not tonight."

Jay moved his hand to stare at the revolver Nelly had poised on her knee, directed at the door. She heard the words coming long before he said them. Felt their ripples. She hadn't forgotten the look in his eyes those seconds before the gun went off. That brief but unfettered brutality of a wounded creature caught in a snare. Quite inadvertently, the revolver began to shift away from the door and toward the bed.

"Before," Jay said, "at the cotillion. You said that 'you know.' What exactly do you think you know, Nelly?"

She did not appreciate that tone. Hiking up her dress to cross one leg over the other, she said, "I *know* that your name is James Glass, not Jay Shorey. I know that you were raised on a plantation in Alabama called White Pine. I know that your parents were killed by a mob. Your uncle, too. I know that you disappeared when you were young after some kind of accusation from a white girl, and no one's heard from you since. From what I can gather, the only true thing you've told me about yourself since the day we met is that your mother was a German dance teacher."

Jay chuckled at her tale, unflappable, and said, "That's not the only true thing."

"You want to talk semantics now, Jay? Or should I call you Jimmy? James? What name would you prefer, since you have so many?"

"There's no shame in me keeping my past to myself."

"I'm not talking about shame. You *lied to me.* Worse yet, you terrorized that poor girl when she caught you dead to rights."

"Poor girl?" Jay propped himself up on his elbows to look at her straight on. "You mean Rose Claxton?"

He spoke Rose's name easily. As though he'd known all along that they would come to this but held back for her benefit.

"We ran into each other yesterday morning during that canvasing they made all the debs do," she said. "She didn't seek me out, if that's what you're thinking. Everything she told me, she told me in confidence. But she told it all."

Jay dug his fingers into his eyes. So hard, in fact, that Nelly—in a fit of madness—feared that he'd puncture them and send vitreous fluid leaking down across his cheeks and hands.

"Rose is a nice girl," he said finally, "and I'm sorry for how I spoke to her in Lake Forest. I was scared, Nelly. Her being there, *here*, it frightened me. Seeing her was like stepping into a living nightmare made up of all my mistakes."

"So, it's true? You won't even try to deny it?"

She'd secretly hoped that he would fight. That he would cry on bended knee that this was just some horrid misunderstanding, but no. Tonight was a night for the truth, acidic and ruinous as it might be.

"I'm not James Glass." He said the name with the discomfort of a foreign language. "I don't *want* to be him. 'Jay Shorey' gets Christmas cards from Mayor Thompson, drinks with film stars, wears custom suits. 'James Glass' ain't no one at all. Just some half-breed orphan born on a wagon train. A prideful fool who condemned the only family he had left because he dared to turn down a white girl born for mischief. 'James Glass' is a body dumped in a creek bed or hung from a bridge, one of hundreds. I didn't lie to you, Nelly, because there's nothing to fucking lie about."

Jay's voice broke, a sound like fracturing ice. The tears seemed to shock him as much as they shocked her. He swiped at his eye with the heel of his hand and looked at the wetness with an astonished contempt.

"I'm assuming Mr. Jackson isn't really your godfather, then?" Nelly asked.

"God-uncle," Jay said, "and no. He *did* know Captain William Shorey and the extended Shorey family out in California. He figured that name would be respectable, recognizable among Colored folk of note, but too far removed to confirm. His plans for me required some pedigree."

Jay spoke resentfully of Dan's "plans." He sounded like a prisoner living off of scraps and thin sunlight.

"You must have known Mr. Jackson was a criminal when you met him," she said. "Known enough not to get caught up like this."

"Oh, Nelly. I can't tell if you think well of me or terribly of everyone else. *I* was the criminal when I met Dan," he said. "I'd finessed my way into a posh club operated by Teenan Jones, a big-time saloonkeeper and a friend of Dan's. It was a white-only club. Dan caught me out almost at once. Teenan had every right to slit my throat; he'd lose half his clientele if they knew they'd lost their money playing cards with a cheating Negro who made quick work of their money. But Dan liked my style. Liked my brazenness, my ability to blend in. He liked that I was a Southerner with a damn big chip on my shoulder, too. He offered me legitimacy and a real influence. All things I couldn't achieve on my own."

Nelly took his cold hands in her own and rubbed them together until they took on her warmth.

"You're one of the most capable people I've ever known," she said. "You demand the respect and affection of everyone you meet. *I've seen it.* You speak, and folk listen because they're struck by you. God, sometimes, I hate you for that, Jay. I couldn't manage a fraction of all you seem to do so effortlessly. You don't need some vice lord to give you legitimacy. You could do and be whatever you want on your own."

Jay's smile was mournful, and when he squeezed her hands back, there was a condescension to his embrace. Like an adult comforting a child too innocent to know when they are standing alone in the valley of the shadow of death.

"People back at Wood Acre liked to tell the story of a man from slavery days called Lincoln," he said. "Lincoln had an ear for tongues like musicians have for pitch. White folk would travel from all over to observe him, test him, rub his head for luck. One day, a foreign diplomat came to see the spectacle. He talked with Lincoln for a week in everything from Russian to Welsh. At the end of that week, the diplomat demanded to know why Lincoln's owners hadn't freed him. Such a skill could end wars, save lives. Change the world. And you know what they said? 'A parrot may sing "Yankee Doodle," but that don't make him General Sherman.'"

His hands held *her* now. Fiercely, to the point where if she even wanted to pull away, it would be a struggle.

"They used to play that as a joke, a parable," he said. "Even other Negroes. No matter what, Nelly, the best I can be is a talking parrot to all of them."

"But there is a right way to do this. A safe way that doesn't involve getting shot by the Italian mafia!"

Jay snorted in her face.

"A right way? You mean schooling—which takes money. A trade—which takes money. An enterprise of some sort—if you can swing it. Then there's of course the problem of me being Colored. No matter how I may look, that's who I am. Just because your father managed to somehow surpass the limitations of his race doesn't mean we all can."

Nelly yanked her hands away from him and sat as far back as she could.

"That's not fair," she said. "My father—my family—isn't some paragon for what Negroes can achieve. We raise racehorses, for Christ's sake. That ain't nothing but luck and good weather!"

"*And time.* I don't have ten or twenty years to make my fortune. I don't have twenty hours if the hole near my heart is any divination. Cecilia meant to teach me a lesson when she slandered me, and she did just that. If I don't make something of myself, someone else will. Vice running may not be good for my health. But it is quick. In a year, I'll be able to buy Dan and the other investors out of their Lantern shares. I won't need a university degree then, and I damn sure won't need a political campaign."

Jay kept around more cash than Nelly had ever seen in one place, but she knew that wouldn't be enough. The Lantern thrived in the midst of its illegality. Good music, good booze, every kind of gambling, and a freedom to socialize across color lines were all precious gold. Dan Jackson and his associates would be worse than fools to let it go for less than a king's ransom.

Nelly said, "How do you plan on swinging that, Jay? You're not exactly flush. With ego, maybe, but not with cash."

Nelly heard a faint scratching sound, assumed it to be mice burrowing through the walls, but then she noticed Jay picking at a bloody scab that was once the cuticle of his thumb.

"You remember the polo game where you spotted me?" Jay asked.

"Of course. You were surrounded by swooning white women."

She meant that as a dig to lighten the weighty mood, but he shook off the effort.

"The people who shared my pavilion own some restaurants in Lake Forest that still have alcohol and spirits on the menu. Export fees out of Canada are steep, and the Italians lack a certain refinement. These country-club types can buy the same or better quality from me, and all without forsaking their usual comforts. It doesn't take long for back alleys and warehouses to lose their allure."

"They deal with you on behalf of Mr. Jackson?" Nelly asked, but she knew the answer. He shook his head. The nail bit into his thumb until it gushed.

"No. Just me."

Now Jay's precautions made sense. Why he had a home on the far side of town that no one knew about. Why he refused Dan's doctor, why he didn't go to him when he was shot. Why he had stacks of money hidden in a Polish attic.

"You're stealing from him," Nelly said.

"They're my stills." His voice quaked. "My contacts, my work, *my idea.*"

"But his money."

Jay gave up on using his finger and began to pull at the cuticle with his teeth. Nelly couldn't stand such a thing. She snatched his hand away and held it down with his wrist flat against the bed. He looked at her with pupils dilated by the pain, and all of him exposed. Down to the scar tissue. But even amidst that fear, there was no regret in Jay. Everything he did, he did without looking back.

"I won't be a talking parrot forever, Nelly," he said. "Not for anyone."

Nelly never took Jay to be a man of faith. Raised under the eaves of a chapel or the canopy of a revival tent, maybe, same as her, but the image of him reciting his nightly prayers was absurd. Yet, this kind of blind determination could only be due to the stubborn conviction of old-time religion.

"Do you think less of me?" He sounded abandoned, as though speaking from an opposite shore concealed in fog.

"My opinion doesn't matter," she said.

"It's the *only* opinion that matters. You know more about me now than anyone alive, I think. There's no one left to judge me."

Jay was tired. Near fevered by his injuries, depleted by all he'd unburdened. Lord willing, he wouldn't remember half of this conversation in the morning. Already, the distant horizon was changing from black, to purple, to blue. It would be a whole new day soon.

"You have to sleep," Nelly said. "*I* have to sleep."

Jay was already there. His eyes were closed, his body had gone lax. That confession seemed to take the last bit of whatever he'd been withholding since the cotillion. Nelly looked him over and wondered at the kind of boy he'd been in the days before they ran him out of Wood Acre and set him on this road. Rose had described him as aloof, pensive. Carrying around a marked-up book in a town where others struggled to write their own names. Smart enough to know the right thing to say, but quarrelsome enough to say the opposite instead. Weighed down by all the souls he carried and the dead he mourned. A considerate boy. A careful boy. A boy doomed to die.

CHAPTER THIRTY-THREE

Nelly woke with a start and regretted it immediately. Her neck was twisted in an unnatural position that stuck like a dirty hinge. It hurt to breathe, and every muscle felt stiff and overused. The perils of falling asleep in a rocking chair.

She opened her eyes to an apartment stripped of all the evening's clandestine mystery. It was just an attic in the end. Grimy and cramped and forgotten. She could still smell the blood galvanizing the floor, but within that, there was bacon. A visceral and strange scent stolen of a dream she half remembered. Sunday breakfast, Elder answering a knock at the door, a hidden guest just beyond the threshold. She understood then—in the way one suddenly understands what is lost in dreams—that the voice she'd heard laughing with her brother was Jay's.

Jay.

When she saw his bed neatly made and empty, she nearly screamed. Her mind jumped to the most extreme of conclusions. Italians snuck in while she slept, slit Jay's throat, and disappeared out the window.

He died in the night and Dan came to collect his body. Or worse still; he had simply left her.

"Good morning! Pardon, *good afternoon.*"

Jay stood at the stove, as spiffy as Easter Sunday. All the way down to his combed-back hair. The only jarring difference was his bare chest and the layers of clean bandages wrapped tight about his shoulder, waist, and right arm. He even whistled some banal tune like "Danny Boy" or "Keep on the Sunny Side."

"What on earth are you doing?" Nelly asked.

Jay looked down at the cast-iron skillet full of thick pig fat, then back at her.

"Making breakfast," he said, as though it was the most obvious thing in the world. "I borrowed some bacon from the Kamiński family downstairs, and a loaf of black bread from the landlady. No one had any eggs, but I guess I can run out and—"

"Stop."

Nelly held up her hand to silence him and squeezed her eyes shut until she saw colors.

"Did I imagine last night?"

Jay chuckled and said, "Well, if you did, you have a very vivid imagination."

"I'm serious. You were death's own dear creature when I fell asleep. I wake up, and you're cooking. It doesn't make any sense."

Jay flashed a doting smile as he wiped his free hand with a rag tucked into his belt loop. It was an image so contrary to what she thought she knew about Jay Shorey. Domestic and homey. Proof that he was indeed a living man, not just a well-tailored pair of pants and a skimmer hat.

"It still hurts like hell," he said, "and I can't use this arm properly for a month. But I've come through the valley in half-decent shape, I'd say."

As muddled as Nelly was, having Jay upright and conscious was a relieved end to a gruesome play filled with melodrama and bloody near-deaths. Picking the crust from the corners of her eyes, she said, "When did they come back? Tomás and the seamstress."

"About an hour after Dan left. Kasia sewed me back together and applied some awful tincture to keep it sealed. I couldn't sleep a wink after, so I changed out the sheets and cleaned up what I could."

Nelly glanced about and noticed just how "cleaned up" everything was. The floors were scrubbed. The dust was swept away, and the bedsheets had been folded down with military corners.

The sounds of a busy street filtered into the attic apartment in drafts. Honking cars and hawking peddlers, even a few horse's hooves on cobblestones. The bells were ringing at Holy Innocents Church, and Nelly could hear parishioners idling on the steps to chat. They weren't the sounds of early morning. What little light the room had was hot, bright, and jarring as the noonday sun.

"What time is it, exactly?" she asked.

"After one. Maybe three o'clock."

"You're joking!"

Nelly looked down at herself and her wonderful dress, stiff with Jay's dried blood. When she tried to thread her finger through her hair, it tangled in dense coils that were once as smooth and shiny as a hubcap. Her mother would have a field day over this. Her mother, who hadn't seen Nelly in hours. Who didn't know if her daughter was dead or alive.

"Christ on the cross," she said. "I have to get home. My folks will think I ran off, or worse."

Jay held out the skillet and said, "At least have something to eat. I'm no cook, but you can never go wrong with bacon."

His cheeriness was aggressive enough to be uncanny. Nelly narrowed her eyes to assess the turmeric glaze over his own.

"Have you taken something?" she asked.

"Just a little dope, for the pain. Gave me some pep."

Nelly was no prude, but still, the casual admission scandalized her.

"You use cocaine, Jay?"

"Only when I have to," he said. "Forty-eight-hour workdays aren't uncommon. Usually, I can manage on coffee and good times, but . . . Well, like I said, it helps with the pain."

Nelly wouldn't judge him, not now. But the jittery flexing of his fingers made her curious and slow to leave him on his own. She buttoned the duster straight up the middle, as far as it would go, but she somehow looked even more suspicious without the gore and the mess.

"Is Tomás still here?" she asked. "They'll never let me in a cab looking like this."

Jay pointed at the street.

"Round the corner. I offered him the bed, but he insisted on sleeping in his car. Said that would be the 'gentlemanly thing' to do." His laugh sizzled as he pushed the bacon onto a plate.

"He's been out there all day? *Shit.* My father's gonna ship me back to Kentucky in a damn crate. Listen, I have to go now, but I'll come back to check on you if I can get away."

"You shouldn't," Jay said. "I appreciate it, but you shouldn't. If the Genna brothers come looking for me and find you, I'll never forgive myself."

"Didn't last night teach you that I can take care of my own hide?" she asked as she lifted the Smith & Wesson from her pocket and left it on the chest top.

Nelly tarried by the door, reluctant to leave.

"Are you sure you'll be okay?" she asked. "If you don't want me to come back myself, I can send someone."

"Despite appearances to the contrary," he said, "I can take care of myself, too."

She didn't know how to say goodbye. Such a sentiment felt contrived. Nelly couldn't remember ever properly saying "goodbye" to Jay. Usually, they just broke apart like glaciers, drifting on their own until they occasioned to crash together again.

"When can I see you?" she asked.

Jay's face was burnished red from the heat of the stove.

"I'll get in touch when it's safe. It won't be long, though. I promise."

Nelly leaned against the doorknob as though it was the only thing keeping her upright. All she had to do was turn it, but she couldn't seem to figure how.

"Well," she said at last. "I'll be seeing you, then."

When Jay touched her arm, Nelly felt thankful for the excuse it gave her to stay.

"I said a lot last night. Things that I had no business telling anyone," he said. "Especially you. You have every right to tell Dan, to tell the police even, about what's been going on. But I hope our friendship is worth more than that."

"Your secrets have been safe with me so far, Jay. That's not about to change."

His hand on her elbow was tender and caressing, just as it had been during their dance under a glass sky. Already a memory they would cling to in the slums of old age when all the wonders of the world became nothing more than a ticking clock.

"I never did thank you," he said. "I did everything but. You saved my life."

"Please. Tomás did the brunt of it."

"But he wouldn't have bothered if not for you. He's very honorable—maybe the last honorable man in the world—but you were the one who convinced him to help. You threatened to kill or be killed for me, Nelly Sawyer. You know now what happened the last time someone stood between me and damnation. If anything like that ever happened to you, and because of *me*—"

"I'd do more than that."

Jay's mouth hung open, caught mid-breath. He inhaled, and inhaled again, but didn't let anything go.

"I don't care what you call yourself, Jay," Nelly said. "I don't care about where you come from, or what you've done, or what you plan to do. Fuck, I mean, *I do care*, and that's the point. I care about *you*. Lord knows I should after everything you've risked to help me."

"So, that's all it is?" The earlier softness to his face began to harden right before her eyes. "Last night—you, here with me, right now—is just 'paying me back'?"

"It should be. But I don't think it is."

The small fraction of sense that remained to Nelly demanded that she turn and leave Jay locked up in his elevated tomb, where he belonged. But everything about him was a challenge. To avoid him or deny him was too much like a surrender.

His movements were infinitesimal, but she sensed them, just as one sensed the rising tide.

"It doesn't have to mean anything," he said quickly. Covering his own ass, as always. Nelly sneered and shook her head until her teardrop earrings chimed like discordant wedding bells.

"Don't. That's not what I want. What you want," she said.

Jay took a deep, slow breath.

"All right." Nelly felt his hand move up from her elbow, to her arm, to her shoulder, to her neck, to the new, soft hairs curling under her ear. "Let it mean something."

And she closed her eyes.

CHAPTER THIRTY-FOUR

Nelly found Tomás in an alley half a block down from Jay's apartment. He slept curled like a cat across the car's only two seats. He appeared completely unaffected by the previous night's chaos. This could very well be any other day in his world. Even the bloodstains looked like dried corsages.

The Stutz Bearcat's upholstery was ruined, and Tomás had to let down the canvas top to clear out the meaty smell. The roadster was fast, and Tomás drove it like a racer. Above them, a large red-tailed hawk took its stately time coasting on an eastern wind. Spotting one alone was a glum reminder of home for Nelly, where hawks the size of dogs traveled twenty deep. As a child, she was fascinated by birds of prey. Even now, when she closed her eyes and let her head fall back, she could imagine herself sprouting copper wings and soaring among the city's spires and steeples until all the world looked like a dollhouse below her. But even that familiar fantasy couldn't dislodge the way her lips ached. Jay hadn't been gentle, and she hadn't pulled away.

"Penelope."

The name sounded so new coming from Tomás, as though she'd never heard it before. Instrumental and layered, a lyrical fugue that turned every syllable into an orchestral movement. And it was her given name. Although they had passed most of their time together entirely alone, he never dared refer to her as anything other than "Ms. Sawyer."

She turned her head to him, but he kept his eyes on the road. Both hands were curled around the steering wheel and every muscle, from his fingers up to the tendons in his neck, was tense. She took this restrained posture to be born of anger, but she couldn't be sure.

"We'll be near your home soon," he said. "We should discuss what we are to tell your parents." His leather driving gloves made a pitchy, pinching noise that Nelly felt in the back of her ear canal. "Unless we mean to tell them the truth."

There was no question in that. In a less forgiving light, it might have even been a command.

"And what truth is that?" she asked.

Tomás's eyes were far too sophisticated to be panic-stricken, but they were dancing just south of that.

"A man was shot and nearly killed last night. That is the simplest and purest truth I know."

"The simplest truth, but not the purest. My parents most likely saw the gun go off, but they don't know what happened after. We can let that remain a mystery. Jay's already in enough trouble."

"*Jay's* in trouble? Penelope, to associate with such a man is to be in constant danger. You could have been shot along with him, or worse."

"It's more complicated than that. Besides, Jay's not going to let anything happen to me that he can help."

The wheels shrieked as Tomás shifted gears and passed into a new lane.

"I found that woman Kasia," he said, "but it took hours to convince her to come with me. When I mentioned Mr. Shorey, she began to pray. She said an evil eye was upon him. I've never seen such terror in a person, not even during war and rebellion. Her hands trembled as she mended his wounds."

Tomás meant to scold Nelly with his story, or was preparing to scold her. When they rode, and danced, and ate together, he'd appeared quite young. Jovial and generous. But now she saw the age in him. The years he'd seen, and the imagined authority he planned to wield over her.

"I won't presume to know what your connection with Mr. Shorey is," he said with diplomatic delicacy. "I don't dislike him myself. He intrigues me, as I'm sure he intrigues you."

"I beg your pardon? Jay Shorey is my friend, not some roadside attraction, Tomás."

"Forgive me," he said, but it was a token gesture. He meant to speak his mind, her forgiveness be damned. "I don't say this to be cavalier. My deepest concern is for you and your safety. And your clear attachment notwithstanding, I sometimes doubt the same is true for Mr. Shorey."

Of course, he could never know the whole convoluted business of her "attachment" to Jay, and just how much she owed him. Even if he did, judging by the remote world-weariness that colored his features now, it wouldn't change his mind.

"I can never thank you enough for helping him," she said.

His sigh conveyed a mature disappointment that wore her thin.

"I helped him for you. I'll help him again, for you, if that is what you want. But I won't deceive you. My sincerest hope is that you never have occasion to speak with Jay Shorey again."

The wind picked up and Nelly felt the chill reach like probing claws through the jacket and under her skin. She wouldn't deceive him either, so she chose to say nothing at all.

The Hyde Park house was flanked by police cars. A shiny black battalion of them. No light seeped through shuttered windows, and a chain had been pulled across the drive to stop vehicles from coming through. Armed men stood in the lawn, tapping cigarette ash onto the azaleas. The splendid and novel mansion had been transformed into a citadel. Nelly's neighbors were out in force—children, pets, in-laws, and all. Heads shaking, fingers wagging. If they didn't look so hateful, one would think they were waiting for the Fourth of July parade to pass by.

Tomás had relaxed into the curve of his car seat, one arm extended along the back of hers in a show of protection. He watched the armed men with strict suspicion, as a soldier should.

"Listen," Nelly said. "I don't know what we'll find inside here. For all I know, my father's put together an army of mercenaries who'll have all kinds of questions. And I plan on lying to them.

Every one of them. If I get caught in these lies, then Jay's trouble will be the least of my worries. You have every right to leave and let this be the end of it, of us. Your courtship, if that's what you want to call it. No one would blame you."

Tomás's fingers closed over hers, and when he lifted the back of her hand to his lips, Nelly felt a thread snap in her chest. Strangely, she thought of Jay's mouth with all its force and desperation. Compared to Tomás's tenderness, Jay was a slow-burning brush fire that turned forests to embers and left her mouth forever tasting of ash.

"I'm not going anywhere."

"I haven't promised you anything," she said as a kind of apology.

Tomás kept her hand where it was.

"Darling Ms. Sawyer. You'll never have to. Stranger or lover, I'd insult my mother's memory if I let you face this on your own. We're blood-bonded now, you and I. However far this tale goes, we go there together."

Cops scurried over every inch of Nelly's house like those invasive black ants that, once in, can never be forced out. Plump faces in identical blue uniforms ate in her kitchen, smoked in her drawing room, took books down in her library, and gathered around paintings Florence had so obsessively curated with the snide little expressions of those who despised art only half as much as they resented it.

Nelly found her parents in the dining room. The lace table runner and porcelain settings had been cleared away, replaced with detailed maps of each Chicago district. Police captains and sergeants loitered about with cups of coffee, barely looking useful. Her father was still in his white waistcoat and shined leather shoes, while her mother was dressed for a hard ride in canvas trousers and a yoked shirt. It would've been a comical clash if not for the shadows under their eyes. Nelly hadn't seen the like since the day Elder was pulled from the river. It was a grim sight that made her feel as though she'd turned a corner and walked in on her own funeral.

Commissioner Fitzmorris was the first to notice her. He was a short, neatly arranged man who lounged in the upholstered dining chair placed in prominence at the head of the table as though waiting for the show to begin.

"Ms. Sawyer," he said, rising. "You've raised quite the ruckus, young lady."

Ambrose and Florence fell upon Nelly like buzzards on a kill. Plucking at her, inspecting her, covering her with a smothering concern.

"Jesus, Nelly," Ambrose said. He held her tight, just as he had when she was young and he could lift her up into the sky and spin about until her legs looked like the spokes on a wheel. "They said you'd been kidnapped."

"Kidnapped?" she said. "No, I wasn't—"

"Hush!"

Florence pressed her finger against Nelly's mouth to silence her. She glanced at her husband, and nodded with squirrel-like quickness toward the commissioner, who leered behind them all.

"Welcome home, Ms. Sawyer. We're all so happy to see you back safe. Your parents and I were starting to assume the worst."

He held out his hand for hers to shake, but she kept them both buried deep in the duster's pockets. The last thing she needed was to show a cop her literal red hands. When it was clear he'd get nothing from her, he rubbed his fingers and let the hand fall.

"As I said, we were starting to assume the worst. You seem well, though, thank God. Unharmed." This was dotted with a fair amount of irony. Nelly knew she looked like something dredged out of a marsh. "I'm sure we'd all love to hear about your thrilling adventure in our fair city."

Florence was shielding Nelly before she could speak.

"Let her get in the door first, Commissioner," she said. "Can't we save your questions till after I've cleaned her up?"

The commissioner looked at Florence like a blemish on an otherwise flawless crystal chalice.

He said, "It's best that we do these things immediately, before the girl forgets finer details."

Ambrose joined Florence in her blockade.

"She's in shock, Fitzmorris. You can see my daughter hasn't made a peep since she walked in the door."

Fitzmorris's jaw made a cracking noise when he flexed it. His thumbs hooked the edge of the thick black belt that held his loaded standard-issue pistol. It was as understated a threat as a man like him was likely to give.

"You know this is more than just a missing girl now, Mr. Sawyer," he said. "A boy is dead."

"Dead?" Nelly said. Fitzmorris inhaled at the sound of her voice. He even chanced a peek around her parents to catch her eye and detain it.

"That's right," he said. "You didn't know?"

This was impossible. When Nelly left Jay an hour ago, he was more chipper than the day before. Unless the Gennas had waited outside all night. Biding their time until she left him alone with no witnesses and no one to call for help.

Tomás had remained respectfully silent thus far, but his timing was martially precise.

Speaking with a faintly British, smart, social-club inflection that he threw on like a cashmere scarf, he said, "I'd be happy to answer any questions you may have. I was with Ms. Sawyer at the time of this terrible business."

Fitzmorris lowered his eyes at the money-laden weight of Tomás's voice. It was a shade of power he recognized and halfway respected.

"And who are you, sir?" the commissioner asked with a deference he didn't once offer Nelly or her parents.

"Tomás Escalante y Roche, officer. As I said, I was with Ms. Sawyer last evening. I've been with her all morning, in fact. She was understandably upset by the whole affair, and I thought it best to get her away to safety during the worst of it. She slept under my roof as my guest. I should make clear before we begin that I'll need to contact my lawyers if you see fit to relocate our conversation to any station or precinct. Is there a language you prefer? I retain a firm in New York, Paris, London, Mexico City—"

Under the cover of Tomás's name-dropping, Florence spirited

Nelly up the stairs and away to the premier suite. It was a bedroom the size of most houses with an attached bathroom styled after the Raffles Hotel in Singapore. A curved wall of windows looked out over the back garden, where the hawthorn was in bloom over a translucent koi pond.

Florence locked the door behind them, then put her ear to its seam. After a few seconds, she began to speak.

"Go on, now," she said. "Take all that off."

Nelly had stripped down to the flimsy underthings the dress required when Florence returned from the bathroom with a bowl of warm water and a towel. In an armchair opposite Nelly, she sat with her legs wide, her shoulders slumped, her hair tied back with a scarf. It was the Florence that Nelly knew best, but in the far-removed way one knows the color of the paint in the schoolhouse where they learned arithmetic. Her mother's recent metamorphosis into a woman who wore a straight bob wig and sequined tea gowns was as strange as it was absolute.

"Clean yourself up the best you can," Florence said. "We don't have much time. While you do that, you're gonna tell me exactly what the hell happened last night."

The blood took some scrubbing to come off. Florence had to refill the bowl twice before they were through.

Nelly told her mother the truth. About the shooting. The flight into the Polish Patch. The late night keeping Jay alive. But everything else, she kept in the dark. Where it belonged. Florence nodded along with all of it in silence. She didn't pry or demand further explanations, but the more Nelly revealed, the more she could see the fine embroidery of her mother's plans unravel.

"Is Tomás willing to lie to this policeman for you, Nelly?" she asked.

"He damn well insisted."

"Thank Jesus and all the angels for that. And the man still wants to court you?"

"He insisted on that, too."

Florence shook her head. As much as she admired Tomás's loyalty and discretion, like Nelly, she could hardly believe it.

Florence gathered up the jacket and dress while Nelly put on her father's massive brown wool robe. She thought it ridiculous when her mother suggested it, but as she gauged her reflection in the standing mirror, she understood. The robe made her appear penitent and purged of all the fixings that Fitzmorris found so unnatural on a Negro woman. Tomás would wear him down with his bilingual lawyers; by the time the commissioner got to Nelly, he'd be spent.

"What're you going to do with that?" Nelly asked, as Florence shoved the dress deep down into a trash bin.

"Burn it in the furnace," she said. "What else?"

They stood at the top of the stairs together. Down below, Nelly could hear Fitzmorris's laughter and Tomás's musical tenor. She'd be surprised if the commissioner got around to his questions at all in between the schmoozing. Before Nelly came home, they were at war. Now, all was hot coffee and butter cookies, nary a trace of foul play in sight.

"Momma." Nelly held her mother by the arm before she could lead them down. "Fitzmorris said that a man died last night, but Jay isn't dead. Should I lie to him about that, too?"

Florence looked at once relieved that Nelly'd finally asked the question, and annoyed that she was the one who had to answer it. She squeezed Nelly's hand and poured a fraction of her Herculean strength into her daughter.

"You stick to your story," she said. "After the gun went off, you saw nothing and no one."

Hastily, Nelly pressed, "Sure, but if they think Jay's dead, that changes everything. Doesn't it?"

"He wasn't talking about Jay Shorey, Nelly. He was talking about Dr. Younger's boy."

A mind in distress leans on the logical, and Nelly's immediately wondered how Lloyd was tied up in Jay's bootlegging. He was well-connected. Maybe he made an introduction or two, but how would the Genna brothers know? And why would they care about some doctor's son from Georgia? All this she wondered in vain.

"A ricochet killed him, according to the police," Florence said. "Bounced off a pillar and hit Lloyd in the back of the head. Poor child didn't even see it coming."

Nelly thought of Dr. Younger's hand. The way it came up and struck Lloyd so hard and so fast that he—a young man they could have named hurricanes after—was felled to the ground.

"No," Nelly said. "No, I don't suppose he ever did."

CHAPTER THIRTY-FIVE

The great secret of Jay's Alabama origins was secret no more. In fact, it was all anyone could talk about at the memorial for Lloyd Younger, held three days after his death.

Dr. Daniel Hale Williams hosted the gathering in his modest house on Forty-Second Street. Dr. Williams and Dr. Younger had attended medical school together, and Dr. Williams was Lloyd's own godfather. The Youngers weren't there, of course. They'd packed up Lloyd's body and fled back to Georgia in the fog of the morning, presumably to never visit Chicago again.

Thirty to fifty people managed to slot themselves like dominos into the one-and-a-half-story Queen Anne home. The food served was bland and dense, the drinks were appropriately dry. The only music came from a waning gramophone that played the same record of monastic hymns over and over again. To sob too loudly would have been presumed too demonstrative and inappropriate. The memorial for Lloyd was different from Elder's funeral in almost every way, except for one. It had nothing to do with him. The people cried true tears, but they cried them out of spite. A show of loyalty to the Youngers that turned the home into a battleground that separated Jay and the Sawyers from everyone else.

I knew the Shoreys back West, and I can say for a fact there ain't never been a "Jay" among them.

A charming young man. Yes, spoke perfect French and everything. Paul and I thought it was some kind of terrible mistake.

That explains the suits. You know what I mean.

I never cared for him, or his shiny grin. Always seemed so damn eager, that Jay Shorey. Makes sense for a gangster like Daniel Jackson to put him on. That old grave-digger's greasier than a basket of fried fish.

He was dancing with Penelope Sawyer when it happened. And you can bet they didn't find a speck of blood on that overpriced dress. Flora Mae already has her decked out like a duchess. Doubt the fellow will propose now. Nobody wants a murderess for a wife.

Nelly walked through the gossip and the sneers like tall grass. It brushed against her clothes, tickled her hands, and left its seeds embedded in her skin. Not a week ago, these same people were complimenting her on that "overpriced dress." Shaking her father's hand, congratulating them on such a successful showing. Now they looked at her with horrified eyes, as though she'd guided the bullet that killed Lloyd Younger herself. Their opinions about her and her family never really had changed over the two months they'd been in Chicago. If anything, those opinions had calcified like stalagmites.

Sequoia held court in the home's one proper sitting room. In the absence of Lloyd's direct family, it appeared that she was mourning in their stead with all the accoutrements that such a role demanded. Her fashion was political in its acuity: black velvet from neck to ankle, opaque lace veil. A widowed queen in a Greek tragedy seconds away from tearing out her own hair. The young people she'd hand-selected for her entourage stood all about her, fulfilling the role of the tragedy's chorus decrying humanity's failings.

"Hello, Sequoia," Nelly said rigidly. Then, to the others: "Everyone."

Effy Syphax was the first to step away from the group and embrace Nelly. She pressed Nelly's cheek with her own, wet and smelling of warm milk.

"How're you holding up, dear?" she asked.

Before Nelly could answer, Mabel Ford was saying behind an embroidered kerchief, "It's a shame, isn't it? Our little club's only been together twice: once with Lloyd, and once without him."

"It ain't a shame," said Nathaniel Terrell of the DC Terrells. "It's a murder. It's a damn crime."

His seething had a smell like when farmers purged their fields of dead crops. He made a point of avoiding lingering too long on Nelly. When he did look at her, those handsome eyes were hateful.

"It must've been horrid," Effy went on. "What with you being so close when it happened."

Nelly didn't quite know where to focus when they all talked at once.

"No, I wasn't close to Lloyd when he died," she said. "I only knew about it a day later."

"But you were close to Jay Shorey." Effy grinned like a prosecutor upon catching a witness in a lie.

So, this was an ambush. When Nelly shook Effy off, the young woman she'd once considered akin to a friend recoiled as though burned.

"Yes," she said to them all. "I was with Jay. And you're right, Effy, it *was* horrid. He's my friend, and he may be dead, too, for all we know."

Mabel looked upon Nelly with a church mother's evangelical concern for a sinful and irredeemable soul.

"He wasn't really your friend, though. Was he, Nelly? I mean, you didn't even know him. None of us did."

Nelly strived not to read into the way Mabel used *wasn't*. It implied that whatever connection she had with Jay prior to the cotillion was long dead and buried. Most of them, like her, didn't even live in Chicago. In a few weeks, they would pack up their lives and vanish to the four winds, only mentioning Jay Shorey when thinking of poor Lloyd Younger, gone too soon. Give it ten years, or even five. It would all be myth and legend soon enough.

"Jay's as much a victim in all this as Lloyd," Nelly said. "This terrible thing is not his fault."

"No, it's not Jay's fault. It's yours."

Sequoia rose until she stood like a great black obelisk in the middle of the Williamses' living room.

"I told you who Jay Shorey was," she said, "and I told you who he wasn't. I practically begged you to leave him alone, Nelly, but you persisted. He's a liar who skulks at the edges of our community like the scavenger he is, and you flung open the damn door and let him in!"

Now, this was far enough. Nelly was willing to accept her lot in what had happened, but she would not drag around Lloyd Younger's soul.

"Don't lay this on me, Sequoia. I wasn't the one who fired that gun, and neither was Jay."

"But Jay was there because of you. He was at the cotillion *for you.*"

Nelly smirked at the accusation, but it was a weak derision held up with string. She said, "He was there on his own business. The cotillion was announced and confirmed before he even knew me. What happened to Lloyd was awful, inexcusable—"

"Don't you dare say his name!"

Sequoia's voice spiked to a crow caw that silenced everyone around them. Deep inside the home, the record of hymns continued to drone. Scratchy and ancient and sorrowful.

"There are a million ways for someone to die," Sequoia said. Spent sobs rattled around in her throat. "Sickness, violence. Pointless accidents, like your brother. Old age if you're lucky. But for Lloyd to die from a bullet meant for that cancer Jay Shorey is an insult. To Lloyd, to his family, to all of us!"

Nelly looked at Sequoia like the stranger she ultimately was.

"'All of us'? The two of you couldn't stand each other, Sequoia. I saw the way he sliced and diced at you. The cruel things he said. Lloyd Younger hated you, and Lord knows you probably hated him. This performance of yours may fool 'all of us,' but it doesn't fool me."

Sequoia came at her like a rogue wave. She was a tall woman and monolithic in her fury. Nelly retreated until the back of her legs collided with a roll-top desk.

"You ignorant, spoiled little girl." Sequoia did not yell. She spoke with a deliberate softness that turned every word into an intimately personal curse. "What could you possibly know? Lloyd and me, we grew up together. This society was built by us. For *us*, not outsiders like you. You pass yourself off as so aloof and dignified, but you don't know how to function without the money you pretend to despise. That's why Jay chose you, you know. Not only can you be fooled, Nelly Sawyer, you can be *easily* fooled."

Nelly's chest strained with held-back, pathetic tears. She glanced to either side and saw the faces of distant acquaintances drinking in this scene with a decadent fervor. She knew those capricious eyes from the last funeral. Licking their lips for something worth the price of admission.

"Maybe," Nelly said, "but I'm also free. I can leave this 'society' and all its bigoted, restrictive rules whenever I want. But you, Sequoia, you're shackled to your father's pulpit. You'll always be here, forever. No matter how many clothes you borrow or secrets you sell."

Sequoia's smile was livid, devastated, thirsty for blood. But Nelly also knew that, in that moment, her friend was quite proud.

The front door of the Williamses' home banged shut behind her. Florence and Ambrose followed like a stampede.

"I refuse to stay here and embarrass myself," Nelly said in full retreat.

Ambrose called after her, "Baby girl, you can't just leave. This is a somber occasion; we all need to stay."

"Why?" Nelly spun at her parents. "They think Lloyd died because of me. It was more disrespectful to be here at all than to stay away. And they're not wrong. It is my fault."

Nelly anticipated some denial from her parents, to comfort her fear. But their silence offered nothing but affirmation.

"This will undo everything we've worked for this summer," Florence said.

"Oh, Momma, spare me! Don't tell me you believe that. Either of you. This isn't the summer we entered Negro society, or the summer you were inducted into some club, or the summer that I made a stunning debut. This is the summer Elder died! His memory is wasted on them, on us. You two can go back if you want, but I'm through here. Chicago has had its way with me. I'm going home."

Murphy—the attentive, borderline insolent chauffeur that he was—stood at the ready next to the Rolls-Royce with an open door. Nelly breezed right past his crooked smile and breath reeking of snuff.

"Miss Nelly?" he asked cautiously.

"I'm walking."

"Walk?" he said. "We're an hour's hike from Hyde Park."

"I'm not going to Hyde Park. I don't know where I'm going, just away from here."

Murphy spat the black remains of his chewing tobacco into the street.

"This is silly, Miss Nelly. You were just abducted. Think of your parents!"

Whatever Murphy saw when he looked into Nelly's heartbroken face was enough to make the stalwart veteran take a step back.

"Follow me if you can, Murphy. But if you want me in that car, you'll have to hog-tie me and throw me in yourself."

CHAPTER THIRTY-SIX

And so, Nelly walked north with her back against the wind. It was well into the afternoon when she stumbled with sore feet into the lofted confines of the Gold Coast. The distinction was easy to spot. Even so close to the rabid city center, the air in that neighborhood was serene. Birdsong filtered in as though from a gramophone, and all smelled of fresh linen. Ambrose had initially wanted to build on East Goethe, but the founders had closed ranks. Plenty made threats when he chose Hyde Park, but only the citizens of the Gold Coast swore to follow them through. That memory rotted the grandeur of the neighborhood, and Nelly rushed to be clear of it.

Ahead of her on the sidewalk, a small crowd had formed. Three to four bodies pressed in close together. Cops, she realized, several of them, all gathered about a young man in a floppy checkered cap that obscured his face.

"I'll ask you again; what's your business here, lad?"

"And I'll *tell* you again. I know people in there."

Nelly knew him as soon as she heard him. It was a voice she could never forget, not since hearing it whispering in her ear as the life was choked out of her. She couldn't see Rowan Byrne's eyes under the long brim of his cap, but she could see a curl of red hair and the the reedy trail of smoke floating up from his slow-burning cigarette.

One of the cops looked up at the gothic gray townhome to their right and said, "Who the hell could you ever know here? Last I heard, the president of the Dearborn Company didn't entertain little shit micks."

"Then clearly," Rowan said, "you don't know the president of the Dearborn Company."

An officer with an old-fashioned handlebar mustache gave Rowan a hard shove that sent him stumbling back but didn't uproot his balance. He was a brawler, as Nelly remembered.

"Never mind your smart mouth," the mustached man said. "Ain't no loitering round here. Now get, and be quick about it."

When Rowan lifted his chin to look up at the townhome, Nelly saw the overcast day's hoary light catch in his eyes. He knew how this altercation would turn, but he also knew there was no avoiding it.

"Fellas, my boss needs me here. So here's where I'm going to stay."

"Who's your boss, then?" an officer asked. "Some paddy rumrunner, I'd wager."

"I could say the same thing about your boss." Rowan spat out his cigarette and stomped it under his boot heel. "You fucking pig."

The blow came fast, and boxer or not, there was no way for Rowan to dodge it. His head bounced back as though tugged on a string. When he brought it back up, a bloody gash ran down the center of his nose. Nelly was running before the second blow could land.

"Hey!" she shouted.

They all turned and looked rightfully stunned to see a Colored girl dressed for a homegoing sprinting at them down the sidewalk. The cops then remembered themselves and the hierarchy of the street. Some Irish tramp and Negro madwoman meant less than nothing to them.

"Mind your business, missy!" one of them yelled. He waved his club in the air between them like a torch meant to scare off wolves in the wilderness. She slowed and held up her hands as she approached.

"Sirs, I know this man," she said. "Please, leave him be. He's harmless." The lie came easily.

Rowan stood on the other side of the cops' human-shield wall, squinting. If he recognized her at all, he didn't give it away.

The man with the handlebar mustache laughed and looked between Nelly and Rowan. He had a giddy expression, like a kid at a carnival, eager for the next act. Maybe the bearded woman, or a fish-tailed squirrel preserved in brine.

"You work for his boss, too, girl?" he asked.

"No," Nelly said, "but . . ." She glanced at the townhome and its dark windows, its imposing fencing. "I'm a cook here. I've seen him in this house before, dining at the main table with the family."

One of the cops stepped close to her, and she wrinkled her nose at the musky scent of his wool uniform.

"You don't look like a cook," he said. Nelly wanted to sneer and ask him how exactly he thought a cook should look, but she held her tongue. Being insolent would get her nowhere with this lot.

She checked her posture—hunched her back just so, lowered her eyes, became the downtrodden servant they expected her to be—and said, "I just started, sir."

One of the officers made a low, skeptical sound while his hand drifted from his belt to the butt of his billy club.

"All right, say that's true. But people have reported this vagrant hanging about for weeks. Maybe you two are in this together. Yeah, maybe you tell him which houses to case. Pinching some silver and the old lady's jewels, eh?"

"Even if that was true," Rowan said, laughing, "that's not how it works."

The mustachioed cop raised his stick in warning.

"I swear it, sir," Nelly said. "I can go in and fetch the missus myself. She'll tell you it all, though she doesn't take kindly to interruptions during her beauty rest."

There weren't many things that could stop a man determined to get his own way. But the threat of a rich woman's vexation was one of them.

"Right," said one with a pronounced potbelly. "We'll leave you two to your business. But if we see you—either of you—round these parts again, we'll be taking you on a long ride out to the boonies."

Nelly didn't cower under their menace. Lord willing, she would never see any of these men again.

The officers carried on down the street away from them, chittering like chickens. Next to her, Rowan was doing a poor job stanching his nose with the sleeve of his cotton shirt. Nelly offered him Jay's handkerchief. The very one he'd tied about her neck to hide the evidence of Rowan's own abuse. Rowan accepted it with that same button smile from when they first met, defanging him, even through the dripping blood.

"My, my, Miss Nelly," he said. "And here I was, thinking that you hated me."

Nelly squinted up at the steadily clearing sky. The blue was brilliant and speckled with thick white clouds. If she strained, she could hear the seabirds fishing over the lake, and the waves lapping against the beams of the boardwalk.

They shared a cigarette on a townhouse stoop, unmolested. When Nelly asked Rowan why he was there in the first place, he said, "waiting on a package," and left it at that. The streets were busy now. Vehicles rumbled by, spewing exhaust, and small children in matching blue-green jumpers toddled behind schoolmarms like living dolls. And behind even them was a legion of Negro women in uniforms, tethered to their charges.

"Shame about your face," Nelly said.

Rowan sucked up a disgusting mixture of mucus and blood and spat a glob of it into the street.

"It wasn't much of a face to begin with. Besides, I deserved it."

"From the police?"

"No. From you."

When his eyes met hers, Nelly didn't flinch away. He deserved every bit of her still-seething anger. She didn't need him comfortable. And frankly, she didn't want it.

"I'm sorry for what happened at the Ebony Masque," he said.

"Yes." It was an old song, and she didn't care to hear it again. "We've established that."

"Well, I mean it."

"You can apologize until the seventh seal breaks, but there's no excusing what you did to me. I have every right to hate you! What else should I expect from a member of Ragen's Colts?"

"It's an athletic club."

"Don't fucking insult me, Rowan," Nelly said. "Are you daring to tell me that you didn't know about the threats, the murders? The riots in 1919? You're plenty old enough to have participated."

"I could never," he said with such sincerity that Nelly was tempted to believe him. "I'm just Mikey's bagman. I have no stomach for that rough stuff in the Black Belt. I grew up with people of every stripe, including Negroes. The man who got me into fighting was darker than you."

Rowan was awash in a hopeful glow of absolution, as oblivious to Nelly's outrage as he was to the ignorance of his own excuses.

"Tell me," Nelly queried. "Would you treat these Negroes you remember so fondly as you've treated me? Lured into a trap, nearly killed, then trussed up for dangerous men to threaten?"

He spared himself the indignity of refuting her. Yes, he would. He wouldn't enjoy it, but he wouldn't hesitate. Impractically, Nelly had hoped for better. Rowan flicked the burning remains of his cheap tobacco into the closest flower bed. The smell corrupted the carefully arranged aroma of gardenias, lilies, and bearded iris.

"How's your search going?" he asked. "For the Mayor?"

The friendliness of the question muddied the clarity of Nelly's annoyance. She wanted to talk to someone, be distracted by another's unbiased presence, but by God, why did it have to be *him*?

"I gave up on it," she said.

Rowan barked a laugh.

"Like hell."

"Not that you should care, but I'm telling the truth. The cartoonist I gave up, the one who told me about the Ebony Masque. She died."

Rowan's freckles stood out like coal in snow when his face blanched, perhaps from shame. He tapped the cigarette again without taking another drag.

"Don't feel guilty," he said. "You did what you had to do."

As rebuked as his empathy was, Nelly took his validation and added it to the hoard that kept her on the right side most days.

She said, "You can keep your hoodlum, kill-or-be-killed logic, Rowan. What I did was wrong. Maybe when I've wrecked the same score of lives as you and your Colts, I'll be numb enough to think otherwise."

"You're damn lucky, Nelly. In the old days, before the Mayor, you would've been killed right along with her. Count that woman's death as the blessing it is."

His words were callous, but not his sentiment. Rowan really did half expect her to drop to her knees and thank God.

"You're saying the Mayor did this?" she asked. In the weeks since she'd allowed herself to spare a kernel of thought for the Mayor of

Maxwell Street, he'd decayed back into a spirit of tricks and favors, a ghost story. But Rowan spoke of corporal murder.

"It wouldn't be the first time. I wasn't there at the start, but Mikey was. And the man likes to pontificate when he's in his spirits. Back on that veranda, if you'd asked me without deception for me to tell you what I knew about the Mayor, I would've told you, Nelly."

She would tell herself later that curiosity drove her. Or maybe just the sound of someone else's voice, and words not spoken in judgment. But in her bones, she knew the truth. She might have abandoned the Mayor of Maxwell Street; he had not abandoned her.

"So tell me now."

"It started a couple years ago. Mikey got an invitation to some high-stakes blackjack game at a hole-in-the-wall saloon in the Levee. But Mikey wasn't the only boss there. Italian. Colored. Russian. The Jews, the Poles, even the Cubans. A few big-time politicians, too. Mikey thought it was some kinda setup, but the dealer explained that a nameless man had brought them all together for a reason. He proposed a network connecting all of Chicago, where trouble could be settled in private without interrupting business. They'd make more money working together than warring over turf in the streets. This city's its own continent, you see, with dozens of little countries all jostling for power. Boundaries always shift, and peace never lasts for long. And politicians, they just collect their cut and pretend not to see a thing. Everyone has always accepted the rules for what they are and buried their dead along the way. What the Mayor promised was an end to all of that uncertainty."

"Bold of him to promise the impossible."

Rowan smiled as though they'd shared a fond and touching memory.

"You ain't kidding," he said. "Mikey and all the rest thought the same. Not only would they never work together, they damn sure wouldn't trust some outsider to oversee it all. But that was before."

"Before?" Nelly asked.

"Before the secrets came out. This Mayor had something on all of them. Personal shit, things that no one could or should ever know. That was enough to get their attention. From there, a code of honor was enforced. What was discussed at the table, stayed at the table. They'd work together to run the city, and if any trouble arose that impacted the majority, the Mayor would handle it. Trouble like you and your questions, Miss Nelly."

"You make it out like they were forced into this," Nelly said. "Seems to me like it's the best deal for everyone. No bloodshed, no old-world pettiness, and more oversight."

Rowan's lips drew back as he said, "The bloodshed *was* the oversight. It kept everyone in their place. Without what you call 'old-world pettiness,' anyone could go anywhere, do anything. It maintained the natural order."

Nelly had heard such talk before. Usually from men who looked very much like Rowan as they held forth on the uniqueness of the Sawyers and their presence in rooms that they would otherwise live and die without ever seeing.

"Right," she said. "The same reason why when Colored folk move south, east, or west of the Black Belt, their homes are bombed, and black-faced gangs run around setting fires."

Rowan coughed and glanced down at his scuffed, secondhand shoes.

"Yes. That exact same reason. This place was built on 'me and mine.' Any unity, from the gutters all the way up to city hall, is a threat. I figure that's why the Mayor hides his face. If word ever got out about who he actually is, they'd find him swinging from the top of the water tower. No one man should have so much power."

Nelly disagreed. Instead of stockpiling power, as all the other bosses had done, it seemed to her that this Mayor was distributing it. Collecting it like rations and dispersing out a morsel at a time. Just enough to keep forever-hungry men fed.

"And no one's *ever* seen him?" Nelly asked incredulously. "No one at all?"

Rowan ran his thumb's dirty nail against the pad of his index finger until it turned red. "No one in Ragen's Colts. One of the Italians claimed he was an Englishman once, because of the Savile Row suits he wore, but that's only gossip."

It was a weak and haphazard connection, but it was a connection all the same. It dragged the Mayor of Maxwell Street out of the mists she'd banished him to and began to give him shape.

"And this man—whoever he is—maintains all of this for nothing," said Nelly.

"He's paid in information," Rowan clarified. "More evergreen than cash. But there was this one time, if you can believe the ravings of a drunk man. Some playboy was racking up a lot of debts around town. Flush and Colored, too. They let him gamble in all the neighborhoods because people vouched for him. But when the bill came . . . Well, these men tend to get their due one way or another. They asked the Mayor to follow through and settle the score, but he refused."

Nelly started.

"He refused his own terms?" she asked.

Rowan nodded, still baffled by a story he knew well enough to tell by heart.

"The Mayor wouldn't take money or favors, or a night with a beautiful woman. The bosses even offered to tell him where the bodies were buried. It came down to a life for a life. The Mayor would take care of the gambler, make an example of him, but only if this good ole boy from down South didn't see another sunrise. A couple of Colts were sent to Alabama to snatch him up, and they didn't go easy."

What kind of man demanded the life of a dime-a-dozen white boy over confessions and cash? Still, intriguing as it was, some unidentified Southerner was no kind of useful lead. Especially if he was dead.

"What happened to the one with the debts? The playboy?" Nelly asked.

"Just what was meant to happen," Rowan said. "The Mayor's not the flashy sort. He used an automobile accident or some such, something untraceable."

Nelly felt a sharp prick at the base of her skull. An insistence as though from beyond the grave. How many automobile accidents were there in any given day? Fifty? A hundred? And there were twice as many reckless playboys with debts as long as her arm in Chicago. No. Such a thing was impossible.

"This playboy," she said, "he have a name?"

She watched his lips to avoid meeting his eyes. Rowan took a drag, deep enough to hollow out his cheeks, and in a cloud of putrid smoke, he said, "Elder, I think. Ain't that a peculiar name for a Negro?"

Nelly stared into the smoke. It burned her eyes and brought on stinging tears. The light of the sun was suddenly too much. The noises of glee and lives lived in ignorant peace grated on her ears like the cries of the damned.

"Elder Sawyer."

"Yeah, maybe. I never heard his Christian name," Rowan said. "Why? That sound like someone you know?"

She laughed at his question and how the invisible strings that bound them all together were so apparent to her now.

"I had a brother named Elder," she said, and left the rest to him. Rowan was a bright young man, quiet as it was kept. It didn't take him long.

"Oh." The word came out of him like a final breath. "Oh, Miss Nelly—"

He reached for her, but she was up and reeling from him.

"I didn't know," he said. "I swear to God, Nelly, I had no idea."

Nelly put her face in her hands and took that second of insulated silence to breathe. And to think.

"At the Ebony Masque, did they know who I was?" she asked. "Who I was to Elder?"

Rowan shrugged helplessly.

"I don't know. Maybe Tony did, or Mikey. Maybe Jay—"

"No!"

Some truths she could take on the chin, but not others. She began to walk, but there was nowhere to go. That house in Hyde Park was not her home, and if she saw her parents now, she'd be tempted to tell them all just to share the burden. But they could never know. There were a dozen "to-the-grave-never-tell-Momma-and-Daddy" secrets Elder and Nelly had held between them over the years. This one would be the last.

Nelly recalled her first conversation with Richard Norris, back in that dingy little cafeteria long before the stinking pits of this city gave up their secrets to her. He'd said that truth had no room for vengeance, but that justice was always vengeful. She'd feared him burned-out and cynical at the time. An old man who'd wasted his short supply of decency on delusions. But it was clear now that he'd spoken not of platitudes, but of prophecy. Nelly *would* write her article. It would be truthful. It would be complete. It would be perfect. And it would be vengeance.

CHAPTER THIRTY-SEVEN

The Hyde Park house was often dark. After all, there were only the three Sawyers and a handful of sleep-in staff. On an uneventful night, Nelly would eat with her parents at seven, sit with them for a spell, and then they'd recede to their own separate isles. Lights out by nine. Silence like the grave by ten. That's why when Nelly stepped through the kitchen door at midnight and saw the hunched shape of a man at the breakfast table, she screamed.

"Nelly, shush! You'll wake your mother!"

The light above the table clicked on, and Nelly saw her father sitting alone with two whiskey tumblers and a stack of loose papers spread out before him. The smoking butt of a used cigarette in a caramel tin made the kitchen smell like a candy shop on fire.

He was dressed down to his suspenders and undershirt, and Nelly was momentarily unsettled by the sight of his bare arms. When they were children, she and Elder would tell strangers that their father was the strongest man alive. Stronger than John Henry. That was all the fancy of excitable kids at the time, but a part of her believed it like a private dogma. Believed it still. Seeing Ambrose now, she was forced to reckon with her own skewed memories. His skin hung thin and limp from stick-like biceps. His once imposing shoulders were narrow and knotted. The truth about Elder's death served to break some kind of glamour that held her family, her world, suspended in a time out of time. Nelly's father had aged while she wasn't looking. The time was long past to put away childish things.

Nelly closed the kitchen door as softly as she could, then whispered, "It's the middle of the night. What the hell are you doing, sitting up alone down here?"

"You want to play twenty questions with me now, girl?" Ambrose said. "How about I tell you why I'm awake at this hour, and you tell me exactly where you've been all night."

There was no way out of that particular standoff. In truth, she'd been on the El. Riding every line in every direction until she was forced to pick up pennies in the street to stay in motion. She thought her best when moving. In the absence of a stallion, the train had to do.

Nelly joined Ambrose at the table, and the loose papers glowed under a yellow spotlight. Some were handwritten, others typed. One or two were tiny letters cut out of magazines and pasted to the kind of strong stationery that came with books of paper dolls. Nelly wiped the sleepy, soul-tired scales from her eyes and tried to focus on individual words. *Ours* stuck out often. Along with *uppity, haughty, corrupt,* and *nigger.*

"I didn't think there were so many," she said.

Ambrose flattened his hand over the threats and pushed them all to the far end of the table.

"Nothing to worry yourself with," he said. "It's all just hot wind. If they wanted to, they could come and tell me how they feel about my family and my business to my face. I ain't afraid."

Ever since the notoriety, the Sawyers had received unsigned correspondence calling them unworthy, telling them how they were owed a debt of violence. Neither of Nelly's parents ever had much time for posturing and would save each letter like a warrior's trophy. Nelly wasn't so dismissive. If the last few days had taught her anything, it was that a fired bullet *will* find its target, come hell or high water.

Ambrose picked up his tumbler and said, "I'm sorry about today. At the memorial. We should've gone without you. Exposing you to all that nastiness was the wrong thing to do. You had every right to walk outta there, and if I had half your sense, I woulda walked outta there with you."

"One of us has to behave, Daddy," she said while holding his rough, dry hand. "Elder isn't here to stir up trouble anymore, and if I'm replacing him, then you have to follow Momma's rules from now on."

Ambrose chuckled, but it was cold. Weary and abnormal, not at all like the "Daddy" Nelly knew and took comfort in. It was a terrifying thing, to see one's parents brought low.

"Are you all right?" she asked.

Ambrose crouched forward to kiss the crown of her head. He still smelled the same. Cigarette smoke, cinnamon-and-pepper cologne, and fragrant undertones of hard work. She wished she could capture that scent to wear in a locket around her neck.

"I'll be just fine, baby girl," he said. "Hell, after all this drama, if I manage to stick around long enough to see you settled, safe, and well-endowed, then I'll know I have God's grace."

That spark of pride in her father's eyes shouldn't have wounded Nelly as harshly as it did.

"Is that all you want for me, Daddy?" she asked.

"Of course," he said. "What else is there?"

The impulse to cry welled up from Nelly's chest, but she tamped it down. To challenge him, or refute him, or argue that there was *so much more* would only be a disappointment. Someday they would have that conversation. When they were both older and more prepared for the consequences. So instead, she picked up the second glass of whiskey and threw it all back in one go. Her father liked to drink the brutal stuff that folk brewed on the side of the road like the witches in *Macbeth*, but this vintage was richer, smoother, and distinctly more expensive.

"Did you break out the good stuff for me?" she asked as she set down the empty glass.

Ambrose could not hide that conniving glint like a drawn sword in his right eye. That's when the kitchen door opened, and Nelly turned to see Tomás standing in the darkness.

She tried to rise but failed when her legs buckled against the table and forced her back down. There'd been not a peep from Tomás since the day after the cotillion. No cards, no calls. After weeks of speaking almost every day, she took his silence as a decision and accepted it for the sensible thing that it was. Having him in her kitchen—forced into a private moment—felt like a cruel surprise that left her staggering.

"How long have you been here?" she asked. It was a rude and sorry greeting, but she figured they were past pleasantries now.

"Tomás and me have been drinking for hours," Ambrose said. "Guess the time got away from us. How's the old girl settling in?"

Tomás rubbed his hands against his trousers, leaving what looked to be bits of straw on his khaki breeches. He appeared unusually casual in tall socks and rolled-up sleeves. To Nelly's father, he said, "Beautifully. It's a bit tight for her in the carriage house, but I think she's just happy to be home."

Nelly's attention leapt between the two of them.

"What are y'all talking about?" she asked Tomás. "Did you ride Estrella all the way here?"

He sat down in the neighboring chair, reeking of horse. He reached for what she now took to be *his* whiskey glass but paused when he saw it empty.

"Blue Sonata," he corrected, "and I did. I planned to make a dramatic, romantic entrance right at sunset, but we ended up stuck in traffic of all things. By the time I finally did arrive, it was dusk, and my suit was soaked through with sweat. Your father kindly offered some spare clothes. I'm also a bit drunk, I fear. We inevitably drank all the whiskey."

Tomás's eyes were big and shiny, and his head swayed as though caught up in a tune only he could hear. She'd never seen him tipsy, and his inebriated asymmetry made her smile.

"You both probably needed the exercise," she said. "But if you think to ride her back, she won't be fit and rested in time for your next match."

"I won't be riding her back, Ms. Sawyer. Blue Sonata is yours."

Nelly was too tired to be excited or thankful. She only had enough energy to be rational.

"Tomás, I didn't mean what I said way back. You're an excellent rider. One of the best I've ever seen. Willful as she is, that horse was born to be your polo pony. Why on earth would you give her up?"

Tomás wouldn't answer her. His full lips curled in on themselves in an expression of skeptical hesitation, and he began to fidget with that same coral ring. Round and around and around and around. Nelly was suddenly afraid. She looked to her father, who immediately moved to stand and excuse himself from the table.

"I'll say good night," Ambrose said, then left them alone.

A car sped past outside, and the scream of rubber on asphalt made Tomás jump. His skittishness only fed Nelly's apprehension. When she spoke, it felt obtrusively loud, like a cough during church.

"Lloyd Younger's memorial was today."

Tomás maintained his silence but nodded to show his regard and regret. He'd seemed to have legitimately enjoyed Lloyd's company at the cotillion and the NNBL dinner. Even if his deference was merely a product of polite routine, it came from a heartfelt place.

"I couldn't take it," Nelly said. "The guilt made it impossible. So I ran away and kept running until I looked up and didn't know where I was. I'm sorry I wasn't here when you came."

Tomás waved her off and said, "It is not my place to say what guilt you should or shouldn't feel. I threw myself into a war to outpace my guilt. A long walk in a strange city is no less rational."

"Maybe, but it's not exactly respectable, is it?"

"I'd rather you be anything and everything but respectable, Ms. Sawyer."

He picked up one of the papers still littering the table. Strangely, Nelly felt embarrassed. So much of their relationship thus far had the taste and feel of a game, or an act. She played pretend princess with him in a way she never could before, even as a child. After all, there were no fairy-tale stories where Negro girls with country accents, uneducated parents, and dark complexions were swept off to a castle in the clouds by a handsome prince. Those threatening letters could very well shock Tomás out of whatever madness drove him to pursue her and remind him that he was one thing and Nelly was something else altogether.

But that didn't happen. His hands began to shake until the paper tore where he pinched it between his fingers.

"This is abominable," he spat. "These men should be found and shot. How can such base, savage threats be condoned?"

Nelly marveled at her own apathy. Yes, those men should be found and shot and displayed as a warning for all the world, but that was not their reality. One white man would never condemn another for speaking what they all took to be the indisputable truth.

"They are condoned because they're condoned," she said.

"Not by me. Not ever. Not when it comes to you."

The fear had ebbed with the flow of their natural conversation, but it flared in Nelly again with Tomás's declaration. His delivery might have been messy and drunken, but no less undeniable. When he reached into the pocket of the borrowed breeches and placed a small velvet box on the table, it felt like a foregone conclusion.

Blame it on the late hour or the long day, but Nelly senselessly began to laugh. Tomás's pouty indignation only made her laugh all the harder.

"Entiendo."

His fingers curled like talons around the box.

"No," Nelly said, still laughing. "No, you don't. I'm not laughing at you, Tomás. I'm flattered—"

"Flattered?"

"But we're strangers!" Nelly knew her parents squatted at the top of the stairs, listening. They needed to hear this most of all. "How long have we known one another? Since July, if that? Two months of friendship is not much to stake a life on. You don't know enough about me to want to marry me."

"On the contrary," he said, "I know more than enough. I know of your character, and your bravery. Your iridescent beauty. How you can handle a horse better than most men. And I know that my head's been full of you since that day at the stables when you called me an imposter to my face. If that's not the stuff of marriages, I don't know what is."

Nelly folded her hands over her eyes and wanted to scream. It was hilarious, and tragic, and beautiful. More than she could ever hope for, and more than any reasonable person could bear.

"You know a charade," she said. "The night of the cotillion was a look at the truth, the whole wretched mess of it, and it only gets worse from there. I put you in terrible danger, Tomás."

"Do you think I'm afraid?"

"I think you don't love me. And if I'm being honest, I don't love you. I admire you and respect you. I'll say without blushing that I'm attracted to you. I will value our friendship for the rest of my life, but if I accepted that ring today, it would be based on a lie."

Tomás's grin came as a shock. She'd just turned him down in no uncertain terms, yet there he sat, beaming like a fool. He had every right to curse Nelly's name after what she just had the nerve to say.

"Why're you smiling?"

He pocketed the ring with a magician's sleight of hand and said, "I'm an athlete and a soldier, Ms. Sawyer. I appreciate a good fight, and I never regret a win. You may say no today. You may say no tomorrow. You may turn me down every day for the next twenty years, but one day you *will* say yes. And that is the day you will love me as I do, and always will, love you."

Such a stirring profession should have enchanted Nelly. It proved beyond a doubt that Tomás was earnest and perhaps cared for her more than she ever thought someone could. But all she heard at the heart of his devotion was a countdown. Her time was running out, and she still had much left to do.

The calling card was still tucked in a vanity drawer, where she'd stashed it. Nelly refused to sleep, or even to move, until the sky erupted with the morning's first sunlight. She feared the lull of a warm bed and the self-preservation that came with rest. If she allowed herself even a moment's reflection, she'd forget that she had no other choice.

Nelly picked up the phone at eight o'clock exactly and gave a bushy-tailed operator the number. It rang twice, and then a male voice answered with "It's too damn early, what d'you want?"

"Yes, hello," she said in odd response to so gruff a salutation. "My name's Penelope Sawyer. I'm calling for Antonio Genna. We met last month at the Ebony Masque. He'll remember me."

There were only a few minutes of waiting before she heard a sharp intake of breath on the other line.

"Ms. Sawyer." Tony Genna's tight, dignified voice betrayed no surprise. For all Nelly knew, he'd been sitting by the phone for weeks, anticipating her call.

"Mr. Genna," she greeted him. "You offered your services not too long ago. Are you still amenable?"

She heard the groan of a leather chair when a body leans as far back into it as it will go.

"Oh, we're always amenable," he said, and Nelly made her deal with the Devil.

CHAPTER THIRTY-EIGHT

Nelly took a page out of Sequoia's book and chose red.

A slinky, formfitting number with a matching turban to hide her unwaved hair. She couldn't risk having someone awake so late to style it and witness her sneaking out, so she made self-sufficient choices. It wasn't her best look of the Chicago summer, but it would serve.

She stood at the corner of Thirty-Fifth and State as instructed. It was a bleak time of night when men passed like unfettered souls in low-tipped hats and jackets with popped collars. Their foreboding presence implied that everyone in the world had someplace to be, and those who found themselves alone on the outside would be outside forever.

This is for Elder, she reminded herself. For him, for her. Their shared legacy was wrapped up in this venture now.

A ways down State Street, a car stopped and parked. Nelly shielded her eyes from the glare of the headlights as two men and a woman stepped out in blurred silhouette. She couldn't see their faces or hear their voices over the engine's noise, but she felt them studying her.

The doors slammed closed. The car revved, then sped into the street and away, leaving its passengers at the curb. Nelly heard the woman's heels on the sidewalk as they approached.

"You're late," Nelly said.

Tony Genna removed his black fedora as he stepped into the flickering light of a marquee. He was still handsome, and dressed as he was in a beige double-breasted suit, he could've been easily mistaken for a McCormick of McCormick Reaper acclaim on his way to the yacht club.

"Perdonami, Ms. Sawyer," he said. "We were delayed." He pointed at the woman by way of explanation. She was plump, impish, and pretty, sporting a red dye job that clashed with her tanned skin.

"What can you expect when you tell a girl she only has an hour to put on something smart?" she asked unironically. "I live with my folks, and these things take time."

She spoke soft and sultry, and Nelly had to lean in to understand her. The woman took that as some kind of invitation and kissed Nelly on both cheeks.

She said, "I'm Irene, Tony's gal. He never mentioned we'd be stepping out with a Colored girl. I don't mind, of course. I work with plenty of you all at the cabaret."

Nelly gave the woman a tight-lipped smile and tried her best to appear friendly.

"I'm Nelly," she said, "and I didn't realize I was playing third wheel."

When she and Tony had planned out this infiltration and the closest shot she might ever have at scratching the Mayor's veneer, she was under the impression that only the two of them would be involved. The fewer people, presumably, the better. It would be hard to explain why Nelly Sawyer was cavorting with Antonio Genna and his girlfriend; harder even than explaining why she was with Antonio Genna alone.

Tony didn't bother defending himself. Instead, he motioned at the fourth member of their party: a boy, gawky in his padded suit jacket and long shoes. He looked downright ashamed to be there, and turned red every time his eyes strayed in Nelly's direction. Tony squeezed the back of his neck and steered him forward.

"This is my nephew, Greco," he said. "You'll be his escort tonight."

Nelly looked the boy over. Sixteen and skinny and clearly quite scared.

"This is not what we discussed. You said that *you* would get me into this blackjack game, so I assumed—"

"I'm not responsible for any of your assumptions, Ms. Sawyer. You wanted in. This is your way in. These men know me very well; throwing over Irene for you would be unexpected, to say the least. Fetching young Greco, though, wouldn't be that hard to believe."

Nelly doubted that logic, but she reluctantly accepted it. Gals and mistresses were always welcome. A pretty girl was the equivalent of a fur overcoat to these men. Much less of a threat than an interloping journalist out to expose their deepest conspiracy. Still. It wasn't what they'd discussed.

She held her hand out to Greco, who accepted it with surprising care. His skin was soft, and his nails were manicured and clean.

"Charmed, miss," he whispered at his feet.

"See?" Tony said. "You'll make a lovely couple. Who knows, this ploy may lead to a match."

"Wishful thinking, right, Greco?" Irene winked her bright green eyes at a boy who was ready to melt into the gutter.

"What if I'm recognized?" Nelly asked. She had a fake name prepared, but there was always a chance.

"Tell them the truth," Tony said. "This wouldn't be the first time a rich girl has slummed it with an Italian boy from Elmwood Park. Speak when spoken to, smile and laugh, drink what is offered and only what is offered, and you'll vanish into the wallpaper. Now, you told me that all you wanted was to observe. That implies a certain degree of *silence*. If you should break that silence, there will be consequences. Do not harbor any delusions about me defending you should you open your presumptuous little mouth and talk yourself into deep, deep waters."

Nelly shut her "presumptuous little mouth" and resolved to play nice. This man was not Jay and would not humor her because of some mutual infatuation.

"I have no delusions about you, Mr. Genna," she said. "I recall how you once offered to 'break me' when Mikey Hannigan couldn't manage alone."

Tony's smile stretched his mouth grotesquely, like a grinning skeleton.

"Yes. And depending on how this evening goes, I still might. My record is twelve hours, but experience tells me that you can beat that easily. I've read that Negro women have a strong tolerance for pain."

Through a fierce smile of her own, Nelly said, "Just because someone has lived through pain doesn't mean they can, or *will*, tolerate it."

"Hmm," he said, unimpressed and unintimidated. "Perhaps it's best you give me my payment now."

Nelly took a step back.

"That wasn't the deal," she said, then looked back at Irene and Greco. "*None of this* was part of the deal."

"You are welcome to leave at any time. You're the one who called me, remember?"

Nelly did remember. And while she didn't regret the decision, she certainly didn't count it as one of her best.

From within the matching change purse that hung from a golden chain at her wrist, she pulled a single piece of paper. Tony took it, opened it, and spent a New York minute reading it over. His eyes betrayed nothing, and Nelly figured that was intentional.

"Does anyone know about this?" he asked.

Nelly shook her head, and the feather poised like a third eye at the top of her turban bobbed. Tony opened his mouth to speak, closed it, then stood firm in his conviction and tried again.

"You do understand that if this gets out, your family will be ruined, right?" he said. "You'll be banned from every respectable racetrack in America. Your stock won't be worth their own manure if the sires can't run to win. All of those rich, pompous 'Whites Only' breeders have been looking for an excuse to lock your family out, and this will be a damn good one."

Nelly didn't need to be reminded of the risks and the visceral, ever-present danger. The payment Tony demanded was high. As she'd learned, intel was evergreen, and there was no better intel than a rigged horse race. What she needed from Tony was for him to think that they were wrapped up in that danger together.

"I trust a man like you knows how to protect his investments," she said.

Tony folded the paper and tucked it into the top of his sock for safekeeping.

"As I'm sure you'll find this evening, Ms. Sawyer," he said, "even the best of us are prone to errors in judgment."

The famed Dreamland Cafe wasn't just empty, it was dead. The vibrant lights were all dimmed to black, and the famous stage stood alone collecting dust. The manager, a man called Redd, met them at the door. He was a slicked-back Negro with a flashy grin, like a ringleader in the world's biggest circus.

"Welcome to Dreamland," he said. "Please. Follow me."

As they trailed Redd through all the dance halls, and the theaters, and the saloons that the Dreamland was known for, Irene sidled up next to Nelly.

"Just stay close to me tonight, hon," she said. "These things can get so very boring. It'll be great to finally have someone to chat with."

"How many times have you sat in on one of these games?" Nelly asked.

Irene rolled her eyes, as though counting off the dates in the air.

"Five or six. They happen nearly every month. Though I

wouldn't call it a 'game,' or at least a game that I wanna play. All they do is shift the cards around the table and grumble at each other, and it always ends in a tie. Doesn't seem worth the trouble to me, but oh well. Such things we sacrifice for a good time, right?"

Redd led them to a closed, locked door in a quiet corner of the club. Tony knocked three times, and Jay was the one who answered.

The memory of their kiss submerged and choked Nelly like a wave. His hot, insistent need and the desperation with which she'd clung to him. It had been a week to the day since the cotillion, and yet that recollection still left a bruise on her lips. She even reached up to touch them, if only to simulate the sensation, but stopped herself. Jay was a surprise—as always—but she couldn't let him shake her. The very instant she allowed herself to fall into the delirious bog of her feelings for him, there would be no climbing out.

"Thank you for coming, Tony," Jay said like a proper host. He wore a discreet gray suit, muted and dreary. His right arm was still bound up in a sling, and every jerk made him wince. Other than that, there was no way to know that he'd been shot near dead only a few days before.

Tony didn't address Jay. Instead, he spoke over his head and into the room behind.

"As if I had a choice. Is this all of us?"

"The Mayor set this up to be small," Jay said. "Private. If the other players knew the specifics of our falling-out, they might be tempted to take sides."

Tony grunted and said, "So this won't come down to a vote? That's very convenient for you, Jay Bird. You remember Irene, of course, and my brother's son, Greco. He wanted to bring his girl along. I hope you don't mind."

Jay's eyes went wide, and every part of him seemed to seize. He stared at Nelly without breathing as she watched his shock turn to fear, then to panic, then to rash anger. He was seconds away from blowing this whole hopeless, mad scheme to perdition.

"What the hell are you—"

"Jay Shorey!" Nelly met him in the middle. She squeezed his hand and prayed that he was half as clever as he claimed to be. "I haven't seen you since that awful night at the cotillion. Are you all right? We've been so worried."

Nelly could see her words filtering through and making him see sense.

"Thank you for your concern, Ms. Sawyer," he said after a long exhale. "I'm doing much better. Forgive my outburst, I was just . . . not expecting you."

Tony hovered at the edges of their conversation, missing nothing.

"She's accompanying Greco," he said.

"Greco Genna?" Jay asked. He looked at Nelly, and his smile was brittle enough to peel away. "You're stepping out with Greco Genna? The people who tried to kill me?"

Tony tutted and waved one of his aristocratic fingers at Jay in warning.

"Allegedly, Jay, allegedly. Or are we jumping to conclusions now? I thought this sewing circle existed specifically to avoid that kind of speculation."

Tony hungered for a reaction from Jay. A curse, an insult, a disrespectful slight. Anything to justify violence. Jay, to his credit, didn't bend to the lure.

"If you think to use her against me," he said to Tony, "it won't work. We're here to settle business, not get under each other's skin."

Tony patted Jay's cheek as a brother or uncle might, but with the flat of his palm. It left a blotchy handprint that made the color rise in his cheeks.

"Not everything is about you, boy."

From within the cloistered room, a female voice said with a Polish accent, "Can we begin? Some of us have places to be."

The Genna party filed on in, but not Nelly. Jay gave her arm a tug and kept her next to him.

"Do I really have to tell you how dangerous this is?" he whispered, enraged, against her ear.

"I'm not a fool," she said just as severely. "But I had to take some initiative."

"Initiative? You told me that you'd given up on finding the Mayor. If you wanted back in, I should have been your first call."

"Telling you was out of the question."

"Why?"

"You know why."

"Dammit, Nelly! You said you didn't want any more trouble, but what the fuck do you think this is? This world isn't some record that you can stop and start when you see fit. Once the wheels are turning, there's no going back. I don't know how you managed to convince Tony to go along, but I for one won't allow it."

"You?" Nelly had to moderate her voice. He chose the most inconvenient of times to be conceited. "Who the hell do you think you are? I'm Tony's guest, and if I leave, it'll be with him. You have no idea what I had to do to get here, *so don't fuck this up for me.*"

Jay stared at her with a frightened but resolute awe.

"Let's just get through tonight, Jay," she said. "I know what I'm doing."

The room was so cramped that, with the card table, there was barely enough space to sit. Nelly and Irene were forced to stand behind Greco and Tony like choirboys, and while the position was socially uncomfortable, it gave Nelly an excellent view.

Daniel Jackson sat with Jay on one end of the table, yawning and stretching like a bored tomcat. Dan, for his part, appeared delighted to see Nelly. He rose and embraced her when she came through the door. He even complimented Greco on proving worthy enough to share in her company. However, once they were all settled, Nelly noticed his grim gaze. He never spoke to her, but he didn't have to. The thin line of his mouth told all: *Jeopardize this meeting, Ms. Sawyer, and they won't have a body for your funeral.*

The lone woman at the table was dressed completely in black. Her red lip rouge was the only color she sported, with her tight mouth jutting out like a pointing finger. Unlike the men, she was there without a second. Either she was too important to fear being outnumbered, or too insignificant for it to matter. Tony called her "Ms. Saltis" when he greeted her.

Once Redd made sure drinks were replenished and cigars lit all around, he bowed out and left the five players alone at the table. It was a bare gathering. Not at all like the sprawling network of powerful men and women that Rowan had described. If some dance-hall-tipsy flapper unsteady on her feet picked the wrong door one night and walked in by mistake, she wouldn't suspect a thing. Just chalk it up as some low-stakes backroom game as random as it was harmless.

A curtain shifted, and a young woman dressed in a precisely tailored waistcoat and trousers stepped into the room. She had dark, even skin and bright eyes. There was something in the turn of her features that Nelly thought she recognized. No one acknowledged her as she stood at the dip of the crescent table and began to shuffle three decks of cards. The speed with which she dealt was sharp and efficient.

Ms. Saltis made the first bet, and the game began.

"I must say, Dan," Tony said when his turn came, "I can't recall the last time we had the pleasure of sitting at a table together. See a dog without a leash enough times, you start to figure him for a stray."

"Are we really gonna waste this game trading insults? What we all want is to be friends again, Tony," Jay said as the next in the order. He made his bet quickly and carelessly. Irene's insight had not been far off; they really did just shift cards around the table.

The dealer revealed her hand. The house won, and the game continued. Ms. Saltis chose to hit without saying a word.

Tony stood. "Fine, then. Let's be friends. As a friend, you can pay back what is owed."

Jay stood. "Owed? The lead in my shoulder isn't payment enough?"

"Call it interest, you leccaculo."

"No going out of order. You know the rules."

These were the first words Ms. Saltis had spoken since Nelly walked in the room. Well, then. She was just playing witness. Nelly looked again at the dealer. A very young woman indeed. Not long out of high school. If the dispute was between Jay and the Gennas, and Ms. Saltis was only there to witness, then the dealer must have been the Mayor's proxy. His eyes, his ears, his omnipresence. A continued way to maintain anonymity.

Nelly twisted her head and tried to catch the girl's eye. She could not shake the notion that she knew that face. Perhaps she'd seen it in a dream.

"Let me apologize on Jay's behalf," Dan was saying. Distracted, Nelly had missed a few turns. "He was acting in the best interest of our people. You know how these young bucks are. Always pushing boundaries, trying to be better than the ones that came before. We should support upstarts like him. Even when they make a mistake."

"But it was no mistake," Tony said. "Everything you did, you did on purpose, Jay. The only mistake is that you got caught."

The cigar hissed as Ms. Saltis left a burn mark on the card table's green baize, then flicked it into a corner. It sailed like a fading comet as she said, "The rules, Antonio."

Tony stood so suddenly and violently that it shook the table. Chips clattered to the floor, and if this had been a real game, there would be no telling where one bet ended and another began. Greco reached for his uncle and tried to pull him back down.

"No!" Tony yelled. "Fanculo le regole! I will not sit here and let this pup worm his way out of what he has rightfully coming. In the old days, there would be none of this sitting, and talking, and playing. A man does a thing. He's punished for it. It may be an old rule, but it's the primary rule for a reason. If the Mayor has an issue with that, he can show his face and take it up with me himself."

Jay kept his seat throughout Tony's tantrum.

"You're right," he said calmly. "In some ways, the old days were better. Certainly faster. But they weren't perfect. Look, Tony, you've already made a valiant attempt on my life. Almost sealed it for good, too. But this is bigger than just the people at this table now. You acted rashly, and a person died for it."

"Just another nigger whelp," Tony said. Nelly visibly shrank away in revulsion. Somewhere in their entanglement, she'd convinced herself that she had his respect. How insipid must she look to these people—standing behind a man who didn't see past the color of her skin or the money in her hand.

"That's where you're wrong," Jay said.

"Jimmy." Dan spoke, but Jay held up his hand and silenced him at once, like a command.

"Lloyd Younger wasn't just some 'nigger whelp,' as you so chivalrously put it. He was the son of a very powerful Colored family back in Georgia. A family with federal connections. If pointed in the right direction, they could bring the house down on you and your brothers for a whole slew of things, murder included. By the end of it, whatever dip in your profits I might have caused will be small potatoes. None of us want that kind of heat. So, please. Sit down and let the process work."

Tony appeared amused, and possibly even impressed with such a veiled and plausible threat.

"It's a shame," he said. "I've always liked you. I vouched for you at every turn. It's only right then that I do this myself."

Tony's Smith & Wesson was almost identical to Jay's. Only cleaner. Newer. And much more deadly.

"No guns. The rules!" Ms. Saltis spoke as though on automation while helplessly staring at the gun.

Greco yelled at his uncle in Italian but was subsequently ignored by everyone. Dan had seen this coming, Nelly figured. His gun was a shiny streamlined Colt with a heft that Nelly felt in her knees when he thudded it on the table. Greco made this unbearable whining noise, fumbling around for a gun of his own, and Irene giggled as though this was all some slapstick matinee at the Haymarket.

Jay didn't flinch.

"You know this won't solve anything for anyone, Tony."

"No, it won't," Tony said, "but I'm an engineer at my core. I like to finish what I start."

When he pointed his Smith & Wesson at Jay, the dealer screamed. And there, *there it was*. It was only a sliver of a moment, but it was enough to shake that part of Nelly that never forgot a face. Or a voice. Florida bred an accent so embedded in the souls of its children, it even came through in a scream.

The guns went off all at the same time.

Nelly dropped to the floor with her head pressed against her knees while above her, bullets bounced and ricocheted, blood made red constellations on the walls. People yelled in fear, in shock, in pain. Some were dying. Down on a bare wooden floor littered with peanut shells, Nelly and the dealer found each other. Now that she could name the resemblance, it was uncanny. Might as well have been Marta's own gray eyes staring back at her.

This way, mouthed the girl Nelly now knew to be Becky Harjo. She lay flat on her belly and began to crawl. Nelly followed and cried out when searing-hot bullet shells landed on her back.

CHAPTER THIRTY-NINE

Becky ran on swift feet through the labyrinth that bordered the Dreamland Cafe. So fast, in fact, that Nelly almost lost her in the rigging behind a stage.

"Becky!" Nelly shouted, and the name echoed up and all around them. "Becky Harjo!"

Becky stopped and turned. She panted hard enough for Nelly to see the heat of her breath dissolving in the air. She reminded Nelly of a hare she'd once hunted on a frigid December dawn. It froze in her crosshairs, ready to run, but just a second too late.

"I don't know you," Becky said. It was impossible to mistake the similarities now. Becky was a younger, healthier version of Marta down to how she stretched her vowels.

"No. But I knew your mother." Nelly approached Becky slowly, cautiously. She only had one chance to make this right. "My name's Nelly Sawyer."

Becky's lips drew back in a snarl. She was no hare, but a fox with foam dripping from her fangs. She lunged at Nelly, and they fell to the ground together. Nelly had never experienced a proper fight, but she knew what it was to be beaten. And Becky beat her like a woman undone. She used her fists, her nails. She drew Nelly's blood with everything but the sharp ends of her teeth. Her sobs became battle cries as terrifying as any banshee, and the shrill wretchedness stabbed at Nelly until her own tears mixed with the mucus and the blood.

"It's your fault!" Becky screamed. "You lying bitch, they killed her! My ma is dead because of you!"

With her knuckles, Becky thrashed Nelly's abdomen until cramps rolled through her stomach and made her gag. Struggling to catch her breath, Nelly briefly wondered if Becky meant to beat her to submission, or to death—whichever came first. But soon, the girl's breathing evened. Her arms lost the strength needed to fight just as her spirit did.

"They killed her."

Becky repeated this like a prayer, like an accusation, with eyes on the club's beamed ceiling. She cried out as though God Himself might answer, speaking divine words of comfort to erase the horror of weeks, of years. Hell, even of the past few minutes. It was a ridiculous folly: that all the infinite glories of life could be reduced in the seconds it takes for someone to die.

"I'm sorry," Nelly said in a voice made hoarse by all the screaming and the running. "I'll be sorry for the rest of my life, Becky. Your mother offered me aid, and I betrayed that confidence. But I think I know how to fix this."

Becky's hand pulled back and slapped Nelly square across the face. She coughed and tasted copper in her mouth.

"There's no fixing this!" Becky cried. "What, you can bring my ma back?"

"You know I can't."

"Then you can save your pity." Becky stood and loomed above Nelly, awash in a barbarous power. No more a child than an ancient goddess of vengeance and war.

"I'm not some charity case," she said. "You think you can absolve yourself by throwing your money around and erasing everything my mother was, everything she could've been?"

Nelly sat up and felt every one of Becky's blows.

"I can't take any of it back," she said as she struggled to stand. "I can't even in good conscience apologize. What I can do is shine a light on the people who did this to your mother. People who dispose others as soon as they become inconvenient or uncontrollable. People like the man you work for."

With her hands rooted on her hips, Becky looked very much like her mother.

"You mean Redd?" she asked.

Nelly paused.

"No, no, I mean the Mayor of Maxwell Street."

Becky knew the name. Her eyes became acute, like the eyes of some omniscient cat.

"That's the man Ma drew in her comics," she said. "The shadow. You think I work for someone like that?"

Nelly observed Becky again, and her crisp, androgynous casino uniform. This was a job for a grown woman of experience, not a girl who should have been tucked in bed, preparing for a new day at school.

"How the hell did you even get this gig?" Nelly asked. "What are you, fifteen? You shouldn't be working in a place like this."

Becky straightened her spine and lifted her flat chest in an unconvincing show of womanhood. She said, "I'm plenty old enough to deal cards. My daddy taught me how before I could even speak."

"That doesn't mean you're good enough to deal tables at the Dreamland. Your ma said you wanted to be an accountant."

Instead of raging at the thought of her mother, as she had before, Becky wilted. No doubt, she saw those dreams of college and a respectable, dependable job as visions from another life. Marta had stoked those dreams. Without her, they dried and died.

"It's only supposed to be temporary," Becky said. "Redd is offering me protection, and Jay said I should make myself useful while I'm here, to show my gratitude."

Nelly had been ten years old when she made the grave error of all country children and roused a beehive. Dozens of them descended upon her, pricking every inch of bare skin. It took Florence hours, but she managed to pick out every barbed stinger but one. The longest one, the deepest one, directly in the center of Nelly's left hand. The wound closed over with time, and the only proof remaining of the attack was a black line in her palm. The pain eventually faded and became lost to memory.

But when Nelly heard Jay's name, she felt that sting again.

"Jay Shorey got you this job?" she asked.

Becky nodded.

"He told us what you did. He came to warn us, but Ma knew we wouldn't get far if we ran. She asked him to fulfill a promise instead."

Nelly's promise. The one that guaranteed Becky's safety should anything happen to Marta. Nelly did not know if she was grateful to Jay for following through on what she could not, or furious at him for allowing her to believe he had done nothing at all.

"So, you don't know what tonight's blackjack game was even for?" Nelly said. "What it meant?"

"Redd told me to just deal the cards. If I'd known it would turn into all that madness, I woulda said no. This city ain't gonna kill me like it killed my ma."

The whole of Nelly's ramshackle theory balanced on the dealer. She could accept that the Mayor wouldn't show his full self to them, especially if they changed with every venue. But there must have been *someone.* Someone he confided in, listened to, spoke through. Such an outfit couldn't run on smoke and mirrors alone.

"Were you told to report to anyone afterward? Other than Redd?" Nelly asked.

"Yes," Becky said at once. "Jay. To pay me."

That pang in Nelly's hand was intense enough to make her cry out. She looked down and half expected it to be on fire.

"We need to go."

Both Nelly and Becky jumped at the sudden intrusion of a new voice. Jay stood behind them, bent double at the waist. Everything from his neck on down was covered in blood.

"Oh my God," Becky said.

Jay immediately assured them, "It's not mine," then looked at Nelly properly, with all her bruises and shallow cuts. "What happened to you?"

"Becky and I had a score to settle," Nelly said. Jay didn't wait for further explanation.

"We need to go," he said again.

"But—"

"Not now, Penelope, please! For the love of God, just listen to me. People are dead."

His use of her given name was meant to silence her, but it only spawned more questions.

"Who?" she asked, selfishly hoping it was Tony. If he had died, then that little piece of paper in his shoe and the information that could doom her family would die with him.

"Hanna Saltis," Jay said. "Dan caught one in the arm, but he'll be okay. Tony's girl, and the boy."

Nelly had known Irene and Greco for all of forty-five minutes, but the image of their once-lithe bodies disfigured by death broke a piece of her in two. Those were faces that neither she nor anyone else would ever see again.

"Tony?" she asked.

"Down, but not out. He'll call his brothers, and we want to be as far away as possible when they get here."

Jay crossed over to Becky and shoved a wet, folded stack of cash into her hand.

"That's for tonight," he said. "Extra, for what you had to see. Go back to Redd's house and stay with his woman. You'll hear from me soon."

Becky's hand closed over the money and the blood stained her fingers. When she looked at Nelly, that grief-stricken passion marked her, along with an acceptance that resembled bitterness in one so young.

"I hope you find him," Becky said, and then she ran on down the hall until the club's living darkness swallowed her whole.

CHAPTER FORTY

It was only as Jay polished off his third serving of fried catfish, succotash, and biscuits drowned in gravy that Nelly realized she had never seen him eat before.

She'd seen him in the *vicinity* of food—the Marigold tea service, the NNBL dinner, even that thrown-together breakfast in his drafty apartment—but never actually consuming it. There was that tangy Cuban pear he'd shared during the Sunday Market, but that had been barely enough to fill the stomach of a child. Nelly couldn't rightly say where he found his energy. Maybe he did manage on just coffee and good times.

The waitress came with his fourth plate of food. Nelly could see her actively trying to ignore the red blood turned brown coating the front of Jay's suit, and failing. The only reason they were allowed a table at all was because the owner lost over two hundred dollars at the Lantern Club and had yet to pay it back. Jay told the man as much to his face when the owner explained that—in their condition—Nelly and Jay would drive away his customers.

Fine, Jay had said. *Then pay what is owed now, or end up looking just like me.*

After that, they were given the restaurant's finest booth toward the back, away from the street-facing windows, with every meal on the house.

Jay glanced up from what must have been his tenth or twelfth biscuit and eyed Nelly's peanut soup, now gone cold.

He said, "You should eat. This place has the best Southern-style food in the city."

The soup's velvety yellow finish made her stomach turn.

"I can't eat right now."

"Well, I'm hungry," he said and resumed his meal with fervor like a newly domesticated dog, accustomed to going days without a good meal.

The restaurant's only music came from a creaky player piano that rolled through a catalog of antebellum work songs and old-timey hymns. It was meant to create a specific kind of atmosphere to go along with the cuisine, but after so many off-key renditions of "Shenandoah," Nelly started to feel like a wax figurine trapped in a museum display.

"What happened back there?" she asked, just to get Jay talking. He'd been curiously quiet ever since they slipped into a street behind the Dreamland and ran through alleys and private gardens until blocks stood between them and the club.

Jay picked a fish bone from between his teeth and spat it onto the plate.

"That," he said in a thin, flat voice, "is what happens when folk take things personally. What transpired between me and the Genna brothers was just business. Sure as shit not enough to bring a gun into a game over. Of all the rules, that's the one that matters most."

"Why?"

"To keep situations like tonight from happening. Emotions run high, things get out of hand. If just Irene and Greco were gone, then we could claim blood for blood and call it even. But Hanna's death complicates things. She was Polack Joe's favorite niece, his right hand. It won't take long for the others to pick a side, and I guarantee it won't be in the Black Belt's favor."

He emptied his glass of lemonade in two strong gulps, then motioned for the waitress to bring more.

"You and Dan are in big trouble," she said. "Aren't you?"

"We'll see. Tony was the one who broke the rules. The final word lies with the Mayor."

Nelly drew swirls in the condensation of her water glass. She hadn't forgotten what Becky said about Jay being her contact after the game. Or how Rowan implied that Jay was fully aware of the circumstances of her brother's death. The revelation painted him in a smoky relief not too unlike "Salome." Face preserved in darkness so the viewer can never see whether she is sobbing over the body of the man she's condemned, or laughing.

"You didn't tell me that you found Marta," she said.

He cut his eyes up at her through long lashes.

"You never asked."

"Oh, fuck you, Jay!" Nelly yelled. Several patrons turned to glare at them, but once members of the staff whispered who Jay was, they kept their curiosity on their fried green tomatoes.

"You know what Marta's death did to me! I gave up on my life's dream to atone for that, and the entire time, I assumed she died because you didn't get to her soon enough."

"No." Jay jabbed his fork at her like a fencer's rapier. "She died because you gave her up to Big Bill and all the rest. I told you that I would warn her, and I did. What'd you expect? Spiriting her out of town in an apple cart?"

"How can you joke about this? About any of this? God, Jay, if I didn't know you, I'd think you didn't care at all."

"I care about you."

There was no sentiment when he said this. He sounded regretful, pained, as though compelled at gunpoint. Picking over each word like a crusted scab, he said again, "*I care about you.* Marta was a talented, determined woman, but she was no fool. She knew exactly what she was doing, and as much as you may try to deny it, Nelly, so did you. I only warned her for your sake. I only took in Becky for your sake. So, no. I won't sit here and cry over them, because they're not my dead to carry."

"You could have at least told me that Becky was safe," Nelly said.

"No, I couldn't. I was hard on you at the time, but honestly, I was glad when you gave up on the article. Something had to knock you to your senses. If I told you that Becky was alive and well, you'd strike up the band again. I guess there's no stopping fate, though. How much did you pay Tony to tell you about the blackjack games?"

Nelly folded her arms and stared Jay down with a defiant desire to see him unravel.

"Tony didn't tell me about the games, Jay," she said. "Rowan Byrne did."

His forkful of succotash fell in a wet clump on the plate. She was finally hungry, she noticed. She plucked a biscuit from his plate and soaked it in cold peanut soup so it could dissolve in her mouth.

"They sent Rowan after you?" he asked.

Not even Jay's note of concern could extinguish Nelly's smugness.

"I ran into him last Wednesday, after Lloyd's memorial," she said. "He told me everything he knew about the Mayor of Maxwell Street. The blackjack games, the network, everything."

If Nelly had blinked, she would have missed it. That twitch under Jay's right eye. It was as clear a tell as she'd ever seen. So, when he lied, she wasn't surprised.

"Rowan is a low-level grunt who made his bones shining Mikey Hannigan's shoes," Jay said. "I could fit everything he knows about anything in a shotgun shell."

Nelly leaned far across the table. The tassels on her satin dress dipped into the gravy and made strokes like ancient calligraphy across his plate. Looking into his eyes was akin to looking into the summer's brightest, clearest sky. Brilliant enough to blind.

"Did you know how Elder died?"

"Of course," Jay said without hesitation. "His Roadster hydroplaned in a storm."

Nelly slammed her hand down on the table with enough force

to topple Jay's glass and send a waterfall of lemonade splashing and spreading across the floor.

Her voice like gravel, like buckshot and nails, Nelly said, "Yes. But did you know *why?*"

Jay didn't speak. He didn't have to. For the first time since that fateful day when she asked him for a cigarette and he took her hand, Nelly could decipher his whole churning mire without a word.

Nelly did not know where she was after she stormed out of the restaurant, or where she was going. She didn't even recognize the obscure South Side street she was on. All she knew was that Jay lay behind, and to get away from him, she must go forward. Her sobs came on in wracking waves so violent that they made her chest hurt from heaving.

"Nelly!"

She closed her eyes and walked on in darkness. To see him would be to unspool before him until there was nothing left.

"Nelly! You can't be out in the open, it's not safe!"

His hand took hold of her so suddenly, so unyieldingly, that it made her cry out. He was a strong young man. When he had a mind to hold on to something, there was little she could do.

"Get the fuck off of me, Jay!" she shouted. "All this time, you've known that the Mayor of Maxwell Street killed my brother, and you just let me go on searching out this man like a fool!"

"But I didn't know, Nelly!" he yelled, shaking her. "Look, I did lie to you when we first met, okay? Elder wasn't just some passing acquaintance to me. He came into the Lantern Club on Fridays, and we'd share a drink. Trade stories. I don't have many of what you might call friends in this city. People I owe, or who owe me, maybe, but Elder was different. I could be whoever I wanted with him, and he didn't demand a thing for it. Kind of like how it is when I'm with you."

Nelly retreated from the soft pulse of his voice, the caress in his eyes. That same transformation had come over him in the seconds before they'd kissed, and all the rules had changed.

"You say Elder was your friend," she said, "but you let him die. You could have saved him!"

"You don't know what I did for your brother. I begged him to stop. He said his parents would help if it came to that. And you know what they did when he told them about his trouble, your mother and father? They ignored him, Nelly. They left him to hang in the wind like dirty laundry."

Nelly slapped him hard across the face. She felt the impact travel up her arm and settle in the roots of her teeth.

She said, "Don't you dare turn this back on my family. *You* had every opportunity to tell me about Elder, but you didn't. Why? What possible reason could you have to keep this all from me if you weren't working with the Mayor yourself?"

Jay began to laugh. The sound, as sweet as it was, drove through Nelly like a stake.

"Quite the journalist you are," he said. "I never anticipated seeing you again after the funeral, Nelly. The whole story didn't matter if you'd only be gone off to Kentucky the next day. But you stayed. And as I found myself more and more in your company, saw all of your maddening, beautiful ways . . . I didn't want my history with Elder to shape my future with you."

Nelly hated how his words stirred her, moved her. "You are a bastard, Jay. You have lied to me from the moment we met. What future could we ever have based on that? Tell me the truth, right here, and right now. Have you known who the Mayor of Maxwell Street is this whole time?"

"No."

"Do you know who he is now?"

"No!"

"See? I can't believe a word that comes out of your mouth. Christ, why did you even agree to help me in the first place if you knew what I was walking into?"

"I agreed to help you," he said, "to protect you."

"Are you sure? Was it not just to influence me? To control my time, my attention? My affection?"

Jay scoffed and said, "Don't flatter yourself, Nelly Sawyer. As much as I care for you, as much as I—and yes, I'll admit— ardently want you, I would never put either of us in that kind of danger just to woo you. I should hope my methods are more direct than that."

Nelly had convinced herself for weeks that what she felt for Jay was gratitude. Compassion. A kindred friendship born of sacrifice and trust. But when they kissed, the earlier shock of grief and fear brought clarity to a sentiment long cloaked in uncertainty. Her attraction to him was more than physical. A part of his soul called out to her, and even now as she dissected every moment they'd ever shared, her own soul answered.

"I agreed to help you because you and I are the same," he said. "We will both do whatever it takes to get what we want. And we both know *exactly* what we want."

"I am nothing like you, Jay," she said.

"Oh, Ms. Sawyer. You are more like me than my own shadow."

And of course, he was right. Right in a way too wretched and too wicked for Nelly to accept.

Their Yellow Cab driver was a cantankerous Persian who chewed snuff and kept a military-grade pistol on the dashboard. *For the Checkers*, he'd said when Nelly asked.

He had some doubts about taking two roughed-up Negroes into the heart of the most affluent neighborhood in the city in the dead of night, but after Jay passed him two ten-dollar bills, the man kept to himself. Nelly offered to make her own way home, but Jay wouldn't hear of it. Tony might count her as a witness to the night's butchery; Dan, too. Both were currently in the process of drawing up a list of names, and hers would be very near the top.

The ride into Hyde Park was unnaturally silent. Every house seemed especially shuttered: drapes drawn, lights out, windows shut against the first refreshing breeze in months. Nelly almost told the driver to turn them around back toward the city, but she dismissed her suspicions as the last willful cinders of her anger at Jay and ignored them.

"You should keep your head down for a while, if you can," Jay said from his exile at the far opposite end of the cab.

"The sooner you can get out of the city, the better. When are y'all going home? Back to Kentucky?"

"Kentucky?" Her laugh was wry and just south of cruel. "We're not going back to Kentucky. Tomás proposed."

A stench came off of Jay like seared meat. It pleased her, his indignation. Somehow, it made all the horrors and betrayals of the evening feel worthwhile.

A single lamplight danced in the Hyde Park house's parlor window, and Nelly knew that her great escape had been a failure. Either one or both of her parents were currently seated and waiting to meet her at the door and lay into her until she lost the will to ever leave her room again.

However, even with the lamp's beckoning glow, the house projected a dread. The drive was suddenly especially long, and the door very far away.

"If I asked you to run away with me, would you?" Jay asked. He stood next to her in the house's shade, waiting for what, she did not know.

"You're deranged," Nelly said. "Run away where, and why? You are a selfish liar who made a consistent fool out of me, Jay. Even if I loved you, I could never go anywhere with you."

"So, you're saying you don't love me?"

Nelly felt the dizzying sensation of rising déjà vu. Tomás had made similar assumptions, similar protestations, mindless of whatever truth she carried.

"I won't say that Tomás is an unworthy man," Jay said. "Anyone else vying for your affections would've left me shot and bloody on that dance floor. But he picked me up, packed me into his very expensive little car, drove me home, and stood guard outside my house all night. He's the best of them. If there was no other choice for you, I would want nothing less. But you do have a choice. You'll always have a choice with me."

His words were rose-scented, but they were a fabrication. More deceptions made to lure her into a stasis that never asked questions or embraced uncomfortable answers.

"Jay, I don't know you," she said. "How am I even meant to see you?"

"See me as I am, Nelly. See everything I have tried to hide, and bury, and eviscerate since the night I left Wood Acre. Tomás can give you all the glittering wonders of this world. Security, wealth, prosperity that folk like you and me will only see on Judgment Day. In time, he *will* give you love, but I can give you a life worth living."

And what a life it would be. Fierce and dangerous, forever teetering on the edge of disaster. But free.

That brisk evening breeze stirred up into a full-on wind blowing in from the lake, and a smell caught in Nelly's nose. Cloying and manufactured. It triggered a strong nostalgia for pickup trucks and those last few miles on an empty tank as they pushed on to the sole filling station in Richmond that would serve Negroes.

"Do you smell that?" she asked.

Jay lifted his nose to the sky like a deer scenting a hunter.

"Yeah," he said. "Something's burning."

Afterward, Nelly would swear on the Bible that the explosion came from the basement, but only because she felt the blast rumbling under the earth in the seconds before the mansion went up in flames and smoke. The truth? It came from the garage. The dynamite was but a match to a fuse. The Rolls-Royce's powerful engine—left running for half the night—did the rest. They never could find Murphy. His letter of resignation included no forwarding address, just a single line written in a near illegible, tear-stained script: *You lot have always been good to me, but a man must have his dignity.*

CHAPTER FORTY-ONE

When Nelly woke in the penthouse suite of the Blackstone Hotel, Jay was gone, but Sequoia was there. She sat at her bedside in a virginal white dress, billowy as a choir robe. A King James Bible was open in her lap, and her mouth moved as she read aloud to herself. The shades were all drawn, and the room felt thick with the smoke of burning incense. There was no telling whether it was day or night.

"Are you praying for me?" Nelly said, but her voice came out creaky from lack of use like a well gone dry. She closed her hand over her throat and coughed.

Sequoia's eyes jumped up to Nelly's. Immediately, she pressed the Bible to her forehead and began to cry out in prayer.

"Thank God," she said. "Thank God, thank God! I thought the old bastard didn't listen to me anymore."

Nelly tried to smile, but her lips were so parched that they split and cracked with every twitch. Sequoia offered a wet handkerchief before Nelly could ask. With her color so high, she took on a gloss like burnished leather.

Nelly reached up to touch her friend's face and said, "You're beautiful."

Even when crying, Sequoia was glamorous. The tears sat like crystals atop her cheeks, perfectly poised as though waiting for a stage direction.

"You've been out cold for three days, girl," Sequoia said, "and that's the first thing you think to say to me?"

"Three days?"

Nelly absorbed the room and all its empty space. She only knew it as the Blackstone because her family had visited before—one of the few luxury hotels in the city that accepted their money without the dramatics of a public sacrifice. It was her father's favorite place to stay in maybe all the world. The wood paneling, masculine colors, soaring ceilings, and impeccable white-glove service were all the props he'd grown to associate with a successful life. They were no longer fantasies that men in the clubs he worked when he was twelve years old would lord over him while he shined their shoes. He could stand in the middle of the grandest room in the grandest hotel, look out over the city's lustrous skyline, and feel protected, shielded. Invisible.

Behind a closed door, Nelly heard voices speaking like the voices of the ancestors across the veil.

"Where are my folks?" she asked.

One of Sequoia's hands came to rest on Nelly's knee through the bedsheets. The other tapped the top of her Bible with the frantic pace of a fly trapped under glass. Looking at her, Nelly saw someone new. Or rather, someone who had been artfully hidden beneath the chic clothes and witty repartee. Thin-haired, sunken-eyed, and still impossibly faithful to a church that decried her as an abomination.

"Your mother's still in the hospital," Sequoia said. "They think she'll be all right, but it's in the Lord's hands now."

Nelly closed her eyes and tried not to visualize her mother laid up in a grimy hospital bed, surrounded by strangers. She was the indomitable Florence Sawyer. A fighting chance was all the chance she needed.

"But your father." Sequoia's hand squeezed until her nails dug into the fleshy space below Nelly's kneecap.

Nelly began to scream, but with her voice still so weak, all she really did was open her mouth and bare her teeth.

There were no days or nights. Just eyes open and eyes closed.

The suite remained dark, so Nelly relied on Sequoia's outfits to mark the passage of time. She would sit with Nelly for hours and talk about her mother's progress, about the weather, about Tomás and how capably he'd stepped in. A legion of private detectives was apparently stationed outside her door twenty-four hours a day, armed to the teeth. All manner of attorneys and estate planners and journalists joined them in the outer recesses of the hotel. And beyond even that—cluttering the streets with horses and barking dogs—were the police.

Tomás made it clear that not a one was allowed to disturb Nelly's rest under threat of prosecution, and possibly even death.

Although Sequoia rarely stayed for long, Nelly was never alone. Elder liked to pace the floor at the edge of her bed and tell stories. Ambrose stood at the window, looking down on the street with the unsympathetic discontent of one who has been cheated. Marta and Lloyd were there, too, but they didn't speak. Only stared at Nelly and exuded a slight annoyance, as though they'd just missed the train. Then there was the Mayor.

She never saw his face during those fevered dreams, but she knew him, sitting in Sequoia's chair with legs crossed and hands closed in his lap. He wore a top hat and suit. Black as spilled ink and lined with bloodred silk.

"I suppose I should apologize," Nelly said on the second week of her confinement. They were the first words she'd uttered in days.

Sequoia sat cross-legged on the bed with her face behind a fan of cards. She was terrible at gin rummy, and Nelly won most rounds without even trying. Looking at the cards, Nelly thought of Greco's puffy face and Irene's rouge-stained teeth.

Sequoia sneered at her hand then said, "Apologize for what, dear heart?"

"The last time we were together, at Lloyd's memorial," Nelly said. "I had no business speaking to you like that. Your grief was genuine and rough, and I used it against you. I think we both said things we didn't mean—"

"Oh, I meant them."

Nelly laid her cards down face up.

"What do you mean?"

"Just that," Sequoia said. "I probably could've chosen my words better, but I didn't exaggerate. And I imagine you didn't either."

"What I said was merciless," Nelly said, disbelieving.

"Doesn't make it untrue."

Sequoia discarded her own cards and flexed elegant fingers, now dry and wrinkled after washing Nelly's hair. Without Florence's oversight, it had gone days without being combed or hydrated, and now shone from the fresh attention.

"My father wasn't born to be a bishop," Sequoia said. "He was born to be a philandering indigent steel worker like my grandfather. He always had a talent for showmanship, though, and there's no finer stage than a pulpit. Or more eager an audience than a congregation. But without that telltale legacy that the talented tenth and their like love so much, becoming a legitimate 'first family' proved difficult. If not damn near impossible. Unlike you, I didn't have any money or other practical excuses for our peers to tolerate me. So I became *impractical.* A good-time girl who can always get you in the fun parties, introduce you to the right people. I still can't afford good clothes, so I win them. Or borrow them. Or steal them, in a pinch.

"I don't despise Jay Shorey just because he's a manipulative little cockroach. Looking at him is like looking in a mirror, or a time machine. It takes a certain degree of sacrifice to build a new destiny. I'm reminded every day of what I had to give up for mine, but Jay has bigger dreams than me. I imagine the price he paid was much steeper."

The voices outside Nelly's door grew ever more frantic, and the ghosts grew ever more bold. The longer she stayed in bed, withstanding their intractability, the more she felt the rot of madness creep into her gray, sunless world. She would not survive going insane any more than she could survive living without her father, so on the morning of the fourteenth day, Nelly got up, put on something clean, and opened the door.

Immediately, a dozen flashing light bulbs struck her blind.

"Ms. Sawyer!" a voice behind a camera called out. "Ms. Sawyer, do you have anything to say on the death of your father?"

"Do you mean to sell the ranch?"

"There're recent rumors that Hawthorne has been fixed in your favor, is that true?"

"When will you announce your engagement?"

The words came at her like a gale, and she held up her hands as though to ward them off.

"All right, that's enough!"

A wide shape stepped into the line of Nelly's sight, and the cameras ceased. Tomás silenced the reporters as easily as Moses split the Red Sea.

"Ms. Sawyer's lawyers will make a statement," he said. "Until then, we ask that she be undisturbed at this terrible time. So, please, leave her in peace."

Tomás snapped his fingers and a small battalion of men in derby hats began to herd the journalists out the door. With the suite's sitting room cleared out, Nelly could see the excessive amount of flower arrangements plainly. Hundreds of them. Massive, gaudy constructions that spelled out "Deepest Condolences" with tulips. And the smell of them was as noxious as mustard gas. Nelly began to cough and could not stop until Tomás placed a glass of water in her hands.

He'd grown thin in the numberless days since she'd been entombed. His bronze glow had dimmed from lack of sun, and his suit was hectically askew. But he was just as striking as ever, and Nelly clung to that vigor without shame after so many hours alone with the dead.

"Penelope," he said, then kissed her for the very first time. He was gentle, as she'd always expected him to be.

"I'm sorry I haven't been in to see you," he said when he pulled away. "With the police behaving with such carelessness, I thought it best to help where I could. Ms. McArthur established herself as your protector at once and has refused to leave your side. It thrills me to see you up and standing after so long."

"Yes," Nelly said. Her voice was unaccustomed to speaking above a whisper. "It's good to see you, too. And thank you. You didn't have to do any of this."

Tomás kissed her again, with more pressing force, like a seal leaving its mark in hot wax.

"I will do anything for you, Penelope. Especially now. Your father was a great man."

Nelly tried not to think of her father. It was easier to imagine that he'd never existed at all. Even as his ghost peered into the street and reminded her to put the studs out to pasture.

"Has my family come?" she asked. She hadn't seen her grandmother in years, but now she wanted to throw herself against the old woman's weather-worn embrace and disappear. Even Samuel would be a welcome sight. He'd take one look at the mess of her life and know what to do.

Tomás touched her cheek, showing more affection in minutes than he had in months, and ran his thumb along the shell of her ear.

"I told them to keep people away," he said. "As to not disturb you. We need to get your strength up before throwing you to the wolves."

"My family's not 'the wolves.'"

"Perhaps not. But the reporters are, and they will latch on to anyone close to you and your parents for a story. This is for the best right now, darling, just you and me. Until you're stronger."

Tomás's compassion wrapped Nelly up in its generosity. She could feel in every word that he was acting with no other motivation but her safety. Yet, she felt something lock around her as he spoke. Not a cage, not exactly, but the bones of one. She needed her family. Whatever strength she could muster, she'd muster from them.

"I'm strong now," she said. "A little banged up, but I don't need to be bedridden anymore. Tell me what's going on, and I can take over from here."

"I've taken care of everything," said Tomás. Nelly stared up at that handsome face and wondered if he'd gone quite mad, too.

"Everything?" she repeated.

"Your father's business manager came on the fastest train. We've been making your arrangements together. Rest assured, Penelope, that all you have to do right now is be still and recover."

Her father's business manager should have known better. Tomás was an outsider; a friend of her family, sure, but not someone who should ever have access to One Oak's inner workings. Such privileges only belonged to the closest family. Unless . . .

Nelly separated from Tomás and drifted to a table piled high with more flowers, and cards, and the odd casserole. One note came in a familiar square envelope, small enough to fit in the palm of her hand. The stationery was thin and un-embossed, but the signature was in the most florid calligraphy. Nelly had come to memorize the hills and valleys of such handwriting after a year's hidden correspondence.

On one side of the card, it read:

Dearest Ms. Sawyer,

My deepest condolences on the loss of your father and your beautiful new home. We are all praying for your mother's recovery, and the swift apprehension of whoever enacted this heinous attack. With your permission, the Defender *would be honored to dedicate a full spread to Ambrose Sawyer's obituary. Negroes throughout America will weep at his cruel and untimely murder.*

With all my love, Richard B. Norris

But on the other side, scrawled as though by an unsteady hand, were only three words:

Maybe next time.

She'd been close. Close enough to touch the truth, to comprehend it in all its brutality. If Richard wanted to wash his hands of her, very well. But she would follow the Mayor of Maxwell Street's trail of blood all the way to the bitter end.

"Tomás, one of those reporters mentioned an engagement," Nelly said. "You didn't announce something, did you?"

"I would never do that without your approval. But I am ready to. I would very much like to."

He didn't drop to one knee, for which Nelly was grateful.

"What I feel for you hasn't changed," Tomás began. "But what I can offer you as a friend, as a husband, and as a partner *has*. I don't need to tell you that One Oak Ranch without Ambrose Sawyer is barely One Oak at all."

That same tone of compassion had not wavered, turning all of Tomás's devastating words into the promises of a childhood sweetheart. It made Nelly sick to her stomach. As though she'd eaten too much cake and would pass an endless night hating something for its saccharinity.

"One Oak still has me," she said.

"Of course. I've seen how capable you are, and I know how well you can manage on your own."

"So, what are you asking me?"

"I'm asking for a life," Tomás said. "A shared life, a protected life. Nothing like this will ever happen again to you, or your mother, if God willing she should live, or our children. The work of our marriage will be sustaining your well-being, and all that your father built. Loving you will be the indulgence."

"That's not very romantic," Nelly said, at a loss.

"Would you rather I prostrate myself? Profess the depths of my adoration? I can do that, if that's what you want. But I thought such displays were above us."

As much as Nelly resented his frankness, she knew that any other way would be unacceptable. He'd already performed the dashing suitor's besotted role. He came to her now as a man of some years and means. Fully aware of what he wanted and willing to offer up the world to have it.

Tomás played the inconspicuous golden boy effortlessly. So, when the tactician who orchestrated attacks that killed hundreds began to show, it was a jarring possession.

"It is what your father would have wanted," he said. "He told me himself."

Nelly glared at Tomás and felt his persistence staring back at her. It was just as he'd said from the start: he was an athlete with a love for competition. If his devotion couldn't win her, then his intimidation would.

She asked for time. He gave her three days.

471

When she opened the door to the suite's bedroom and saw Jay sitting in Sequoia's chair, Nelly took it for a vision. Or a new ghost come to yoke itself to her torment. But Jay looked to be the one in agony.

He was a mess. Inelegant, grubby, and reduced to the spindly and unforgiving bits that made up the soul of a person. He wore not one of his colorful suits, but a senseless collection looted from the bodies of the dead. Wrinkled twill workpants, a military-surplus shirt, and an army vest with another man's name sewn over the right pocket. His hair's natural curl pattern was loosed and ran rampant over his head, and the shadow on his neck and chin came in thick. Nelly had yet to meet "James Glass," but she assumed that—if left unbothered and unchanged—he could have grown to look something like this.

Jay stood as the door closed. He held his finger to his lips, then touched his ears, listening for the sound of Tomás's retreating steps. Only when a second set of doors closed and locked did he speak.

"Nelly," he said.

That was all it took. His appearance there, in that room, was just another costume; she could have found him in the pitch darkness at the end of the world.

He opened his arms, and she ran to him.

CHAPTER FORTY-TWO

Nelly had yet to cry in earnest over her father. She'd tried, in the solitude of her bed, but the effort left her emptied and sore. Crying for him would be as much of an end to all she knew of her life as a curtain call. She could not accept that. But she was stronger now. Her body had what it needed to weep.

Jay pressed his nose into her hair and took deep, bracing breaths full of her.

"Let go," he said. "Let it go, my girl."

When he touched her face to blot out her tears, Nelly felt how hardened his hands had become. As though he'd dug through clay with nothing but his nails. Two weeks had passed since the bombing, but Jay's beard and reedy body made Nelly think that, like Rip Van Winkle, she'd fallen asleep and let a hundred years pass by. His blue eyes remained as luminous as ever, but they were tired and half-wild.

"I left you there," he said. Nelly shook her head, not understanding. "After the bomb. You were knocked flat, hurt, *bleeding*, and I left you. God alone knows how sorry I am, Nelly."

She held his face in a rough embrace of her own. Touching Jay again held the same sensation as touching a live wire. A shock ran through her, and she was alive.

"I know. No doctors. No police," she said. "Were you hurt?"

Jay looked down at his mismatched body and took a shallow inventory.

"It all blends together after a while. But your parents, Nelly—"

"I can't, Jay. I won't. Not yet, and maybe not ever."

Jay nodded and did not express his condolences again. She ran her hand over his vest and his shirt, all coated in grime.

"You look awful," she said, which made him laugh.

"That's one way to greet an old friend."

Nelly was too worn for jokes, and judging by all appearances, Jay should have been, too. His thinness was the thin of the starving.

"I'm serious, Jay. What's going on?"

He broke from her and began to pace through the suite. His shoulders were hunched like a vagrant's after wandering into a rich man's house. When he lingered by an untouched plate of chicken and potatoes, Nelly insisted that he eat his fill, but he shook his head and moved on.

"You remember," he said, "the night of the cotillion, when Dan said that he'd turn me over if I caused any more trouble?"

She did. Nelly wrapped her arms around herself and waited for the scythe that she always knew would come for Jay to swing.

"They came knocking at Dan's door and threatened to raise the Italians, the Poles, and Mikey Hannigan's Colts to wage holy war on all the South Side unless he gave me up." Jay stopped again by Nelly's bed. He ghosted his fingers over the sheets as though playing an invisible piano with the utmost care. "He didn't give me up, exactly. Just told them he wouldn't stand in their way."

Nelly recalled Daniel Jackson's talk of "our boy" and "mourned you like a son" and hated him. She would rue not shooting him then and there, right on Jay's doorstep, for the rest of her life. Even on her most forgiving of days.

"You said that the final word lies with the Mayor," she said with the upward turn of a question.

Jay shrugged, and Nelly could see the bony spikes of his shoulders underneath his shirt.

"He might have the final word, but it won't do much against half of Chicago's gangsters. I sometimes think these men went along with the Mayor of Maxwell Street's whole sham just to add some color to their lives. They never meant a word of it."

"Christ, Jay. If they catch you, they'll kill you."

"Oh, sure. But first they'll have to catch me."

If he was scared, Nelly couldn't tell. Perhaps he'd expended all his fear in those weeks hiding and foraging. All he had left was survival.

She asked, "How'd you get in here?"

The suite was allegedly locked down from the inside out, but Jay smiled as though all Tomás's guards and precautions were little more than creeks to be crossed.

He gestured toward a wardrobe that Nelly had yet to use or open and said, "There's a door behind the back panel. These old hotels always have a secret entrance for the posher rooms. And this isn't my first time here."

"I can't hide you," she said at once. "You can't stay. Sequoia is always stopping by, and doctors come in and out without announcing themselves. And Tomás will notice something before long—"

"I'm not here for that, Nelly. I almost didn't come at all, but I had to see you before I left."

Nelly was surprised at her own indignation. Leave? Leave where, how? In what reality could Jay Shorey exist anywhere outside of Chicago, Illinois?

"What do you mean?" she asked. "Leaving the city?"

"If I stay, they'll smoke me out. There's nothing stopping them without Dan to back me."

It was all happening too fast. In the span of three months, she was to say goodbye to twice as many people. Never mind her feelings for Jay; she'd come to rely on him the way she relied on the rising sun. His hands were suddenly holding hers, and he pulled her as close as two people could be.

"I asked you once before to run away with me."

"And I said no," she said. "I'm saying no again. There's no reason for me to run. Tomás is willing to support me, to save my family's legacy, and I have a duty to accept him."

Jay heard all this while shaking his head, denouncing every word.

"What family? Forgive me, but that family is gone. Who's left? That indigent cousin of yours?"

"My family is more than my dead," she said. "They're my aunts, grandparents, my ancestors!"

Jay's face contorted in bitter scorn.

"The fucking ancestors. You are an individual person, Nelly. A beautiful, exceptional woman who deserves to live under your own terms. The ancestors aren't stalking us through eternity, waiting for the absolution in death that they were denied in life. Marrying Tomás won't scour away hundreds of years of blood."

"Then my folk died for nothing?"

Nelly's breathing became shallow and fast. The panic shook her, and all over again, she was lying on her back on the lawn of the Hyde Park house while burning shards of plaster and wood floated down like falling stars. Jay held her by the shoulders and leaned into her with all his weight. She felt her body grow roots and cement her to this room and this moment, instead of lifting away with the smoke that made storm clouds over what was once her home.

"There's no honor in suffering, not even for the ones we love," Jay said. "If you can be happy, *then be happy*. Be happy with me."

Jay's words were persistent in their calm and affection. The more she listened, the more she wanted them to be true.

"Look at yourself, Jay. You've been underground for weeks. Is this what 'running away' would be with you?"

He released her and marched to the wardrobe and its secret door. He pulled out that same carpenter's bag from his apartment—the one with the useless gun and a small fortune's worth of cash.

"I have eighty thousand dollars," he said. Nelly felt the mass of each one.

"Whose money is that?" she asked.

"It's mine."

"You mean Dan's?"

"It's money I earned," he bit out. "More than enough to set us up in style. This may be the end of the Mayor of Maxwell Street's story, but there are thousands of mysteries just like him out in the world, waiting for all your stubborn determination. You told me once that I didn't need a vice lord to be legitimate. You don't need the fucking *Chicago Defender* to be a journalist."

The ghosts stood in their respective corners, watching. Their mouths were open and moving, screaming even. The day would come when their sorrowed and maligned screams would be all Nelly could hear in the world. But this was not that day.

"Okay," she said, then repeated, "Okay. Okay. Let's go."

Jay didn't give her a moment's chance to change her mind. He took her hand and—with nothing but the nightdress and robe on her back—led her through the wardrobe's hidden door. The ghosts didn't follow. They stayed interred in the President's Suite of the Blackstone Hotel, and Nelly didn't hear the warning in their cries until it was far too late.

CHAPTER FORTY-THREE

They returned to where it all began: Maxwell Street on a sweltering Saturday night.

The tenement building stood sentry on the far edges of the market. Jay insisted on using the fire escape, a rickety contraption that clung to the brick siding by a single embedded rod. When they finally reached the top floor in one piece, Jay knocked on a window as easily as he would a door and waited. From so high, the putrid and familiar smell of horseflesh from Maxwell Street's stables wafted up into the wet air. Nelly inhaled and thought of her father and her home, a life she was prepared to abandon forever. She glanced at Jay and saw him studying her.

"I'm fine," she said.

Suddenly, the window was flung open and both barrels of a Winchester shotgun were pointed at Jay's face.

"Abraham!" he whispered with hands raised. "Abe, it's me! Put that thing away."

Abraham lowered the gun just enough to show his face. It was that same onyx brown, now lit from within like a sapphire by the evening light.

"Jay?" The tailor fumbled for the glasses in the chest pocket of his pajamas. Once on, he looked again and groaned. With weary exhaustion, he said, "It's the middle of the night, Jay."

Jay bypassed Abraham completely and threw his laden carpenter's bag through the window. It landed with a hard *clunk* that the neighbors probably heard two floors down.

Abraham cried out, "Jay, my God! Laura and the children are sleeping. And you've brought Ms. Sawyer."

Nelly grinned apologetically at Abraham as Jay helped her through the man's window. It smelled of baked bread and sewing thread and stepping into his kitchen was like stepping into someone else's memory of everything a family life could be.

"We'll only need the night, Abe," Jay said, "then we'll be out of your hair."

"Hmm. Is that the same 'one night' as last time? Or will it be three? Or five?"

Jay reached deep in the canvas bag and produced without flair a wrapped stack of cash. More than six hundred dollars. Abraham stared at it as though it carried a hex, then measured its weight in his hands. Nelly wondered if he'd ever held so much money at once before. The feeling must have been akin to caressing a brick of solid gold.

"Just the one," Jay said again.

There were a hundred more questions that any sensible person might ask, but Abraham left it at that.

"We've had a couple more children since the last time you stayed with us," he said. "You'll have to sleep on the roof."

The roof of the building was surprisingly sturdy considering the general wobbliness of Maxwell Street itself. Abraham's children had little to no access to open grass, so the roof was their secret garden. Lovingly tended flowers grew from pots, and quilts and pillows were piled into child-sized nests. Above, around, and beyond, the city lit up the sky like a thousand lanterns. It was a charming place, and as tired as Nelly was, she thought it ideal for dreaming.

Abraham shook out the quilts, sending cookie crumbs and abandoned toys into the air.

"Apologies," he said, coughing from the dust. "It's not what you're accustomed to, Ms. Sawyer, but it'll have to do."

Nelly smiled at Abraham in earnest and said, "I think it's magical."

"Yes. Magical, and moldy. There are the rats to contend with. I wouldn't recommend leaving food up here." Abraham then observed Nelly and a pall fell over his face. He looked at the rudimentary bed as though it were Scheherazade's cursed silken sheets.

Bashful and more than a little scandalized, he said, "There isn't much in the way of privacy for you, miss."

"Oh." Nelly glanced about. He was right.

Before she could speak, Jay was saying, "It's great, Abe. Thank you."

Abraham grinned at Jay with aggrieved acceptance, but his eyes on Nelly were dubious.

She squeezed his hand in a show of appreciation.

"We're fine."

Abraham left them, descending the fire escape, and the noise of the Maxwell Street Night Bazaar was suddenly very loud. Nelly could feel the pulse of each queer instrument, hear the pain or ecstasy of every crooner.

Jay stood perilously close to the roof's edge. A hard breeze could have tossed him headfirst into that deafening sea. Nelly came to stand next to him at his bow, and they stared into the night together.

"What's next?" she asked. Next for today, for tomorrow, for the next five years. They hadn't discussed the particulars when Jay absconded with her. She'd acted on an intoxicating adrenaline that was now beginning to run dry.

"Canada."

"Canada? We're leaving the country?"

He looked at her as though she'd slept through the last two hours and was just now coming round.

"And Europe after that. If we stay in America, we'll be found," he said. "I stole a lot of Dan's money, and with his go-ahead, the Gennas will call on every Sicilian from Boston to Los Angeles. And Tomás will say I stole you, too. Don't give me that 'he would never.' We have some time before he thinks to consider me, but when he does, he won't stop until you're found. No, getting out is our only fighting chance."

"But *Canada?* What the hell are we gonna do there?"

"Wait. I have a friend overseas who can help us with the passports and paperwork, but that'll take time. For now, we bed down in some sleepy Canadian outback and keep to ourselves."

When Nelly reached up to pull at the hairs along the back of her neck, Jay's hand was ready to intercept her. He held her fingers entwined with his and kissed them.

"Don't worry," he said. "In three months, we'll be shiny new people in a shiny new world. I can finally see if my Spanish, French, and Hebrew stands up to the real deal."

Jay would be resplendent in old-world finery, Nelly thought. All those cathedrals, palaces, and royal courts where charm was the only currency they had left. She would enjoy watching him thrive in such places. To observe his meteoric rise would be an adventure in and of itself. Nelly looked to the night sky.

"Where are the stars?" she asked.

Jay glanced up. "What do you mean?"

"There are no stars here."

"Of course there're stars here. Look closer."

Nelly peered farther into the flat sky above them, vision shoddy as it was, and *did* pick out a lone spark like a far-off lighthouse. And another. Thousands and more, but all with such space between them.

"Back in Richmond, looking at the moonless sky was like looking into the a clear, deep pool. It was fathomless, vibrant, and *full* of stars. One of my earliest memories is standing under a starry sky and feeling absolute terror. It was all too big and too beautiful for me to comprehend. My mother says that a night sky is the nearest to God we'll ever get, and when I did have occasion to pray, I prayed out in the open. The South has not been kind to me, or mine, but I will miss Southern stars."

Of all the things to break her heart, Nelly had not expected it to be Chicago's bland, drowned-out night. She mourned over the home she'd left, the home she'd lost, and the home she would never have.

"I grew up in hill country," Jay said. "When I was a boy, I hated it. I hated the bugs. And the animals. The dirt roads and the constant mud. I hated the smell most of all. Manure, stagnant water, and cook fires all melding with an atmosphere thick enough to swim in. I envied my father when he told me about his time in San Francisco. By then, I'd never seen a theater, or a museum, or a dancing school like my mother's. I would cry and ask why he moved us back to Wood Acre if things were so much better in California. He said that we would be an example to all his people. Living, breathing proof that a Negro with a fraction of the will it takes a bird to fly from one tree to another can be free of Wood Acre and all its horrors. But it was a lie. My father never left Alabama, and neither will I. Wash me white as snow, and you'll still smell it on me."

Jay closed his eyes. The city's notorious wind lifted the hair swaying limply over his brow. Nelly sniffed and felt the burn of a cook fire itching her nose. They'd passed hours together closer than this, and she had never caught the smell of it before. Not under the cologne, or the tobacco, or even the blood. When Jay opened his eyes again, there were no questions. Or doubts. Or expectations. They could have been anywhere in the universe in that moment; even a musty tenement roof on Chicago's West Side, playing make-believe like children.

"I don't remember what it is to be loved," he said. "I don't want to. Not if God sees fit to snatch it away from me again. But whatever it is to love someone, that's what I feel for you, Nelly Sawyer."

He offered up that declaration like some small, paltry sacrifice, and not the king's ransom that it truly was.

"Then love me."

Jay moved as she stayed still. His breath was becoming one with hers when she stopped him.

"I will never forgive you for Elder," she said for the first and last time.

He kept his head close to hers. When his mouth bloomed into a smile, Nelly felt it as though it came from her own lips.

"Good," he said. "There will always be at least one honest thing left between us."

They lay down together that hot night on rat-eaten quilts and pillows full of chicken feathers. And they made their own stars.

Nelly woke to the sound of a cowbell. Cold had come with the dawn, and she shivered in her cotton nightdress. Jay slept curled in on himself like a dying spider: knees tucked to his chest, hands over his head. But his face was relaxed. He slept as deep and secure as the dead.

The cowbell belonged to a foreman walking the streets. A line of men followed behind, called out of their homes to go all together to the factory, or the yard, or the warehouse; no different from the herds of men they shipped in from neighboring counties for harvest season down in Richmond. A place that Nelly might never see again. But she couldn't think about that. Richmond was a memory, and as with all things, it would fade with time.

Abraham sat alone at his kitchen table, head bent over the hem of a pristine wedding dress.

"I didn't know you made women's clothes," Nelly said as she crawled through the open window.

Abraham grinned up at her through his glasses.

"I don't," he said with a cigarette clamped between his teeth. He threaded a needle and pulled the knot tight. "But my wife's niece is getting married in two days. Her seamstress contracted diphtheria and left the dress in an unacceptable state. No one else could be found on such short notice, so I told her I would do what I can."

It was a beauty of satin and lace and silver taffeta. Nelly had never allowed herself to harp much on weddings and wedding dresses, but seeing one up close rustled an unfamiliar yearning in her.

"May I help?" she asked.

Abraham looked mildly impressed by her offer.

"How are you with a needle and thread, Ms. Sawyer?"

"I can sew in a straight line."

He handed her a needle with a long white tail and said, "That will do."

To the waking calls of mourning doves, the two of them worked in tandem hemming the dress. Abraham moved with preternatural speed, covering yards while Nelly labored over every inch. She didn't figure she was helping much, but the sense of camaraderie and creative purpose calmed the frenzy of the last twelve hours.

"Your family's sleeping?" Nelly asked after a stretch. She knew of the wife, and the children, but the only proof she'd seen of them was secondary.

"I am always the first awake," he said. "Dawn is the best time for my kind of work. Once the day begins, there will be a thousand demands on my attention, and I will get nothing done. Is Jay still asleep? I'm not surprised, after your exertions last night."

Nelly's mortification could have reached up out of the floor and dragged her down to Hell. She kept her eyes on her work only to avoid Abraham's tickled smirk.

Chuckling, he said, "No need to be embarrassed on my account. I told you that Jay needed a good friend. A good lover will do the trick just as well, I think."

"We're not lovers," Nelly jumped to say. Abraham's eternally moving hand stopped. "I don't know what Jay and I mean to each other, but we're not lovers. Not yet."

Abraham pierced the silk with his needle. He used his tailor's skill at accurately gauging a client's mood and changed the subject.

"How is your article progressing? The one on our elusive Mayor of Maxwell Street."

Nelly cried out when the point of her needle slid under her thumbnail.

"Suspended," she said as she sucked the blood away. "After my parents, I . . ." She shook her head and started hemming again. "It all went up in smoke, anyway. All my notes and journals. I'd have to either start from scratch or write it all from memory. Not that it matters anymore. Tomorrow, I'll be someone else, and the Mayor of

Maxwell Street will still be a ghoul haunting the streets of Chicago."

Abraham took a long drag of his cigarette, then passed what remained to Nelly, which she accepted with a thankful smile. She understood now why Jay found such refuge in Abraham's company, outside of him being an excellent tailor. He didn't need to delve into the innermost sanctums of her soul to see her disappointment, or loss, or grief. He saw it in the fine lines of the little she shared, the same way he saw a finished suit in pleats of a fabric.

But there was one question that remained unanswered.

"I'm curious," she said. "Did that package from your friend abroad ever come?"

Abraham slapped his knee and cried, "You know, it did! For last month, and this month too. Forgive me, I never thought to call."

"Are you saying that you *still* have the packages? Both of them?"

"The boys never came," he said. "Not for weeks. I couldn't justify the cost of sending them back, so I brought them home. I'm thinking of giving them to Jay, so he has something presentable to wear on your journey."

"It's a strange thing, though. Isn't it?" Nelly asked. "This friend of yours going through such trouble. And all for a custom suit? Not money, not information?"

Abraham's laugh was distant, full of memories from a time before a business, and a wife, and children to raise. She could envision that young boy from Barbados stepping into New York's steel jungle and a man like Sam Mason waiting there to greet him.

He said, "There is rarely rhyme or reason to the things Sam takes it in his mind to do. Why, when he met me, all I knew of custom suits came from observing white men on the street when they passed from the hotel curb to a waiting Cadillac. Sam saw potential in me that I could never see in myself."

"He sounds like a good friend to have," Nelly said.

Abraham's smile was suddenly not quite so sincere. A polite mask for something more ominous.

"Sam is a good friend. But he's a better enemy. I told you, Ms. Sawyer, that he was an actor of sorts, and that's true. He takes on roles that allow him access to high society. Prince this, duke that. His transformations are arresting. Once embedded in these communities, he robs them within an inch of their lives, and all in the name of vengeance."

"Vengeance against who?"

Abraham motioned broadly toward the sky.

"Anyone. Everyone. He claimed it was to right the wrong of his treatment in that boarding school, and perhaps it began that way. Those assimilators stripped him of all power, all agency, and these schemes tend to give some of it back. And he would collect children along the way. All abused and abandoned. Disciples to carry on his doctrine of 'Become what they hate, take all they love.' It became an education in how to deceive. He even asked me to join his 'family' once, but I turned him down. So much hate corrupts the soul and turns you more beast than man."

Nelly pricked her finger again but ignored the pain. She thought of Abraham's packages and the Mayor's identity, shifting and mercurial as quicksilver.

"Might the Mayor be one of Sam's disciples?" she asked.

He bit off the last thread with his teeth. "That is a notion. I wouldn't put it past the old player. But then, I must tell you, Ms. Sawyer, if the Mayor did learn his trade from Sam, then you'll never find him. Oh, careful!"

Nelly looked down and saw a bright red spot spreading across the dress's hem. Four of her fingers were pricked from the needle and bleeding directly into the silk.

"Oh, my God!" She threw herself back from the table, hands in the air. "I've ruined it. I've ruined your niece's wedding dress!"

Abraham lifted the fabric to assess it closer and clicked his tongue.

"No, no, we can fix this," he said. "Nothing some cold water and salt can't clean out. But don't tell Laura. *Never* tell Laura. She'll cancel the entire wedding if she finds out."

Nelly asked, "Over a bloodstain?"

"Haven't you ever been to a wedding, child? Blood on a wedding dress will only lead to disaster."

"What are you two busybodies up to?" Jay asked from the fire escape's window. He was clean-shaven and bright after a good night's rest. When he approached Nelly, he kissed her on the cheek and whispered good morning as a husband would. She hadn't even a day to adjust to this new form of their relationship. It's not that she disliked it, but the fit was snug. It would take some getting used to.

"Sewing," Abraham said, "and gossiping, of course. Ms. Sawyer has all kinds of fascinating insights to share about you, Jay Bird."

"Nothing you didn't know already, Abe."

Jay filled a cup with coffee warming on the stove and downed it—piping hot—in one go.

"We'll need to move fast from here," Jay said to Nelly. "Leaving in broad daylight is risky, but not impossible. It's just our luck that the ferry never leaves at night. And I have a new outfit for you, something unassuming that will help us blend in."

"When did you get a new outfit for me?" she asked.

"Yesterday."

"Yesterday? Before you knew whether or not I'd come with you?"

Jay didn't miss a beat. He seemed to relish such challenges, especially when they came from her.

He winked and said, "I had a hunch you'd say yes."

Nelly was left to change in the privacy of the kitchen, while Jay changed on the roof. The skirt and blouse he'd selected fit her perfectly. It was not an outfit chosen in haste by a man on the run. Nelly wondered if Jay'd been holding on to it for some time, waiting for the moment when she'd follow him over the edge.

When Jay came back through the window, he looked like a prince. Specifically, the Prince of Wales.

The double-breasted white flannel suit had an immediate transformative effect. Men out on the streets hunting for "Jay Shorey" would look at him now and only see a handsome traveler returning home from a US holiday. To see the suit on anyone else would have been a sacrilege. Thin and worn as he was, there was no denying that the outfit was made for him.

"Impeccable," Abraham said as he adjusted Jay's lapels. "Nothing quite compares to Savile Row. Promise me, Jay, that wherever you go, you set yourself up with a real clothier. Pay whatever they demand. Just don't go back to dressing like a peasant."

"Never again, Abe." Jay crossed to Nelly. "Not with a princess on my arm."

A hunger returned to his eyes. Not lustful, or wistful, but ravenous.

"Your ticket," he said, handing it to her. Another sign of his forethought. "My friend has British citizenship, so they were purchased in his name."

"What about when they ask for *our* names?"

"They won't. I've taken steps to ensure that."

Jay and his steps. Some things would never change.

Nelly went to pocket the ticket, but her eyes caught on the passenger's name. Then she began to shake. Her mouth dropped open, and she stood gasping, fighting to fit air in a chest that clenched like a grown man's closed fist. There were only so many Sam Masons in the world. So many Ojibwe conmen who lived overseas and shipped suits that fit Jay like a second skin to a Black Jew tailor in West Side Chicago. No, not "so many" at all. Only one.

"Ms. Sawyer?"

Nelly's eyes jumped up to Abraham, and Jay standing behind. Of course. *Of course.*

"It wasn't the dealer," she mumbled in a daze. The room spiraled down, down into darkness. Her head felt engorged from all the lies. All the truths, too. "You didn't need a proxy. You were already there, in the room. In every room. Every time. I just never saw you."

Those fool enough to go looking always expect to find him at the bottom.

Down here in the mud and the hustle, with us. Most never stop to look up. Where the air's clean and the living is easy.

Up toward the sky. And sky-blue eyes.

"Are you quite all right, Ms. Sawyer?" Abraham said, reaching for her. "You're talking nonsense. Do you need to sit down? Jay, go wake Laura and tell her to call the doctor."

Nelly jerked away.

"No," she said. She blinked, but her vision blurred. The ringing in her ears smothered her own voice. "No, I'm fine, I just . . ."

Jay watched her. Already, whatever care he felt for her was dissolving into suspicion. No one knew where she was. No one was coming for her.

"I need to use the bathroom before we leave," she said. She hoped Abraham took the shakiness to be illness and not fear. "Abe, is there a washroom here?"

"Yes, behind the building. It's just an outhouse—"

"I don't mind." Already, she was backing toward the window and its escape. "I'll be back in a minute, then we can go."

Jay took hold of her with none of the tenderness shown the night before. He squeezed until her arm went numb.

"I'll walk you down," he said, but it was not an offer she had leniency to refuse.

He was silent, but she heard his voice loud in her head: *Didn't you learn your lesson?*

Nelly squared her jaw and met him head-on: *Isn't it too late for that?*

"I'd rather be alone," she said. "Please."

They stared each other down just as they had so many times before. For all his capabilities, he'd never managed to intimidate her. Humble her, frighten her, but nothing Jay Shorey ever did or could do would turn Nelly's head. Not with all his threats or his warnings, or the lies he fired like bullets, heedless of where they landed.

And so, he let her go. He watched her as she scampered out the window and down the fire escape. She felt him track her steps from the street, around the corner to the weedy garden in the back. He could not watch her forever. When his eyes saw her no more, she kicked off the shoes he'd picked for her and ran.

The Sunday Market was awake and frothing.

People crowded in on all sides, and Nelly had to push folk out of the way as she ran. She cried out for help, but her voice became lost among the hundreds of hawkers, and peddlers, and traders. The world's wares washed up on Maxwell Street's shores. But for all the treasures that came in, they did not flow out again. The street had a hunger of its own.

He was calling her name. Of course his voice alone pierced through the pandemonium and found her. Jay had always been adept at tracking Nelly. In every room, every house, every city. She could run the length of the globe, but at the end of it all, he would be there. Smiling. Hand open and stretched out for her.

When Nelly turned into an empty alley, she didn't recognize it. But the smell brought it all back.

"The Lantern Club always calls its children home."

Jay stood behind her, at the mouth of the alley—flawless and dapper, even after chasing her down a busy street. His Smith & Wesson gleamed with fresh polish. Adept and fatal as the day it was made.

"I thought you didn't carry a gun."

Jay observed his finger softly fondling the trigger. He looked mystified, as though someone had slipped the gun into his hand while he wasn't looking, and now he had no other choice but to use it.

"I guess I learned my lesson," he said.

Nelly wanted to hate him. Despise him, curse him, damn him to the lowest, coldest ring of hell. But that would mean the end of his story, of *their* story. And just when they were getting started.

"You should've stayed away," she said.

Jay sobbed, "I tried! At every crossroads, I tried. How was I to know that just seeing you would bind me to you forever?"

"But you had a choice in it! I never forced you to do this, to use me."

"Use you? You were the one who sought me out, Nelly. You had a choice, too."

Jay shook his head. At the waste of time, of life, of potential. Then he raised the gun.

"This is the only choice that matters."

EPILOGUE

THE LAST SONG OF JAMES GLASS

What do you see?

Jimmy saw a glorious wedding. Hundreds of smiling faces gathered about the loving couple like sheep surrounding a trough. He saw a wealth so bold that it exuded its own heat. He saw the blinding truth of their love, and he saw the deception at its core.

One Oak was not White Pine, but it was familiar. The bright green lawn dotted with lamp-lit pavilions, stretching on for acres, was more maintained, but limitless all the same. One Oak was another house on another hill, and it was grand in all the ways White Pine never could be. Where White Pine was in the last, pathetic throes of its death, One Oak was on the brink of a brilliant new life. The smell was the same. Blood, and meat, and shit. A working man's final drop of sweat. Showing up there was like coming home for Jimmy. In the same way he was told dying would be like coming home.

He sat at a remote table, as removed from her as the farthest city star, but even at that distance, she could not be avoided. He regretted many things in his life. Failing to tell Nelly Sawyer that she was the most radiant of creatures every second he spent in her company was prime among them.

Even her in-laws' shattered illusions couldn't refute her glow, and they did try. Jimmy watched them crouch like buzzards over a carcass in the road—contrary and reeking of violent death. *Anyone but her*, he heard them whisper in all their aristocratic Spanish, and French, and Portuguese, and English. *Anyone in the world.* But Tomás had been persistent; Jay would give him that. His pride in his new bride was the color of gold, glinting in the last rays of September sun.

"Now, tell me again, old boy, about this business you're in?"

The man sitting across from Jimmy was already capping off his third bottle of champagne and had this strange habit of harping back to previously answered questions when drunk.

"Show business," Jimmy said in his new voice. The British dialect wasn't difficult to get right generally, but the devil was in the details. A solicitor from London could spot a cobbler from Brighton in the lengthening of a vowel, and vice versa. Becoming an Englishman without origin or history took hours of meticulous design that still showed its cracks. Sam had advised him to grow a beard. Still all the rage in England, it did the bulk of the work that got Jimmy into the wedding undetected in the first place.

He cleared his throat to settle the baritone deep in his chest and said, "I help introduce American talent to the English market.

Nothing quite rivals a Negro blues singer from Louisiana, and we just can't grow those back home."

The man nodded like a doll with a broken head. Bobbing freakishly up and down as though a critical screw had come loose in his neck.

"Yes, I get all that," he said, "but how do you know this family *in particular*? Their lot isn't too partial to show folk and gypsies."

Jimmy smiled. Smiling was one of Sam Mason's first lessons after he'd fished Jimmy out of the Mississippi, scraped the mud and dried tears from his face, and set him on this path of vengeance for vengeance's sake. It was a language unto itself, and once mastered, it could open any door, to any room, in any house.

"I don't know the family personally," Jimmy said. "Either of them. I'm a plus one to an old Oxford buddy of the groom's. He brought me along as a kind of payment for a favor."

The earl's son in question was currently on the dance floor, trying to tango with Sequoia McArthur. Sequoia grimaced as though she'd been forced to drink a bottle of poison one drop at a time while a squat young peer stretched to press his cheek against hers. Jimmy had done an admirable job of avoiding Sequoia's discerning eye thus far, but in that moment, he wanted nothing more than to march right up to her and laugh in her face. If he had to suffer through the entitled vainglory of Lord Reginald Crosby, then he wouldn't do it alone.

The man was still talking, though it could have been to anyone. "—known them for years, mmhmm. Since the grandfather started buying up oil shares. A storied family, a respectable family. Good bones from stem to stern. But I'll tell you the truth, old boy; I just about swallowed my tongue when I heard Tomás was marrying a Colored gal. Even one as rich as her. His father tried his hand at marrying below him, and we all know how that turned out."

Nelly and Tomás showed their bravery when they decided on one massive affair instead of smaller gatherings scattered throughout the globe to accommodate regional guests. His Mexican family sat with her Kentucky family. The European elites from Paris sat with the Negro elites from Boston. Everyone was forced to join together in a mass so diverse that it reminded Jimmy of Maxwell Street. But he stopped that memory before it could begin. Maxwell Street was a stretch of road in a Midwestern city built on a swamp. A tack on a map. Nothing more, and nothing less.

And yet, when Nelly stopped at his table to shake his hand and thank him for coming without a *moment's* recognition, Jimmy knew such affirmations were wasted on him. Maxwell Street was as much a place as it was a galaxy that encompassed the whole of his existence. The beginning and the end of everything he ever was or could hope to be.

She was alone.

He found her a good eight hundred yards from the big house, in the twilight hours when the energy of the wedding began to pop and crackle. The booze was well and truly flowing, and whatever polite reservations that kept folk from enjoying themselves were all checked at the door along with hats and mink shrugs. The old heads retired while the young people wound their spines and their hips until the earth itself quaked. It was the perfect moment to disappear.

Nelly sat perched on a fence post in the shadow of a hundred-year-old crape myrtle. Jimmy heard the twinkling of bells as he approached it; once close, he saw that it was strung with dozens of blue bottles like the ornaments on a Christmas tree.

She held her lace veil swaddled against her chest. The silken hem of her wedding gown was tucked into her belt to keep it from catching dirt, and her feet were bare. She smoked with the anguished intensity of a woman on the last hour of her last shift. She'd take a deep inhale, then lean her head back to let it all out in a chorus line of thick smoke rings. Add in a flask and a jazzy tune, and she'd be fit for the cabaret clubs. No more a wilting country mouse bewildered by this flappers' age. She was now a fixture in it. The girl who stumbled into the Lantern Club in search of a story would look at this woman and be undone.

"Can I bum one of those?" Jimmy asked in another man's voice. There was a paralysis to her impassive expression. Either she'd finally released the vigor that he'd always thought so juvenile and alluring, or it had been taken from her.

"Are you friends with Tomás?" she asked. She really didn't see him. Even though Jay Shorey was gone, Jimmy had hoped that Nelly might still be able to find him. Recognize the ghost, and by acknowledging it, give it life.

He said, "Not directly. I'm here with one of your husband's old school friends. The first words I ever spoke to the man were 'Congratulations.'"

Nelly slanted her eyes at him, weighing his sincerity, then decided in his favor. She unhooked a pack from her garter and tapped a Chesterfield out for him. He still couldn't quite abide smoking. The campfire taste of the tobacco reminded him too much of his parents and the night they died. But *not* smoking wasn't an option, not anymore. Nelly might have been the first to mention his full cigarette case, but she hadn't been the first to notice. It was a limp in his stride that could not trip him up again.

"Does the bridegroom not allow you to smoke?" Jimmy asked as he put a match to the cigarette and watched it burn.

"That's quite the impertinence," Nelly said. Jimmy didn't apologize. "I'm sure he wouldn't mind if he knew, but there aren't many secrets between Tomás and me anymore. My smoking is just the last little thing I'll keep for myself."

Nelly did not say this with resentment, but rather, a kind of solace that Jimmy found hard to swallow. He'd wanted to stumble upon a sullen girl in runny makeup, dragged to the altar by her hair. Not this woman of stone who walked the path before her with the steadfast countenance of a saint.

"This is a lovely property," he said. Nelly glanced toward the big house and grinned like someone in on the joke.

"Thank you. I can't take any of the credit, but thank you," she said as she reduced another Chesterfield to embers. "Tomás hired a new steward to prepare everything for the wedding while we were abroad. The man did a fine job. Dug out all the old photos and everything. It's appropriate, I suppose. Before today, I was the last Sawyer. Now there shall be no more."

Another thing Jimmy reluctantly appreciated about smoking; it made people loose and friendly. A group of strangers will vow a blood oath over a shared cigarette.

"My deepest condolences for your losses, ma'am." Nelly threw him a questioning look, and he went on. "The gentleman I came with mentioned that you were an orphan."

"Not an orphan," she said. "My mother still lives. She stays at a spa in Switzerland."

Jimmy knew this. He'd been to the spa. Sat with Florence Sawyer in the arboretum under the guise of a weary traveler and learned about her daughter's stunning success.

"Switzerland? That's quite a distance, and to be separated from your mother at such a time."

Nelly shrugged. She'd had this conversation a thousand times before, but with her own conscience.

"I wanted the best for her," she said, "and we were told that the best spa for this type of thing is in Switzerland. Tomás's family—*my* family—collects those kinds of connections."

Yes, the Escalante y Roche clan were all apt collectors. Horses, property, trophies, people. Jimmy had discovered as much when he cultivated the relationships that allowed him this access. He didn't want to believe that Nelly was just another addition to the family collection for Tomás. Didn't want to believe that she would allow herself to be so easily sold.

"You're some manner of writer, are you not, Ms. Sawyer?"

Nelly choked on the weak tobacco.

"You'll think me dubious, but I know you," he said. "Or *of you,* although I didn't realize it when my friend first invited me to this wedding. I saw your byline in a publication out of Chicago some months ago. The *Defender,* I think it's called."

Nelly tried her best to maintain that apathetic polished exterior that he imagined kept all the cousins and blue-blood relations at bay. But Jimmy managed to dent it and leave her, even for an instant, as exposed as their last seconds together.

"Yes," she said after letting the crickets fill the silence awhile. "That's right. But I didn't think they read the *Chicago Defender* overseas. At least not in enough numbers to remember one name and one article."

Jimmy defied convention and stepped closer to her.

"I was quite struck by it," he said. "You painted the story of this 'James Glass' character with such vividity, such talent. It was very entertaining."

"It wasn't meant to be a penny dreadful, sir. James's story was a warning. And I still don't know the half of it."

"And you're sure he's dead, Ms. Sawyer?"

A lightning bug passed by her face, illuminating the suspicious glint to her eyes. She reached out to touch it and it blinked off like a light.

"You seem to know all of my names, but you've yet to tell me one of yours, sir," she said.

"Edmund Rutledge," he said. "Pardon me for never introducing myself."

Nelly nodded her head.

"Well then, Mr. Rutledge, take it from the horse's mouth, since you're such a fan. James Glass is dead. The Mayor of Maxwell Street is dead. I watched them both die with my own eyes."

"Your article was some kind of obituary?"

"No. An homage. To all the people who think they have to cheat, and steal, and lie until they have no memory of the truth just to be free of oppression. James was one of thousands."

"Mmm," Jimmy said, enjoying the aftertaste of her fervor. It brought back a hundred memories of times when her obstinance made the impossible possible. "Do you count yourself among their number?"

Nelly threw down what remained of her cigarette and crushed it under her naked heel without a wince. She couldn't look him in the eye before, but now they faced off as equals in more ways than one.

"What the hell is that supposed to mean?" she asked, already simmering. "Do you think, like all the rest of Tomás's crowd, that I managed to steal him away with hoodoo magic?"

"I wasn't referring to that, Ms. Sawyer."

"That's not my name!"

"It's your only name to me."

Some people become so accustomed to an accent that they barely notice when it's dropped. But not Nelly. He gave her just an inch, and that's all it took.

"We had a deal, Jay," she said. What had he expected? A kiss? Passionate protestations of undying love? No, he hadn't expected that. But by God and all the saints, he'd allowed himself to dream.

"Jay Shorey. Another dead man."

Nelly flung her hands at his clothes in a barbed kind of gesture.

"Am I to call you Edmund now?"

He released himself from a year's worth of constraint and touched her.

"Call me Jimmy," he begged. "I'm Jimmy, Nelly. You know me."

"I have never known you!" She wrenched away from him. "You promised me that you would leave. You swore it on the soul of my brother, the man you killed."

"I told you, what happened with Elder was—"

"Fucking save it! You are my enemy, Jimmy, and I will *never* forgive you."

Without the heat of her body close to his, he was suddenly deeply and profoundly cold. And that frigidity made him heartless.

"And what about the promise you made to me?" he said, advancing on her. "I told you I would only let you go if you took the story of my life and resolved to make something of your own. Not turn and run to Tomás as soon as you saw the back of me!"

"You tell me to call you Jimmy, but I listen to you, and all I hear is 'Jay.' That same selfishness. You can make sacrifices to survive, and I can't?"

"Marrying Tomás Escalante y Roche is no great sacrifice, Nelly. I told you once before that you were just like me. Telling the same lie over and over again until it becomes your truth. You didn't do this for duty or survival. You did this because you wanted an easy way out."

She closed her eyes and began to count. As though they'd been here before, and all she had to do to break the spell was wake up.

He touched her hand again, gingerly and slow, and she did not pull away.

"I came back for you, Nelly."

She opened her eyes and smirked as if to say *Damn. You're still here.*

"And you do this on my wedding day? Your sense of timing is as fucking histrionic as ever."

"A happy accident."

He smiled, and it was all for her. Taunting and sinuous, delighted with itself. But for once, Nelly didn't smile back. In fact, she looked close to screaming.

"I did try," she said. "That Mayor of Maxwell Street article was good. *Really* good. Richard Norris all but begged me to write more as a permanent member of the *Chicago Defender* staff. But as good as I believed that story to be, it wasn't on the first page, as promised. *My marriage announcement was.* Can you imagine? Being upstaged by my own self. I was angry for a while. Considered running away, finding you. Then, while walking down a Spanish street named for my husband's sixth great-grandfather, I understood something. When the names of my children are chiseled into some palace or monument or boulevard, they will be called Sawyer first. This ranch and all it meant to my parents will be spoken of in the same breath as cathedrals and battlefields, Jimmy! Marrying Tomás, becoming his wife, loving him—it's not about me. And it's not about you either."

A cheer went up from the main house. The band struck up a new tune: "My Man" by Fanny Brice and the Follies, of all cruel things. That window Jimmy had into her heart and into her mind closed and bolted shut like St. Peter's gate on the sinned and sinned against.

"Shit," she said. "I'm late for the last dance."

She untucked her hem, put on her shoes, fluffed out her veil until the lace undulated behind her like wings.

"I have to go."

"You're not serious!"

He stood in her path, but she charged him with the force of all the hundreds of horses she now solely owned.

"Get out of my way, Jimmy."

"I'm offering you a way out," he said. He held on to her to keep her still, but it was a show on her part. There was no holding her anymore. "A real one. I've done good work since you last saw me, Nelly. More money than I ever made in Chicago, a name that folk can respect. You don't need Tomás's pedigree to give you a legacy anymore."

The pity in Nelly's eyes is what proved to him that it was all truly over. It would've been easier to bear if she despised him. That, at least, was subject to change. Anyone could grow to love anyone, with time, but once you pitied someone's lot, you were likely to pity them forever. No matter how fortune's wheel might turn.

She caressed his face. Ran her fingers over his brow, his eyes, his nose, his mouth. No, not *his* face. Edmund's. Jay's. James's. She did not know this "Jimmy," and now no one ever would.

"I pray I don't see you again."

Nelly passed through his hands like the finest sand and headed back toward her new husband and her new life. For the first time, Jimmy refused to watch her walk away.

He heard a barking noise. The ghostly, phantasmic yelp a fox makes; the one that wakes children with a scream. It had always been far too human a sound for Jimmy's liking. No animal could ever be so mournful.

He started at the crack of a rifle shot. All the world was silent in its echo. No critters, no animals, no ghosts. No names to whisper. And no one left to suffer for but himself.

ACKNOWLEDGMENTS

Before anyone and everyone, I must thank my mother, Cheryl Pesce. All of who I am now and who I am destined to be is due to her unconditional love and unfaltering support. She is my rock and my light, the source of every experience that has formed me. I love you, Momma. "Thank you" will never be enough to express my gratitude.

I must also thank my father, Louis, who indulged my ambitious whims at every turn, even going so far as to read the first chapter of my adolescent fan fiction and offer unbiased feedback.

I thank my brilliant siblings—Candace, Alea, and Alex—my devoted family, and the legion of Aunties who inspire me each day to do my best in all things. And thank you to my dear friends for being my greatest cheerleaders, critics, and coconspirators.

I wish to acknowledge my teachers and professors, as well, who saw potential in me when I failed to see it in myself. Specifically, those who taught me at Rose Hill Middle School, University School of Jackson, and DePaul University. I could not have asked for a more stellar education.

Now, to thank those who made *The Mayor of Maxwell Street* possible. My mentors Rebecca Johns Trissler and Melissa de la Cruz; these incredible women guided my every step professionally and creatively. A very special thank-you to my agent, Richard Abate, for taking a chance on me and fighting in my corner. To my editors, Adam Wilson and Cassidy Leyendecker; their keen insight took this novel from a loose idea to something beyond what I ever could have imagined. Also, thank you to my legal representation, Channing Johnson and Brittany Berckes.

Thank you to my two student interns and fellow DePaul alums, Grace Brown and Ava O'Malley, for making sense of my vague ramblings. And a huge thank-you to the entire Hyperion Avenue team from copy editors, to designers, to formatters, to marketers, to publicity, and the dozens of others whose tireless work breathed life into this project.

My gratitude for their early and constant support goes to all of my mentors—especially Noni Carter, Jamey Hatley, Kwame Alexander, and Troy Wiggins—and the DePaul Writers Guild. And thank you to the now shuttered Davis-Kidd Booksellers. I was all of three years old when they gave me the world in a well-told tale, and I haven't looked back since.

And finally, it goes without saying that I must thank my Bernese Mountain Dog, Grizzly, for staying up with me through all-nighters, rising early for dawn writing sprints, and glaring at me every time my keyboard fell silent.

There are hundreds of others I could thank for showing me love, support, and encouragement throughout my life. I hope that if any of them should happen upon this book and do me the honor of reading it, they will know how appreciative I am. And how much I wish to make them all proud.

© 2024 Andrea Fenise

AVERY CUNNINGHAM is a resident of Memphis, Tennessee, and a 2016 graduate of DePaul University's Master of Arts in Writing & Publishing program. She has over a decade of editorial experience with various literary magazines, small presses, and bestselling authors. Avery grew up surrounded by exceptional African Americans who strove to uplift their communities while also maintaining a tenuous hold on prosperity in a starkly segregated environment. The sensation of being at once within and without is something she has grappled with since childhood and explores thoroughly in her work of historical fiction. When not writing, Avery is adventuring with her Bernese Mountain Dog, Grizzly, and wading waist-deep in research for her next novel. She aspires to tell the stories of complex characters at the fringes of history fighting for their right to exist. *The Mayor of Maxwell Street* is her debut novel.